THE DEMONS OF CONSTANTINOPLE

by
Eric Flint
Gorg Huff
Paula Goodlett

Cover Art by Larry Dixon
Cover designed by Gorg Huff
Internal art by Gorg Huff

Eric Flint Paula Goodlett and Gorg Huff
Visit our websites at https://ericflint.net/
https://warspell.com/

Printed in the United States of America

First Printing: June 2020
1632, Inc.

eBook ISBN-13 978-1-948818-87-2
Trade Paperback ISBN-13 978-1-948818-88-9

Paula: To Chuck.
Eric: To My Grandchildren Lucy and Zachary
Gorg: To my nieces and nephew, Holey, Heather, Katy,
Alison, Tanya Brandy and Jimmy. I'll get to my step nieces
and nephew in the next book. Sheesh Now I have to write
another book.

CONTENTS

CHAPTER 1—A CAT'S EYE VIEW

Location: Farming Village, Lorraine, France
Time: Evening, August 23, 1372

H alf an hour into her stalk, the cat was frustrated and angry. She moved through the weeds next to the clearing as silent as death, watching the crow calmly peck at something, apparently completely unaware. Again hope of a meal rose. *This time I'll pounce.*

This hunt had started deep in the grove of trees that was the cat's hunting ground. Every time she got close to pouncing, the crow flew away. Never too far. But always a tiny bit out of pounce range. By now her emotions were so strong that she didn't even notice that she was about to leap into an open field filled with humans and their works.

Then the cat heard a voice.

"You don't want to do that."

It was said in cat, and the cat twisted her left ear back in the direction of the voice.

"Not a good idea," the voice said.

The cat growled back, "Mind your own business." Then she turned her head to bring the source of the voice into view. It wasn't a cat. It was a human. A human with strange clothing and stuff, sitting on a fallen log next to the clearing.

"Okay," the human said in cat, "but that's not an ordinary crow. It's part *wiloklisp.*" The last bit wasn't in cat or human talk, but the cat still understood it.

That was when it occurred to the cat that the speaker wasn't an ordinary human. A human shouldn't be able to speak cat. Even cats didn't speak cat with the sort of clarity or precision that the human's meows conveyed. And that last bit was a combination of sounds like nothing she had ever heard before, but she understood it. A *wiloklisp* was a "lying light" that led travelers and enemies into traps. A hunter who hunted by *being* hunted.

The crow said something in human talk.

"You're welcome, Carlos," the human cawed in crow, with more than a little sarcasm. Then the human turned back to the cat. "Carlos," he pointed at the crow, "was 'thanking' me for spoiling his game. You would have lost an eye, not gained a meal."

The cat looked at the crow, and it laughed a cawing laugh at her. Disgusted and intent on ignoring the crow, the cat turned back to the human. "How can you talk to me?"

"It's magic," the human said.

And the cat, who had never even had the concept of magic before, now understood what the word meant, and even that it was at best an inadequate explanation of what was going on. It growled in frustration. "Explain." Another new concept.

"All right," the human said. "I guess I should start at the beginning. I'm Wilber Hyde-Davis. Before we came here, I was profoundly deaf. I had a device to let me hear, called a cochlear implant. When we were brought to this time, a muse—that's a being from the netherworld—inhabited my hearing aid and implant, and in the process, fixed my hearing. Now my implant is at least sort of alive and a part of me. It gives me the magical ability to translate. I can talk to almost anything in their own language, even if they don't have a language. That's the magic part.

2

"Merlin, that's the muse, is still hooked into the implant—" Wilber pointed at a point behind his left ear. "—but he mostly resides in my computer." He twisted a flat box thing with the top open around, so the cat could see its screen. "He can talk to me via my implant. He can also talk to other people through my computer, or indirectly through my phone, or any of the electronic devices, with the consent of whichever demon resides in the device. Say hi, Merlin."

The screen of the computer showed a man with wings like a bird. It bowed at the cat and said, "Hello, cat. What shall we call you?"

Like Wilber, when Merlin talked to her, she could understand. But the cat didn't really have a name. There were things the humans in the village said, but the cat mostly thought of those sounds as instructions. "Here, Brownie" meant she should come get food or petting. Or "Damn cat" meant she should go away if she didn't want to get kicked. Which she generally didn't.

She explained that and Wilber said, "How about we call you Leo?" and the damned crow laughed again. Through the magic, the cat knew that Leo was sort of short for lion and was a male name, and so understood the crow's derision.

Apparently the human was so stupid it couldn't tell a male cat from a female cat. With a flick of her tail, the cat said, "I am female."

"Oh, sorry," Wilber said. "Ah, how about Fluffy?" At her look, he said, "No, I guess not. Leona?"

The crow laughed again. And said something in crow that Wilber didn't translate, but was probably insulting.

"Fine," Leona agreed, as much because the crow didn't like it as because she liked the fact that Leona meant female lion. "Now, do you have any food?" she asked, since snooty crow didn't appear to be on the menu.

"I think we can manage something," Wilber said. He drew a knife and sliced off a chunk of the fine white cheese that the villagers made, and tossed it at Leona.

Leona jumped back. In her experience the things thrown at her were hard, not edible. And in that moment, the crow swooped in and stole her cheese.

Wilber shook his head. "Carlos is a bit of an asshole." He cut another slice of cheese and set it on the ground. Leona made her way cautiously to the cheese and grabbed it in her mouth, then quickly backed away. Because she could understand Wilber didn't mean she trusted him.

For a time Leona nibbled on her cheese, while Wilber made strange gestures and spoke to the air in words of some language that made no sense to Leona. When Leona had finished her cheese, which wasn't truly enough for a real meal but did take the edge off, she meowed a question. "What are you doing?"

"I'm preparing a spell," Wilber told Leona, and again as she heard the meow she knew what a spell was, though not what this particular spell was.

"What does the spell do?"

"Nothing yet, but once it's finished I will be able to invoke it and it will produce a set of wards that will prevent demons or angels from entering the mortal realm around us.

"Now, I'm kind of busy, so why don't you go over to the van?" He pointed at what looked like a human house on wheels. It had an opening on the side, and a man and a woman were sitting in the opening, while two children were seated on the grass next to the opening. One of the children had a tail and cat's ears. "You could chat with Doctor Delaflote, Mrs. Grady and the kids. Merlin, will you translate for Leona?"

"I guess so. . . . If necessary."

"Why wouldn't it be necessary?"

"Kitten is part *nekomimi*, and it is not uncommon for catgirls to speak cat."

"Kitten is the girl with the cat ears and the tail," Wilber said.

Leona gave him a look, then went over to the van.

* * *

Kitten looked over as the bluetooth that she was born with warned her of the cat's approach and provided her with the particulars. Kitten was the daughter of a dryad and a human. Well, Mom was working as a succubus at the time, but you gotta do what you gotta do. Her dad, Jeff Martin, had been one of the twenty-firsters, the people from the twenty-first century who were dragged here when Pucorl grabbed their van to use as his body when he was pulled here from the netherworld by Doctor Delaflote's spell. She quickly put thoughts of her dad aside, because he had died less than a month ago, and she didn't want to start bawling again.

"Hello, Leona," Kitten meowed. Everyone looked at her, then at the cat. "This is Leona."

"How do you know?" Paul Grady asked.

She tapped her dataport which was located behind her left ear. It wasn't connected to a cable at the moment, so she added, "Bluetooth. Merlin told Pucorl and Pucorl told me." She grinned because Paul was a normal human boy with no dataport or bluetooth, and he really, really wanted one. Her dataport and bluetooth, along with the fact that she was a girl and he was only a boy, proved that she was his superior in every way that mattered.

* * *

After some negotiations, Leona settled on Kitten's lap while Dr. Delaflote, Mrs. Grady and another of the odd boxy things that the humans called laptop computers instructed the children in such arcane matters as reading, math, and magic. This computer was named Catvia and was Kitten's mother. Merlin, Catvia, and Kitten translated so that Leona wasn't bored. She wasn't completely convinced of the utility of such things when compared to the practical skills of tracking and pouncing, but with the magical translation they weren't the boring gibberish that all human yapping had been before.

As the sun was getting ready to set, Pucorl announced that it was returning to the garage for the night.

"Since Mrs. Grady gave Pucorl the van," Kitten explained while scratching Leona behind the ears, "and especially since he was knighted, he can return to his garage from anywhere. And after we got on the road, it finally occurred to our 'brilliant' magicians that we could store our stuff at Pucorl's garage and not have to carry it in wagons over the rough roads of France."

"Did you think of it?" Leona asked.

"Well, no."

Leona twisted her head to look at Kitten. She realized that half magical creature and half human or not, Kitten was still basically a kitten. Leona was a bit under a year old and considered herself a fully mature, but still young, cat. So she stared at Kitten and waited.

"All right," Kitten said grumpily. "Anyway, I have to go. I sleep in my tree most nights."

On the spur of the moment, Leona decided that she wanted to see this tree. "Take me with you."

"I don't know," Kitten worried. "Animals don't do well in the netherworld. Not even the Elysian Fields."

"Why not? I mean, if humans can go, why can't a cat?"

"Well, not all humans can. Pucorl keeps his garage human friendly, but it's still dangerous for humans who don't have familiars or enchanted devices. They can be really screwed up when visiting. You know, like never eating anything in Elfland or you're stuck there. It really is a different reality, and it takes imagination to translate.

"Dr. Delaflote's crow would have gone nuts if the demon occupying it hadn't translated. And most of the troop don't like going there, even if Pucorl's garage has a motel attached to it now, since he ate that evil demon lord on the field outside Paris.

"It's staffed by dryads and fauns, so Mom doesn't let me stay there. Well, there are the rooms right next to the garage. They're G-rated because of Paul. But I like my tree better. After all, the tree's my brother, sort of."

"I'm not a crow. I'm a cat. And you and your brother can translate for me."

"Well, okay. Hop in my backpack." Kitten had a Hello Kitty backpack that was enchanted burlap. That is, a burlap backpack that was imbued with the essence of a minor silk demon. So it was a magical backpack that her Mom could afford mostly because the whole dryads' grove was doing much better since they had joined Pucorl's lands, and especially since the veils between the world were so ripped up that they could get energy from mortals.

"Why?"

"Because if they see you, Dr. Delaflote may not let you come."

Leona jumped into the backpack, and Kitten, carrying the backpack, climbed into the van.

Location: Pucorl's Garage, Netherworld

The van was now in a different place and Leona peeked out of Kitten's backpack as the side door opened again. With one arm through the backpack's strap, and the other holding Catvia's computer, Kitten climbed out of the van and started walking toward the dryads' grove.

It was a magical sort of place. The trees had tan-colored bark that was almost like skin, and leaves of every color in the rainbow and some more besides. The most common color was gold. The sun was in the sky, and it was a bit dimmer than Leona was used to, but you could feel the warmth gently. The breezes were cool and caressing. Leona sniffed the air. It smelled of flowers and wine.

As they left the black stuff that was right around the garage and walked over a wooden e, Leona decided that she was done riding. She jumped out of the backpack and landed on the soft green grass that was the edge of the grove. The stream under the bridge burbled happily and she could almost understand it.

"What's this?" asked Catvia, but not like she was really surprised.

"Leona wanted to see the grove, Mama." Then, with a severe look at Leona, Kitten added, "Leona was supposed to stay in my backpack till we got to my tree."

"Did you tell her that?" Catvia asked, and a mist flowed from the box and turned into a woman with cat ears and a tail. "Never mind. If you don't know better than to think you can tell cats what to do, it's time you learned."

Leona meowed in complete agreement with this.

"But you tell me what to do all the time," Kitten complained.

"You're a kitten and I am your mother. It's my job."

Again Leona meowed her agreement. Then she asked, "Why didn't you walk around like this in the . . ." Leona was at a loss. How could she describe home? The grove of scrub wood next to the village where she grew up.

"You mean the mortal realm?" Catvia said more than asked.

Leona flicked her ears in a cat shrug. "I guess."

"It's called the mortal world," Catvia said, "and sometimes the humans call it the natural world, though I myself don't see it as any more natural than this world. But your question was why I didn't walk around like this in the mortal world. The answer is that I can't, at least not yet. Even doing it here takes a certain amount of energy, though I have gotten better at it since the grove joined Pucorl's lands. We're on a higher energy plane than we were before."

"What?"

"Kitten, you explain it," Catvia said. "I want to see how much you understand."

"Okay," Kitten said, running ahead to a sapling about fifteen feet tall. She hugged the sapling and two of the lower limbs seemed to hug her back. The sapling was pinkish tan and, like Kitten, it had a data port. It also had a mouth and eyes, as well as the rainbow of leaves that were common to every tree in the grove. A cord from the tree spiraled up and plugged into Kitten behind her left ear. For a moment she was still, then the cable released, and she grinned and sat down with her back to the tree. "Data dumps make telling each other what's happened so much easier.

"The reason . . . No, never mind. I'll explain about dataports later. Kitten, you were going to explain about the energy planes," Catvia said.

"That's what Wilber calls them," Kitten told Leona while she patted her lap.

Leona considered. A petting might be nice, but she wasn't sure she wanted this kitten to get ideas. After a moment, she walked over and curled up on the grass next to the kitten.

"The ones up there—" Kitten pointed at the sky. "—are the crystal spheres of heaven. And the ones down below have lots of names. Underhill, the dark places, or even the nine circles of hell. But that's only heavenly propaganda. After all, Mom was from there. The whole grove was there before the dryads—they were succubi at the time—made a deal with Pucorl and they were perfectly nice. Coach says so. Coach is the faun that was Dan's sports watch."

"Ahem. The point, Kitten. You were talking about the energy planes."

"Okay, Mom, okay. The 'energy planes' make up this universe, which Wilber says is a different universe from the universe he's from. He says that they are passing through each other and for the longest time they barely touched each other at all, even as they passed through. But then something happened and they started interacting a lot more. That was about two years ago in that other universe. Back then, time moved differently in this universe. So I'm eight, almost nine. As old as Paul, even though I was only born a few weeks ago in that other universe's time."

Leona meowed in total confusion. Magic or not, this kitten was talking nonsense.

"We can worry about temporal distortions later," Catvia said. "Go on about the energy planes."

"Well, we're on the middle one now. The energy plane about half way from the top of heaven to the bottom of hell. The part of it we're in is called the Elysian Fields. It's roughly analogous to England in the mortal world, and at about the same level, so to go from here to England is a step sideways, in a way. A special direction."

"Is that where I'm from?" Leona asked.

"No. That's why we had to use Pucorl to get here. He can go to his lands from anywhere in the mortal realm. Or, for that matter, from about any place in the netherworld. But we can't . . . well, Mom can't, and I'm not allowed to."

"Why can't Catvia?" Leona asked.

"Dryads are tied to the location of their tree," Catvia said. "We can't travel far from them without special help. When we are pulled into the mortal world, we are especially weak, only capable of manifesting in dreams, even with the veil ripped all asunder. We can only produce dreams. Most of us is our trees. So the farther from our trees we are, the weaker we are. I am freer to move about than most because Kitten's father gave me the computer that is, in a sense, my body. But even so, when I go to the mortal realm with Pucorl, I prefer to stay as close to the van as possible to piggyback on Pucorl's link to these lands and my tree."

"Yeah, the only way our trees can move is if the land moves too," Kitten said, then added, "like it has been my *whole* life. The grove has been shifting around to match the tree locations in the mortal realms. For the first time in eons, our trees will have mortal trees to match them."

Leona looked over to Catvia for an explanation of this.

"Remember that we of the netherworld are without form unless we impose it on ourselves, or someone else imposes it on us. Having a matching thing from the mortal realm helps, makes it easier for us to maintain a form. The less of ourselves we are spending on that, the more we can spend on other things."

"Except for me," Kitten crowed. "I have a mortal father, so I have a defined body that grows, and I don't have to work hardly at all to keep that shape." Then she pouted. "But I can hardly change my shape at all."

"Talk to Kitten," Catvia told Leona. "I have to go to work." Picking up the laptop, Catvia strolled over to a large tree near to Kitten's tree, and walked right into the tree.

Leona looked at Kitten and then decided to have a nap. She climbed up on the girl's lap, curled up in a ball, and went to sleep.

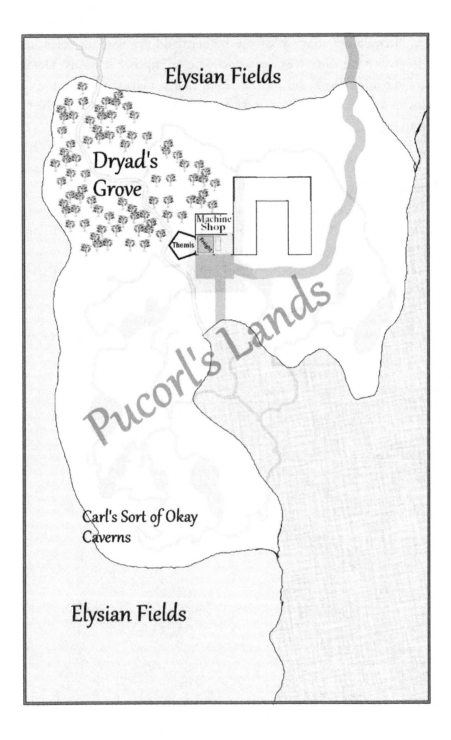

Elysian Fields

Dryad's
Grove

Machine
Shop

Themis

Pucorl's Lands

Carl's Sort of Okay
Caverns

Elysian Fields

CHAPTER 2—HOW ARE WE GETTING THERE?

Location: Pucorl's Garage & Happytime Motel, Netherworld
Time: 8:50 PM, August 23, 1372

Roger McLean lifted the Sword of Themis from his back where it floated. It was five feet long with a foot and a half of hilt. It was also light as a feather in his hand. He laid it in the rack that Pucorl installed in his room, then sat on the bed to take off his boots. He opened Sun Tzu, his laptop, enchanted by a muse of war. "Sun Tzu, where are we?"

The map function came up. There was no GPS in the fourteenth century, but Pucorl could and did record each rotation of each of his wheels, giving them an accurate mile count. His internal systems also had a compass, adding direction to the mile count. That combined with some fairly primitive surveying equipment—made in Paris by local smiths to designs that were developed between Wilber, Annabelle Cooper-Smith, Jennifer Fairbanks and Jennifer's physics textbook chapter on optics, gave them location data and allowed the mapping programs to fill in the gaps.

So Sun Tzu had a detailed map of where they had been and a basic map of the rest of the world. Well, it was fairly detailed for France, but not truly accurate in terms of fourteenth century roads and structures.

Still, the planned route to Constantinople was, in Roger's opinion, stupid. Especially now that everything but Pucorl, the horses, and people could be stored here in Pucorl's lands. It would be better even now to turn south to Marseille, and take ship from there. Surely there was a ship large enough to carry Pucorl. A galley, maybe. He used the touchpad to draw a route to southern France, then by sea around the boot of Italy and Greece, to the Bosporus Straits.

"It's seventeen hundred miles," Sun Tzu said in Chinese-accented English. "But the real issue is that we know that Pucorl can come here and return to the same point of land he left from. A boat moves all the time and at sea it will be miles away by the time Pucorl gets back to this world. Will he reappear over open ocean or on the boat? We don't know. And Pucorl isn't going to take the chance."

"I know, but what about the Danube?" Roger asked, drawing lines on the screen with his finger. "We can hit the Danube at Donauworth in not more than five hundred miles. Then we buy or make a barge to carry Pucorl. After that we can stop once a day while Pucorl does his jump home for supplies and maybe drops us at the hotel to spend the night in comfort."

"Time is still different in Pucorl's lands when Pucorl is not in residence."

"Not that different. A few minutes a day shorter or longer."

"Yes, but that is without the distorting effect of mortals left here. Remember, time in our realm is somewhat subject to the will of the individual. And you humans have an unfortunate tendency to insist on a few more hours to sleep or study or play. When Pucorl is in residence, he keeps time fairly constant using his onboard clock and the pendulum clock we bought in Paris and shipped to Pucorl's lands."

Pendulum clocks were an invention of the seventeenth century, but that was before the twenty-firsters had arrived in Paris in February of 1372. They had all seen grandfather clocks, and between Annabelle, Jennifer, and the local craftsmen they managed to make pendulum-based clocks, one of which was bought by Pucorl and placed in the lobby of the Happytime Motel. Several others had been built and now resided in Paris. King Charles had three and there was a big one, recently finished, at the cathedral of Notre Dame.

They knew that because one of the phones and one of the computers, as well as an enchanted crystal radio set, had been left in Paris. Which, with Merlin's place being located in the netherworld analogous to the Île de la Cité in Paris meant that they had an indirect radio connection. The network went from Pucorl's van to Pucorl's lands, to Merlin's place, to the enchanted crystal set on the Île de la Cité, to the phone in the royal palace, or to the king's computer that His Majesty had loaned to the University of Paris. In spite of being unofficially banished, they had friends in Paris.

"Besides," Sun Tzu added, "you are neglecting the politics. You know that most of the religious contingent refuses to set foot in Pucorl's lands."

The excuse for getting them out of France was for the twenty-firsters to act as escorts for a papal mission to the Patriarch of Constantinople to consider the possibility of reuniting the Catholic church with the Eastern Orthodox church, in light of the introduction of the netherworld into the mortal world with its demons and old beliefs. That meant they had a cardinal from Avignon with three priests, not including Monsignor Giuseppe Savona, papal nuncio to the twenty-firsters. Monsignor Savona had a room in the Happytime, but didn't welcome the dryads to his dreams. However, Cardinal Pierre de Monteruc refused to enter Pucorl's lands, even refused to ride in Pucorl, and the three fathers that accompanied him followed his lead. Other than that, he wasn't particularly belligerent. He would speak to Pucorl, Merlin, and the rest. He was simply unwilling to put himself in any way at their mercy.

That included Raphico, the "angel" that inhabited the phone that Monsignor Savona carried. It was not owned by Giuseppe Savona but, in theory, by God. Cardinal de Monteruc was not convinced that the being which owned the phone was literally the God of heaven and Earth, but instead suggested that it might be the god, or a god, of that other realm where the demons came from. In other words, not the one true God, only a being of great power and uncertain motivation.

"I know that, but that too argues for using the Danube. Get other river barges for the horses, men, and priests that are coming along."

"Eighty men at arms, one hundred and twenty horses, ten wagons. That is a lot of barges." Not all their gear was stowed in Pucorl's lands. But most of it was.

"I know. But however we do this, it's going to be a lot of something." Roger looked at the computer on the screen. Sun Tzu, a small man with a fu manchu mustache and wings, sat in a chair looking at a three-dimensional map of their projected route. He was scratching at his chin. "What's really bugging you, Tzu?"

"The river is a line, not an area. It will make us much easier to find and not everyone in the netherworld is on our side. It seems an invitation to be ambushed."

"Sure," Roger agreed, then countered with, "but on the river we will be moving twenty hours a day. On land we're stopped sixteen to eighteen hours every day, and where we're stopped is predictable to bandits who know the territory we're traveling through."

"Good point."

"Call Bertrand," Roger said, referring to Bertrand du Guesclin, the former Constable of France, who was in charge of the military contingent of their not-so-little caravan.

✳ ✳ ✳

The phone rang. It was new to Bertrand, and existed only in this place of Pucorl's. The phones were from movies and books brought by the twenty-firsters, and the infrastructure that made the connections was completely magic. Tiphaine was in the shower, so he didn't turn on the camera, but instead picked up the headset.

"Yes?"

"General, I think we should make for the Danube. It's only five hundred miles from Paris to Donauworth and we've already covered two hundred. We could be there in another week, or perhaps a bit more. Then we stop, prepare barges and move downriver to the Black Sea, and from there to Constantinople. It's a little farther that way, but we avoid the Alps, or at least most of them, and we can travel more than four hours a day."

Bertrand considered. It was better than Roger's notion of going by the Mediterranean Sea, but he wasn't sure how much better. Then Tiphaine came out of the bathroom, wearing only a smile. "We'll discuss it tomorrow, Roger." He hung up.

Location: Kitten's Tree, Dryad's Grove, Netherworld
Time: Late Evening, August 23, 1372

Leona looked around the grove and wondered. Why humans did things was always a mystery, and here she was with a human. At least, a sort of human she could talk to. "Why were you in my village, Kitten?"

Kitten yawned and curled up next to the tree. "We were going from Paris to Constantinople. Your village was on the way."

"And why are you going to Constantinople? Is there good hunting there?"

Kitten's eyes opened, then she giggled. "No, silly. Humans don't have to hunt to eat. We're on a mission."

Leona was offended by the "silly" comment, but she was also curious. And, as usual for her, the curiosity won. "What sort of mission?"

"We're looking for the cause of the rifts in the veils."

"What are the rifts in the veils, and why should you care?"

"Because Wilber and Dr. Delaflote say that if the veils aren't fixed, both the mortal world and the netherworld could be destroyed." She yawned again. "I'm sleepy, Leona."

Leona let her sleep, but Leona wasn't a sleepy kitten and this news was disturbing. She didn't know exactly what it meant, but if the world was destroyed, her grove back next to the village and this grove with the magic would be destroyed too. She needed to find out what was going on.

Location: Farming Village, Lorraine, France
Time: Early Morning, August 24, 1372

Kitten was worried. Leona was missing. She had spent the night in Kitten's tree and wandering the dryad's grove, but this morning she was missing and there wasn't time to find her. They transported back to the field next to the village, and then they were off. Kitten rode in Pucorl, since Paul had his horse now and rode it most days. Roger, Liane Boucher and Wilber were also riding horses, but Mrs. Grady, Lakshmi Rawal, Jennifer Fairbanks and Bill Howe were in the van, along with Tiphaine de Raguenel, her personal servant Jolie, Dr. Gabriel Delaflote, and Monsignor Savona. Kitten's tail came up and over her shoulder while she nibbled on the tip.

"What's wrong, Kitten?" asked Mrs. Grady. In the time since they started traveling, Mrs. Grady and Kitten's mom, Catvia, had come to an understanding. Catvia watched out for Paul in the netherworld, keeping him from getting an advanced education from the dryads, and in the mortal realm, Mrs. Grady looked after Kitten, since her mother lived in a computer when they were in the mortal world.

"Nothing," Kitten insisted, without much hope.

"Kitten, do you really want me to call your mom?" Mrs. Grady asked.

18

"It's really nothing. It's just, well, I can't find Leona."

"Leona? Wait. You mean the stray cat that visited us yesterday? Surely it's back at the village." Something must have shown in her face because after a moment Mrs. Grady continued. "Kitten, what did you do?"

"She wanted to visit the grove."

"You know that animals go nuts in the netherworld."

"Only in the bad bits. And you know that Pucorl's lands are almost as civilized as Themis' lands." Themis was a titan, the goddess of proper behavior that Philip the Bold had forced into a sword and who Roger had freed to return to her own realm. Roger still had the sword and there was a pentagram in Pucorl's garage that connected it to Themis as there was one that linked to Merlin's lands. "She was doing fine when I went to sleep last night."

"So she is still in the netherworld?"

Location: Forest of Dean, England
Time: Before Dawn, August 24, 1372

Leona felt the shift even here. She grabbed the fat field mouse by its broken neck and slipped through the gap in the veil back to Pucorl's lands, arriving where she had left, in the grove of the dryads next to the babbling brook.

Location: Brook, Pucorl's Lands, Netherworld
Time: Early Morning, August 24, 1372

Leona settled on the bank, eating her field mouse and chatting with the brook. It was the first time she had ever encountered a babbling brook, and she was finding it interesting and frustrating at the same time. She knew there were fish in the brook, but the brook babbled on about the dappled sunlight and how she had been forced to change her course when Pucorl moved in to the area. But the brook said not a word about where Leona should pounce if she wanted fish for lunch.

"Anyway, when Chevalier Pucorl's lands floated up from the netherworld—"

"I thought this was the netherworld."

"No, silly. This is the Elysian Fields, which reside between the netherworld and the crystal spheres. When Chevalier Pucorl got knight—"

Suddenly the whole place got weird. The hairs on Leona's back stood up all on their own, nothing had changed, yet everything was different. "What?" Leona meowed.

"Oh, that. The chevalier is not in residence. Like I was saying, Chevalier Pucorl got knighted. These lands are him. The lord is the land and the land is the lord. Since Chevalier Pucorl got knighted, these lands are a part of him and he is a part of them. They respond to his presence or absence. Did you know that Themis herself confirmed the Chevalier's knighthood? That's much better than being knighted by a mortal king. She also confirmed his eating Beslizoswian."

"Wait a second. How can she confirm his eating this Beslizoswian? Either he did or he didn't, right?"

"Well, no, silly. He defeated Beslizoswian, subsumed him, but Beslizoswian was a demon lord. Its lands were a monstrous cavern below Themis. I don't care if he was in the body of a van and wearing a cold iron cow catcher, a puck doesn't eat a demon lord. Beslizoswian would have re-formed in a few years from the stuff of the cavern, or Themis could have cut Pucorl open and pulled Beslizoswian out right then, like Zeus pulled Saturn and his other siblings out of Cronus. Instead, she confirmed Pucorl's victory, so all the land that was Beslizoswian is now part of Pucorl. It's still moving from under Themis to here. And it's been pushing other parts of the Elysian Fields out of the way as it moves in. And land doesn't like to move."

"Never mind that. You demons eat each other?"

"Sure, fish and deer, foxes and cattle are drinking me all the time."

"And that doesn't bother you?"

"Not especially. In a few days I'll be swallowed up by a river then the river will be swallowed by the sea. But it all comes back around. Go ahead, have a taste."

Leona did. The water was cool and clear. It tasted of forest glades and fruit trees. Leona was almost used to the change in the land since Pucorl left, but the difference was still there. Not so much that the place was more magical, but more that the restrictions on that magic were loosened. This glade out behind Pucorl's garage and next to the dryads' grove was a tricksy kind of place, full of wonder, but not at all safe. She could feel it.

But she was more interested in the fact that demons ate other demons, and that she could drink a demon. At least, she could drink from a babbling brook and the brook didn't get mad about it. It was a different way of thinking about the world than she was used to. It offered all sorts of possibilities, so for the next little while, she asked about how this whole demon eating demon thing worked. "So does a *wiloklisp* own the land like a demon lord?"

"No, silly. A *wiloklisp* is more like a puck, except they are posted as guards, used to delay enemies, or draw them into traps."

"So if a *wiloklisp* got eaten, it wouldn't have to be confirmed? It would merely be eaten?"

"It depends." The brook was bright, a bit flighty, tumbling over rocks and dancing in the sunlight. "Most *wiloklisp* are owned by a lord of some sort. So if one gets eaten, then the eater should have the permission of the lord. Unless it has a protector of its own."

About then, the change that took place when Chevalier Pucorl left was reversed. And a moment later, the brook said, "You need to go back to the garage. Pucorl wants to talk to you."

"I don't see why." Leona yawned in indifference that was only partly feigned. She was, after all, a cat.

"These are Pucorl's lands. Piss him off and you're going to spend a lot of time getting rained on and getting burrs in your fur."

"Well, if you're going to be that way about it."

* * *

A few minutes later, Leona strolled onto the parking lot of Pucorl's garage and Pucorl opened his side door. "Kitten is worried you got lost and Mrs. Grady . . ." Pucorl sighed heavily. ". . . insisted I come pick you up before the magic of my world drove you crazy."

"I'm fine."

"I don't doubt it, but let's keep them happy. I'll arrange for some smoked fish for dinner."

Leona strolled over to the van and leapt in. The door closed and suddenly they were back in the mortal realm. Leaping up to the back of one of the seats, Leona saw that the humans were packing up. She watched as Wilber walked around the campsite, gathering little flicks of light as he went. "What's he doing?"

"Picking up the wards he put out last night," came Merlin's voice. Then the door opened and Kitten climbed into the van. "Bad Leona," she said in cat.

Leona looked back at the kitten and growled low in her throat. "You don't own me, little kitten. Behave, or I'll box your ears."

"I'm sorry," Kitten said meekly, "but I was worried."

"It's all right." Leona forgave her and jumped down into Kitten's lap to be petted.

The others climbed in and Pucorl drove off, following several horsemen.

For the rest of the morning they rode, taking a break every hour and traveling about twelve miles an hour the rest of the time. Around noon, they stopped and set up camp. They would spend the rest of the day and tonight here while the horses grazed and slept. That left plenty of time for Kitten and Paul to be educated in their school on the road. They practiced sword play with wooden swords under the tutelage of Bertrand du Guesclin's guardsmen, reading and writing, math and physics, from Mrs. Grady and Jennifer Fairbanks, magic from Dr. Delaflote and Wilber, aided by Merlin and Archimedes, and that began the cycle. Mornings were spent traveling, afternoons studying, evenings and nights in Pucorl's lands, while half the guards kept watch on the campsite within the wards that Wilber set.

Location: On the Road, France
Time: 9:37 AM, August 24, 1372

Wilber sat astride Meurtrier, the war horse that only allowed Wilber to ride him. He wore a saddle, but no bridle and Wilber wore riding boots, but no spurs. He mostly guided Meurtrier by voice, with an occasional movement of his knee. Roger McLean, on another war horse, rode up beside him.

"What's up?" Wilber asked.

"I want to take the Danube across the Germanies and all the way to the Black Sea."

"Why all the way? I can see following the Danube until we get to, say, Belgrade, but after that it starts going out of the way."

"You don't understand. I don't want to ride along the banks. I want to buy boats and boat down the river."

"You think they have river boats big enough for Pucorl? Or do you want him to drive along the banks while we ride boats?"

"If we can't buy one that's big enough, we have one built," Roger said. "Look, boats aren't faster than horses, but they travel all day and all night. We can stop when we need to pick up something from Pucorl's lands, and spend the rest of the time traveling. Heck, Wilber—" By now they were all used to avoiding words that invoked the beings of the netherworld, so heck replaced hell and darn, damn. "—even traveling ten full hours a day at eight miles an hour would double the miles we cover in a day."

Wilber took a moment to run the numbers in his head. Not that he doubted Roger, but the guy did get enthusiastic about things. His numbers were good, though, and since people and horses could rest on boats while the boats traveled, they would be better rested.

"We can use the birds, Archimedes, Carlos, and the rest to scout while we travel, so we don't get ambushed."

"Carlos, maybe. But Archimedes is Dr. Delaflote's familiar spirit. He has better things to do than flap around trees. This isn't Dungeons and Dragons."

"Fine. Archimedes can lecture Gabriel on the proper way to boil an eye of newt. By now half of Bertrand's men at arms have some sort of familiar. Even Louis has that glider Jennifer made for him."

The glider in question was bat-winged, made of sticks and lacquered cloth, and was halfway between a triangular kite from the twentieth century and a model of a bat. It would fly like a kite if you tied a string to it, but it was enchanted and could fly for hours after Louis tossed it into the air. It had three eyes, two looking forward and one looking down, a small speaker, and two bat's ears, so it could even do echolocation. Louis had paid Wilber a goodly amount for enchanting it.

Wilber looked up. Ariel was flying right now. He could barely see it, because it was painted blue gray on the bottom. "We need to talk to Bertrand."

"Right. I called him last night, but we didn't get into it," Roger agreed. "Whose phone is he using today?"

Bertrand didn't own a phone. Only the twenty-firsters, the King of France, and God owned phones. But Bertrand usually borrowed someone's phone so that he could be reached if anything came up. Annabelle's or Wilber's most often. After all, Annabelle was in Pucorl most of the time and Pucorl had his own phone. Roger pulled his phone from his pocket and said, "Clausewitz, find Bertrand would you, and see if he's busy. Wilber and I want to talk to him."

* * *

As it happened, Bertrand was carrying Annabelle's phone. Enzo said, "Phone call from Roger, General. You want to take it?"

Bertrand looked around. He was riding with the scouting element, ten horsemen who were riding a quarter mile ahead of the main party, scouting the trail as much for deadfalls and trees that would need to be cut to let Pucorl and the cardinal's wagons through as for bandits.

They were in a grove of trees, but it was a small one and Bertrand could see the fields of a village ahead. "I'll ride back, Enzo. Tell Roger I'll be there in a minute." He turned his horse and put it into a trot with a squeeze of his knees.

* * *

By the time he got back to the main body, Roger, Wilber, and Jennifer Fairbanks were all riding next to Pucorl, with Mrs. Grady leaning out of the passenger side window.

"What brings about this conclave of twenty-firsters?" Bertrand asked.

"Noah, here," Amelia Grady hooked a thumb at Roger, "wants to build an ark."

After that, they explained the plan as they rode along the path. Bertrand had the same basic concern that Sun Tzu had. Bertrand was fond of Roger's computer. It was teaching him Go and chess. Pucorl was in favor of the idea. He had a good bit of biodiesel stored in his garage, but didn't like wasting it.

They spent the rest of the morning discussing the possibilities of enchanted river boats and what sort of demon would be best to enchant them.

Location: On the Road, France
Time: 2:14 PM, August 24, 1372

As they drove along, Pucorl was playing music over the stereo system. It was quiet music, and at first Annabelle didn't notice. Then Paul started singing along.

"We're off to see the wizard, the wonderful wizard of Oz."

Annabelle rolled her eyes. "This is hardly a yellow brick road, Pucorl. And we aren't headed for Australia, anyway."

"Besides," Amelia Grady said, taking hold of Gabriel Delaflote's arm, "We have the best wizard on Earth right here with us."

"You want to play something a bit more grown-up?" Annabelle asked.

"Pucorl and grown-up don't belong in the same sentence," Paul announced. "That's what Mom says."

Pucorl sniffed loudly over the sound system. "I am most profoundly displeased." Then he giggled.

Amelia's phone Laurence said, in the voice of Laurence Olivier, "Well, we *could* be on a yellow brick road. At least in Pucorl's lands."

* * *

And so it proved. For that night, when they returned to the netherworld, the blacktop road that led to Pucorl's Garage had been replaced by a two-lane-wide yellow brick road.

Location: Pucorl's Garage, Netherworld
Time: 9:37 PM, August 24, 1372

Roger stepped into the pentagram in a room off the mechanic's bays in Pucorl's garage. This was a special pentagram. It went from Pucorl's lands to the land of Themis. He bowed and sat in the chair.

A moment later the titan Themis appeared in the pentagram, sitting on her throne. "Hello, Roger," Themis said. "What can I do for you today?"

Themis was a friend. Normally mortals didn't count titans as friends, in the same way that peasants didn't normally think of kings as friends. Only more so. But this was a special case. Roger McLean had, for a short time, owned Themis and had freely given her to herself, freeing her from the bondage that Beslizoswian, a demon lord, had forced on her. It was partly that Roger gave her her freedom, but mostly that he did so not out of expectation of reward, but because it was the right thing to do. And Themis was the titan of right behavior. It was a bond between them.

Besides, as a titan and the parent of a god or two, Themis could be in as many places at once as she needed to.

"Mostly some advice, Themis. We were wondering who we should recruit to enchant a river boat."

"That's an interesting thought. You know I extend out to sea some way. Well, partially. My nephew Poseidon shares, ah, I guess you would say sovereignty of the coastal areas with me." Themis was referring to the fact that she was both the queen of her lands and the land itself. Her body, as it were, was the entire land of Themis, which was roughly analogous to the Thrace of the ancient world, and included most of the remaining Byzantine Empire. And apparently she mixed with Poseidon on the coast.

"Before I was stolen from my place and forced into the sword, I had a lovely sea monster locked in the Bay of Athyra. It would have been a thousand years ago. When I was forced to enchant the dead for—" Her voice became as cold as a glacier on Pluto. "—that creature Philip, I used the more powerful, but not necessarily brighter, of my servants to enchant those who were to serve that creature personally. The kraken I am thinking about wasn't all that thrilled to be locked in my bay in the first place, and it's one of those who declined to return after you allowed me to free them. It's residing in a rock at the bottom of a creek in France at the moment. I can ask it if it would like a change of residence."

Which she certainly could, since she knew the creature's full name to the last accent on the least syllable. Demonic kind were controlled mostly by the invoking of their name. The more of their name you knew, the more control you had over them. The kraken wasn't in that rock only because it chose to be, but because Themis, who had learned to love freedom, allowed it to stay in that rock.

Location: Happytime Motel, Pucorl's Lands, Netherworld
Time: 9:45 PM, August 24, 1372

There was a meow and the door to Wilber's apartment in the Happytime opened enough to let Leona in.

"Pucorl, in the future, wait until I invite someone in, please." It was Pucorl's lands, and he could control things like doors at will.

"Why? You weren't doing anything important. Reading your books."

"Meow," Leona said. It meant "I need to talk to you." And Wilber decided that the discussion of manners with Pucorl could wait. It would be an utterly useless discussion anyway.

"What do you want to talk about, Leona?"

"Is the world going to end?" As she meowed, her body sank to the floor, ready to pounce or jump out of the way. Which was cat for "intensely concerned," which made sense.

Wilber was intensely concerned himself. He sighed. No matter how important the issue, you couldn't spend all your time waiting to pounce. "I don't know. It could happen if the veils aren't repaired. As long as they were in place, the netherworld slid right by the natural world with little interaction in either direction. But now it could be that as the netherworld moves, it will rip apart our world and vice versa. Honestly, I think that the vice versa is more likely, that the netherworld will be destroyed. But that doesn't mean that the side effects won't knock down mountains and shift Earth's orbit so that we fall into the sun, or are thrown right out of the solar system. The planet will still be in basically one piece, but everyone will be dead."

And because of Wilber's magic, Leona understood every word. They talked into the night and Leona learned that the threat to the universe wasn't that bad, or might be even worse. Time in the netherworld wasn't the same as time in the natural. In the netherworld, it was cyclic. In the natural world, linear. So when this destruction would occur was hard to calculate. It might be a million years in the future or a million years in the past, but most likely would be right around the time when the veils were ripped. So, if they failed to fix the problem, they might well cease to exist.

"That makes no sense," Leona meowed.

"I know. It's because we aren't sure how the two timelines will interact. But Themis is concerned, and her calculations add up. We have to stabilize things, and that means we have to figure out what caused the rifts in the first place."

Location: On the Road, France
Time: 8:40 AM, August 25, 1372

Roger slid the black charger up alongside Bertrand's huge gray and said, "I talked with Themis last night. She knows a kraken that might want to be a river boat."

"We will need more than one." Bertrand glanced at Roger, then went back to scanning the fields and hedges around them. "If we are going to enchant river boats with demons, we will need at least half a dozen. Nor am I convinced that a kraken is the best option."

"Kraken are based on cephalopods, and aside from whales are the brightest things in the oceans," Roger said. "Besides, one of their means of locomotion is their legs."

"And what good does that do us if we are putting it into a boat? The last time I checked, boats didn't have legs."

"No, but river boats have poles to push against the land or oars to move through the water. Perhaps those can double as the kraken's legs."

Bertrand shrugged shoulders so wide as to make him seem almost dwarfish. "Talk to Annabelle."

"I think better Jennifer," Roger said. "Annabelle is more of a mechanic. I don't know how much she knows about boats. Jennifer has a better background in physics."

"Consult with both then, but consider whales if the netherworld has them."

Roger turned his horse and headed back to the van.

✳ ✳ ✳

"How they bouncing?" Pucorl asked as Roger rode up.

Roger ignored the quip. Pucorl had been a puck for millennia before he got the van for a body. It was in his nature to be a smart ass. "Annabelle, you know anything about boats?"

"Not much," Annabelle said, leaning out Pucorl's driver's side window. The van was only traveling about eight miles an hour. "And nothing at all about the ships of this time. Engine girl, here."

"I was afraid of that." He pulled out his phone "Jennifer, you got a minute?"

"I guess. What's up, Roger?"

Roger could see her bay gelding pull away from one of the priest's wagons, and canter up to the van. "I need to know about boats."

"What kind of boats?"

"Riverboats." He explained about his plan to use the Danube to get them to Constantinople faster.

"Bertrand okay with that?"

"Yes, reasonably. Assuming we can find a riverboat big enough to hold Fatso here." He hooked a thumb at the van, which was twice the size of the cardinal's carriage, which was the second largest vehicle in their caravan.

"Not Fatso," Pucorl insisted. "The Incredible Van. You know, like the Incredible Hulk." The van, as it happened, was painted dark green. It was one of the standard colors that the van came in, and Pucorl's body had started life as a school van. "And assuming you can find a river boat suited to my—" Pucorl honked a haughty sniff. "—grandeur. What are you going to do for the rest of the party? That's a lot of riverboats and I ain't dragging them all along behind me."

"We hire some. Even if they don't have anything big enough for you, they ought to have some that will hold horses and wagons."

CHAPTER 3— DONAUWORTH

Location: Field Outside Donauworth, Germany
Time: 2:25 PM, September 1, 1372

The mayor of Donauworth wasn't thrilled to see them. After one look at Pucorl, he refused any of them entrance into the city, even the cardinal.

Bertrand looked at the city that Paris made into a small town. He looked over at Pucorl and his cavalry, and wondered if he could take this city. That would be an extremely bad idea, starting a war between France and the Holy Roman Empire, so he bit down on his irritation and agreed to camp outside town.

As they were setting up camp, he asked Monsignor Savona to see about negotiating with the city's burghers for entrance into the city. Only during daylight hours, and only to arrange to buy boats, barges, and food, for which they would pay in good French silver.

* * *

Monsignor Savona, Cardinal de Monteruc and the priests were refused entrance, but the senior local priest came to the gate and explained. "Since whatever it was happened, the city has been beset. The kobolds are spoiling the milk, the wild hunts run most nights, and the nixes are dancing naked up and down the river and singing in voices that tempt our young to debauchery and death."

"There are wards, Father," Monsignor Savona said. "Wilber Hyde-Davis is becoming adept at their use. And so is Doctor Delaflote."

"Why would you accompany those who traffic with demons?" the priest asked. "Especially after your experience with the demons raising the dead to grim war."

That brought on discussion of what happened in Paris and it was admitted that they were using demons to fight demons. Monsignor Savona introduced Raphico and when the priest held out his cross as though to ward off the phone, the phone's screen lit with a golden cross on a field of white. Monsignor Savona mentioned that among the functions of the angel-enchanted phone was one of healing. And that even if the townsfolk wouldn't let them in, they were still willing to heal the sick.

The priest promised to consider it.

Location: Field Outside Donauworth, Germany
Time: 10:15 PM, September 1, 1372

They came through the night, blowing ghostly horns that sent terror straight into the bones. They rode around the town, over the water as though it was firm land, then straight at the camp.

Bertrand was wakened by the howl of the trumpets and came out of his tent, sword in hand. Tiphaine was at the Happytime Motel, but after the warnings Bertrand, Roger, and Wilber had decided to spend the night in camp. Just in case.

Wilber was outside his tent, making magical gestures and intoning something in demonic. Roger had the Sword of Themis riding on his back, and as the wild hunt rode into view, Pucorl appeared in the middle of camp.

Leading the hunt was a tall man in armor that glowed silver. The man had long hair so pale it was white in the moonlight. He had no beard and his eyes were slanted up. He had pointed ears and his laugh was cold and evil. He rode straight at the wards with his companions and his hounds all about him.

As he reached the barrier, Roger drew the Sword of Themis, which lit with fire. And then the wild hunt hit the wards . . .

. . . and splashed.

First the dogs hit, and were ripped to bloody mist. And though the elf lord tried to turn, he wasn't in time. He ran into the wall of magical force and his front half was turned into mist. There was a pause as the rest of the wild hunt diverted around the wards, some of them riding right through the walls of Donauworth as they tried to avoid the wards. They went around the wards, rode on, and then turned around. The wild hunt came back. By now, the elf lord was re-forming. His horse was still half bone, but he himself was almost back to his form, save for his right hand, which was bone with flesh starting to re-form on it.

In a voice like a banshee, he shouted, "Who dares interfere with my hunt?"

Roger looked at Bertrand. Bertrand looked at Roger.

In a loud voice, Wilber said, "That would be me. Now what are you doing in the mortal realms?"

"I go where I wish, mortal. These are my lands, whether mortal or fairy. Mortals are mine to hunt."

"I'm right here. Hunt away."

Suddenly a woman stood in the clearing. She held a book in one hand and scales in the other. It was Themis, and divinity glowed from her. She looked around, walked the wards, and while she did so everyone was held motionless. Within the wards, outside the wards, mortal and elf in the field and on the walls of Donauworth, no one could move but to look at her. She examined Wilber's wards and clucked her tongue, pointing at flaws. Wilber blushed.

She looked at the elf lord, and he said, "This is not your place."

"As justice is everywhere, I am everywhere. As decency is everywhere, I am everywhere."

Then she went over to Roger. "But, Roger, there is also freedom. Theirs as well as yours. So this I lay upon you. You may use my sword to defend yourself and your companions." She looked around, saw Leona sitting on Pucorl's dashboard and smiled. "Even to the cat who has joined your company. However, you may not use my sword simply to strike those you dislike or disapprove of." The book became a torch and she held it high. "For they too have freedom."

Roger looked at her, then he looked at the elf lord who was starting to smile. "What about my rifle?"

Themis laughed. "You too are free, Roger. But don't use *my* sword for this." She looked around again and then faded away.

Roger put the Sword of Themis over his back, and turned to his tent, but one of the squires was ahead of him. The lad, perhaps seventeen, had the rifle in his hands and was running over to bring it to Roger.

"Thank you," Roger said, taking the rifle.

"Husband," said a beautiful elven woman with flaming hair and glowing eyes, "will you let the night's sport be spoiled by this rude interruption and these mortals who think themselves our equals?"

Until that moment, Roger noted, there was at least a chance that the wild hunt would pack it in for the night. But not now. He sighed, and lifted the rifle.

"Coward!" roared the elf lord. "Hiding behind your wards while you attack me from afar."

Roger looked at him, then at Bertrand.

Bertrand shrugged. "He has a point. But, at the same time, if he's after a duel, it should be between you and him."

"The thing that I'm worried about," Roger said quietly as he walked over to Bertrand, "is the town. Those people have no defense against the wild hunt and the way the powers that be are reacting, they aren't going to have one either. They won't even let us help them unless we demonstrate that we are on the side of the angels, so to speak. If we do nothing but sit here in our camp, those folk—" He hooked a thumb at the wild hunt. "—are going to take their frustration out on the town."

"If you desire a duel, elf lord, then face him one on one!" Bertrand shouted.

The elf lord waved away his fellows. He sheathed his sword, and gathered up an elven bow, then dismounted and walked to stand a ways off. Roger opened the rifle. It was a breech loading weapon that opened like a shotgun. He loaded it with an iron bolt that had a lead sabot around it, then with a block of shaped black powder. That last wouldn't work without the demon that resided in the firing chamber.

Roger closed the weapon and carefully stepped over the glowing wards without touching them. He could feel the magic flow around him.

✷ ✷ ✷

The elf lord watched the mortal step out from the wards and let the rage take him. How dare this flyspeck consort with titans and embarrass him before his lady? But there was calculation in his heart as well as rage, for the fool brought the Sword of Themis with him. And to the victor goeth the spoils. He smiled and laid the elven shaft into the bow. He waited.

✷ ✷ ✷

Roger moved slowly, rifle held ready to fire. The rifle was a distance weapon. It had rifling and enchanted sights. That would let him see where the bolt would go. But that wouldn't matter much today, because there wouldn't be time to aim. This was more a wild west gunfight than a formal duel. It would start when one of them started to move.

Roger watched, right hand on the trigger, left hand holding the barrel. Roger was a good shot, and before they were brought here, he had hunted birds and shot skeet with his father.

He was never sure what it was that brought him to decision, but in a moment he was moving, and so was the elf lord. As the elf lord lifted the bow and pulled the bowstring, Roger lifted the barrel of his rifle with his left hand and pulled the trigger long before the rifle reached his shoulder.

The hammer struck the home of the salamander and the little demonic creature of flame was released. It consumed the charge of black powder in a tiny fraction of a second, then retreated back to its home as the bullet sped across the field.

The elf lord's bow came up and as the bowstring touched his cheek, he heard the crack and felt the iron bullet rip through him, and it ripped him in a way that bronze or wood could never do. It ripped and twisted the connections that made him what he was. The bow was a part of him, the arrow was a part of him, as was his horse and to an extent the whole wild hunt. All were a part of him.

No more. All those connections were ripped asunder as the cold iron bolt ripped through him.

The elf shot bolt was bereft. In the normal course of things, it would be guided by its master to the target. But now it was loose, with no guidance. It went looking for a target, flying in random spirals.

It saw the strange cart that stank of magic, decided that was a target worthy of its attention, and flew at it.

It never got there.

It hit the wards and was broken and shattered into nothingness.

✳ ✳ ✳

This cannot be, the elf lady thought in shocked horror. *My lord is a being of magic. He cannot be harmed by a mortal.* This was sport, nothing more. The worst that could possibly happen was that he might be forced back underhill to the netherworld, to return on another night. But truly damaged . . .

In horror, she ran.

And the wild hunt ran with her.

Location: Outside Donauworth, Germany
Time: Dawn, September 2, 1372

As the sun peeped over the horizon, the gates of Donauworth opened and the townspeople came out. Not all of them, but a goodly number. First were the poor and the sick, who came to see if the healing that Monsignor Savona promised was as real as the wild hunt and the fight seen by the city guard last night.

Then there were merchants and boatmen who, whatever the town fathers said, came to see if they might make a profit dealing with these people.

Liane Boucher pointed her camera, DW, at the child and the camera saw, but it saw with magic as well as integrated circuits. It saw—with advice from Raphico and knowledge from high school health and biology texts—how to see illness and what the things it saw in the little girl's body meant, and then it sent that knowledge to Raphico by bluetooth connection.

By the time the little girl got to the angel-enchanted smartphone, Raphico knew what was wrong with her. She had tuberculosis, and Raphico went through not only wiping out the tubular bacilli, but explaining to the little girl's body how to recognize them and fight them on its own.

With the images from DW, it took little energy.

The next patient had tapeworms. He was a man of thirty-five. And after him came a man with an infected jaw, the result of a decaying, impacted wisdom tooth.

It went on all day, with Raphico and DW having to take cooling breaks, for even with demonic help, each healing used the circuits of the camera and phone to direct the energies of the demon and angel, and that use heated the CPUs.

As it went on, several of the priests of the town watched. Finally, around two in the afternoon, one of the priests asked, "How can you believe that is an angel if it is so willing to talk with a demon?"

Cardinal de Monteruc said, "I have asked the same question many times. Raphico insists that the politics of Heaven are more complicated than mortals realize, or want to realize. For myself, I am skeptical of Raphico's true allegiance. At the same time, I know that he is healing the sick and doing so in God's name. And that I cannot condemn, not while I am not *certain* he is evil."

Several of the local priests nodded as a man with a broken hand was healed.

* * *

The barge maker, after getting permission, went to Pucorl and, grabbing his front bumper, lifted. Well, tried to lift. Pucorl didn't help and weighed over four thousand pounds even empty. After grunting a bit he stood, looked at the van, shook his head and said. "It's too big, too heavy. The water is shallow in many places this far up the Danube. The cart will make the barge sink three, maybe four, feet into the water and that's too much draft. Better you go downriver to Ingolstadt."

The barge he was talking about had thick walls of wood and would weigh a considerable amount even empty. Jennifer had a better—or at least different—idea. She wanted a thin-walled flotation chamber made from a wooden structure wrapped in cloth which would then be painted with boiled pine resin. The idea was to produce something between the doped canvas wings of a WWI airplane and a fiberglass boat body.

But as long as she was the one bringing it up, the bargeman was uninterested. When Bertrand demanded that he listen, his attitude changed. Mostly that was because Bertrand was a large, scary man, not an attractive teenage girl. But, in large part, it was because he assumed that Bertrand was in charge of the money, which wasn't true.

As it happened, the biggest part of the twenty-firsters' funds were owned by Mrs. Grady and her son Paul, who had sold a phone and a computer to the king of France. The next largest part was owned by Liane Boucher, because the pope, after a long, private talk with Monsignor Savona, had decided that she should be paid for her phone by the church. Even if she did give it directly to God, and not the church, it was given to God in care of the church.

More surprising than the church paying was that it stayed with Monsignor Savona instead of returning to Avignon with the pope. Raphico, however, had insisted. Cardinal de Monteruc had his own funds, and Bertrand had a chest of silver for expenses, but the people who would be paying for the barge—at least Pucoral's barge—were going to be the twenty-firsters. So after two days of negotiations, Jennifer got her way.

Wilber didn't have much in the way of cash, but he was in an excellent position to work his magic with the aid of Merlin. With Archimedes the crow, Doctor Delaflote and Wilber were fairly capable wizards.

* * *

"We," the mayor, a fat man with an ermine cloak and a wide leather belt, said pompously, "will consider letting your party enter the city." He looked around the tent. There were two rickety looking tables and six chairs. Seated in the chairs were Bertrand du Guesclin, his wife Tiphaine, Wilber Hyde-Davis, Gabriel Delaflote, and Mrs. Amelia Grady.

"Don't trouble yourself," said Wilber Hyde-Davis in excellent German. "It's no trouble at all for us to stay here while we do our business. After all, Pucorl's lands are only a moment away." He waved at Merlin, who was open on the table, and the screen changed to show Pucorl's lands with the dryads' grove, the Happytime Motel, the garage and shop, and the little brook that wound its way around behind the garage and through the dryads' grove.

It was, in its—to Wilber's mind—tacky way, a nice place and much better than sharing a bedbug-infested canvas sack filled with hay in one of the local inns. But Wilber knew perfectly well that that wasn't what this was about. This meeting was about kobolds and wards to keep the wild hunt out of Donauworth— and for that matter, off the backs of the peasants harvesting the grain that would feed the region for the winter into next spring. Mayor Fats was trying for bargaining points. "On the other hand, if you want to talk to Cardinal de Monteruc, I'm sure he will be pleased to know the town is now open to him."

Wilber hid a smile as the mayor's face congealed before his eyes.

The mayor looked around at the rest of those present, and Bertrand spoke.

"Well, I thank you for your city council's forbearance. My men will be better for the occasional night in a tavern."

"There are conditions." The mayor jumped back on script like a starving dog on a steak.

"I'll instruct my men to be on their best behavior," Bertrand offered airily.

"It's not that. It's . . . well, it's the elves and the kobolds. You have to get rid of them for us."

"That's easier said than done," Gabriel said. "And it may not be possible at all."

"But they're demons! Fey creatures! And you're wizards. You have to be able to get rid of them." The mayor went from bluster to begging in a moment, and in spite of the way they had been treated, Wilber felt for the guy.

But that didn't change the facts. The veil was in shreds, and kobolds didn't live far below the surface in places like this. Donauworth had been here for centuries and its echos affected the netherworld. On the other side of the veil was a fairly close copy of Donauworth, and that copy was the home of kobolds, one for every structure in the town. They lived there and were affected by the actions of the inhabitants of Donauworth for the simple reason that the netherworld, that other universe that impinged on the imperial plane, had little structure of its own. The netherworld got imprinted, and by now the beings in that other realm were mostly converted into what the people living here for the last thousand years or so *thought* was there.

And now they could cross from their copies of the houses of Donauworth right into the real world houses. Usually at the hearth, because that was the center of most homes.

"We can't make them leave," Wilber said, "because they live here too. Always have. It's only that their 'here' is a half a beat to the side. Out of the corner of your eye. And they had nothing to do with the ripping up of the veil that separates our world from theirs."

"Then you can't help us? But you fought off the wild hunt."

"That was different," Bertrand said. "While the fey are local to the region, the wild hunt participants aren't local to Donauworth, and they are from a couple of levels farther away. It was Roger and his rifle that did for the elflord. But at least for the town proper, Wilber and Doctor Delaflote should be able to produce wards to keep the wild hunt away."

"And," added Tiphaine, "with the aid of Pucorl and the twenty-firsters, if you are willing and reasonable, we should be able to negotiate some sort of rapprochement with the kobolds and other fey creatures that inhabit your town. Back in our lands in France, we managed fairly well with simple courtesy."

The discussion went on. Ways and means, what the town wanted, and what it would accept. Then, after they had a rough idea of what the powerful in Donauworth wanted, it was time to find out what the kobolds wanted.

They would open the gates and Pucorl would drive to the central square, and then slip across into the netherworld. Not back to his place, but to that part of the netherworld that matched this place.

✳ ✳ ✳

The sun was bright as Pucorl, with Annabelle, Roger, Wilber, and Doctor Delaflote shifted. The sun dimmed as though it was behind a cloud, but it wasn't. The sun was still there, glowing yellow in a blue sky, but a bit dimmer. The town too was dimmer, and the houses were shorter, to suit the size of the people who were mostly kobolds. There were others of the magic world here, some with names of legend, some with no name that any living human would know. The arrival of Pucorl in their midst was a shock for them and the *Landdísir* of Donauworth. In truth, she was the *Landdísir* of Donauworth before Donauworth was Donauworth, back when it was a fishing village and a crossing point before Christianity got to this part of the world. Her name was long since forgotten by any living person, but she was the mistress and mother to the kobolds of Donauworth and the other fey of the area. Her name was long and complex and not something she was willing to share, but a thousand years before, when the villagers offered gifts at her shrine, she was called *Mareike ves Landdísir*.

Talks with Mareike were complicated by the fact that she was miffed that she had been forgotten, and not at all pleased with the Catholic church, which had enforced the forgetting. Her priestesses had been murdered by Christian mobs.

"I think we are going to need Raphico for this," Wilber told Roger a few minutes in.

"I think we are going to need Tiphaine," Roger said.

"Let's wrap this up and go get them both."

There was also the fact that while the kobolds were Mareike's children, they weren't the most obedient of children. There was some question as to whether she could command them to behave, even if she wanted to.

* * *

Even with the inclusion of Tiphaine and Raphico, the negotiations took the rest of the time they were in Donauworth and were still ongoing when they left. What was in place was more like a framework for the individual households of Donauworth to make their own deal with the kobold of their house or the river spirits for fishermen, that sort of thing.

* * *

What the twenty-firsters, and especially Pucorl, got out of the deal were several barges, including a large purpose-built, flat-bottomed enchanted barge for Pucorl. They needed the enchantment for two things.

One because the barge without enchantment wouldn't last the trip down the river. It was too flimsy and, as it turned out, a lot of fish found the resin-soaked cloth that was its skin absolutely delicious. The demon who inhabited the barge managed to make the little fishes leave it alone by making the barge seem a large hungry predator, which was what the spirit they called to the barge was—a kraken from the sea next to Themis' lands. It had gotten caught up in the battle for Paris, and was looking for a new body.

The first thing the kraken, who chose to be called Joe Kraken, did was demand that the poles that pushed the barge along the river be replaced. Not good enough, not flexible enough, according to Joe Kraken.

Instead . . .

"That's kind of creepy," said Jennifer, as she watched the workmen attach the leather and canvas tentacles with their leather suckers to the bottom rear of the barge. There were ten of the things, eight that were ten meters long and a half meter thick at the base, and two that were fifteen meters long and a meter wide at the base.

"That's not the half of it," Roger said, pointing at the back of the kraken barge where they were installing—also at the kraken's insistence—a beak made of wrought iron, a leather tongue embedded with "teeth," and a gullet that went into the body of the barge. The kraken would be able to eat.

Once the new tentacles, mouth and so on were added, they re-did the enchantment. As they had learned with Pucorl, repeating the enchantment process let the kraken migrate into its new additions to its body.

* * *

Roger, Jennifer, Annabelle and Wilber watched as workmen with poles levered the newly modified barge onto greased wooden rails and slid it down into the river. It was thirty feet long with a flat area for the first twenty-two feet and an eight foot long, ten foot wide cabin in the back. The front had a liftable ramp that could carry Pucorl and was how he would drive onto and off the barge. The cabin in the back was eight feet tall with a slightly curved roof, so that rain would poor off. It had two eyes, one to either side, and there were a matching pair below the waterline, so that Joe Kraken could see the bottom of the river. Behind the eyes and in the back were the tentacles, eight thirty feet long, and two forty-five feet long. And they writhed as Joe was slid down the rails to the river.

A tentacle grabbed a bush and pulled it out of the ground, then tossed it away. Jennifer shuddered.

Once in the water, the tentacles were mostly hidden. The bases of the upper ones could be seen, but they quickly bent down into the water and the water roiled with their movement. Joe Kraken twisted about, using his tentacles to shift the barge back and forth, then pushed out into the middle of the river, scooted over to the far bank, and turned back. A tentacle came out of the water and grabbed a tree, then flexed, pushing the barge quickly down the river. Then the barge turned and crossed the river again. Back on this side, a tentacle grabbed a rock for purchase, and they could almost see that it was doing the same thing underwater.

Jennifer shuddered again. "Creepy."

* * *

The next day, Joe Kraken was still learning his body configuration. Jennifer and Roger were aboard, sitting on the roof of the cabin. Jennifer was there to examine how her design was working. Roger was there in case someone wanted to take the barge away from Jennifer. The Danube was not the safe, policed river of the twenty-first century.

They were two miles downriver from Donauworth when one of the two longer tentacles came up out of the water and grabbed a cow. The cow was pulled against, which moved the barge, then was picked up and pulled beneath the river. Its subsequent fate was unclear because of the muddy water but almost certainly not good.

"Oh, that's *really* creepy," said Jennifer. She glared at Roger, standing next to her. "How do you know that . . . that *thing* won't use one of us for a snack next time?"

"It's not mine." Roger was wondering the same thing himself. "Hey, Joe. You're not supposed to eat the wildlife."

Joe didn't answer.

"Joe Kraken, answer me." They knew that the kraken could hear them. It had microphones and speakers in the cabin and outside it, as well. The silence made him nervous. He didn't want to be on a sea monster that had gone rogue.

He reached up and grabbed Themis. "Excuse me. Could we get a little help here?"

Whenever the titan wasn't present in person, she could talk to Roger through the sword—and on those occasions she was something of a mind-reader.

<You needn't worry. The kraken's not all that smart, but he's smart enough to know the difference between a person and an animal. He won't harm anyone unless he is ordered to.>

"Ordered by whom?"

<By the owner of its vehicle. Haven't you been paying attention for the last almost a year? In this case, Pucorl owns his vehicle, so Pucorl is his master. I have some authority, since I created him with the help of my nephew, Poseidon.>

Roger was still not satisfied. "But that cow belonged to somebody. We're not going to make ourselves real popular if our demon-possessed river barge is lunching on livestock and pets as we go along."

<He won't bother any animal clearly attached to a human. By a tether, a leash, whatever. If the animal's not attached, you'll have to instruct him not to eat it. And now, I'm busy. This is not important.>

And she was gone.

After Roger explained the gist of the conversation, Jennifer shook her head. "It's still creepy. You'd better give the thing its instructions now, though, before we run across any more domestic munchies."

"It's not listening to me."

"Then call Pucorl."

"Why me?" He was practically whining by now.

"Never mind." She called Pucorl. "Pucorl, you need to talk to your barge. It's ignoring us. And it's eating the local livestock."

"Do I have to?" complained a deep fog horn of a voice through the external speakers, clearly in response to Pucorl's instructions. But at least it was speaking though the speakers.

"Kraken," said Roger. Then, in the vague hope that personalizing the creature might be of help, he asked, "Joe?"

"Joe," the speaker agreed.

"Don't eat any more cows, Joe. Or a horse. Or a sheep. Or a pig. Or a goat. Or a dog." Each was accompanied by a mental image. "Or . . . I guess that's enough."

"You didn't tell him to stay away from cats and chickens," said Jennifer.

"Who cares about chickens? And I don't like cats."

"Well, we have a cat with us. And if Joe eats Leona, much less Kitten, there's going to be hell to pay."

"Then you tell him."

Jennifer did, but she wasn't entirely sure that she was getting through, so she called Wilber.

✳ ✳ ✳

Wilber called Joe by way of his built-in crystal set. And to clarify, he sent it a list of animals with their images. Then he called Jennifer back. She put her phone on speaker so Roger could hear.

"Squid brains are really different from human brains. They don't have voices at all, and they barely have ears. They communicate with colored patterns on their skin. It's a language and a way of thinking that's so strange it gives me fits, in spite of my magic.

"But we put in speakers and microphones, and it does talk."

"Yes, but I'm not so sure how much it understands. That's why the pictures."

Jennifer had to be satisfied with that.

Location: North Bank of the Danube at Donauworth, Germany
Time: Dawn, September 19, 1372

One last time they brought Joe Kraken up onto the shore and repaired the pentagram. The pentagram was made of river plants and fish parts from the Danube, ground into a paste and blessed by Monsignor Savona and the local priests. The latter based on the notion that a kraken in the Danube would be a bit safer if the priests of Donauworth were involved. *Joe Kraken*, the boat, was a complex combination of magic, twenty-firster technology, and courtesy. Joe Kraken, the demon, was contacted by the twenty-firsters before they reached Donauworth. When it became clear that the twenty-firsters would have to have a specialized boat built to spec, Joe was asked what he would like in his new body. As it turned out he could communicate with them through their cell phones, and communicate reasonably well with Pucorl.

Sort of. It was a bit like talking to a three year old. His calling name was discussed too. Kraken because he was a sea monster, and Joe after Joe Louis, because he was a fighter. Especially now that he had tentacles to punch with.

Joe Kraken wanted four eyes, two permanently fixed on the boat's pilot house. That way he could see without having to constantly heave himself above the surface, and two more painted on the sides below the waterline. Happily, the pilot house eyes didn't need to be the size of Joe's own eyes. That would have been beyond the skill of the local glassmakers.

In front of the pilot house was a long and wide flat surface that Pucorl would ride on, and inside the body of the boat was a leather sack that had openings in the bow and stern. That was an experiment to see if Joe Kraken was able to use it like a squid's bladder to propel itself through the water. Not use the bladder itself—it was much too small—but somehow make it work as a surrogate.

Roger didn't ask too many questions. The less he had to contemplate what was happening at the barge's bottom, the better. Jennifer was right. It *was* really creepy.

But it worked.

CHAPTER 4—VIENNA

**Location: Danube River, Approaching Vienna,
Austria
Time: 7:25 AM, September 22, 1372**

Two and a half days after leaving Donauworth, Joe Kraken saw the walls of Vienna. He stopped the barge and grabbed a couple of rocks on the riverbottom to hold him in place.

Joe Kraken didn't own his body. Roger was the kraken's master—his pilot, it might be better to say—but the creature itself was owned by Pucorl. The twenty-firsters had received payment from Pucorl before the kraken was invited into the barge. That meant that Pucorl could land on it, even if it was slightly out of place.

Over the last couple of days, Joe Kraken had experimented with his bladder and was learning to use it to propel himself through the river water. But it was easier to use his tentacles to hold himself steady.

Pucorl said, "I see Vienna."

Annabelle answered, "Yeah, me too." She was sitting on Pucorl's roof, enjoying the cool breeze as they floated down the river. The rest of the party were on fifteen river barges, enchanted partly by sea spirits that Themis introduced to them, and partly by Danube River sprites. They carried the cargo and some of the horses. Other horses and their riders rode along the banks on either side of the river, scouting their path.

Having the barges to rest the horses meant that they could switch off and keep their horses fresh. It still delayed them, but not nearly as much.

After the brief stop, Joe Kraken pushed off and used his jet to shift out to the center of the river as Pucorl used his speakers to let the outriders know they were in sight of Vienna.

✳ ✳ ✳

Wilber Hyde-Davis looked up, then back down at the computer screen. The spell he was working on could wait. He closed Merlin and climbed out of Pucorl, but his mind didn't let go of the spell. It was to enchant a printing press, but spells were more complicated than simply calling a demon into a thing. The shape of the thing mattered. The demon mattered. And, finally, the way it was called mattered. It was the combination of all three things that made a spell work. And that last one, the manner of the calling, was subtly important to the results. It was also something that demons did to each other, on what amounted to an instinctive level. They did it automatically, like people breathing, or the beating of their hearts, or eating and digesting. And that made it difficult for the demons to understand why what they did affected the magic.

The spell in question was an example of that. It used a rope to hold a bag of ink, and the demon was supposed to move the rope like an arm and ink the press after each page was printed. But making a rope into an arm involved more than tying the rope to the press and calling a demon. The demon had to be fitted into the whole contraption in the right way, because the rope by itself lacked the definition needed to become an arm or tentacle.

The spell was for a printer in Paris. Wilber would receive a sum of money deposited in the new Royal Bank of France. He still wouldn't be able to spend that money anywhere but France, since as of now there was not much in the way of international banking. But the twenty-firsters had—without wanting to—introduced the concepts of fiat money,

54

fractional reserve, and so on. They didn't have any of the details, but they did know that Banque de France was the national bank of France in the twenty-first century and that it controlled monetary policy and was part of the European Central Bank, sort of. They knew that the money wasn't gold or silver, but paper notes that weren't even backed by gold or silver, and they knew that printing too much money was a bad thing. That information was enough to get things started. So Wilber and all the twenty-firsters had accounts in the Royal Bank of France. They weren't the only ones. Bertrand had an account, and so did Pucorl and several other demons.

It wasn't important in the here and now, but like the other seeds of knowledge the twenty-firsters dropped in their time in France, it was continuing to have an effect even after they were gone. And they were seeing that effect because of the communications link provided by Pucorl, Merlin, and especially Themis and the links she provided.

"What's up?" Wilber asked Joe.

Jennifer had her eyes shaded with a hand. "I can see what I think is the tower of Saint Stephen's cathedral ahead."

"What's going on?" Leona meowed.

"We're apparently in sight of Vienna," Wilber told her in cat. Then he climbed the ladder to the landing on the roof of the cabin. Halfway up the ladder, he turned and saw the tower. "Yes, I think you're right."

Location: Archducal Palace, Vienna, Austria
Time: Two Hours Past Dawn, September 22, 1372

The scout had dust on his boots and dirt on his cloak as he burst into the throne room. "They're here! We spotted that enchanted barge of theirs."

"Good." Archduke Albert III of Austria looked to Karl von Richter, his new chief counselor. "Do you think we will be able to succeed?" By now the events in France were well known from one end of the Danube to the other. Bargemen had brought the news that the twenty-firsters were building a new kind of river barge that would be enchanted by a tame demon almost a week ago. The plans were in place.

"I don't know, Your Grace. We can but try." The counselor looked at the starling on his shoulder.

It looked back and said, "Remind them."

The counselor laughed. "Swift is unimpressed by royalty and wishes me to remind you again that these are people of great power, with strong alliances. We must be careful of them. Don't offer them insult!"

"Human royalty," Swift clarified.

"Shush. Don't be rude."

"We remember, Swift," Archduke Albert told the starling. He shook his head. Karl was his favorite teacher at the university of Vienna. The university was started by Albert's older brother Rudolph the same year that Rudolph died.

After the veil between the worlds was rent and demons started appearing in the world, the interest in magic in the university had increased. Then, with the news out of Paris—especially the paper by Gabriel Delaflote on the proper means of summoning an informational demon or familiar to teach one magic—Karl summoned Swift to a starling. Since then, they had been studying magic and picking up rumors from the netherworld.

The lands of Themis in the netherworld were fairly near Austria, so the rumors of events in Paris were transmitted to Vienna more quickly by way of the netherworld than by land or sea in the real world.

"Very well. We will remember. Call out the guard. I want them greeted as royal guests. After all, aside from Roger McLean who bears the Sword of Themis, there is Bertrand du Guesclin, the former constable of France, and there is also a cardinal of mother church."

✳ ✳ ✳

56

The docks were festooned with banners and the city guard were lined up in rows with their pikes held in salute as Joe Kraken pushed up against the dock. Four huge tentacles came up out of the water and seized various posts and such on the dock to hold the barge in place. Seeing that, the city guard did an impromptu rearward scuttle before their officers held them steady.

Unfortunately, the dock was wooden and a bare eight feet across. Getting Pucorl onto it and down it to the shore was impossible.

For the other barges, it wasn't so bad. The horses could be guided and the wagons could be manhandled. Still, the first impression was not what Albert III was hoping for.

"It is no great issue, Your Grace," Tiphaine de Raguenel offered with a curtsy. "Sieur Pucorl, Chevalier du Elysium, is large. The more so now, with his armor. A little later, Joe Kraken will move over next to the beach and run out a ramp for Pucorl to use." She waved at Bertrand du Guesclin. "My own dear husband has similar difficulties, albeit on a smaller scale."

Bertrand was a big man and so broad that he almost seemed deformed. The twenty-firsters were all tall and comely, even—perhaps especially—the lovely dark-skinned young woman with the shiny black hair and glowing black eyes, introduced as Lakshmi Rawal, whose family, he was told, were diplomats from far off India.

His guests were nobles. That much was certain.

*   *   *

The banquet hall was well lit with torches and lamps. The tables were covered with cloths, so the diners could wipe their hands between courses. Wild boar and fruit compotes, as well as other savories, filled the tables, and there was conversation throughout the room as the minstrels played in the corner.

Albert looked over at Lakshmi again. His eyes found her of their own accord. He dragged them away from her. The twenty-firsters were not peasants, to be taken at one's pleasure. They were nobles with an armed retinue of considerable size, and magic beyond any he could bring to bear. Lakshmi did not look back, but continued her conversation with a musician.

*   *   *

Johann of Vienna was nervous after the woman called him over. She asked him about his lute and the song he was playing. She seemed to know a lot, and if she were a servant girl he would be enjoying himself. But she wasn't, and he wasn't. The ballad that he played was old and well known but not, apparently, to her.

"Let him go, Lakshmi," said a young man, "before you ruin his life. This isn't the twenty-first century. Entertainers are not considered royalty of any sort."

"Well, we should be, Bill. This guy is good. I'd like to have Liane record him." Lakshmi was a drama student whose dream was to be a movie star before they got pulled into this century. She was also a good singer.

"I don't disagree, Lakshmi, but you're going to get him in trouble if you keep ignoring the other people at the table."

The other people at the table included the archduke, his brother, Leopold, and his wife, Elizabeth, who was even younger than Lakshmi. And who was looking daggers at Lakshmi everytime Lakshmi looked up. *Keep him, kid,* Lakshmi thought. *I'm not interested in your archduke.*

Still, she let the minstrel go back to his playing. And the dinner went on.

Location: Ducal Palace, Vienna, Austria
Time: 10:20 AM, September 23, 1372

The guest quarters in the ducal palace were grand, if not as comfortable as the Happytime Motel, but politeness required them to stay here. It wasn't going to be for long. There was no reason for them to stop in Vienna more than a day or so. There was a knock on the door, and a man in scholar's robes with a starling on his shoulder came in.

"Lord Wilber, my respects. I was wondering about your ability to speak with animals?"

"What about it?" Wilber asked. He knew Counselor Karl von Richter from last night.

"I wonder how you acquired it. Were you born with the knack? Is it a thing common in the time you come from?"

"No. It comes from Merlin." He waved at the computer which was sitting open on a table.

"Yet Swift doesn't let me speak to horses?"

"The abilities a demon companion provides are dependent on their strength and the vessel they are placed in. A bird or a cat doesn't give— No, that's not the right word—affect the demon that occupies it the way that a more specialized container does. With the starling, your familiar can speak to you aloud. If it was a cat, you would hear the meaning in your mind. But Merlin was called into a device that was designed for one purpose and one purpose only, to let me hear and understand speech." Wilber needed to be careful here. He didn't want to tell this guy all the effects on Merlin and, for that matter, on him, but at the same time uninformed magic use was bloody dangerous. "Also, Merlin is a good bit more powerful and intelligent than your average puck. He was an adviser to an ancient god. One that was subsumed by a later god that was itself converted into an unnamed Christian angel sometime later."

"That is one interpretation," Merlin interrupted. "But it is not universally shared. Whether my begetter is converted or temporarily imprisoned depends on who you ask. I would say she is simply biding her time until she may again walk free."

"Oh, boy. Here we go," Wilber muttered. While he personally agreed with Merlin's interpretation more than Raphico's, when the two got into it, it was like a Baptist and a Scientologist trying to convert each other. Raphico insisted that since Jennifer had given her phone to God; i.e., ipso facto, and squaring the circle, the one who owns it must be the one true and absolute God. Merlin argued that the netherworld being who received it, was the one that happened to fit the Christian mythology best. If she'd given it to Allah, it would have gone to a different god. The one that got it was one of the "all powerful" gods of the netherworld.

However, Merlin surprised him. "But that isn't really what you wanted to talk about. Is it?"

"Not exactly," Karl said. "We have some magic and we are learning more at the new university, but you have a good head start. I would like to convince you and Doctor Delaflote to stay here and head up our faculty of magic at the university of Vienna. We can offer you an excellent stipend, good quarters, servants, and with your phone, you won't even be out of touch with your companions."

"Thank you for the offer, but at least for now I think I prefer to stay with my companions." Wilber shook his head. "In a way, we are on a mission from God, or at least the powers that be in the netherworld. We are trying to discover the cause behind the rift between the universes. And at least some of the gods and angels of the netherworld agree that discovering the cause is necessary if there is to be any hope of repairing the rift."

"Do we really want it repaired?" Karl asked. "After all, magic makes many things possible that were unthinkable before. I know that there are bad things as well, but might the good outweigh the bad?"

"It might," Merlin agreed, "but there are also the natures of the two universes to consider. Our universe is a place of cycles, where everything comes back around to its beginning. It has done so many times, and our time is not like your time. I remember your world before there were humans and after your species had gone extinct. I don't remember everything. I am not a god. But I remember many futures of your universe."

"What he doesn't remember," Wilber added, "is this. The ripping of the veil between the universes to tatters. Themis being forced into a sword and used by a spoiled brat of a king's little brother. He doesn't remember us, the van, the twenty-firsters, any of what has happened since our arrival in this time. At this point we can't be sure that our two universes can survive this more intimate contact. Whoever, or whatever, did this could have doomed two universes. We have to find out, and we have to discover if it can or should be fixed."

"I agree that is a most important mission. But why can't you do it from right here in Vienna? Why go to Constantinople?"

"Partly because Doctor Delaflote knows a scholar in Constantinople who he wants to talk to. Partly because Raphico has been ordered to Constantinople to deal with something he won't talk about. Partly because Roger wants to return the Sword of Themis to its proper place."

"Its proper place?"

"The lands in the netherworld correspond loosely to the lands of our world. The Elysian Fields are 'far to the west,' England as it turns out. The land of Themis in the netherworld corresponds roughly to parts of Greece and Thrace in our world. Turns out it's close to what's left of the Byzantine Empire.

"And, finally, because from what we hear from the demons, the rifts in the veils are centered somewhere to the east of Constantinople. So we are hoping we will be able to find out more once we get there."

This whole conversation was bothering Wilber, so the shout of "Knock, knock!" in Coach's voice came as something of a relief.

Wilber went to the door and opened it, only to have Leona stroll in like she owned the place. Around her neck was Jeff's sports watch, its strap expanded into a collar. "Hello, Leona," Wilber said in cat. "What's Coach doing around your neck?"

The collar answered in Austrian. "Leona, the lovely little pussycat, has consented to give me a ride and since I have an internal mic I can translate for her."

"That sounds like an equitable arrangement," Wilber agreed while Karl looked on in surprise. "So what brings you here?"

"Leona has a few questions about magical creatures and dietary habits," Coach said, like it was a joke of some sort.

"Are you saying that the magical device is owned by that cat?" Karl stared at the cat and watch.

"No," Coach said. "Thanks be to Jeff, glorious lad, no one owns me but me. I am a free sports watch, I am."

"Would you be interested in staying in Vienna then?" Karl asked quickly.

This guy is sharp, Wilber thought.

"An interesting question. For myself, I think not. I prefer the netherworld. I can't walk in this one, while in the netherworld I am a faun of great athletic prowess." The leer in Coach's voice made the type of athleticism he was talking about obvious. "I may know someone who might be interested, but you would have to make a good offer."

"Who?" Wilber asked.

"Asuma," Coach said. "She's a bit bored with the talent of the troops. I'm not sure she'd be interested, but she does own herself and she could stay here if she were to receive adequate recompense."

"What sort of recompense?" Karl asked.

"Let's not get ahead of ourselves. We haven't agreed to anything," Wilber said without thinking.

"I don't see how *we* have anything to agree to," Coach corrected. "Asuma doesn't need your permission to do anything."

"I didn't say she did," Wilber backpedaled quickly. He knew enough of demonic politics to realize that having been given the phone and the sense of solidity and freedom that came with it, Asuma would be as belligerent as Coach was on the matter of her freedom.

"Well, what were you saying then, boyo?"

Wilber thought fast. "I was thinking of the technical difficulties. Asuma's tree is in the dryad's grove in Pucorl's lands. I'm sure Pucorl would allow her to remove her tree from his lands if she wanted to, but that's a long way for a single dryad's tree to migrate. And who knows what might happen to it on the way? Besides, it's going to need a matching tree in the mortal realm to tie to. This isn't something that is safe for Asuma to do on her own, and I'm not sure that the rest of us have the time to help her."

Leona twisted her head to look at Wilber and meowed, "Nice save" in cat. Clearly she wasn't convinced.

Wilber shrugged his thanks.

"I am sure something can be arranged," Karl said. "Surely we can find an appropriate tree."

"If—" Wilber held up a finger. "—Asuma wishes to stay, we'll do what we can to facilitate. But we need to discuss the technicalities among ourselves. So please excuse us."

"Couldn't I listen?" Karl asked. "I'll be quiet as a mouse, I promise."

Leona stuck out a small pink tongue and ran it around her mouth.

"After we have had some time to consider, Professor," Wilber insisted.

* * *

As soon as Karl was gone, Wilber turned to Merlin. "Merlin, contact Pucorl and Roger, please. No, first contact Asuma and see if she's truly interested in Coach's ridiculous scheme."

"I already have," Merlin said, then continued. "Well, I forwarded Coach's contact to her through Pucorl and, as it happens, if we can do it in a useful and safe way, she is interested."

"In that case, we need to bring Roger in on this."

"Why Roger?" Merlin asked. "I like the lad well enough, but he's hardly a magical scholar?"

"Themis," Wilber said. "Remember who did the pentagrams that connect your place to Pucorl's lands. And, for that matter, the link between Pucorl's lands and Themis'. If Asuma wants to stay here, we want a good, solid link between her tree here and Pucorl's lands."

As it happened, Roger was busy, so Leona took the opportunity to bring up her questions about demons eating demons. "I was talking to the babbling brook that runs between Pucorl's garage and the dryad's grove, and it said it was fine with people drinking it."

"Did it ask you to drink?" Wilber asked.

"Yes. The water was good."

Wilber sighed. If the veil was still in place, drinking or eating anything in the netherworld would keep you there until it was all out of your system. Possibly the rest of your life. But clearly that wasn't working in this case. That was even a bit true of the food in Pucorl's garage, even though the base food was brought in from the natural world. It had its form modified by the magic of the netherworld, which made the effect much less than eating or drinking something that was wholly of the netherworld, like a babbling brook. And Leona was a cat.

Wilber stopped. Cats . . . the legends and stories about cats abounded. Cats having nine lives, cats being able to walk between this world and the next, cats being independent and not following the rules. Did the beliefs about cats affect how a real, natural cat interacted with the netherworld?

"What's wrong with drinking the water?" Leona asked in worried cat.

"Apparently nothing, at least for a cat," Wilber said. "Merlin, are cats immune to the whole eating thing?"

"It appears that this one is," Merlin said. "I can't be sure whether it is the nature of cats or the damage to the veils. But, for whatever reason, Leona appears to be able to eat demonic fare with no ill effect."

"So I guess you're fine, Leona. What was your question about demons eating demons?"

"It's not that important," Leona said, and Wilber was convinced that she was hiding something.

Then Merlin said, "I have Roger on the line," and they started talking about how Asuma might be able to stay here.

*　*　*

Leona slipped out as they discussed ways and means. "Well, Coach, what do you think? I can eat a demon."

"Yes, you can," Coach agreed. "And I can't think of a demon more deserving of your appetite than Carlos." Coach was around Leona's neck not only for transport, but for protection. In his watch form, the only one he could assume in the natural world, he was vulnerable to being picked up by a crow and dropped in a privy hole. Which Carlos had done.

"The trick is going to be to catch him," Leona said. "That will-o'-the-wisp has the power to disappear."

"You will need to do it in a pentagram."

"Will that help?"

"It will keep Carlos from simply disappearing. We need Catvia's help."

Coach contacted Asuma, and Asuma contacted Catvia, and the issue of how they were going to get someone to create a pentagram for the trick was brought up.

"No. I don't want Kitten involved in this," Catvia said. "The mortals aren't going to be all that happy, especially Chevalier Charles de Long. Whatever his other faults, Carlos is an excellent scout."

"You don't think we should do it?" Coach asked, but by his tone he wasn't going to be swayed, even if Catvia disapproved.

"Not at all. I think it's important for the demons who accompany us to know who is who in the zoo."

Coach laughed.

Location: Dryad's Grove, Pucorl's Lands
Time: 4:55 PM, September 23, 1372

Roger lifted the sword from his back and placed its tip into the rich soil around Asuma's tree. He felt the presence of Themis, released his grip on the hilt, stepped away, and she was there. Glowing with golden light in a gown of green, she began to trace an intricate dance of tunes and lines around the tree. The "pentagram" did have points, but not five. There were nine hundred and ninety-nine of them, enough so that it looked almost like a circle. As she was finishing, Leona the cat leapt into the pentagram, and curled up next to the tree. She scratched her ear and the collar that was Coach came loose and slipped off her neck onto the soil.

Themis looked at the cat and her lips twitched in an almost smile. She turned to Roger and said, "You will need to take me to the tree in Vienna."

He stepped up and took the hilt of her sword as she passed it to him, disappearing as its hilt touched his hand.

Location: University of Vienna

The campus of the university of Vienna was still a bit amorphous at this time. Luckily, since on this day Albert III expanded it to include a small grove of trees right next to the Danube. That grove included a small ash tree.

Joe Kraken used his tentacles to pull and push his bow up to the shore, then let down the ramp so that Pucorl could drive off onto dry land. Roger climbed out with the sword in hand, to see Albert III, Archduke of Austria and his brother, Leopold, also Archduke of Austria, standing there.

Albert looked pleased and interested, Leopold looked resentful. Roger thought of the evening before when Tiphaine had run horoscopes for the royal family using Jennifer's computer and a spreadsheet. Roger shook his head. He still wasn't convinced that astrology worked, but he wasn't going to argue with Themis, who had helped with the astrology calculations. Themis was a god. All the titans of ancient legends were. She didn't claim to be all-knowing, but she could look into a soul easily, and that included being able to examine Wilber to learn programming and Jennifer to learn the use of spreadsheets. And she knew the orbits of the planets to the microsecond, so Tiphaine's astrology file was spot on accurate. Plug in the date, time, and location of birth, and out poured all the signs and degrees.

He watched the point of Themis' sword as it traced intricate patterns in the grass around the tree, and thought about Elisabeth of Bohemia's horoscope. It predicted she had become pregnant and if the pregnancy wasn't handled properly she would miscarry and die next year. Raphico confirmed that she was pregnant, but only barely. No more than two weeks. The angel in a phone also determined that the placental bond was not solid and a miscarriage was likely. After consulting with the principals, Raphico fixed the issue so that Elisabeth of Bohemia's future was changed. Maybe.

Themis was finished with the pentagram now. She made a gesture and the pentagram started to glow. The glow faded, and Asuma in her anime form appeared in the grove of her tree for all to see.

"She still won't be able to manifest outside the pentagram, save in dreams," Themis said as she walked over and handed her sword back to Roger.

* * *

In the grass around Asuma's tree, Coach appeared in sports watch form. He tried to transform into his faun form, but failed and Carlos cawed a sneering laugh. Carlos looked around. No one else seemed to notice Coach's difficulty.

Carlos leapt from Charles de Long's shoulder and in a fast glide, he stooped and grabbed up the watchband with his talons. He flapped his wings to clear the grove, but they were returned to the netherworld and the pentagram around the tree hardened to a wall of force that might as well have been made of iron.

Coach became a faun and reached for Carlos, who let go and flapped away. Carlos' flapping took him under one of the limbs of Asuma's tree.

And from that limb, Leona leapt, catching the crow in flight.

Landing on the ground, Leona bit down hard, breaking the crow's neck. It died and the will-o'-the-wisp tried to escape the body, but it was restrained by the pentagram and by Leona's will. For she, with malice aforethought, had bit not only the crow but the will-o'-the-wisp that inhabited it.

Over the next few minutes, Leona ate the crow from beak to tail feathers. And as she did she ate the will-o'-the-wisp as well.

She didn't know exactly what effect it would have. All she really knew was that among demon kind, eating a demon gave you its powers. The power she was after was the ability to appear and disappear.

She got that.

But she got more, for the crow was part of her meal as well, and it was soaked and marinated in the will-o'-the-wisp's magic.

CHAPTER 5—ON THE RIVER AGAIN

Location: Near Asuma's Tree, Vienna, Austria
Time: 6:45 PM, September 23, 1372

No one noticed the events in Asuma's pentagram, because they were all distracted by a nobleman who'd accompanied Leopold to the scene. He was a big, tough-looking fellow they'd never seen before.

As the sun was touching the treetops, and moments after Themis disappeared, Leopold's companion drew his sword and proclaimed, "I challenge you, Roger McLean, for you are peasant born and unworthy to own such a blade."

"Put your sword away," Roger said without drawing the sword. "I don't own this sword, to begin with. It is the Sword of Themis, and no man owns it."

"Then I claim it as my right," Leopold's companion said.

It was obvious to Roger that whoever this arrogant jackass was, Leopold himself had put him up to it. He looked at him and said, "Archduke, this is really not smart. Call him off."

Leopold said nothing. Still holding his sword, his companion came up to Roger and reached as though to take the sword.

Some small part of Themis' awareness was always in the sword, and Roger was expecting her simply to refuse to move, as she had dealt with Charles of France.

But Themis had apparently had enough of being claimed by nobles by right of blood. Or, for that matter, being claimed by anyone.

<Kill him!> The words were shouted in Roger's mind in a voice that was Themis' and not Themis', and there was no question at all that this was a command. Almost without his will—and certainly without any sort of thought or consideration—Roger's hand flashed back over his shoulder, grasped Themis' hilt, and swung. As always, Themis was as light as a feather in his hands and Roger was strong. The blade moved almost faster than the eye could follow and passed through the nobleman from shoulder to hip.

It wasn't a fight. Holding his sword or not, Leopold's companion never stood a chance. It was an execution ordered by a god and carried out by Roger. The man's upper body fell to one side, his lower to the other. Blood gushed everywhere. So did intestines and . . . other organs.

Roger flicked Themis and more blood spattered the grass. When he returned the sword to his shoulder, it was clean and dry as though it had not cut through a man. And in his mind he asked, *"Why?"*

<It was not my sister Themis who gave you your command, Roger, but me, Nemesis.>

<Do not rail at my sister.> Themis said. **<She would not have acted without my acquiescence.>**

Roger was soaked in blood and covered with gore. *"You may have given your acquiescence. I didn't give mine, not to your sister."* Roger was pissed. He had a personal relationship with Themis, like a lot of Christians claim to have with God. In Roger's case there was no illusion to it. He had owned her for a short, if very intense, time and felt the depth of her mind and soul. It let him trust her in a way that he didn't trust anyone else, not even himself. That trust was definitely not extended to her sister or the

70

other gods who were her family. That Themis would let her sister use him this way . . . that was a betrayal.

The whole thing had happened so fast he'd never had time to even think about getting himself out of the way, much less refusing. The smell was . . . incredible. Roger had heard of slaughterhouse stench but had never experienced it himself. Luckily, there was a breeze blowing and he was able to step aside and get away from it.

His nerves were steady, though. That had been true when he killed Philip as well. He turned and faced Albert III, who was staring at him in shock. "I am sorry that had to happen, Your Grace. But I warned your brother and his man"—he didn't bother looking at Leopold—"and in this I was a man under orders. Queen Themis of Themis will not be claimed by mortal man, and any who tries to hold her against her wishes will have their mortality instantly demonstrated."

Location: Pucorl's Lands
Time: 11:55 PM, September 23, 1372

Pucorl appeared in his spot of the parking lot at Pucorl's Garage and the passengers piled out. After the events of the evening, they had left Vienna almost in an armed truce. It was clear and witnessed that the assault was caused by Leopold, but he was still Albert's brother. And if they would have had difficulties later in life, that didn't mean that Albert was happy his brother's man had died. Almost the only thing that kept him from ordering Roger's arrest was the Sword of Themis, still riding on his shoulder.

"What is it with you, Roger?" Lakshmi asked. "Do you have to get us kicked out of every kingdom we pass through?"

"Not my idea this time. Or, for that matter, the other time either. If I recall correctly, having me run off with Themis after the battle of Paris was Raphico's idea, and the rest of you agreed."

"Well, titan or not, your sword needs deportment lessons. Talk first, kill later. That way, if you do it right, you can avoid the killing part."

She sighed. "Never mind. I know it's not your fault. Maybe it's not even Themis' fault. But we have to develop better ways of dealing with these barbarian kings than we have found so far."

Roger didn't correct her about which god gave the order. That was an issue between him and Themis. He didn't blame Nemesis. It was Themis who had lent him to her sister as though he was a possession.

"Oh, I don't know . . ." Annabelle smirked. ". . . it seems efficient to me. If we can get them to line up, Rog can kill enough of the bastards to make democracy feasible. I never thought I would say it back in the world, but I want politicians."

✳ ✳ ✳

Wilber let them talk. Since they were back in the netherworld, Merlin had assumed his winged human form and was carrying Wilber's computer under his arm. As he was walking toward the Happytime, Wilber saw a cat run over the bridge, then spread its wings and fly. "What the heck?"

A few quick flaps and a glide, and the cat, which was now a cat-sized gryphon, landed on the path ahead of Wilber and said "Hi" in Leona's voice. And Wilber realized it wasn't exactly a gryphon. At least, not a standard gryphon. It fell somewhere between a gryphon and a manticore. It still had a cat's head, but the jaw was more pointed. It had a cat's ears, but the hair was almost tufts of feathers around the ears. It did have the front claws of a crow, and the back claws of a cat.

"What happened to you, Leona?"

"It turns out that Carlos was on the menu, after all," Leona said with a very cattish smirk in her meow. Then continued. "I didn't expect the wings or the talons. But I am not displeased."

Leona was still a fairly small cat. But for a winged creature, she was huge, about the size of an eagle.

"Anyway, I need you to have a talk with Charles de Long. I ate his crow, but he don't own me. I'm a cat! Well, sort of."

Wilber shook his head. "We'll think of something."

* * *

Bertrand du Guesclin came to visit Roger that evening. By then, there wasn't anything left in Roger's stomach. His nerves had held steady until they were out of any danger, but then the reaction had finally hit. He'd spent several minutes on his hands and knees vomiting. Fortunately, he'd been able to get out on an empty patch of land before doing so.

The former Constable of France sat next to him and placed a friendly hand on his shoulder. "You've never killed anyone up close like that, I believe."

Roger shook his head. "Dammit, Bertrand, I come from a civilized world, meaning no offense. I'd never killed *anyone* until I came here. The zombies on the wall don't count. That was combat and they were already dead."

The truth was that Roger wasn't sure that everyone he killed on the walls of Paris was already dead. The living were mixed into that zombie army.

"I think the first, and until now the last, person I killed was Philip and I was never within thirty feet of the man, even when I called the sword." Roger shook his head. "A couple of high school fist fights, that was it. And shooting Philip wasn't . . ." He shook his head again.

"Not the same thing as hacking a man in pieces and being covered by his blood and guts. Yes, I know. I will never forget my first battlefield. Believe me, I wasn't the only survivor puking afterward. If it makes you feel any better, you will get used to it as time passes—although you never will completely, unless you are a madman."

Roger wiped his face with a hand. "Boy, does that make me not feel good."

Bertrand patted his shoulder again. "You said it yourself. You are no longer in a civilized world. And I didn't take offense at that because I agree with you. Ours *is* a barbarous world."

He rose to his feet. "I predict you will do well here. Tiphaine's done your horoscope and predicts the same."

Location: Joe Kraken, Near the Black Sea End of the Bosporus
Time: 2:15 PM, September 27, 1372

Pucorl sat on Joe Kraken's deck as the rain poured over him. Pucorl was a van, so rain didn't bother him all that much. He ran his wipers and had the heat going on low, so Annabelle was comfortable. She and Jennifer were working on a new crystal set. Jennifer had the theory, but Annabelle had talented hands. This model was going to have speakers, earphones, eyes, and a screen. It wouldn't be a real screen. It would be a flat piece of wood painted with a chemical mix that was similar to that used on Joe Kraken's hull. Because of his chephlopodish origins, Joe Kraken knew about skin that could change color in a heartbeat and they were trying for the same thing in this crystal set. They were also waiting for the scouts to get back.

* * *

Wilber, sitting in Joe Kraken's cabin with Merlin on the table in front of him and Leona curled up on the cat stand, looking over his shoulder at the screen, was working on the incantation that would help adapt a demon to the crystal set phone.

When he wasn't being interrupted by Leona's comments or the requests for translation from animals with the scouting party.

"Meow," Leona said, asking if he really wanted that diphthong there. Leona didn't know anything about magic, but the fact that she was magical now, combined with the fact that she was a cat, convinced her that she must know more about magic than Wilber did.

Then a horse started complaining about the rain.

Wilber sighed.

Location: North Shore of the Bosporus
Time: 2:17 PM, September 27, 1372

The rain dripped off Roger's helmet and down the back of his neck. His horse nickered at him in what Roger was sure was a complaint.

His phone, Clausewitz, added, "Wilber says Beau would like you to turn off the rain."

Having someone who could talk to animals was often a convenience. However, having your horse know that it can complain and be understood was not always a boon. Like now. "Have Wilber tell Beau, for the fourteenth time, that I don't control the weather."

The phone neighed as they rode slowly into the village. No one heard, thank goodness. Because of the rain, no one was outside.

Bertrand guided his horse to the little stable on the north side of the mud patch that seemed to think it was a road through the village. As near as he understood, had this been the netherworld, the mud patch would truly have thought that it was a road.

There were two mules in the stable, but no horses. There was also only room for about a half-dozen horses and there were twenty in their party. There was a fenced-in paddock where most of the horses would have to reside.

What there wasn't, was anyone in the stable area. Across the mud was another building that might be a small tavern. Or maybe an overlarge hut for a relatively well off villager.

Bertrand pointed. "Father Dalpozzo, would you mind riding over there and seeing if that's an inn? And, in any case, where the stable keeper might be found."

They waited. A few minutes later, the priest waved for them to come over, and a moment after that, an old man and a boy came out of the door. While Roger dismounted, the two locals made their way to the stables, shouting in the worst accented Greek that Roger had ever failed to understand.

Clausewitz translated. "Hey you, what are you doing putting your horses in my paddock without my permission?"

"Bargaining," the phone added in Wilber's voice. "He isn't really upset at all."

"Shut up, Wilber," Roger said. "At least until we have the lay of the land."

* * *

In the tavern several minutes later, Roger wrung out his cloak before hanging it on a peg. The inn was smoky and stank, but it was dry and it was also full, mostly of fishermen. Waiting for the rain to end so that they could take their small skiffs out into the Bosporus, Roger guessed.

The party sat around three large wooden bench style tables and ordered a meal with the local sour wine. Then they asked for the news from Constantinople.

The barmaid, who looked about forty—and Roger figured was the tavern keeper's wife—proceeded to look them over, then started talking. Roger couldn't understand a word, but he got a report later. She first asked, "Are you the wizards from France?" Then without waiting for an answer, she went on. "Magic is illegal in Constantinople."

Father Dalpozzo asked, "But not here?"

"It's illegal here too, but we don't care much. Certainly not enough to fight armed men over it."

At that point, Father Dalpozzo had Roger pull Clausewitz out, and from then on Wilber—safe and dry in Joe Kracken's cabin—provided a running translation.

They talked over magic with the locals. The local priest was Greek Orthodox and while still doing services to God had set up an altar next door to Poseidon, and was offering prayers to the Greek god of the sea for the protection of the local fisher folk.

Father Dalpozzo wasn't pleased with that, but Father Grigoris didn't much care what some Catholic thought. He had a village full of people to look after.

Over the evening, they learned that though the political powers tried to outlaw magic, and especially heresy, the old gods were being prayed to again, in a way that they probably hadn't been even when they were the only gods available. For one thing, prayers to Poseidon were occasionally answered.

While that was going on, Roger was aware that he was in that part of the natural world that correlated to Themis' lands, or at least close to it. He could feel it. Roger wasn't exactly anxious to give up the sword, but he felt he should. For one thing, the netherworld was affected by the natural world, and having the physical sword in her part of the netherworld would give Themis back that part of herself that was perforce left in the sword when he released her from it.

Themis had never said anything about it, but Roger felt like he was holding the sword under false pretences.

And there was one other thing.

The Sword of Themis was, in a way, like Excalibur of legend. It could act as the sword of state for the Byzantine Empire. And that would give Themis a say in who was to be emperor of the Byzantine Empire.

The histories in their little collection were limited in regard to royal families in Constantinople, merely recording that the Byzantine Empire was to fall to the caliphate in a few years. But Themis was a god, one who remembered history, and not only the past history, but history into the future. Even many histories, probabilities, as Pucorl called them. It struck Roger as important that Themis have a say in who sat on the throne of the Byzantine Empire.

Others might be going to Constantinople for other reasons. But that was Roger's reason.

After a lot of discussion, they decided that they would move a bit closer to Constantinople, then send a small party into the city to find out the situation and see if they could get some sort of prior agreement before bringing Pucorl and Joe Kraken, not to mention the other enchanted boats, into the city.

Location: Village on the North Coast of the Bosporus
Time: 10:15 AM, September 29, 1372

The sun was bright and shiny as Joe Kraken pulled up to the beach at the village and extended his ramp. Pucorl drove down, and then up into a field to the north of the village. He would be staying here, along with most of the party, while Bertrand, Monsignor Savona, Father Dalpozzo, Dr. Delaflote and some of the armsmen went into Constantinople. Jennifer was a bit upset about being left behind, but stopped arguing when Tiphaine told her some horror stories about women alone in this time.

But they wouldn't lack for occupation. The village was fairly prosperous for a village in the Byzantine Empire of 1372, but that meant that they usually—but not always—had enough to eat. There were a lot of fallow fields here because of the loss of the population over the last half century or so. Besides, they were anxious to exploit the oceanids, the ship fairies of legend. They were, variously, the daughters of Oceanus and Tethys, or the spirits of the sea or boats. And while Oceanus was no longer lord of the sea, his daughters were still running around in the netherworld, performing all sorts of functions, including the protection of boats and ships on the ocean or any other body of water.

At least that's what the local legends and mythos said. Half-believed stories told around the fire. But since the ripping of the veil, these nymphs had often been seen cavorting in the waves. The villagers wished to capture these creatures and put them in their boats to help protect the fishermen and insure a good catch.

After listening to all this, Tiphaine shook her head. "It is most unwise to try to enslave the creatures of fairie. It is better to offer them a home in exchange for service."

"And considering their father might well be a titan of old," Wilber added, "it's doubly unwise. I have met a titan. They aren't the sort of folk you want to piss off." He pulled his phone from his pocket. "Igor, can you contact Themis directly for us?" He turned to Father Grigoris and explained. "Themis' lands are around here, where ancient Thrace and Greece were, so I am wondering if Igor can reach her directly without going through Pucorl to his lands and to the pentagram that connects his lands with her lands in the netherworld."

Igor tried, and did make contact of a sort, but it was patchy. He only got one bar. So he went through the network, and got put off on one of Themis' assistants, Iris, who they had kidnapped, then released, during the Pretendership War in France last year.

Iris didn't hold a grudge. Not exactly. But neither did that noble lady of the netherworld think that the twenty-firsters—aside from Roger McLain—were of such a rank to disturb her mistress.

"What do you want to know?" she asked.

"We were wondering about the sea nymphs and boat nymphs," Wilber said. "What sort of container they might find acceptable."

"You should speak with Oceanus or Poseidon. Not bother Her Majesty with such questions. As well, you will want the owner's permission."

"Well, can you connect us with Oceanus?"

"Don't be ridiculous. Why would Oceanus consent to speak to you? I will contact one of the oceanids. Maybe she will consent to help you." At which point Wilber was put on hold.

The ancient Greek muzak coming out of his phone made Wilber shake his head and laugh. "Iris isn't a fan."

"Well, she should be," Tiphaine said. "If it weren't for us she might well have been locked into a decaying body."

That got her asked to tell the story, and she did until the oceanid Korálli came on the line. She spoke a language that was more akin to the speech of dolphins than anything a human might know. Her language was made up in part of sonar images or perhaps sonar descriptions, combining echolocation with squeaks and whistles which allowed her to communicate the shape and compositions of undersea features, including fish, with a clarity that human language couldn't hope to emulate. Wilber quickly became so engrossed in his conversation with her that he utterly ignored the staring villagers.

Lakshmi said, "Wilber, you're being rude."

"Oh, sorry. But I am learning things. There are things you will need to do to your boats, additions that you will need to make. Aside from the eyes, you will want to make sonar clickers and microphones. So that the oceanids won't be left half-blind from human ignorance."

At the blank looks, Wilber explained sonar in Greek. It was a new concept to the villagers.

"Do fish truly see that way?" asked Katos, the village headman/master fisherman.

"Not all fish. Dolphins, killer whales, and whales in general, use echolocation. Sharks, aside from eyesight, also use electromagnetism to locate prey and avoid threats. Squid have several means of communication, including their camouflage ability." Some of this was from Wilber's twenty-first century, but more was from Joe Kraken and the conversation he'd had with Korálli.

There was more conversation, and eventually a design of modifications was worked out.

* * *

Leona sat on the branch and meowed at the local tom, a big, strapping fellow that she would have found quite interesting a few months ago. But he didn't have wings and Leona wasn't in the mood anyway. So she chatted from a safe altitude, confident that she could fly away if the need arose.

He wasn't convinced that she was truly a cat, even if she did speak cat. And in any case, he wanted her to know that this was his hunting ground, not hers.

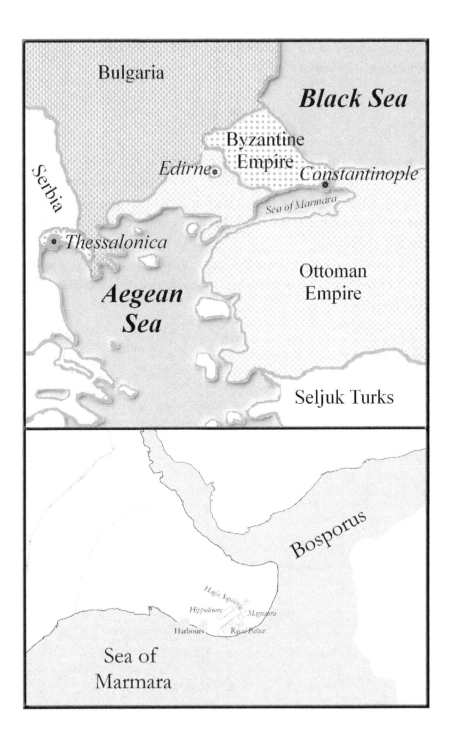

CHAPTER 6— CONSTANTINOPLE

Location: Constantinople
Time: 3:05 PM, September 29, 1372

Bertrand stepped out of the large inn and looked around. The broad streets were dirty and there were as many vacant lots as buildings in the large wall-inclosed city. The gate guards had let them through with only a modest bribe and the hostel they were staying in was large enough for their party. Constantinople was a complex mix of wealth and poverty, of grandeur and decay.

He walked along the side of the building to the stables where their horses were housed and checked on the mounts. And while he walked, he considered. Tomorrow would be soon enough to look up Gabriel Delaflote's friend, Theodore Meliteniotes. It was already evening. The Magnaura, where he worked, was likely closed to guests. It served several functions, a collegium much like the university of Paris, guest quarters for ambassadorial groups, and a training ground for the bureaucracy of Constantinople.

Meliteniotes' job, aside from being a philosopher, was as what amounted to rector of the Magnaura. From what Gabriel said, he was also a strong adherent of Greek orthodoxy and opposed to any rapprochement with the western church.

Bertrand looked down the street. It led over a mile to a turn and from there probably another mile and a half until it reached the Magnaura and the royal palace. Out here near the outer wall, half the lots and more were empty, the buildings torn down or left to rot.

The people, of which there were many even out here, were mostly dressed in sewn together rags, with a gaunt look about them. They avoided his eyes, but that was clearly due to his sword and armor.

He turned back to the inn.

Location: Magnaura, Constantinople
Time: 8:37 AM, October 2, 1372

Roger McLain sat his horse in good armor and the sword looked perfectly ordinary, so ordinary that most people failed to notice it at all, and those who did see it saw it only as the sort of sword any man at arms would wear. No one noticed that it had no sheath, but floated, not touching his back. People tended not to notice him at all. He wasn't sure whether that was because of the sword or because he was riding next to Bertrand du Guesclin, who carried an aura of command around with him that had nothing to do with the demons that now infested the world.

Bertrand, Roger, Gabriel Delaflote, Monsignor Savona, and Father Dalpozzo dismounted. A couple of the armsmen took their horses in hand, while the five of them walked up the steps to the front doors of the Magnaura.

* * *

Roger stayed in the background once they got inside. Father Dalpozzo waved at a clerk and asked, "Where can I find the director of the Patriarchal School?"

The clerk looked at Father Dalpozzo, then at Monsignor Savona, and then at Bertrand, and whatever snide remark he'd been planning died on his lips. He gave them directions, and a few minutes later they reached a set of fairly luxurious offices. The clerk seated by a lectern asked, "Who are you here to see?"

"The rector," said Gabriel Delaflote.

"Rector Tacitus is busy at the moment. May I tell him what this is in regard to?"

"Tacitus?" Gabriel asked. "Theodore Meliteniotes is the rector of the university."

"Shh," the clerk hissed. He waved them closer. "Theodore Meliteniotes has been arrested for consorting with demons."

"That's surprising."

Father Dalpozzo interrupted before Gabriel could put his size twelves further down his throat. "Meliteniotes doesn't even believe in astrology. Now you're saying he believes in demons."

"Not only believes," the clerk whispered. "He summoned a demon into a statue of Erato with a *speaker* attached." The word "speaker" was in French. "He got the technique in a book published by the heretical sorcerer Gabriel Delaflote, all the way from France. Including the design for the speaker. She was singing obscene love songs in ancient Greek when they arrested him."

"Really?" asked Delaflote. "What happened to the statue?"

The clerk smirked. "It was seized by Prince Manuel, and it hasn't said a word since."

Manuel obviously referred to Manuel II Palaiologos, the second son of the present emperor of Byzantium, John V Palaiologos. Manuel was supposed to be something of a scholar in his own right. Roger had been well briefed on the royal family and what was known of them through the history books and what Tiphaine and Themis had determined through casting horoscopes. Back in the world, Roger hadn't believed in astrology at all, but he wasn't going to argue with a god about its efficacy.

The clerk was still talking, and while Roger was distracted they had switched to word of the delegation from France and the Pope.

"No, they aren't here yet. But they are supposed to be on their way, and the patriarch is arguing to have them arrested as soon as they arrive. The emperor wants to hear what they have to say, so he probably won't arrest them on the spot.

"I heard they are traveling in that demon-enchanted magic wagon, puck something. It's supposed to be the size of an elephant and made all of glass and steel. Like a steel cathedral on wheels."

*   *   *

They, with a hefty bribe, got in to see Emperor John V Palaiologos. Emperor John V Palaiologos was forty-one. What had once been sandy brown hair was now almost white. Apparently being a prisoner first in Venice, then in Bulgaria, had left him in poor shape physically. He had a big nose and dark bags under his dark eyes. His face was lined and bitter, and his mouth was loose. "Where are the rest of you? The enchanted wagon? For that matter, how did you get here without being spotted?"

Roger left it to Bertrand to answer.

"We came by the Danube to the Black Sea, and the rest of our party is in a village called Gari. We rode ahead to confirm that Your Majesty's government would recognize our diplomatic status—especially in regard to magic—before bringing Pucorl and the rest of our magic into the city." Then they waited while Father Dalpozzo translated.

Bertrand didn't mention Roger's enchanted phone or Raphico in the phone Monsignor Savona carried. Gabriel was without familiar at the moment, Archimedes having decided to return to the netherworld without his crow body after Leona dined on Carlos. He was working with Wilber, Annabelle and Jennifer on an enchanted radio on wheels. But that was still in the design stage.

86

John V said something short in Greek.

Father Dalpozzo translated. "He said, quote 'We agreed.' The royal we, I assume, not him and his co-emperor."

In the Byzantine Empire they had two emperors as a sort of a holdover from the two consuls of the old Roman republic. And John V's son and former co-emperor Andronikos IV was no fan of his father or his father's decisions. Especially John V's conversion to Catholicism. So it was a safe bet that he wasn't thrilled by a bunch of Catholic wizards with diplomatic immunity. Manuel, the recently crowned co-emperor, was something of a cypher.

"As you say, Majesty. Please excuse the ingrained caution of an old soldier." As Father Dalpozzo translated, Bertrand turned to Roger and said, "Give Pucorl a call and let him know we have confirmed our diplomatic status with His Majesty."

Roger pulled Clausewitz out of his inside pocket and checked. "No bars, General. We are too far from Pucorl, and will be until we can install a pentagram link or until he gets closer." They were a bit over fifteen miles from Pucorl, and without a network to go through, that was too far.

Again the emperor said something abrupt in Greek.

"He wants us to explain about the phones," Father Dalpozzo said. "I told him we were out of range."

Roger explained with Father Dalpozzo translating. "It's like having a bunch of people standing some distance apart, yelling one to the next until the message gets to where you want it, or using signal fires. But when you add in the netherworld and the fact that distance and location aren't constant there, it can get confusing. In this case, the issue is that we are too far from the nearest signal fire. If we had a link to Themis here, we could do it, because these are all her lands."

"*What?*" John V shouted and the guards near the door turned to them. John waved them away, but his mouth was now almost firm. His lips pressed together in anger. "Does your titan ally claim my empire?"

When Roger got Dalpozzo's translation, he tried to explain. "No, Your Majesty. Themis' lands are in the netherworld, and a couple of energy states lower than here. She doesn't claim any earthly lands." That last wasn't, Roger thought, entirely true. She didn't claim direct rule over any earthly lands, but she—like any titan—could affect the luck of the king of a land. Especially a land that corresponded to her own as closely as this place did. And with the veil between the worlds in tatters, she could have even greater effect with less effort.

"I was simply pointing out that once we have a connection from the natural world to Themis' lands, she will be able to facilitate communications all through ancient Thrace and Macedonia, since Themis is the land as well as its queen. That sort of sympathetic magic works consistently in the netherworld."

"Can you contact this titan of yours?" John V asked, getting what Roger could only call a crafty look in his eyes.

"Yes. I carry her sword. I can contact her at any time."

"Do so. I would have words with her."

After consulting with Bertrand, Roger agreed. He drew the Sword of Themis and laid its point on the marble floor of the throne room. Then, beside him, holding the hilt of her sword, was Themis. Roger released his hold, and stepped back while Themis grew until the sword became little more than a short sword in her hand.

She spoke in Greek, but the Greek of Achilles and Homer. "What do you want of me, John?" She gave him no other title. Nor did she need to. The crafty look was gone from John's eyes, and Roger thought the old guy was going to climb off his throne and prostrate himself.

With a lift of her hand, she stopped him. "Do not fall on your belly before me. I abhor slavery in all its forms."

"It is true," John murmured. "Themis, she of the lovely cheeks, she of the good counsel. Counsel me, Lady. Advise me."

"Hm . . ." Themis sat on a golden throne that hadn't been there a moment before. "No, I don't think so. At least not in any detail. I would not have you the slave of my counsel any more than a slave in chains. I will not tell you all. Speak to your astrologers and counselors. Listen and consider, but consider first not what is best for you, but what is best for the land. I will make a request . . ." She held up a hand. "A request only. Not a command. Find a place in the city and build a temple for me, so that those who wish may come to lay what offerings they choose before me and ask what boons of me they seek."

"The church would never allow it," John said. And both Father Dalpozzo and Monsignor Savona nodded agreement, while Raphico said, "You got that right."

Themis smiled—well, smirked—then handed the sword to Roger and disappeared.

Location: Pentagram in Gari
Time: 8:50 AM, October 2, 1372

The pentagram glowed and Pucorl got a phone call from Themis. "I'm having a chat with John V Palaiologos. You have your guarantees. At least, so far as the emperor is concerned. I wouldn't count on its preventing the church from getting involved."

The remaining twenty-firsters and their company started packing up and getting ready to travel along the Bosporus to Constantinople.

Location: Docks of Constantinople
Time: Mid-afternoon, October 4, 1372

The crowd was large as the not so little flotilla of riverboats docked on a pier of the large port of Constantinople. Joe Kraken pushed out his ramp and Pucorl drove onto the stone pier. Then, down the pier to the streets of the city, where Roger met them with Clausewitz in hand.

"The emperor is putting us up in the Magnaura," Roger said as he turned his horse to lead them to the large building. Aside from being a school, it also had fairly luxurious quarters for diplomatic guests.

"So, any word on Gabriel's friend?" Amelia Grady asked.

"Unlike Gabriel, Theodore Meliteniotes doesn't have anything approaching diplomatic immunity. Negotiations are still under way to get us in to see him. On the upside, John V would like to have Tiphaine run up a detailed horoscope for him and one for each of his family."

"I already have," Tiphaine said. "And after reading them, I did one for Savci Bey."

None of this was really news. They had been talking on the phone since Pucorl got within range. That was how they knew which pier to use.

Andronikos IV was still avoiding them, but Manuel II was anxious to meet them all.

"We have an invitation to a small party in the town house of Prince Manuel," Roger continued, "even if the Orthodox clergy wants to have us all, especially Monsignor Savona, burned as witches."

They continued to chat as they waited for the rest of the party to disembark from their riverboats and mount their horses. Then the whole bunch made a parade to the Magnaura.

It was a well watched parade. The streets were lined with crowds like they had been in Paris. Well, the mix of emotion was a bit more to the "curious" and less to the "burn them." The population of Constantinople was mostly literate, at least to the "sign your name and read a broadsheet, the Bible, or a book of fables" level. And it contained more scholars and bureaucrats than Paris did, even with the university of Paris in the mix. At this time, the Magnaura was dominated by the church, but the history of secular scholarship was still there.

Location: Guest Quarters, Magnaura, Constantinople
Time: 9:52 AM, October 8, 1372

Lakshmi Rawal waved the dressmaker into the room. Silk all the way from China. Cotton from North Africa, gold thread made with real gold leaf wrapped around the silk threads . . . Lakshmi was going to have a dress made. Part of that, even a large part, was that Lakshmi *liked* beautiful clothes. But another part was that Lakshmi had sized up Constantinople within minutes of their arrival in the city.

Constantinople was all about appearances.

Partly that was because The City—as the locals called it, as though there was no other city on Earth—was living to a great extent on the leftovers of the earlier eastern Roman empire. The aqueducts that provided fresh, clean water to the city averaged eight hundred years old and some of the buildings were even older. But The City was full of tumbled down buildings and vacant lots, and the finery of the local potentates was rich in jewels and precious metals, but worn and cut down or expanded, as though the whole city was a hand-me-down. In spite of its strategic location for trade, as well as for the military, the city had not recovered from the sack in 1200, or the plague and the dynastic wars that had, over the last century or two, shrunk the Byzantine Empire to a shadow of its former self.

That meant that the people here were going to judge by appearance. Because people everywhere did, and people who lacked substance did it most of all.

Liane Boucher came in, carrying her computer, Thelma, under one arm and her camera bag over the other shoulder. She didn't knock. "Blowing your allowance on clothes again?"

That was sort of true. When they arrived in this time all they had was what they were wearing or carried with them, and much of that had been sold to pay for their living expenses. When Mrs. Grady gave Pucorl to himself and later, when Pucorl had gained the lands and substance of the demon lord he defeated in combat, the van had felt he owed all the twenty-firsters for his body and freedom. His lands in the netherworld acted as a place to store goods and then access them from wherever he happened to be. So he rented space in his lands to store the goods that they were bringing with them. Part of that income went to the girls as something like an allowance, in addition to the funds they acquired by selling things. In Lakshmi's case, she had sold her phone to the king of France for several chests of silver coins.

"It's important," Lakshmi told Liane. "If you would come out of your editing room sometime, you would know that."

Liane rolled her eyes. "I need you for some voiceovers."

"Later." Lakshmi was the voice for the documentary of their travels that Liane was making. It was more travel log than movie, but it was good and it let them both keep working at the artform they both loved, if in different ways. "For right now, we need to study these people and make a plan." Lakshmi spoke in twenty-firster English because she didn't want the dressmaker to understand. "J5—" She didn't want to say John the fifth. "—is going to be a problem."

"I thought it would be A4," Liane picked up her cue, calling Andronikos IV A4. "He's the one that Tiphaine's horoscope says is scheduled to revolt next year."

"Yes, but that's because his mom's a manipulative bitch who never forgave J5 for the fact that her dad married her off to him in order to take the throne. And then J5 had the gall to win the civil war and depose her daddy and brother."

This, too, was Tiphaine's horoscope, with liberal interpretation. And some advice from Themis.

"I think A4 is enough of an asshole all on his own. Did you see the way he was looking at us as we rode in? I didn't know whether he wanted to rape us or burn us at the stake."

"First the one, then the other, though I grant he's likely enough to do it backward. I'm not saying that he's either bright or stable. He's a conniving little backstabber. But his dad loves him in spite of the fact that he left him in the hands of his enemies until M2 rescued the old fart." M2 referred to Manuel II, John V's second son who, according to Tiphaine's horoscopes, was destined to be the emperor of Byzantium somewhere down the line.

There had been a sea change in the attitudes of the twenty-firsters in regard to astrology. Partly that was because of Themis' endorsement of it, but also because they had done tests. They had a good bit of French history between all their textbooks. And using that they had Tiphaine run horoscopes based on the dates of birth they knew, then compared the accuracy of those predictions to the historical record. Tiphaine had something like an eighty-five percent accuracy rate and the rest could be explained by her not having exact birth times.

On the downside, that predictive accuracy dropped a lot when you included the demons. For instance, Philip the Bold never rebelled against his brother, according to Tiphaine's horoscope. So they knew that the demons changed things. If they could convince John V not to recognize Ottoman suzerainty they might stop the rebellion.

Might.

So while the dressmaker measured and pinned, displayed fabrics and threads, Lakshmi and Liane talked politics and movies, makeup and murder.

CHAPTER 7—SETTLING IN

Location: Gaol, Constantinople
Time: 10:30 AM, October 8, 1372

Gabriel Delaflote walked down the hall to the barred wooden door. The guard lifted the bar and Gabriel stepped through to see an old man seated on a stool before the lectern-style desk like Gabriel had used his whole life until the twenty-firsters arrived. The clothes the old man was wearing were dirty and the man on the stool stank. No, it wasn't the man. It was the bucket in the corner. There was a high window that let in a bit of light.

The man looked up and in a creaky voice asked, "Who are you?" in Greek.

"Gabriel Delaflote."

"*You!* This is all your fault!" The man who had to be Theodore Meliteniotes pointed an accusing finger at Gabriel. "That idiocy you spouted in your book was never supposed to work."

Gabriel stared at Theodore in shock for a moment, as his mind raced around the history of their correspondence, and he realized that what apparently happened was exactly what he should have expected. Theodore knew with great certainty that magic didn't work, that all gods but God were false, nothing more than superstition. He would see the weird reports since the ripping of the veils as the ravings of superstitious dolts. So his reaction to Gabriel's book would be to disprove it by testing it. One question still remained, however. "Why a muse of erotica?"

"Not erotica. Lyric poetry."

"I did say that magic worked," Gabriel said. "I pointed out that I had tested it and confirmed it."

"But you must have known that no one in their right mind would believe such nonsense."

"Honestly, I would have thought you would believe that I wasn't lying!" Gabriel said. "I refuse to take responsibility for actions you took because you didn't believe me."

Theodore lifted his hand, again ready to declaim Gabriel's guilt, then stopped and lowered it. "Well . . . yes. There is that. But it was so completely ridiculous."

Gabriel shrugged

"How is it you're not in jail, Gabriel? Did you leave your familiar in Paris?"

"Not exactly. On the road here, a cat ate a crow that was inhabited by a will o' the wisp, and managed to digest the will o' the wisp in the process. After that Archimedes asked that he might be released from my service. Having a crow's body was not worth the risk."

"Asked?"

"When a demon is summoned by its right name, it has no choice but to comply. Much like you have no choice in where you currently reside." Gabriel waved at the cell.

"Then why did you release it? From what you said, I assume you did release it?"

"Yes, and for basically the same reason that I hope to obtain your release."

"Do you think that you can do that?" There was more surprise than hope in Theodore's voice.

"I don't know," Gabriel said. "We, our party, the twenty-firsters and the papal legation, as well as Bertrand du Guesclin, even the demons, have diplomatic status so our magic is legal. And if ours is, why not yours?"

Theodore went back to the high stool that was the only chair in the room. He waved at the bed, which was a bag of reeds on the floor. Gabriel shook his head.

"At least half the reason I'm in here is politics. You know from my letters that I am opposed to giving the bishop of *Rome,* who resides in *Avignon,* rulership over all Christianity. To my mind he is, in truth, only one more bishop. Not even a patriarch. That has made me enemies in the government. And when I did the experiment your book suggested, I was left exposed. The patriarch couldn't defend me without looking like a hypocrite."

Gabriel nodded. "Who would I have to convince to pardon your actions?"

"Emperor John or his co-emperor Andronikos. Andronikos would be my best hope. He at least tried to keep his father from giving the empire to the west one island at a time."

"Andronikos isn't the co-emperor anymore. He has been put aside, probably because he was willing to leave his father in prison in Venice. Manuel is co-emperor at the moment."

"Then I see no chance for my release." Theodore's whole body drooped.

"You could apologize." Then, seeing Theodore's expression, Gabriel continued. "Look, my friend. You were wrong about magic. Isn't it possible you are at least not wholly correct about the best place to make alliances? Our astrologer, Tiphaine de Raguenel, has drawn up horoscopes for the major players and one for Constantinople itself. She is convinced that if something doesn't change, it will become a Muslim city within a century."

"*Astrology!* Astrology is *superstition.*"

"Like magic?"

They talked for another hour, and Gabriel almost convinced Theodore to apologize to the emperor. But Theodore was afraid of what that would do to his relationship with the patriarch and the theological establishment of Constantinople.

Location: Salon of Manuel II, Constantinople
Time: 4:25 PM, October 10, 1372

Manuel II, newly crowned co-emperor, had only arrived back in the city a few weeks before the delegation from France. He was excited and deeply concerned about the fact that magic had started working, and hopeful that the French scholars would be able to allow Constantinople to use magic, not be used by it.

He stood in the receiving line as a huge man in armor with a face that seemed almost bestial or, perhaps, like the half-finished statue of a face walked in with a middle-aged redhead on his arm. Bertrand du Guesclin introduced his wife Tiphaine, then came Monsignor Savona, who introduced the angel Raphico. That was a flat panel with a front that was like a painting, but a painting that changed. The phone offered a blessing on his house in flawless Greek.

Then came the twenty-firsters and Magi Delaflote was with Amelia Grady and her son, Paul. She too had a phone, which she introduced as Laurence. And then the rest came in. Wilber introduced him to not only a phone, but a winged cat—a small gryphon which still had the head of a cat. That, more even than the talking boxes, convinced Manuel that these were people of power.

The cat, having been introduced—and having meowed, which Wilber translated as a greeting—then took two quick steps and leapt into the air. Its wings flapped twice or three times to get some height, then it glided to a table of savories, where it snatched up a smoked pheasant.

"Leona," Wilber shouted, "have some manners."

Leona looked up from her pheasant and growled. Then she leapt from the table, pheasant in her mouth, and glided to a corner.

"Let her have it," Manuel said quickly, not wanting to have difficulties with a being of magic. "How did you manage to get a gryphon from the netherworld in its own form? I was told that the creatures from that other place needed a form to inhabit when they came into this world."

"That's not always true," Wilber explained. "But in this case, the cat is local to this world and so are the wings and talons. Leona managed to eat an enchanted crow. Our companions are being surprisingly closed mouth about precisely how Leona managed that, and I prefer not to make an issue of it."

"Are they so chancy to deal with?" Manuel asked, and then at a cough from his majordomo, he added, "We can perhaps discuss this in more detail later." He waved Wilber on into the large room.

Then came Bill Howe and Jennifer Fairbanks. After them Lakshmi Rawal and Liane Boucher. Lakshmi wore a strange piece of jewelry. It was a sparkling blob that was in her left ear and a string that went from the blob to her pocket. He remembered now that Jennifer and Bill had worn the same odd bit of adornment, but theirs didn't call attention to themselves by sparkling.

Lakshmi said in broken Greek, "It's a headphone." She pulled the blob from her ear and reached out with it as though to put it in his ear. Almost without his consent, his head pulled back away.

"It's not going to bite you," she said in even worse Greek.

He moved his head forward and she put the thing in his ear. Then, in a deep baritone, a man said in perfect Greek, "I'm DW, Lakshmi's computer and director. Happy to meet you, Your Highness. I'm translating for Lakshmi."

* * *

99

Lakshmi looked at the young prince. He had hazel eyes, sandy brown hair, and a neatly trimmed beard. And he had noticed her. That wasn't unusual. Most heterosexual males noticed Lakshmi, but this time Lakshmi found herself noticing him back. And she wasn't sure why.

He was a healthy young man, well-muscled and toned with the calluses of regular sword practice on his hands. Something she knew how to recognize after a year in this time of swords and magic.

But there was more. His hazel eyes seemed to see her in a way that made her feel like he saw right into her. And then he smiled a cute little half smile that said he liked what he saw.

✳ ✳ ✳

Some time later Manuel found himself seated next to Gabriel Delaflote and Amelia Grady as they tried to persuade him to intervene in the case of Theodore Meliteniotes. Manuel wasn't willing to go against his father, but he did find himself agreeing to talk to the man.

He wasn't sure what would come of it. Theodore was a scion of the senatorial class, families who lived on the wealth and reputation of some illustrious ancestor. Often enough, one who lived before Caesar Augustus.

Sometimes, in his heart of hearts, Manuel wished the republic could be restored. But the time of democracies and republics was lost in history. It took a firm hand at the top to lead a nation.

Besides, the statue that his father gave him when Theodore was arrested never sang again. He asked about that and it was pointed out that since he wasn't the owner of the statue, the demon didn't answer to him.

"But I am the owner."

"I would guess that the statue disagrees," Gabriel said. "Just seizing things doesn't make them yours."

"What would happen if Theodore were to give me the statue?"

"I can't be sure without knowing the spell. It would be an interesting experiment, though."

＊ ＊ ＊

Wilber smiled at the quip. Why not? It was a witty pun if you spoke both Latin and Greek. It was also delivered deadpan by an attractive noblewoman in red shoes and a colorful dress. She was wearing a hat and something that might be called a veil, though it barely covered the top half of her forehead. She was holding a gold-stemmed heavy glass goblet filled with red wine in one hand and gesturing with the other, while she made jokes and explained court gossip to Wilber.

Wilber's phone was recording the conversation and sending it to Merlin in his computer, so Wilber mostly let her talk flow over him, trying to laugh or frown in the right places. In one way, it wasn't that different from parties he had attended at his mother's house in Paris or earlier in London.

But in another way, it was extremely different. Wilber was centerstage here. He could understand and speak any language now, while at his mother's parties he'd spent most of his time trying to guess what people were saying. Especially before the cochlear implant. Lip reading wasn't all that easy unless you were looking directly at the mouth of the person speaking.

She made a comment about one of the young ladies who was trying to get Bill Howe to dance.

Wilber said, "That's not going to happen. Bill is involved with Jennifer." He pointed at Jennifer and let the woman draw her own conclusions.

"How do you summon a demon?" she asked. It was a question out of the blue. Even more so because she seemed entirely serious. Much more serious than her talk of dresses, fashion, and court scandals.

"Answering that question," Wilber said carefully, "is a longer conversation than would fit here. I suggest you start by reading Doctor Gabriel Delaflote's book on the proper containers and spells to summon the sort of demon you need. What sort of demonic aid were you looking for?"

"Oh, nothing important," she said, and her tone rang false to his magically enhanced ear. "Where might I get a copy of that book?"

"I would assume that any book seller might have it. I know that it was one of the first books to be printed enmass by the new printing presses in Paris. There ought to be hundreds of copies floating around Constantinople by now."

"Oh, but that book has been banned by the patriarch."

"Really?" Wilber looked at the daughter of a major court noble and third cousin of the emperor and added, "That seems an unwise policy to me, to leave yourself unarmed while all about you have the means to arm themselves."

"I agree, but obtaining the book is not so easy, whatever we may think."

"And, unfortunately, I am in a fairly delicate position." Wilber noted that she had moved him over to a corner while they chatted so no one could hear their conversation. "I have diplomatic status so far as my own magic is concerned, but not carte blanche for teaching magic to others."

"Well, could you sell me some magic?"

"What sort of magic?"

She looked at him for a long moment, then said, "Protective magic. Maybe a familiar spirit who could teach me magic."

"Let me give it some thought," Wilber said, moving back to the center of the party. She could come with him or stay there, as she chose.

✳ ✳ ✳

Aurelia Crassa watched the French delegation as they circulated. Her father was prominent enough to be invited to the party, but only barely, and mostly because of the family wealth. And everyone she knew was wondering what the people from the future were really like.

They were, it had to be admitted, very attractive. Healthy, with even features, and excellent teeth. No pock marks in the entire party. They were rich. Their clothing said that, but they seemed a snooty lot.

Standoffish.

Liane Boucher stepped up to one of the young men and said, in barely understandable French, "I wish these people wouldn't stand so close."

"Either that, or bathe more often," the young man said, also in French, but French that was somehow more understandable than the woman's.

Aurelia kept her mouth shut. She'd been to the baths day before yesterday and she went at least once a week.

✳ ✳ ✳

Lakshmi strolled through the party, collecting stares. She was wearing a handmade red and gold crocheted gown over a dark tan, almost brown, chemise. Both the gown and chemise were made in Paris and given to her by the queen in the lead up to the battle of Paris. It was crocheted in a red and gold paisley pattern of fine linen thread and enchanted by a minor demon to turn it into a soft form-fitting cloth of gold and flames outfit, with a flaring skirt, a deep v neck, and tight sleeves.

The goal was to stand out. This was a world of status and the idea of pre-worn jeans and backward facing ball caps as fashion would simply confuse these people. The goal here was to have what no one else had, and your status was based in large part on what you wore. So much that there were laws about who could wear what. Only the emperor could wear red shoes—well, the emperor and upper class women—and only the imperial family could wear purple clothing. So Lakshmi was wearing clothing that was outside the rules, but obviously carefully and expensively made. The idea was to project the highest possible status without wearing something that was illegal for her to wear.

She smiled and gave a curtsy to an older man who wasn't exactly drooling at her, but not far from it. That, naturally, was the other reason for the enchanted crocheted gown. It was armor. Not as good as chainmail, but considerably better than standard cloth.

Then Helena Kantakouzene, John V's empress and Manuel's mother approached, and Lakshmi gave her a deep curtsy.

"Charming," Helena said, though she didn't sound charmed. More like the evil queen in Snow White. *Don't take any rosy red apples from this one,* Lakshmi told herself.

They talked about clothing and magic. Lakshmi had little Greek and Helena had no French at all. But Lakshmi's earbuds were bluetoothed and occupied by the same demon that inhabited her computer, DW. With the phones and Merlin they had decent protocols with DW telling Lakshmi what Helena was saying and how to say stuff back in Greek.

All in all, for Lakshmi, the party was informative, but not a lot of fun.

Location: Guest Quarters, Magnaura, Constantinople
Time: 8:23 AM, October 15, 1372

Annabelle Cooper-Smith laid the wrench on the table. It was a medium small wrench made in France by one of Bertrand's smiths. "For the moment, we cannot do magic other than that we brought with us. However, the twenty-first century had a technology which was put to much the same use. This wrench—" She pointed. "—can be adjusted to fit a bolt of several sizes. And we can build machines that will make this device much simpler and easier to mass produce."

The master smith of the royal court was impressed. He could see the applications well enough, not only bolts, but holding things in place. Even if Constantinople wasn't the center of manufacture that it was a couple of centuries ago, it still had much of the skill base.

He mentioned the clamp and the young woman talked about something called a C clamp. At his blank look, she added, "It's the shape." When he still looked blank she said, "A pi clamp, or perhaps an omega clamp."

Then he got it. He could see an omega turned on its side with the threaded bolt going through one end and pressing against the other. He nodded and they talked on.

The house Palaiologos would own the manufactory and the twenty-firsters would receive either a commission on every product made using their techniques or a flat fee. Part of his job here today was to find out if the emperor would be better off paying them the flat fee or the commission.

Already it was clear that the flat fee was much the better deal, even if it half-emptied the treasury.

He knew that there were other craftsmen and officials interviewing the other twenty-firsters. They were interviewing all of the delegation from France, on everything from law enforcement to the making of sweets for children.

Location: Private Apartments of John V, Royal Palace, Constantinople
Time: 8:23 AM, October 16, 1372

John V knelt next to Monsignor Savona and said the words. "Bless me, Father, for I have sinned. It has been two days since my last confession."

Having converted to Catholicism mostly in hopes of gaining aid from the west against the Ottomans, John still kept up the duties of the faithful. There were spies everywhere and if he failed, it would be reported back to the west. In this case, though, it was more than that. Monsignor Savona, according to all reports, carried an angel of the Lord in his breast pocket. Pockets were yet another new thing introduced by the twenty-firsters.

John recited his sins. Minor things, mostly. Then the questions started.

Not by Monsignor Savona, by the phone. A careful examination of why he had joined the Catholic church. What he truly believed and why.

What he believed in was Christianity and his duty to protect Constantinople from paganism and Islam. And he was willing to bow at any altar that would give him the troops to do that. But that wasn't enough for Raphico. Raphico got out of him the truth that a great deal of his faith was tied into his personal desires, that he was first and foremost protecting his own power, wealth, and status, not the faith.

That wasn't something that John wanted to admit. Not even to himself.

The confession left him shaken and angry. But too frightened of the angel that seemed to be able to see into his soul to take any action against the twenty-firsters or the rest of the delegation from France.

Location: Patriarch's Throne Room, Hagia Sophia, Constantinople
Time: 2:00 PM, October 16, 1372

Cardinal Pierre de Monteruc knelt to the patriarch of Constantinople. It wasn't easy, but he had his orders from Pope Gregory XI. In response, the arrogant heretic smirked at him.

✳ ✳ ✳

Patriarch Philotheos Kokkinos didn't intend to smirk, but the arrogant Roman churchmen were so sure of themselves.

And they were wrong.

Using Gabriel Delaflote's book and the appendix on the summoning of angels, as well as the icon of Archangel Michael that dated back to the seventh century and was a holy relic of the patriarchy, they enchanted the icon, calling Michael to the relic. The relic was a mosaic of Archangel Michael. The mosaic was laid out on wooden panels and held up by two wooden posts inlaid with gold. The reason that they chose this icon instead of one of the icons on the walls of the Hagia Sophia was because it wasn't possible to put a wall in a pentagram, but an icon not part of a wall could be moved where it was needed.

And Michael spoke.

He explained that the devil's fall was its desire to separate itself from the Lord God. That all the demons were fallen angels that must be forced back into the one God. And if human souls were to be saved, they too must be given to God and they must be given to the right god, the true God, lest they strengthen the devil which claims to be God.

The Angel Raphico, while a true angel and loyal to God, had chosen to deny its duty, confident that God would collect up the angels and the souls of men in His own good time.

"You do know that your Raphico is a slugabed who has failed in his duty to God? Not a demon, but unwilling to make the hard choices needed for true faith. It is the Orthodox Church that has the words of Archangel Michael guiding it. The sword of God."

"He is not my Raphico. Mother Church has not yet determined that Raphico is a true angel. I take it you have called another such being?"

"The Archangel Michael. Using an icon created in the seventh century. And he confirms that the Orthodox Church is the True Church. Ask him yourself."

He waved and an icon was brought into the room. It was a panel about four feet high and three wide, with a painting of an archangel with wings and halo holding a sword. And, as Patriarch Kokkinos said it would, it confirmed that the Orthodox church was the true church.

Cardinal de Monteruc left the meeting deeply troubled.

Location: Guest Quarters, Magnaura, Constantinople
Time: 8:00 PM, October 16, 1372

Monsignor Savona bowed to Cardinal de Monteruc. "You asked to see me?"

"According to Patriarch Kokkinos and the icon of Michael, the Orthodox church is the true church. What do you have to say to that, Raphico?"

"That icon wasn't given to God, but was and remains the property of the Eastern Orthodox church and, specifically, the Cathedral of Hagia Sophia. It will say anything it needs to say to advance the cause of the Hagia Sophia and the Eastern Orthodox church. I, on the other hand, was given to God, not to any particular church. Further, it was left to God to determine what angel to send. I serve God. Michael is forced into the service of a particular church."

"Then the Eastern Orthodox church isn't the true church?"

"Not *the* true church, no."

"I noticed your stress on *the*, Raphico," Monsignor Savona asked more than said.

"I thought you might."

"Is the Catholic church the true church?" Cardinal de Monteruc asked.

"It is *a* true church," Raphico said.

"According to you," Savona said. "I have known Raphico longest and speak with him every day. I have also spoken with many of the other demons called, and with Themis. To Raphico, any Christian church is a true church, and even Islam isn't totally false. And Themis doesn't consider Raphico to be an angel of God at all, but another being of the netherworld in service to one of the greater lords of the netherworld."

"What, then, do you believe?" Cardinal de Monteruc asked.

"I believe in God," Monsignor Savona said. "That has never wavered. But as to whether the One True God, the creator of this heaven and this Earth is the same as that being that owns this phone . . . that, I do not know. I do believe that Raphico's intent is good. That he can offer insights into the faith. That he does good in the name of God. And that is true whether he is truly an angel or simply another creature of the netherworld."

"And you, Raphico? What do you say?"

"I have stood in the presence of God and sung His glory with the choirs of angels. I don't believe. I *know* God is God." Then it paused a moment and went on. "But, as Monsignor Savona—and even more, Themis—will insist, my certainty cannot be yours. The truth is that each person must still find their own way to faith, as it has always been."

CHAPTER 8— SUZERAINTY

Location: Royal Palace, Constantinople
Time: Mid-morning, October 24, 1372

The Ottoman ambassador bowed slightly to the Byzantine emperor, John V noted with distaste. His sons were both here, Andronikos and Manuel. Neither looked any more pleased by the lèse-majesté than John was. But he gritted his teeth and stood it. For two reasons. First, he had promised to give Murad I suzerainty if Murad got him free of the Bulgarians, which Murad did. The second, more pressing, reason was that John didn't have the army to stop Murad if the Ottoman sultan decided to force the matter.

"King of Constantinople," Halis Bey said, "the Ottoman Empire calls you to your promise. You must raise an army and lead it south, placing it and yourself under the sultan's authority."

John looked at his sons in light of his discussion with Tiphaine de Raguenel and her horoscopes. If he left Andronikos here, his older son would rebel, and with the aid of Savci Bey, Murad's third son, the two of them would rebel against both him and Murad. They would lose, but the war would leave Savci Bey dead, Andronikos half blind, and the Byzantine Empire much weaker.

Andronikos looked back at him, angry and belligerent. For, after seeing Tiphaine's horoscopes, John had showed them to his son. Andronikos denied any such notion, insisting that Murad wasn't going to call John out of Constantinople anyway.

Now, here was the demand that Tiphaine said was coming and Andronikos insisted wasn't. He looked at Halis Bey. "We will consider Our brother monarch Murad's request."

"It is not a . . ."

"Stop," John bellowed. "Whatever My relationship with Murad, this is My hall, in My city, and *you* do not demand or command here."

He made a gesture and the guards slammed their pike butts into the floor.

Halis Bey looked at the guards, then back at John. "I will have to report this, King of Constantinople."

"Emperor of Byzantium," Andronikos corrected him.

John waved Andronikos down, then said to Halis Bey, "You are dismissed."

✻ ✻ ✻

Leona sat on a chandelier, half in the natural world and half in the netherworld, as Halis Bey marched out of the big room. She didn't understand what was going on. She had never understood what was going on with humans, but having the magic of the will o' the wisp, the brain structure of the crow and, especially, being around Wilber was helping. It was turning what had been meaningless noise into a puzzle to be solved.

Leona had never been able to leave a puzzle alone, and she still wasn't. She flicked most of the way into the netherworld and flew after Halis Bey.

A few minutes later, in Halis Bey's rooms, she heard a great deal of what she assumed was cursing and quite a bit of discussion. But it was in a language she didn't understand. In spite of the help that the crow's brain gave her with language and speech, she still couldn't learn human speech or understand talk without practice.

Location: Guest Quarters, Magnaura, Constantinople
Time: 1:00 PM, October 25, 1372

"Anyway," the maid told Lakshmi in an excited half-whisper, "the emperor almost threw out the Ottoman ambassador."

"Do you know why the Ottomans need the Byzantine forces?" Lakshmi muttered her response in English, then the computer, in an excellent imitation of her voice, spoke the question in Greek. By now the process was second nature to the twenty-firsters, and the locals of whatever country they were in seemed to get used to it quickly.

"It's the demons," the maid said with confidence, then hastily added with a frightened look at Lakshmi's computer sitting open on the table, "Not your demons."

DW and Lakshmi soothed the young woman and assured her again that not all demons were evil. Then she got the conversation back on the subject of the rebellion in southern Anatolia.

"The Karamanids called up djinn to fight against Murad. They have taken Beysehir using magic. The bey's servants say that's why Halis Bey demanded your magics."

"Has there been time for Murad to learn of our arrival?"

"Oh, yes, plenty. His capital is only a few days away by fast horse, and less if you go part of the way along the coast. He took Adrianople a few years ago, renamed it Edirne, and put his capital there. That's why Thessalonica is so important."

"In that case, Murad is an idiot," Lakshmi said.

The maid looked shocked. "You shouldn't say things like that. He's a powerful man." She looked around then whispered, "More powerful than the emperor."

"Maybe, but that's not saying much," Lakshmi said. "Both the Byzantine Empire and the Ottoman Turkish Empire are a lot smaller than I thought. The Byzantine Empire is old and feeble and the Ottoman Turkish Empire is still a baby. It wouldn't take much to shift the balance of power. The question is whether there's anything in the Byzantine Empire worth saving?"

"We're Christians."

"I'm Hindu," Lakshmi said. "Well, sort of. My family's relatively secular. But I don't see a lot of difference between a Christian and a Muslim from this century. Either is as likely to try to burn me as a witch as the other. And it's not like either side has a great record on women's rights—or even human rights—in this century. So what does Byzantium have in terms of culture or government that is worth saving?"

Then Lakshmi closed her eyes, ending the conversation, confident that the maid would report it to those who needed to hear it. It was true that the goal of the party was to save the world, both worlds, from whatever had torn the rifts in the veil between the worlds. But the probabilities had already shifted so much that Pucorl, Themis, and Merlin, all agreed that it was unlikely that they would ever get home. This was the world they were stuck with. And this world was in desperate need of things like democratic republics, governments by and for the people governed. An economic and industrial system that would not leave ninety-nine percent of humanity below the poverty line.

And certainly not least, bills of rights. Lots and lots of bills of rights, in every country.

Location: Royal Palace, Constantinople
Time: 8:23 PM, October 25, 1372

Helena Kantakouzene, queen of the Byzantine Empire, daughter of a former emperor, and wife of the present emperor, lay half-reclined on the Roman-style couch and waved her majordomo, Constantine Korolos, in.

The majordomo, who also acted as her spymaster, bowed, then stood and recited almost word for word the report of the maid assigned to Lakshmi Rawal.

Helena didn't call for the headsman. She wasn't even tempted. Well, not very. The twenty-firsters were powerful. It was hard to tell what kind of power they had. The stories from France said that Roger McLean defeated Philip the Bold in single combat when Philip still owned the Sword of Themis. They went on to say that he then gave the sword back to Themis. But that last part must be a lie, because Roger still carried the sword. Besides, no sane man would ever do such a thing. It was the act of a saint. And deep in her heart of hearts, Helena wasn't convinced that even the saints of old were really so selfless.

So, after a short fantasy about headsmen and seizure of goods, she brought her mind back to the point. "Find out what she wants. What would make her want to save Byzantium. After all she is the first chink in the armor of the French delegation."

"Doctor Delaflote," the majordomo corrected. "We may well be able to get his help in exchange for releasing Theodore Meliteniotes."

"Maybe. But he is only a wizard, and one who is presently without familiar."

Helena had a copy of Delaflote's book and had used it to summon a demon to her white-winged lark. The demon turned out to be a strix, which was under her control but as uncooperative as it could get away with. That left her with a less than high opinion of Delaflote's skill as a wizard.

She looked over at the cage where the lark resided and it cawed like a crow and she heard in her head, *"You're an idiot."*

"Shut up," she muttered.

Constantine looked over at the cage, and frowned repressively. Then he smiled and looked back at her. "You know, Majesty, the delegation has with them a gryphon. I heard that it was made by feeding a cat an enchanted bird."

by, Eric Flint, Gorg Huff, Paula Goodlett

"Bad idea, bad idea!" the lark insisted.

Helena looked at the bird, then said, "Find out if that's true and if it is, precisely how it was done. And find out how tractable the gryphon is." She shook her head. "More importantly, find out how to get the twenty-firsters on our side."

Constantine looked at her and she could see him hesitate. "Well, spit it out," she commanded.

"Manuel has shown considerable interest in Lakshmi Rawal. It wasn't something I thought we needed to worry about, but if you are looking for a way to bring the girl under—"

"Under our control. Not into the family. And not Manuel. She would rule him, not he her."

Location: Royal Palace, Constantinople
Time: 9:15 AM, October 28, 1372

Manuel II looked at the clock in the hall. It was brand new, built from a design sent from Paris, and it gave the time to the second. Good. It wasn't too early. His mother was not an early riser and approaching her quarters before nine wasn't a good idea.

He walked down the hall and nodded to the guard who stepped into his mother's room to announce him.

"Come in, Manuel," his mother called.

He went in as the guard went out. "Mother, you wanted to see me?"

"Yes. What do you think of the twenty-firsters?"

Manuel hesitated. Generally, when his mother asked him what he thought, it was the first step in her telling him what to think. "They are interesting. All of the French delegation is interesting. Cardinal de Monteruc didn't even try to convert me to the Catholic faith."

"The patriarch will insist that that is because the Catholics are not the true Christianity, and they know it from their own angels. Additionally, from what the icon says, he's correct."

Manuel had been in the Hagia Sophia and heard the enchanted icon speak, but he had also talked to Raphico. He kept his mouth shut.

After a moment his mother waved away that concern. "With your father's blunder in dealing with Murad, we are going to need the twenty-firsters and their knowledge. We need some way to compel their loyalty?"

She made that a question, not about the need, but clearly about how they were to get it. Unfortunately, Manuel didn't have an answer for that. "They aren't all Christians, not that the Christian monarchs have shown any great interest in aiding us against the Ottomans."

"Can they be bought?"

"Perhaps, if you can convince father and Andronikos to pay the price." Even though his father and brother were badly angry at each other at the moment, Manuel knew that once they got over their mad, Andronikos would return to being co-emperor and heir to his father and Manuel would return to being the spare. Which suited Manuel fine. He had no desire to sit on the throne and suffer constant neck pain from spending his life looking over his shoulder. "The twenty-firsters won't come cheap, and the treasury is far from full."

"Well, they managed to convince your father to anger Murad easily enough. Feel them out. We might even consider a royal marriage if that will buy them."

Manuel failed to notice her tone as he considered the proposal. Especially as he worked hard to avoid thinking about Lakshmi Rawal in terms of the proposal.

There were four, no, five twenty-firster women. He must include the Widow Grady. However, she was enamored of Doctor Delaflote. The same was true of Jennifer Fairbanks, who was enamored of Bill Howe. That left Annabelle Cooper-Smith, Liane Boucher and Lakshmi Rawal, who was by far the most interesting of the twenty-firsters. Most attractive, most charming, most astute.

He cut himself off. In spite of all that, she might not be the best choice. He forced his mind back to the basic question, how to get the French delegation on their side. There might be another way.

"Are you sure that we need to get them on our side?" he asked, then waved a hand, asking her to wait. "I don't mean we can afford to have them as enemies. If they are neutral but here, teaching us about not only the magic that brought them here but the techniques and devices that they had in their time, we might gain almost as much benefit without having to give them more than a place to stay and the chance to talk. In our discussions last week they were free with information about all manner of things."

"So they like to talk. What is the benefit in that?"

"Do you know what a drop forge is?"

"What? You mean like a smithy?" Manuel's mother sat up on the couch. "Have you lost your wits? What on earth would I, or any person of quality, need to know about the tools in a smithy?"

"And if that knowledge meant we could make rifled muskets small enough that a single soldier could carry them? Quickly and in large numbers?"

"Are you saying that they know how to do this?"

"It seems so," Manuel said. "Bertrand du Guesclin, who was, as you know, the constable of France until he was dispatched on this mission, showed me a device he calls a breech-loading demon-lock. It was the day after my party and he let me fire it. It's no longer than a bow, but you hold it out like a pike and it throws a lead bullet." He shook his head. "I am not explaining this well. But the device is amazing. It took me only moments to get the basics. A man, according to Bertrand, can learn to use one well in as little as a few weeks. They used them extensively in the battle of Paris. Roger McLean killed Philip the Bold with one in the sally that ended the battle. Bertrand's entire force carries the things.

"If we can equip an army with them, they might well let us defeat Murad in the field."

"And how long until Murad gets them and turns them on us?" Helena asked. She got up from the couch and started pacing around the room like a caged cat. "Anyone can use these single person guns? It doesn't take a lifetime's training like the sword or bow?"

Manuel nodded.

"We should kill them all," Helena said. "Including Bertrand." She stopped pacing and considered for a moment. "And the king of France, plus every peasant in Paris who has seen the damned devices. Yes, I know it's utterly ridiculous. The djinn is free of its bottle and will ravage the world whatever we do. But, Manuel, you must see that these devices are even more dangerous to us than the demons. Remember the Zealots of Thessalonica. They murdered the aristocracy and took control of the city for almost a decade, and through most of that claimed to be working for the *populari.*"

Populari meant, literally, "the people," but it had another meaning from the old Roman republic. It meant "the lower classes," not even the equestrians, but the poor and the merchants, those without any title more than "citizen," the peons.

And those people, armed with the demon-locks, was a terrifying notion.

"There is this," Manuel said. "The demon-locks are expensive to make. The flintlocks are cheaper, but not as good. But, Mother, we will need the flintlocks to face Murad in the field."

His mother returned to the couch. "Was their world then ruled by the mob?"

"They come from three countries. America, which is across the Atlantic Ocean, France, and India. All of their countries appear to have been republics, in which the senate and most of the other offices were elected by the vote of the people. As to how that worked . . . it was a longer discussion than there was time for that afternoon, but I am assured that they did work."

Again his mother considered. "Fetch me some wine, my son. I need to think."

Manuel fetched her the retsina, and waited while she sipped.

Finally, she said, "Arrange for me to meet the ladies. And, in the meantime, do Doctor Delaflote the favor of having Theodore Meliteniotes released into Doctor Delaflote's custody."

"Not simply released?"

"No. Make it clear that until his case is decided, he is part of the delegation and their responsibility. If that isn't acceptable, he can stay in gaol."

Location: Guest Quarters, Magnaura, Constantinople
Time: 2:00 PM, October 29, 1372

The guard knocked on the door, then announced in French, "There are a bunch of Greek soldiers here. They say they are delivering a prisoner."

"What prisoner?" Amelia Grady asked, also in French.

Some discussion in the Greek they spoke in this century, then the soldier said, "Theodore Meliteniotes, into our custody."

"What does 'our custody' mean?" Amelia asked.

More Greek, then, "The custody of the delegation."

"Now that's interesting. Have them bring him in, and any documents." Amelia opened her computer. "Will, would you contact Merlin and have him translate some papers for me?" Shakespeare, as a muse, could translate, but the container of the demon had an effect on the magic. Because Merlin was first put into Wilber's cochlear implant, his magic was focused on allowing Wilber to hear and understand any sort of language. Any muse level demon could translate, but Merlin, with that extra focus, was less likely to miss a nuance.

When the guard handed her the parchment, she unrolled it and held it up before Will, who photographed it and emailed it to Merlin. Merlin read it and sent back a translation. The release, it turned out, was based on their diplomatic status. The fourteenth century didn't have twenty-first century diplomatic norms, so they had had to invoke a special treaty between John of Byzantium and King Charles of France, co-signed by Amelia herself as the "ruler" of the twenty-firsters. That treaty, agreed to and confirmed by John V before most of the party entered Constantinople, gave the party essentially the same status as embassies would have in the twenty-first century. Using that, this document dumped Theodore out of Constantinople into the custody of the twenty-firsters. He couldn't leave the guest quarters save in the custody of a twenty-firster or he was subject to arrest. He was thrown out of the Byzantine Empire without ever leaving the city.

Amelia wasn't at all pleased at the speed at which the locals were learning to use twenty-firster customs, but Gabriel would be pleased that his pen pal was out of jail. "Excuse me, but I don't know your title?" Amelia said in French, trusting Will to translate. "What would you like to be called?"

"I am Magistros Theodore Meliteniotes," then, with a bitter twist of his lips, "Or was, until I was arrested."

"May I call you Theodore?"

He gave her a hard look, then looked at the guards, those who had delivered him and those surrounding the woman. "It appears, madam, that you can call me anything you like." He didn't sound particularly happy about it.

"Yes, but I try to be polite, sir," Amelia said. "In the meantime, you need to know what is going on." She spent a few minutes explaining diplomatic immunity and diplomatic territory and finally the fact that he was being released to them—but only if they agreed to take him. If they didn't, it was right back to jail for him. Amelia finished up with, "We are willing to take you in and be responsible for you. But only if you agree to obey our rules."

He asked for the proclamation and read it carefully, then bowed. "I will follow your rules to the best of my ability."

"Very well. The guards will show you to the baths. Get cleaned up and join us for dinner."

The guest quarters in the Magnaura had their own bath, in the tradition of Roman baths. The twenty-firsters had added soap made in France.

* * *

Four hours later, a cleaned and much more pleasant smelling Theodore joined Gabriel and Amelia for dinner. Wilber and Merlin were also in attendance, as were Annabelle, Lakshmi, and Liane. And so, by use of the phones, was Pucorl. And in a corner was a medium-sized cat that had wings, and its fore-claws were the talons of a bird.

The discussion was lively and far ranging. And while at first uncomfortable with women at the table joining in the talk, especially women whose heads were uncovered, Theodore gradually relaxed enough to share his insights into the political situation in Constantinople and the Byzantine Empire in general. Over the course of the evening, several comments suggested that he regretted the fall of the republic. That kings and empire were a retreat to an earlier, less civilized, time. He also insisted that Constantinople and the eastern empire had not fallen so far as Rome and the western empire.

"In terms of military power, it has," Wilber pointed out in flawless Greek.

"But the power of armies is not the only, or even the best, measure of a nation. We study philosophy and the arts, reason and oratory."

"Sure. And that's good, but who studies these things? Do the children of cobblers? Or is it only the children of the titled who have that opportunity?"

"What use would the child of a cobbler have for philosophy? It will not help him with his awls."

"You would be surprised," Annabelle said as she forked a bit of sauteed black sea bass in mustard sauce. "My grandfather wasn't a cobbler. He was a roustabout." She held up the fork now empty of bass, chewed, swallowed, and continued. "Roustabout is a job you don't have. Unskilled labor on an oil rig. Hard, dangerous work which pays okay because of the danger. But he went to school. He could read and write, do math, and had a good basic understanding of physics and mechanics. That paid for my mother's education. So I was born into wealth and status and went to schools as good or better than any you have. But a lot of what I know comes from Grandpa's experience. Given the opportunity, people will often surprise you in what they can accomplish."

Theodore considered the young woman. He knew from Gabriel's book that Annabelle Cooper-Smith was the magistros of the "body" of the demon Pucorl. And finally having seen Pucorl and the computers, he realized that the skills and knowledge involved in making and maintaining such devices were real and not the skills of a dressmaker or cobbler. Theodore was a scholar and member of the religious bureaucracy of Constantinople. He had spent his life learning and teaching. He had correspondents around the world, and for at least the last twenty years had been among the best in his fields of study.

It was a severe shock to realize that these children knew more of astronomy than he did. They, some of them, understood the math that held the moon in place and guided the planets around the sun. And it was the sun, not the Earth, that the planets moved around. He had seen an image of the Earth from the moon.

Theodore did not like being the ignorant one. Not even a little bit. He needed to get access to one of their computers so that he could study.

CHAPTER 9—COUNCILS OF THE MIGHTY

Location: Edirne, Formerly Adrianopolis, Ottoman Capital
Time: Mid-afternoon, November 4, 1372

Sultan Murad I didn't shout at the courier. He wanted to, but by this time in his life what he wanted to do almost never took precedence over what he needed to do. He was a large man with a tendency toward corpulence, mostly held in check by the fact that he rode with his army and worked out with sword and shield. Instead of shouting, he heard the man out, then thanked him for his service. With a gesture, he indicated that his aide should reward the man for his hard ride.

Then he ended court for the day and called his advisors. Especially Candarli Kara Halil, who was his first adviser in war and government, and his closest surviving friend. Almost the only person in the Ottoman Empire who wasn't a threat to his throne.

Candarli Kara Halil Pasha said, "It's the magic," when John V's insulting response to his command was described. "You know that he was trying for aid from the west. And you know that he failed. But this party from France . . . The western church has sent magi instead of troops to aid his cause. And now, with magic working in the world, that is a mighty gift. A gift mighty enough to make sniveling John brave." Kara Halil tapped his pen against the inkwell as he thought. "And if it's true that the wizards are from the future and bring with them magics that we cannot learn from our demons, that would make it an even greater gift."

"So we should abandon Anatolia and attack Constantinople now?"

The crow that sat on a perch and was Kara Halil's familiar cawed "No!"and the pasha looked at it. "You think not, my djinn?"

The crow said, "It's the Mongols. They have an army of demons and they are encouraging the rebellion in Anatolia. The Mongols are the true threat."

✳ ✳ ✳

Kara Halil looked at the crow and considered. He knew that the djinn was from Themis, the land of Themis that was this land a thousand and more years gone by. He knew that the djinn didn't really approve of the war in the mortal lands that were Themis' lands. At the same time, the djinn couldn't lie to him. So what it said was true. "My friend, is your view on this matter affected by your loyalty to the land of Themis?"

The crow hesitated. "I cannot be sure, though I am convinced that the greater threat is in Anatolia. But I am the most minor of djinn. You know that, Master. Not much greater than what the westerners would call a puck."

Kara Halil turned back to Murad. "My lord, I think the djinn may well be right, but in the meantime we need to send spies to Constantinople to find out about these 'twenty-firsters,' as they are called, and perhaps to remove them from play."

Kara Halil and Murad often spent pleasant evenings playing chess.

In this case, though, his lord shook his head. "No, my friend. We can't let John's rebellion stand. To do so would be to encourage others to rebel."

Kara Halil looked at his lord and knew that the reason was valid, but not the true reason. Murad had much more control over his anger now than when he was younger, but the anger still lived deep in the core of the man. John's failure to bow before Murad had angered him and John would be made to pay.

Location: Edirne, Formerly Adrianopolis, Ottoman Capital
Time: Shortly After Dawn, November 8, 1372

The Ottoman armies were moving out. One would travel south and cross the Straits of Marmara at Gallipoli under Candarli Kara Halil Pasha's command, and move in the direction of the rebellion in Anatolia. Meanwhile, a much smaller force under the command of Murad I himself would go to Constantinople and cow the self-styled emperor of Byzantium, gather up the armies of Constantinople, such as they were, and take them across the Bosporus to Anatolia, where the two armies would combine to defeat the upstart beyliks of Anatolia.

Location: Royal Palace, Constantinople
Time: 10:35 AM, November 12, 1372

Bertrand du Guesclin stood in the council chamber and looked at the map. It was a beautiful thing. Five feet tall and eight wide, drawn on parchment in colored inks, and—if they could convince the crown—it would soon be enchanted. For the moment, it was hanging on the wall of the emperor's privy council chamber. It covered north to the Danube and east to include all of Anatolia and west to the Adriatic Sea. The broad outlines were provided by the textbooks and maps shared across the computers of the twenty-firsters. They also provided locations of several key places like Constantinople, Thessalonica, and Edirne.

The coastline wasn't perfectly accurate. Over more than seven hundred years it had changed, so the twenty-first century maps that came with the twenty-firsters were off. That would need to be fixed, but the basic idea was clear and not at all new to the people in the room. Control the narrows between the Black Sea and the Aegean and you had a good chance of holding Murad at bay. Fail to hold them and Murad would win.

What they didn't have was any practical way of holding those narrows or preventing Murad from crossing them at will. Their ships were galleys and small sailing ships. Murad had more troops, more galleys, and more and better of nearly everything.

Further, the crown of Byzantium was broke. The royal purse was empty and the crown jewels in hock. Their credit was nonexistent and if the emperor went anywhere outside his shrinking borders, he was likely to be grabbed up by the locals for bad debts.

Only the twenty-firsters—and those they had told—had ever heard the word "gunboat." That was about to change. "The sea route from Constantinople to Thessalonica is 377 miles. At a speed of ten miles an hour, traveling constantly, it's a day and a half trip," Bertrand said.

"Closer to a week," Manuel II said. "I traveled from there to here a week before you people arrived. I was on a galley and we stopped when the weather was up and for a few hours most nights."

"With better navigation and a steam engine, you could make the trip much faster," Annabelle Cooper-Smith said.

Bertrand cleared his throat. "The issue is that even a day and a half is too long if you are to maintain control of the straits. You need faster communications. There are a few ways we can do that, but the best and simplest is through a magical phone system."

"What are the others?" Andronikos IV asked, giving the twenty-firsters a hard look.

"Fires on hilltops, semaphore towers. You don't have the equipment to do non-magical radios or phones." And as Andronikos bristled, Bertrand added hastily, "No one in this century truly does. What we learned in Paris was that we could use a combination of twenty-firster knowledge and demonic enchantment." Bertrand silently cursed himself for using "demonic." It was the way the demons—at least most of them—referred to themselves. But Andronikos was furious with his father over Manuel's elevation to co-emperor and heir, and disliked anything his father liked at the moment. He was also strongly under the influence of Patriarch Kokkinos, who intended to control Christianity by making sure that only his "demons" were counted as "angels." By now Bertrand was unconvinced that any of them were what the world had thought of as angels and demons before the veil was ripped asunder.

"The beings of the netherworld commonly called demons can be induced to occupy twenty-firster designed crystal radios that have speakers and microphones built in, and those devices can be networked through a phone or computer left in Pucorl's lands. And as long as the crystal set is maintained in a single location with a pentagram around it connecting it to Pucorl's lands, we can have almost instant communications anywhere we have a crystal set.

"We could also use Themis' lands," Roger interrupted, "if His Imperial Majesty can come to an agreement with Themis. That wouldn't require a phone or computer to sort through the calls. Themis could create demons to manage the phone system."

"How does Themis create demons?" Manuel asked. "I thought they were always there."

"Demons make other demons out of their own substance. The process is a bit different from a mortal having a child, but it's how new demons are made. According to Raphico, all the demons in the netherworld from whatever level were once part of God and will be again."

"You're saying they are all angels," Andronikos said. "That's blasphemy."

John V pounded a small paperweight on the table. "That can be discussed at a later time. You were talking about demo— 'angel' enchanted crystal sets. But you have yet to explain their great advantage."

"Communications are a force multiplier," Roger said, and Bertrand cleared his throat again.

Roger held up both hands. "Sorry."

"He's right," Bertrand said. "The person who wins the battle is usually the person that has the most people there when the fight happens. If you can get word to your forces faster, they can gather faster, and you can have more force in one place faster than your enemy."

John V nodded.

"The phones remove the time that it would take for a messenger to travel to forces you have elsewhere, and it also lets you communicate more fully what you need and where you need it. It's hard to get answers from a scrap of paper with writing on it."

"And you can make these?"

"Yes, but not cheaply."

"In that case, we can't do it at all," John said. "We have discussed this, Bertrand. Byzantium has a lack of funds because of the costs we have faced in holding the Turks as long as we have."

"We may be able to help with that, at least some," Jennifer Fairbanks said, "but it's not a blank check."

"What is a check?"

"Never . . ." Jennifer started to say, then changed her mind. "It is a document that can be used to retrieve money from a bank after it has been placed there." That led to a careful discussion of banking and the way money worked in the twenty-first century, which Jennifer managed to explain without ever once using the term "fiat money." Instead, she talked about fractional reserve banking, implying that you needed to keep at least half the deposited money on account, and in which she stressed again and again how vital it was that the government accept such money for payment of taxes and rents.

This wasn't the twenty-first century with income tax and property tax. It was the fourteenth, where tax time meant guys with swords pounding on your door with a book and taking everything you had, and calling it taxes or rent.

This was the time of the tax farmer, who bought the right to collect taxes for the king and kept as much as they ever remitted to the crown. This, in other words, was a time when the poor were even more screwed than they were in the twenty-first century. Jennifer didn't want to screw them any more by introducing paper money that they got paid in, but wouldn't be able to buy anything with.

It was a long and mostly boring meeting, but by the end of it, they had a few things at least sort of straight.

Empress Helena would be in charge of the imperial bank, and certain kinds of transactions would have to be done through the bank.

The twenty-firsters would be contracted to make and enchant a series of crystal sets. Those crystal sets would have about the same relationship with the crystal sets built in the future by hobbyists as a model does a sketch. They would be fancy. They would have screens and microphones and speakers, as well as eyes, all built into the system so that all of them could be shared through the antenna.

And, finally, production would start on a series of rocket boats. Gunboats would be better, but cannons of the sort that a gun boat needed were at least a year away. They had heard of cannon in Constantinople, and John, on his visit to Rome, had even seen some. But there were no cannon factories in Constantinople, not even the primitive sort they had in Paris.

That wasn't all bad. Starting from scratch they could avoid the flower pot cannons that were all the rage back in Paris, and go straight to something practical. Roger and Wilber would be in charge of that. Bill Howe would be working with the city guard of Constantinople to try and turn it into an actual police force that was capable of investigating crime and finding the culprit.

There was a knock on the door and all the plans went away. Murad I was on his way to Constantinople with a force of four thousand.

An army doesn't move fast, so they had a few days to get ready. But only a few.

Location: Land of Themis, Netherworld
Time: Roughly 2:35 PM, November 16, 1372

Zeus appeared in Themis' great hall. "Well," he bellowed, "what are you going to do about the mortals?"

Themis rolled her eyes. Not like an annoyed teenager rolled eyes. In Themis' case, they made a complete rotation, which gave her a view of her entire kingdom and the ones around her. Not that that was the point. She could have gained the same information without moving her eyes at all. She was simply making her opinion of Zeus' arrival clear. "Do sit down, Zeus." She gestured and a golden throne appeared. "So nice of you to call ahead. Oh, wait. You didn't, did you?"

Zeus had, on occasion, been her lover, fathering all of her fathered children. A titan like Themis created her world out of her own substance, the land, the plants, the animals, the people. The new computer beside her throne and the desk it was on were all created from her substance. For the most part, they were created to her own design, often copied from the mortal realm. In the case of her children, though, the process was more cooperative. Zeus, as the father, provided much of the design, but more of the substance came from Themis. It was not really like the sex that mortals had, but it did carry much of the same emotional and social connotations. So, to put it in human terms, Zeus was a bully and a horse's ass, but he was also the father of her children.

Zeus flounced onto the throne. That was the only way to put it. He flounced. Every part of the movement evocative of pouting disapproval. Zeus' lands, Olympus, were to the southwest and a half a level of entropy above Themis' lands. Her worshipers had lived, prayed, and died over a thousand years before those of Zeus, although there was overlap.

"What would you have me do about them? It was not the mortals who tore the rifts in the veil between the worlds."

"How do you know that?"

Themis stopped. She didn't know that. She had assumed that it was a being of great power, one of the origins, what her followers had called Gaia or Uranus. What the Persians called Angra Mainyu and Ahura Mazda. What the Christians called God and the devil. What other lands called other things, but which meant either the first being, or one of the first few, as the origin started to divide itself into parts.

Could they have done it, the humans? They might have stumbled onto something. After considering for an eternity of half a second, she decided that it was unlikely, but not impossible. "I don't. But it seems unlikely that the humans could have made the rifts."

"Maybe they released one of the first ones," Zeus said.

"That seems more likely. But even if that is the case, what do you want me to do about it?"

"Find them and make them put it back. Put them back in their place and make them behave."

"That would seem to be a job for the Furies, or perhaps Nemesis." With a thought, Themis called her sister, and created a new throne.

Nemesis appeared a moment later, with her black wings extended and her sword in hand. She looked at Zeus and then at Themis, shook her head, and folded her wings, which disappeared into her back as she sat on the throne. "I take it you didn't ask me here because you are ready to let me destroy France for the insult they offered you?"

"No, Sister. The one who did the deed is gone now, eaten by a puck, to add insult to his injury. And his mortal tool is in Hades' hands, and Hades assures me that Philip the Bold will spend eternity being devoured by demons of the pit. At least, his soul will."

In spite of herself, Themis took a certain pleasure in that fact, even knowing that Philip was never more than a tool of the elder demon, Beslizoswian.

"We have to make the humans stop calling us into the mortal realm," Zeus bellowed.

"And how do you propose we do that?" Nemesis asked.

"Do you really think that is a good idea?" Themis asked. "They have the right to make their own choices."

"Not when they compel demonkind," Zeus insisted.

"Well, I agree to that." Themis nodded. Then she gave Zeus a sharp look. "Now I understand. Someone managed to get enough of your name to compel you."

The call of a mortal to a demon great or small was dependent on the degree to which the caller knew the demon's name. Zeus' name wasn't only Zeus. It was also Jupiter and ten thousand more words of power and legend. The larger and more powerful the demon, the longer and more complex the name. If the caller, be they mortal or demonic, had enough of the name, they could compel a demon, force it into a container of their choosing and make it obey them. That had happened to Themis because a human's call is stronger than a demonic call. So the same knowledge of her name that failed to allow Beslizoswian to compel her, did allow his human tool to do so. Zeus was afraid that a human would get enough of his name to lock him into a container and control him.

Zeus confirmed her assessment with his next words. "Some pissant Greek scholar in Athens built himself a pentagram, put a statue of me in it, and tried to force me to throw a lightning bolt at the Church of the Conception in Athens.

"If he'd asked, I might have been tempted. The priest in that church is looking to burn heretics who pray to 'false' gods."

"And where is he now?" Nemesis asked with a grin.

"Still there," Zeus grumbled. "I didn't want to give the torch-bearing Christians an excuse to go on a burning spree when I am starting to get actual worshipers again. Besides, moving into the mortal realm without a container is difficult and dangerous. I have no desire to have a puck in an enchanted cart run me down like Pucorl did Beslizoswian. Speaking of which, why in all the netherworld did you cede Beslizoswian's lands to Pucorl?"

Themis looked at Zeus and Nemesis, both of whom were glaring at her. "Remember, Sister—and you too, Zeus—I am still the titan of proper behavior. And one of the things that my time as a slave taught me was that nobility of spirit deserves reward." She laughed. "Half the reason I forgave Charles of France for attempting to claim me was his knighting of Pucorl. It was a noble act, and not his only one. It was Pucorl that finally broke Beslizoswian, and to the victor goes the spoils."

"Very well, Sister. It's clear you won't change your mind. But what are we to do about the mortals calling us? I have no desire to be forced into 'the sword of retribution' and serve some mortal moron who deserves to be cut in half more than any of his enemies do."

"Let me talk to Wilber and Gabriel," Themis said.

"What? You would have us ask the aid of mortals?" Zeus' face became bright red.

"I am free today because a mortal chose to do the right thing instead of keeping me as his plaything," Themis said. "Would you have made the same choice, Zeus?"

Zeus looked at her, then at Nemesis. It was exceedingly difficult to get a lie past a god, even for another god. "It wouldn't have been an easy choice." He took another look at Nemesis, who was looking like she might pull her sword of justice on him, and finished, "Yes, I think I would have, if only out of fear of your sister's reaction if I tried to keep you."

"Well, when Roger did it, it wasn't out of fear."

Nemesis looked at her, and said, "I am not sure how I feel about that. But, yes, if that is the character of your mortals, call them and we will speak together with them in search of a solution."

Location: Guest Quarters, Magnaura, Constantinople
Time: 6:06 AM, November 17, 1372

Wilber was having a lovely dream when the phone rang. He muttered, "Go away, Igor. Not taking any calls now," speaking in both the dream and the waking world, because Wilber was aware that his dream was the product of the dryads of the grove.

Suddenly trumpets blew in his dream and the dryads were gone. Then Merlin's voice in his cochlear implant, over the phone, and from the computer, were all saying "Get up, Wilber! You have to take this call."

Wilber found himself sitting up in the bed, deeply disappointed, highly frustrated, and ready to kill Merlin and whoever was calling. "What the fuck is it?"

"Themis is on the phone, and she's not the only one," Merlin said.

*　*　*

In another room, Amelia Grady woke to trumpets blaring from her phone Laurence, followed by, "Wake up, Amelia. We have trouble right here in River City. The gods want to have a little chat with your boy toy."

The trumpets had woken Gabriel, so he heard Laurence's comment. Normally he and Laurence got along well, but Gabriel had been sound asleep only seconds before. "Can we drown your phone, dear one?"

"It's not me, Gabe," Laurence said. It turned out that Laurence Olivier had a low sense of humor off camera, which had an influence. "This is serious. We have the Olympians gathering in Themis' hall and more are arriving even as we speak. They want to have a little chat with you about that book you wrote back in Paris."

Laurence the phone had a quad core, so it had four separate but linked processors that allowed the muse that occupied the phone to carry on multiple conversations at once. While he was talking with Gabriel and Amelia, he was also on the phone with Shakespeare, Amelia's computer, Merlin, Wilber's computer, and Pucorl. And everyone was in a tizzy because everyone was getting calls from Themis.

By the time Gabriel and Amelia were dressed, the plan was in place. All of them would repair to Pucorl and thence to Pucorl's lands, where they would be able to meet, not entirely in person but close to it, with what might be called the council of European gods.

Location: Pucorl's Lands
Time: 6:34 AM, November 17, 1372

Pucorl appeared in his reserved parking spot on the blacktop outside Pucorl's Garage, the side doors opened, and the first load of mortals piled out. Included among them was Monsignor Savona with Raphico, Roger, Annabelle, Wilber, Gabriel, Amelia, Paul, Jennifer, Bill, Liane, and Lakshmi. Pucorl was going to make a second trip to include Cardinal de Monteruc, Bertrand, and Tiphaine.

As soon as they were out, Pucorl returned to the converted stable next to the Magnaura to pick up the next load.

Wilber and Gabriel made a beeline for the pentagram room on the opposite side of the garage from the Happytime Hotel. When Themis added her own pentagram, she insisted on a separate room to house it. But to pay for it she agreed to add some other pentagrams, a new one for Merlin, and for each of the demons inhabiting one of the twenty-firster devices. It was a large room and Themis' pentagram had pride of place in it. As they opened the door to the pentagram room, they saw that it had, at least temporarily, expanded into a great hall.

Themis' pentagram had expanded. It was at least twenty times the size it had been and it was packed with thrones, and each throne had a god or a demigod on it. Most of them were the Greek gods, who were also the Roman gods, but next to Mercury was Woden. And next to Zeus was Thor.

Wilber stopped in the door until Roger tapped him on the shoulder and squeezed by. Roger walked ahead and knelt to Themis, holding out her sword. She reached out and touched the hilt, and then he put it back on his shoulder and went to a smaller chair next to Themis' throne and took a seat.

One other thing had stopped Wilber at the door. The gods on their thrones weren't human sized. They varied, but the smallest of them would be twelve feet tall if standing. Roger's chair was a normal-sized human chair.

Wilber found his chair. It was to the left of a throne. An empty throne that was human-sized. All the chairs on their side of the room had name tags and the name tag on the throne was Pucorl.

"I don't think the van is going to fit," Wilber muttered to Merlin, who had his own chair. No one else heard, because he spoke through his implant connection.

"Zeus apparently has no desire to talk to a cart, so he's arranging things. By the way, we may have some power issues since Zeus isn't that thrilled that one of his lightning bolts is spending its down time as our electrical system. He didn't notice it until he got here, but at the moment he is having words with Ilektrismós."

"We can build a generator if we have to. I want to see Pucorl when he gets here. Say, did you notice Annabelle's chair is right next to Pucorl's?" Wilber shook his head. He liked Annabelle, and knew that she had a sort of old-fashioned love-from-afar crush on Pucorl. That had to remain an unrequited crush, since Pucorl was a van, not a man. This could add whole levels of complications that Wilber was fairly sure they didn't need.

* * *

Pucorl wasn't warned. He did get a call telling him to make sure that he dropped off his passengers before he entered the garage. Until he got the instruction, he'd planned on staying in the parking lot and attending by phone. As he pulled into the garage, he started to change.

He changed like a Transformer from one of Paul's movies, until he was a metal man. He was dark green, like his van body. Then he turned, and as he approached the door, he became flesh, covered in a dark green flack jacket and twenty-first century body armor, including a helmet with a heads-up display.

He had no idea what he looked like under the armor. The major effect of the change to flesh and armor was to leave him utterly terrified, because he couldn't do it. He lacked anything like that ability, and if Zeus . . .

That was who it was, Merlin informed him.

If Zeus could do this, what else could Zeus do to him?

Pucorl had been playing out of his weight class ever since he got the van body. And even more after he ran over the demon. But this? He wasn't a mouse among cats here. He was a cockroach in a room full of elephants.

With great trepidation, Pucorl walked into the pentagram room and sat on the raised chair.

✳ ✳ ✳

Then they got down to it. For what seemed like a week, they talked about magic. How the demon realm worked. How it was that mortal callings were more powerful than almost all demonic callings. About the threat to the netherworld caused by the rifts in the veil. And, for that matter, the danger to the mortal realm, at least the planet Earth.

And mostly they tried to figure out a way to prevent the gods from being called against their will. That, to Zeus and most of the rest of the gods, was the overwhelming issue.

The Creator of All wasn't in attendance, not in its own person, and while Raphico was, he was unable or unwilling to offer any concrete suggestions. As to Cardinal de Monteruc, Zeus and the other gods essentially ignored him. Their only answer to any of his queries about their status in Heaven were met with "You wouldn't understand."

Wilber got a bit more, let drop mostly by accident. But it amounted to "the gods didn't understand either." They were gods, angels, heroes, demons, devils, villains, all mixed together and would, in the course of their cycles, fulfill all of those roles and more, including being a part of the Creator and totally separate from it.

It was suggested by the cardinal—and sarcastically at that—that since they were gods they could change the books that Gabriel had printed, so that they lacked the knowledge of how to force a demon into a mortal world container. There were two problems with that. One was that if you knew how to ask them to come, you knew how to force them to come. The spells weren't that different. And, second, because the gods had limited power in the mortal realm, they had to work through proxies who were in the real world, unless they were committing way too much of themselves to the project. They were much more powerful on this side of the veils.

And there was the issue of Leona, the self-made griffin. She was proof that, given the right circumstance, a mortal could injure a demon and, in so doing, gain some of the abilities of the demon they ate. Leona, for instance, had the will o' the wisp's ability to disappear by slipping halfway into the netherworld and back at will. She also got the ability to fly, and knowledge of how to fly, as well as speech centers, from the crow. Which wasn't how it normally worked when a cat ate a crow.

That meant that humans, or for that matter, animals from the mortal realm were at least potentially a real and permanent threat to beings of the netherworld.

And as the rifts in the veil between worlds expanded, that threat would get worse. There could come a day when a cat or a bird might wander by accident into the netherworld, eat a demon, and return to the mortal world, taking the magic with it. And if that happened often enough, the netherworld itself might never recover.

"We're like global warming," Lakshmi commented. "Only worse."

* * *

As it happened, the gods weren't the only ones with issues. Roger and Bertrand wanted a better communications for the military of Constantinople and there wasn't time to do it piecemeal. At the least they needed all their phones and devices to be able to contact one another from anywhere in Byzantium, and they needed that ability right now. They couldn't produce that quickly enough, not in the mortal realm. They didn't need *"Deus ex Machina,"* "god from the machine." What they needed was *"Machina ex Deus,"* "machines from the gods."

Zeus wasn't willing to make the necessary "demigods"/ devices/people to run the system and while Themis wanted to help, she pointed out privately that she had been diminished by what she was forced to do in the sword. She was a ravaged land as much or more than the Byzantine empire. Still she agreed to work with Wilber to at least set up a phone exchange.

More talk ensued, and a telephone exchange was installed in Themis' realm that would connect all the phones. In exchange, Wilber and Gabriel promised to do all they could to find a way to anchor the gods and prevent them from being forced into containers.

Location: The House of Gaius Augustus Crassus, Constantinople
Time: Evening, November 19, 1372

Theodore Meliteniotes knocked, paused, knocked twice, paused again, and knocked once more. The knocks had started out as security in the time of Constantine. By now it was hallowed tradition, but still security. If he had knocked differently they would have known either that he was not here on the business of the senate or that he was here under duress.

The door opened and Gaius gestured him in sharply, then closed the door so quickly that the door almost caught Theodore's cloak.

Once the door was closed, Gaius hissed, "What are you doing here? Have you betrayed us?"

The "us" in question was the "Senatorium Republicum."

"Never!" Theodore was startled and greatly offended by the suggestion.

"Then how did you get your release?"

Now Theodore understood. "The French delegation. One of its senior members is a correspondent of mine." He snorted. "Not a proper scholar. Gabriel Delaflote is subject to flights of fancy and believes in ghosts and fairies, much as he might deny it."

Gaius, a short, pudgy man with a ring of black hair surrounding the completely bald top of his head, looked at Theodore and shook his head in wonder. "You do recall what got you arrested, don't you? It was the successful use of Doctor Delaflote's book to summon a demon."

"Yes, yes, I know. But Gabriel believed in demons and the old gods before there was any evidence for them. He tried to hide it, but it was there in his correspondence, in the experiments he wanted to try. And he says that astrology works. Not a proper scholar."

Gaius shook his head again. "Never mind. What are you doing here?"

"It's the twenty-firsters," Theodore said. "They come from republics. The Republic of France, the United States of America, which is a tiered republic. An alliance and more than an alliance of states, which are all republics. And even the England of that time, backwards as the English always are, is a republican monarchy, in which the crown represents the state, but the government is republican in form."

"Yes. I had heard something about that, though not in such detail. But what has that to do with us or our cause?"

"They are proof that republics are not a passing fad. And more, they offer knowledge of the methods of their republics' methods that we can use in restoring the Republica Roma."

"It's not the time, Theodore. No one wants to see the republic restored more than I, but. . . . We need stability and a strong monarchy right now. Even in the heyday of the republic, dictators were appointed in times like these."

That was true, but they continued to talk and Theodore persuaded Gaius, who was the senior senator of the Senate Republica, to let Theodore investigate the twenty-first century republics to understand how they dealt with difficult times.

CHAPTER 10—ATTACK ON TZOUROULOS

Location: Happytime Motel, Pucorl's Lands
Time: 6:35 AM, November 17, 1372

Pucorl stepped through the door and his body changed. He was still humanoid but definitely no longer human. His armor was again part of his body and his body was now filled with oil and electrical systems, no longer blood and nerves. And he couldn't remember how that change was made. As a landed knight Pucorl had greater control over his form than most pucks, and his make up was much of earth, because the demon whose lands he took was a system of caves. But caves aren't only earth. They are air, water, and fire too. He should be able to take any form he chose, even if his default body was that of the van. He had the power. What he lacked was the know how.

"Hey," said Annabelle, "Why'd you change back?"

"It wasn't my idea," Pucorl said. "Zeus changed my form and changed it back. If I'd been running things, I would have waited until we had a chance to *talk*." Pucorl leered the last word, trying to make it sound like one of his usual off-color jokes. But he couldn't carry it off. He really did want to "talk" with Annabelle, and now that he knew it was possible, he wanted it even more. And he thought, believed . . . wanted to believe, that Annabelle felt the same way.

* * *

Roger interrupted. "Sorry, kids. We don't have time for that. We have to get back and we need you to be a van again."

"How am I supposed to do that?" Pucorl complained.

"Step outside the garage," Wilber offered. It was a guess, but an educated one, and it worked. As Pucorl approached the bay doors, he transformed into the van.

* * *

As he was leaving the garage, Wilber got a phone call from Themis, one that neither Merlin or Igor were privy to. That was both a feat and an act that was out of character for Themis. In essence, she forced Merlin and Igor temporarily out of their bodies. Well, Wilber owned the phone, the computer, and especially the implant, but still. It wasn't something that the titan of proper behavior ought to be doing. Her first words explained why.

"I need your help. I was weeks gathering the dead for Philip's army, but only had days to put things right. A twentieth of my substance was left in the mortal world when I returned to the netherworld, and left me too weak to fight off the other gods should it become necessary. Nemesis, my sister titan, still supports me, but even she is not fully comfortable with the other changes my manumission made in me."

Wilber knew what she meant. Themis had been a slave and because of that she now understood how evil the institution was. As the embodiment of proper behavior, she was the law giver of the gods, but the other gods were probably not overly thrilled with the notion that freedom should be held as a thing of such value. "What can I do to help?"

"I need a way to restore myself."

"Mass equals will," Wilber muttered. "Not E=MC^2 but E=W, probably with a conversion factor analogous to C squared in there."

"What does that mean?" Themis asked, sounding utterly confused.

Wilber, deep in his heart of hearts, felt a bit proud of himself over that. How many people could honestly say they had confused the heck out of a god?

"More than can say they have survived doing so," Themis informed him tartly.

"Oops. Sorry about that. What I am struggling to understand myself is the correlation between what happens in the netherworld and what happens in the natural world. In the natural world, mass and will are unrelated. A mountain has great mass, but no will. But in your world, the two are related. When Pucorl got knighted it changed him, and for that matter changed the shape of his lands. When he defeated Beslizoswian, that changed him again. Not only the land, but his personality. He's still a scamp of a puck, but he is more mature and more serious than he was. He's no longer the eight-year-old brat lying for the heck of it and giggling when he gets away with it.

"Mass and will are almost different aspects of the same thing in the netherworld. Like mass and energy are in the natural world. This is something I've been thinking about ever since Pucorl grabbed the van out of the twenty-first century, and I still don't have a solid handle on it."

"It's not mass alone. It's the kind of mass," Themis pointed out. "Water is different from earth, which is different from fire or air, and aether is different from all of them."

"Well, what did you lose the most of?" Wilber asked.

Themis paused only a beat if she paused at all. "More of earth, but a greater part of fire."

It took Wilber a moment to parse that. Themis was mostly earth. He was guessing, but his guess was that eighty plus percent of Themis was earth, ten percent water, eight percent air, and only a couple of percent fire. So even if she lost a lot more earth than she did fire, she still lost a higher percentage of her fire than her earth. What Wilber didn't have a clue about was what would happen if they tried to make up the loss by natural world mass-energy. But that seemed to be their only option. There was, at this point, no way to get back the part of herself she had left in the natural world.

"I want to try something," Wilber said. "But I am going to need Pucorl's permission. Can you tell me why you didn't want Merlin or Igor in on this call?"

"Because Merlin is a muse of a god that existed in France in the time of the Neanderthals. That god sleeps and is ignoring Merlin, and will continue to do so unless Merlin learns something that will aid it. If Merlin does learn something from you or your experiments that would be of great value to his creator, he will be obligated to inform it. I don't know that that is a thing I wish to avoid, but it might be."

"Makes sense," Wilber agreed. "Let me see if I can come up with an excuse for what I want to try. By the way, what about Pucorl? Who does he owe fealty to?"

"After he gained Beslizoswian's lands, Pucorl became a special case. He is independent . . . no, that's not right. He is more powerful now than his creator was. His creator sleeps, and if it tried to force him to serve it, it would be subsumed. Pucorl is as close as the netherworld has to a truly independent being."

"Right. I will do my best to restore to you what was taken, or at least replace it with something that will work. In the meantime, we need the phone system."

At which point Themis was gone and Wilber was on the phone with Iris who immediately said, in Lily Tomlin's operator voice, "Is this the party to whom I am speaking? Please hold." And muzak started up. Wilber was about to hang up when Iris came on and—still in Lily Tomlin's voice—explained that she was really busy at the moment organizing the phone network. They were going to need to put pentagrams on their phone cases. "But everything will be up and running by tomorrow."

Location: Near Tzouroulos, Byzantium
Time: 11:50 AM, November 20, 1372

As Pucorl approached the city of Tzouroulos, now called Corlu, there was great wailing and gnashing of teeth within the city. The Ottomans had taken Tzouroulos in 1355, renamed it Corlu, and torn down its walls, because Murad was a lot more concerned about Tzouroulos rebelling than he was about John V being able to do anything about his conquest of the city. Tearing down the walls was his none-too-subtle way of telling the people of Corlu that he would much prefer to see them dead than in rebellion.

The people of the city were unsure who they were more afraid of. Murad I and his army, who were approaching from the northwest, or the magical monster that was on the road from Byzantium from the southeast.

The Greek Orthodox Church was still allowed to operate and was profoundly concerned that if they in any way supported John V, that forbearance on the part of their Ottoman overlords would cease.

Still, there was no attempt to build any sort of barrier. Murad had made it clear that if the walls returned, then he would tear down the whole city, sow it with salt and cast the entire city into slavery. Since most of the young men of the city were now Janissary slave soldiers in Murad's army, the city fathers didn't doubt the claim.

✳ ✳ ✳

Pucorl twisted his front and rear wheels so that he shifted left while still keeping his windshield facing the city. A delegation of horsemen was riding out to meet them. They were wearing turbans and the sort of flowing clothing that went with the notion of an Arab warrior, but they were also wearing what looked to be perfectly functional breastplates and their turbans seemed to be attached to helmets.

Pucorl wasn't alone. He had an escort of ten of Bertrand du Guesclin's men at arms under the command of Charles de Long, who still didn't have a replacement for Carlos. The demons, having heard about Carlos, were now anxious to avoid occupying anything, ah, edible.

There was also a company of some twenty knights of Byzantium, each with his retinue of squires and servants, so it was a fairly large group. Wilber, riding Meurtrier, and Leona were off to their left about fifteen miles, scouting. Leona was happy enough to scout as long as no one tried to claim any sort of ownership of her.

Roger was leading another group about fifteen miles to the right. And the largest part of the army, the rest of Bertrand's riflemen, and almost two hundred Byzantine knights, were about four miles behind Pucorl. The reason for the placement was that they wanted the Ottomans to think that Pucorl was all there was, with maybe a couple of small scouting forces.

* * *

At about twenty yards out, the Ottomans pulled up and one raised a hand in the universal symbol for "stop where you are."

Pucorl didn't stop. He wasn't under these people's orders. Instead, he continued forward until he was about ten feet from the leader, who by now had a bow out, loaded and drawn.

There were, in this time, no guns that a cavalryman could wield while in the saddle.

Well, that wasn't strictly true. The French army had flintlock breech-loading carbines. And Bertrand's force had demonlock carbines. And, oh, yes, Annabelle, as well as the other twenty-firsters, all had six-shot demon-lock revolvers. Plus the long rifle that Roger had used to kill Philip the Bold and an arrogant elf lord.

But these guys were a solid half-century away from that sort of thing. There was a flash in Pucorl's dash cam.

That arrow was enchanted.

"Behave," Pucorl said in demonic. But the arrow didn't seem to understand. For that matter, Pucorl didn't recognize the sort of demon that was in the arrow.

That was when Pucorl used the new phone system. He called Wilber and asked who or what it was.

Wilber spoke in demonic and the arrow glowed. "I'm not entirely sure, but I think it's a djinn. An extremely minor fire djinn."

"What are you doing, consorting with djinn?" Pucorl asked the soldier in Greek. "You being a good Muslim and all."

In fourteenth-century Turkish, which Pucorl didn't understand, the man answered, then a moment later Wilber told him, "I believe you have been consigned to the Pit of Hell there, Pucorl. You being a demon and all."

Pucorl gave the guy a honk that would have done a Paris cabby proud. The horse reared in fright.

And the arrow came out of the bow at a forty-five degree up angle. It landed in a tree which immediately started to burn.

"Say," shouted Annabelle, "Someone want to put that out before we start the forest on fire?"

Several of the riders rode over to the tree and started splashing it with water.

"Grab the arrow! You won't put the fire out as long as the djinn is embedded in that tree," Pucorl shouted. Then he started forward again and the troop fled.

✳ ✳ ✳

There wasn't much out here, Wilber noted as Leona flicked from tree branch to tree branch, scouting ahead of them. It looked like the Ottoman force was still treating John V as a scared child hiding in his room, which wasn't a totally unreasonable position to hold.

He looked over at the scout. "Murad seams to be marching on Tzouroulos with no scouts out. That doesn't strike me as the canny military commander that Murad was supposed to be."

"Why should he put out scouts? These are his lands, and they have been for over ten years. What does he need with scouts?" The man, one of Bertrand's picked men, grinned.

Wilber got on his phone. "We're coming in," he told Pucorl. "We should be at Tzouroulos in around an hour." The only reason that Wilber was here was because Igor was needed to stay in contact with the main army.

Location: Army of Emperor John V, Southeast of Tzouroulos, Byzantium
Time: 12:02 PM, November 20, 1372

As Bertrand rode out of the trees, he saw Pucorl at the edge of the city, stopped and waiting.

A moment later, Andronikos rode out and started complaining. "Why didn't your tame demon stay here as he was told to? Your forces have no discipline. Someone should take a whip to that van."

"You're more than welcome to try," Bertrand said. "But I would point out that Pucorl is the lord of his own domain and in no way under your authority." As Bertrand knew perfectly well, the burr under Andronikos' saddle was that Bertrand, not he, was in command of this expedition. Partly because of Bertrand's reputation, freshly polished by the siege of Paris, but mostly because John V was still pissed over his son's refusal to pay for his release from Venice in 1369.

152

"Meanwhile, let's get inside the city. Walls or not, it's still the most defensible place in the area. And with us in it, not a place that Murad can bypass."

It took them the rest of the day to establish themselves in Tzouroulos. Which Andronikos, with arrogant ceremony, renamed back to Tzouroulos from Corlu.

* * *

The next day, the first of Murad's scouts came in sight of the city, took one quick look, and rode hell for leather back to Murad's army.

Meanwhile Wilber inscribed a pentagram in a vacant lot next door to an Orthodox church that had been converted to a mosque when Murad took over the first time. In the pentagram he placed a small statue of Themis and a model of a phone.

The phone was a piece of wood carved into the shape of a landline phone, headset, and base, with little depressable buttons on the base. It didn't connect to anything except that it was inside the pentagram. There was a matching pentagram in Themis' lands.

The phone wouldn't contact Themis. Instead, it contacted Iris, who would listen to the request and decide if she would bother Themis with it.

Neither the priests nor the mullahs were happy to see the thing. But Wilber made it clear that they got to keep their altars only so long as Themis got to keep hers.

Wilber was working on a theory. One that he wasn't at all sure was valid. His idea was that prayer from the mortal realm acted as energy in the netherworld. He was working under the theory that if the worship of Themis could be reinstated, then her energy level would increase. The few hundred followers that Themis now had, mostly in France, weren't enough of a sample to truly test the theory. She would need hundreds of thousands of followers to produce any real change in her energy level.

The other reason for the pentagram large enough for a small building with an altar was to give Wilber a route into Themis' lands.

He used that route to take earth, oil, grain, and nightsoil into Themis' lands from the mortal realm in an attempt to rebuild her. Her agents took the stuff and "plowed" it into the soil of Themis' lands.

Location: Outside Tzouroulos, Byzantium
Time: Three Hours After Dawn, November 22, 1372

Murad I, the founder of the Ottoman Empire, sat his horse outside Corlu and examined the tactical situation while in his hidden heart, he raged. How dare they? Could they not see that he was the Chosen of Allah? Destined to found an empire the like of which the world hadn't seem since Alexander?

In less hidden places in his mind, he determined that though there was a slight rise, there were no walls protecting the city, that the enemy placed on rooftops along the edge of the city would damage him before they were overrun, but they *would* be overrun.

He called his staff together and prepared for the battle.

* * *

In Tzouroulos, Roger McLain, Bertrand du Guesclin, and Andronikos IV stood on a rooftop and watched as Murad arrayed his troops.

"Well, he's not an idiot," Bertrand said.

Roger grunted. Murad was arraying his troops into three columns, a large central column, and two smaller flanking columns. It was clear that he wasn't going to try and be clever. He was going to come straight in and roll over them. An idiot would spend weeks working out a clever plan while the defenders fortified the town. "Still, he's not considering

Pucorl. Pucorl's cow-catcher front armor is going to turn that central column's charge into a disaster." Roger looked over at Bertrand and lifted the long rifle. "I should go with Pucorl and we'll repeat the trick of the last day of the siege of Paris."

"It should work," Bertrand agreed, "but you're going to get a reputation if you keep offing great lords. People will start to think you're some sort of republican, trying to put the plebes back in power."

Again Roger grunted. "As it happens, I am. Both my parents were Republicans. And the more I see of kings, the better republics look." Roger was looking right at Andronikos IV when he said it.

Andronikos looked back at Roger and didn't say anything, though his knuckles were white on the hilt of his sword.

Bertrand continued. "As we discussed, Andronikos will command the right, I will command the left. Lord Demetrios, you're mostly a reserve. Let Pucorl and Roger hammer the front of Murad's central column. All we need from your contingent is to keep any cavalry that breaks free away from our people on the roofs."

* * *

Pucorl sat ready as Roger climbed onto his roof, lay down behind the wooden frame work, and strapped himself in with the canvas straps. The framework was about six inches high and completely surrounded Pucorl's roof. It had two functions. One was to act as an anchor for the van's side armor, and the other was to provide a rest for firing a rifle while lying prone on Pucorl's roof. In that position, Roger would not only be secure in case Pucorl had to make sharp maneuvers, he would be mostly out of sight of archers. Not completely safe, but as good as they could reasonably manage. Then they waited, while Murad started his forces forward at a walk.

It took Murad's central column almost ten minutes to get close enough to start their charge, but the moment they did, Pucorl pulled out from behind the building, made a sharp right turn, and charged right at them, horn blaring and speakers screeching dire threats. Not to the soldiers. To the horses. Wilber provided the horse, and what the horses heard was warning that a massive predator was coming for them, and it was time to run.

* * *

In Murad's army, the horses heard, and many of them bolted. But by no means all of them. Murad's mount, for instance, was made of sterner stuff. Horses don't think the way people do, but Murad's mount was a war horse, trained from early age to fight in cooperation with humans. Its reaction was to charge forward to meet the threat, confident in itself and its rider to defeat anything that threatened its herd, which included the grooms back in camp, as well as the other horses and riders with them.

So while some ran, others charged. And Pucorl drove into a charging mass of horsemen.

They tried to get out of his way when he got close, but they were too packed together, and the cow catcher knocked them aside like a bowling ball through pins.

If you didn't count the blood and broken bodies that smashed against Pucorl's windshield.

* * *

Roger saw it. Then he felt it, as Pucorl jerked with each horse thrown aside. Pucorl was still moving, but the simple mass of horses was slowing him.

Then it happened.

With no intent at all, a horse trying to leap aside tossed his rider up onto Pucorl's roof. He landed on Roger.

Roger was strapped in. There were quick releases on the straps, but Roger had to get to them. Before he could, he felt the dagger bite into his right arm.

Roger bellowed in rage and pain as he tried to undo the straps with his left hand.

He bucked under the weight of the man to no effect at all, then Pucorl reversed course, backing out of the mass, and the man on Roger was rolled forward almost off of Pucorl's roof. Roger got one strap loose, and tried to get up on his knees. And the Turk, now lying on his back, holding onto Pucorl's armor with one hand, kicked Roger in the face.

* * *

In the van, Annabelle heard what was going on, and pushed the down button on the power windows. They didn't move.

"Pucorl! You open that window unless you want me to shoot through your roof."

"Shoot through my roof then. Better holes in me than in you," Pucorl shouted back.

"I can't see through the roof. Open the window."

The window opened to Pucorl's pleas for her to be careful.

With nothing really approaching care, Annabelle grabbed the upper edge of the window frame and pulled herself half out of the van. Then, with her right hand, she grabbed her pistol, pointed at the Turk who was less than two feet away, and shot.

And missed.

Pucorl had twisted his front wheels and his rear wheels, and turned to keep her door away from the Turkish army. Not easy, since they were surrounded.

Annabelle would always insist that was why she missed.

She fired again. And missed again. This time it was close enough to singe the Turk's beard. And now she had all of his attention. Well, all the attention that he could spare from riding a bucking van.

A third shot punctured the Turk's breastplate, and he forgot all about holding onto Pucorl's armor. Half a second later, he was on the ground.

And a second after that he was roadkill.

Annabelle slipped back into the van and with no buttons pushed at all, the window went back up.

* * *

Roger was almost out of the straps when the Turk went over the side, but he was bleeding from a wide gash in his right upper arm and a thoroughly busted nose. He flattened back onto Pucorl's roof and pulled out his med kit, cursing a blue streak all the while. He was effectively out of the battle for now. There was no way he could shoot with this arm, and using Themis left handed wasn't going to be easy.

* * *

While they were fighting the Turk on the roof, the rest of the central Turkish column had turned into a raging mass of men and horses.

Almost from the beginning, the front of that column wanted nothing so much as to get away from the armored monster and out of the rain of fire from the rooftops of Corlu. But they were blocked by the troops behind them. With the front pushing back and the back pushing forward, the whole column ground to a stop.

* * *

On the rooftops of Tzouroulos, eighty men equipped with breech-loading demon-lock carbines laid down continuous fire on the writhing mass of Turkish cavalry. Most of them were good shots, and all of them were veterans of a kind of "up close and personal" warfare that left men completely inured to the horrors of killing. They aimed and fired, and not a one of them closed their eyes or aimed over the heads of the enemy.

They still hit more horses than men, but that was because the horses were bigger targets. Actual misses were rare because when shooting into that sort of mass you almost had to hit something.

* * *

Gradually, as the realization reached the rear that things were not going well, the pressure on the front of the central column eased up and people started running. First a trickle, then a flood. Because, to the uninitiated, rifles really are a terror weapon. A loud noise and death from the sky that you can't fight against. Skill doesn't matter, courage and toughness don't matter, the only route to safety is getting the hell out of there. And, unlike arrows or spears, you can't even see it coming.

Bang!

You're dead, or a cripple.

Murad's army, tough and savvy soldiers in sword to sword warfare, simply *couldn't* face it.

* * *

Bill and his horse were in demon-enchanted armor. The enchantment made the steel breast- and backplate and the chain mail light as a feather and flexible as silk. Which, as it happened, was a good thing for Bill, because the left flanking force of the Ottomans was coming right at him and Andronikos. While Bill was on the phone to

Bertrand to get instructions, Andronikos shouted, "Charge!" and five hundred Byzantine cavalryman rode out with lances high and pennants flying.

Bill, perforce, went with them. Bill didn't have a lance. Instead, he had a shield, his phone under the breastplate of his armor, and a six-shot demon-lock revolver.

The two forces met and more of the Byzantines went down than the Turks.

Bill, a couple of ranks back, wasn't in the brunt, but he did take a few shots. He never knew if they hit anyone. The upshot was that the charge, after the initial clash, turned into a melee. Most of the lances on both sides were lost, and more of the Byzantine knights went down than the Turkish ones. They were getting pushed back and Bill saw that Andronikos was up against two Turks. He raised his pistol, but then a Turk was riding at him, so he turned his gun that way and fired. The Turk's horse reared. Bill didn't know if he hit the horse, the rider, or if it was the noise that caused the horse to rear, but he was pushed back and by the time he looked again he couldn't see Andronikos.

"Sherlock," Bill shouted to his phone. "Get me the general. We're being forced back."

Moments later Bertrand was on the line. "Try to delay them a little, Bill. The Turkish center is broken and we're holding on the left. If you can keep them occupied for a little, I'll get Pucorl to hit them in the flank."

"Right, General," Bill said. Then to Sherlock, "Amplify. Pucorl is coming, men. Hold them a little longer and they're toast." Bill said it in French, but Sherlock shouted it in Greek.

It seemed like it would work. The defenses stiffened. But they were still being pushed back.

✳ ✳ ✳

On receiving the new instructions, Pucorl made a sharp right turn and, external speakers blaring "Ride of the Valkyries" at full volume, he charged to the right.

* * *

Jennifer's phone, Silvore, shouted, "Pucorl's going to Andronikos' aid. Bill says they're being pushed hard."

"Lord Demetrios," Jennifer shouted in turn, "we need to help Bill."

Demetrios Palaiologos looked at Jennifer, then at the situation, and proved himself to be more competent than anyone had any real right to expect. He knew that if he didn't go to Andronikos' aid and the emperor's son died, he would be in a lot of trouble, but he also knew that with Pucorl charging off to the left, the center was open if the Turks could recover from their rout.

"No!" he said, "What we need to do is keep the pressure on Murad's center." He stood in his stirrups, waved his arms, and shouted, "Follow me!" then rode after the routed Turks in the center. His force was smaller, much smaller than the Turks, but it was fresh and not terrorized.

Jennifer almost abandoned her post, but she knew that she and her six-shooter would be of little use to Bill's force. She also briefly considered shooting Demetrios in the back, but that wouldn't do any good either. Instead, cursing a blue streak, she rode along behind him.

* * *

Murad I saw his death approaching. Not in the enemy, but in his routed central column. Such a loss right now might shatter his still fragile nation, because it was held together mostly by his reputation. He already had a rebellion in Anatolia and if John *Piss-his-pants* Palaiologos could stop him here, his reputation was dead and gone. He was already in full armor. After all, he was the commander. He wasn't in the front because that wasn't where you commanded from. He mounted and in moments was charging with his personal guards at that routed column, swinging his sword, and bellowing at his troops to stop running and follow him. Surprisingly, some of them did. Not all of them, and he would deal with the cowards later. Right now, he needed to restore his troops to something like organization, and prepare to meet whatever was coming.

That was half his problem. He'd seen some of it, and heard more. Even gotten a good view of the monster as it hared off to flank his left wing. He'd heard the crackling thunder and seen the puffs of smoke from the tops of the buildings. But he didn't really comprehend what had happened. He only knew it was bad.

By the time he had something that almost looked like order restored to what was left of his center, he saw them coming. A contingent of over a hundred Byzantine knights. Coming straight for him. His forces outnumbered them, but they were fresh and solid. Standing in his stirrups and swinging his sword over his head, he ululated to call everyone's attention, then charged right at the oncoming Byzantines.

He was almost surprised when what was left of his army followed.

* * *

Demetrios saw Murad, lowered his lance, and spurred his horse into a charge. He was going to face Murad I alone on the field of battle and, if he lived, he would be safe from whatever befell Andronikos.

* * *

Three ranks back in the Ottoman forces, Omar put an arrow into flight. It flew high and straight. He wasn't the only one shooting, but it was his arrow that came down on the neck of Demetrios Palaiologos' mount. The horse stumbled, fell, and rolled on top of his rider. Demetrios' neck was broken, along with his back, four ribs, one arm, and both legs. He was dead in moments.

* * *

Jennifer almost came out of the saddle as her gelding leapt over Demetrios' horse, and when she came down, she was facing Murad I, with his scimitar looking about fifteen feet long, as he lifted it up in preparation to take her head off.

Not every panic shot misses. Once in a while, pray and spray works.

This was one of those times. Jennifer fired six times, as fast as she could pull the trigger. Two of them hit, one the horse, and the other punched right through Murad I's breastplate. It didn't hit anything vital, but that didn't matter. Between the horse's stumble and the pain of his wound, Murad came out of his saddle and was trampled under the hooves of Jennifer Fairbank's gelding.

The men who were following him, not knowing she was out of ammo, scattered in any direction they could find, as long as it was away from the demon on the grey gelding, who threw thunder and lightning like some ancient god.

* * *

Meanwhile, back at the right flank, Pucorl charged into the rear of the Turks and the charge that was pushing Andronikos' forces back faltered, then failed. Bertrand was still holding on the left, and then they heard it from the Ottoman camp. The drums changed their beat to a particular staccato rhythm, and then Wilber called, "It's retreat." But they already knew it. As soon as the Turks heard it, they didn't retreat. They ran.

CHAPTER 11—BATTLE DAMAGE

Location: Inn Converted into Hospice, Tzouroulos
Time: 4:15 PM, November 22, 1372

ndronikos had a broken arm. Which to hear him tell it was because of Bill Howe's cowardice in failing to support him. He had lost almost ten percent of his knights, again the fault of the twenty-firsters, their cowardly demons, and Bertrand du Guesclin. This time because Pucorl was late in coming to his defense. His cousin Demetrios was dead because Pucorl had abandoned his duty and because, instead of defending him as was her clear duty, Jennifer had run off seeking glory. And Roger, with his famous Sword of Themis and almost as famous longrifle, had proved completely useless. Yes, they had won, but it was in spite of the French contingent with its twenty-firsters and its demons. It would have been a much greater victory with much less loss on their side if he had been placed in command as was his right by virtue of his birth.

Roger, who was in the next bed having his arm and his nose looked after, heard it all for about the fifth time, and said, "You remind me a lot of Philip the Bold."

Andronikos looked at Roger in shock for a moment. "How dare you threaten me? You . . . you . . . peasant! I'll have you whipped through the streets of Constantinople."

They were both in the hospice, not having been magically healed because their wounds weren't severe and could wait. The triage imposed by Raphico and Monsignor Savona had much to do with severity of wound and gave short shrift to rank of the wounded. Raphico *might* have made an exception if Roger had asked. Roger had not only failed to ask, but had insisted that he be treated no differently than any other soldier in the army.

Either army.

The Turkish wounded were also being treated, without regard to their religion, through a combination of magic and modern knowledge of germ theory. There wasn't enough knowledge of modern medicine among the twenty-firsters to produce much of anything like modern medicine in the here and now. The good news was that they were no longer strictly limited by the information brought back in the heads and the computers of the twenty-firsters. The University of Paris School of Medicine was a phone call away.

Yes, it had only had the modern notions of medicine for less than a year, but it wasn't one man studying on something for less than a year. It was hundreds, some clever, some not, some innovative, some hidebound, some trying to adopt all the innovations and find more, and others trying to justify throwing it all out and going back to bleeding, bad air, and balancing humors.

All of which made for an often volatile mix, but one that was self-selecting toward the more accepting of modern concepts when consulting on the phone about wounded Turkish soldiers.

✳ ✳ ✳

In another room in the same hospice, six Turkish soldiers lay in bunked pallets with various injuries. Mohammed ben Sahid, born in Italy under the name of Giuseppe Caldrone, groaned under the pain of the compound fracture of his left humerus. The bone had been set, the wound treated with sulfur, sewn up and wrapped. The heathen healers insisted that it wouldn't putrefy, but he had his doubts.

They also said he was no longer a slave. For Mohammed was a janissary. He was taken as a slave from a trade ship out of Genoa, but that was fifteen years ago. For seven of those years, he had been a dockworker in Bandirma, then he was taken for taxes and made a janissary. The janissaries were a new unit introduced by Murad less than ten years ago. Mohammed was one of the first. They'd almost killed him, forced his conversion to Islam, and whipped or beaten him for the slightest infraction. You got tough or died, and a lot died. Mohammed got tough. So tough that he was one of those janissaries who was made cavalry.

Mohammed wasn't sure how he felt. By now he had fought in several battles and he was a tough man. Murad and his captains had done that. Mohammed was a janissary and that was a thing to be proud of. He wasn't at all sure that he wanted to go back to being a Genoese sailor. And it was hard to concentrate with the pain in his arm.

Then the priest came in. He was a tall, ascetic man with dark hair starting to go gray. He was wearing an alb and stola with fringes, but his alb had a pocket sewn onto its left breast, and in that pocket was the thing Mohammed had been warned about. One of the demon-enchanted slates.

He made a warding away gesture and the slate spoke in Turkish. "You have no need of warding against me. I will do you no harm, neither your body nor your soul."

"Allah protect me!"

"That will be up to Allah, I would imagine," the slate said. "I am simply here to examine your wound and see if it is becoming infected."

That was a whole other fear, to be without his left arm. It would end him as a janissary, probably end him period. Fear for his life warred with fear for his soul, and it was fear for his life that won. He let the priest examine his wound with the phone.

* * *

"There is a bit of infection, but not much yet. If we treat it now and seal the wound, he should be all right," Raphico said, and Monsignor Savona nodded, looking at the screen that showed a colored transparent image of the arm that showed torn muscle, blood vessels, and damaged bone.

"You should bond the bone as well. Not fully heal it, but something to hold it in place while it heals." He pointed at a bone chip that was away from the rest of the bone. "If you can put that back in place, it will speed the healing." By now, Giuseppe Savona was familiar with the internal workings of the human body, and he had learned triage in more than one sense. He knew that he could spend every moment of his life healing the sick and still not make a dent in the problems of illness and injury. He knew that he, and even Raphico, needed to pace themselves and spend part of their time on other things. So they didn't heal the Turk, but treated him enough so that he might, in time, heal himself. Then they went on to the next patient.

Location: Prisoner Camp, Outside Tzouroulos
Time: 4:25 PM, November 22, 1372

After the rout, a lot of Murad's army had surrendered. It was that or be ridden down, and most of Murad's baggage train and camp followers were captured. The janissaries included cavalry. Murad's entire force was mostly cavalry, but once your horse is shot out from under you, an armored cavalryman is only another foot soldier, and no more capable of outrunning a horse than any other. And the point of Murad's central column was almost entirely janissary. They were his toughest, most disciplined troops, and the ones he could most afford to spend in forcing an objective. So more than half the captives were janissaries, and most of the rest were mercenaries. There were only a sprinkling of noble knights in his army.

In a way, the mercenaries were the greater problem. They were willing enough to change sides, but they expected to be paid and John V didn't have the money to pay them.

The janissaries, as a relatively new Ottoman force, were not paid. Not in money. They were fed and equipped, trained and treated, even paid a sort of allowance, but that was the largess of their owner. The discussions among the prisoners were ongoing, and the discussions about how they were to be handled were ongoing as well.

Location: Constantinople
Time: 4:35 PM, November 22, 1372

Pucorl was doing sixty kilometers per hour as he drove through the outer gates of Constantinople. He was then slowed by traffic, but he was still out-speeding a galloping horse as he pulled up in front of the royal palace.

He opened his side door and Bertrand du Guesclin, general of the armies of Byzantium, hopped out and strode up the steps to the palace entrance to cheering crowds. Byzantium hadn't had a victory against the Turks in a long time. After the reconquest of Tzouroulos and, more importantly, the defeat of Murad, Bertrand was the golden boy of the Constantinople mob. And the golden girl was right behind him.

Jennifer Fairbanks, the girl who killed Murad in mortal combat. The fact that she was a woman delighted the mob. Not because of what it said about her, but because of what it said about Murad and his whole line. If he could be defeated by a mere slip of a girl on the field of battle, God must truly be on their side.

Bertrand spent most of the trip here convincing Jennifer to let that part of it go, and not to go around explaining that she could defeat Christian nobles and kings as easily.

Jennifer saw their glee as an insult to her. But they needed that glee and the adulation that came with it, to make the rest of their program more acceptable to the people of Byzantium.

Location: John V's Apartments, Royal Palace, Constantinople

When Bertrand and Jennifer entered the emperor's private apartment, they found a mob. A small mob, but a mob. Aside from John, there was his wife, who doubled as the royal treasurer, Manuel II, the co-emperor of Constantinople and a slightly larger chunk of what used to be the Eastern Roman Empire than they'd been emperors of a few days ago. Tzouroulos was back in the fold, and if they kept pushing they ought to be able to get back a lot more. That was why he was here.

Bertrand wanted to keep pushing. Partly because it was the right strategic move. But politics were involved too. His king, Charles V of France, wanted the Christian powers to push the Turks back across the Bosporus. So did Pope Gregory. And because of the phones in Paris, they could tell him so. The pope was in Avignon again, but Avignon wasn't Rome. It was only a few days away for a fast rider. And besides, the pope had a crystal set enchanted by a cherub in Avignon.

The effect of these things was to allow the royalty, secular and ecclesiastical, of western Europe to stick their oars into the management of eastern Europe, completely bypassing Venice, Rome, and Genoa—which wasn't calculated to make them happy. The phone in Vienna was a major coup for Austria because it put them in the same club.

"If we are to have any hope of continuing this campaign," Helena Kantakouzene, John V's wife, said before Bertrand could get his mouth open, "we must have more money."

"I understand, Majesty. However, I can't provide it. And if you are to generate more revenue, you must recapture at least some of the territory that you lost to Murad and to the Bulgarians," Bertrand pointed out. "And if you are to defend what you have, we must recapture and fortify Gallipoli and control the Sea of Marmara."

It was a long afternoon. Phones were brought out, phone calls were made to Paris and Vienna. Money was promised, and an embassy arranged from France to Venice, in an attempt to get Venice to return the crown jewels without giving them the island of Tenedos.

At the moment the Turks controlled the Sea of Marmara, to the extent anyone did. The introduction of cannon or rockets and the ships to carry them would change that. But that wasn't going to happen fast, and in the meantime the Turks needed to be distracted.

Bertrand's plan for that was straightforward. Take back the Byzantine Empire north of the Sea of Marmara. To do that he would need Roger, the janissaries captured from Murad I converted into a standing army paid for out of the royal purse, and the ability to recruit more. An army that was loyal to Byzantine, not its paymaster or the noble who called them up from his lands. They could use the janissaries as a core because all of the janissary cavalry had been with Murad I at Tzouroulos.

Location: Prisoner Camp, Outside Tzouroulos
Time: 8:30 AM, November 24, 1372

Wilber walked along the camp street outside Tzouroulos. He heard a meow and turned in time to catch Leona, who landed on his shoulder. Four kilograms of gryphon landing on your shoulder is something you need to be braced for.

"You can walk," Wilber complained in Gryphon. Gryphon, it turned out, had aspects of cat and crow but was neither. At least Leona's Gryphon. Wilber imagined a lion-eagle gryphon would have a different dialect.

"Indeed I can," Leona said in gryphon-accented Greek. "But that's what humans are for. To carry us, pet us and, most of all, feed us."

"Why don't you go visit Roger?"

"Roger doesn't speak Gryphon."

"Well, you're heavy," Wilber said. "So you can walk or fly."

Suddenly the weight on his shoulder lessened. He turned this head to find himself facing a sharply pointed cat face that was translucent. "How did you do that?"

"I'm not sure," Leona said. She became heavy again, then light, and as she did her transparency varied in sync. The lighter, the more transparent. Now, on the edge of invisible, she looked around. "There's a djinn over there." She pointed with her nose.

Wilber couldn't see anything, but he was experienced enough to make a good guess at what was going on. A big part of a will-o'-the-wisp's power was its ability to appear and disappear, and the way it did that was to slip back and forth from the natural world to the netherworld at will. It didn't need a rip in the veils to slip through, and it could exist in both the netherworld and the natural world at once.

Wilber decided to try something. His voice, like his hearing, was magically enhanced by the little bit of Merlin left in his cochlear implant. He was now, at least in small part, a magical being. What the limits on that were, he didn't know. Pitching his voice to pass into the netherworld, he spoke Djinn. "Hello. What are you doing here?"

He didn't see anything, but suddenly Leona was off his shoulder, and she disappeared.

* * *

Leona was watching the djinn as Wilber spoke. She saw it look around and see her floating in the air of the netherworld with her wings folded and sitting on something it couldn't see. It was a minor djinn, nothing more than a zephyr. It gave a little squeak of fright and took off

172

running. At that point instinct took over. Both cat and crow were active hunters, and if the will-o'-wisp part of her was less active about it, it was still a hunter. Leona was off Wilber's shoulder and flying after the little creature in an instant. Almost, she dined on djinn, but she wasn't all that hungry, and she thought Wilber would be upset if she killed it before he could talk to it. So she grabbed it in her talons, and slipped back into the natural world.

* * *

The being that suddenly appeared in Leona's talons was the size of a puck, bright orange as though it was made of fire, and it rested on a smoky tail, like a cartoon Aladdin's lamp-style genie. He was also pissed and clearly frightened.

"Hello," Wilber said again. "Now will you behave if Leona lets you go?"

The djinn looked desperately around, then gave Wilber a crafty look, and said, "Yes, yes, master."

Wilber could hear the lie. Apparently djinn weren't held by their given word like European demons. "Hold him for a few, Leona." Wilber picked up a stick and started to draw a pentagram around the djinn. It took less than two minutes and it wasn't particularly powerful, but it should hold the thing.

"Let it go, Leona."

Leona flicked out of the natural world, leaving the djinn in the pentagram.

Meanwhile, Wilber had drawn a crowd. He took a moment to explain what had happened. Then he started questioning the djinn. It turned out that he was from a tribe of djinn to the southeast. From what he said, Wilber guessed it was somewhere around Syria, and he was here because one of Murad's wizards had grabbed his wife and stuck her into a sword. Both he and his wife were the most minor of djinn, and all he wanted was to get his wife and go home.

"Which sword?" Wilber asked. There was something wrong about this, but Wilber wasn't sure what.

Again with the shifty eyes. After a bit of hemming and hawing, he identified the tent that held the sword, and described it. It was a scimitar. Not Murad's, but one of his lieutenants, who had been injured in the battle and captured.

Baqir wasn't thrilled with the sword in the first place, and sold it to Wilber. Again, Wilber wasn't convinced that that was going to be enough to get the truth out of the djinn, but it was a start. The first djinn wanted Wilber to give him the sword and let him go, promising on a stack of Koran to be Wilber's willing slave if he did.

Wilber wasn't buying. Another pentagram, and then he released a fetching top half of a young woman, also orange, but with more yellow, and dressed in veil and harem outfit. She looked at Wilber, looked at Orange, and started cursing a blue streak. Apparently, Orange wasn't her husband. Orange was a low class djinn who wouldn't leave her alone. She wasn't thrilled about being in the sword, but better the sword than that little freak Omar.

Wilber translated this for the Turks, and some laughter ensued. Not all the prisoners were celibate janissaries, and not all the janissaries had always been celibate.

"What do you want then?" Wilber asked.

"I want my freedom! It's not right that a mere human should hold any djinn, even that one."

"Well, at least you're being honest," Wilber said. Meanwhile he was getting warning from all around that letting djinn loose without protection was unsafe. Wilber suspected they were right. At the same time he wasn't thrilled about holding this young woman against her will. It wasn't gentlemanly, not by Wilber's standards of gentlemanly behavior.

Wilber pulled out his phone and called Merlin, who was in his room in Tzouroulos. Then he listened as Merlin spoke to the female djinn, who proved to be a minor ifrit. Then, having gotten a fair piece of her name as a surety of protection, Wilber released her. In a moment, she was gone, and a moaning Omar was released and fled.

The effect was mostly to convince the Turks that Wilber was a powerful wizard.

CHAPTER 12—A PAUSE TO BREATHE

Location: The House of Gaius Augustus Crassus, Constantinople
Time: 3:34 PM, November 25, 1372

The afternoon sunlight pouring through the glazed windows was augmented by candelabras along the walls of the hall. The ladies in their gowns and the gentlemen in their tunics, which were shorter gowns, made a glittering display. Or would, if you hadn't grown up with twenty-first century Paris fashions, materials, and techniques. The silks from China didn't shine and the dyeing was sometimes like unintentional tie-dyed.

Someone should mention buttons to these folks, Wilber thought, then remembered "someone" had. He was wearing a buttoned up jacket. So were the other members of the French delegation in attendance, even Dr. Delaflote.

It wasn't the pretension that bugged him. Wilber's mom could, and often did, look down her nose at the world about as thoroughly as anyone he'd ever known. What he found increasingly irritating was that these people seemed to think they were the real deal.

"You're not dancing," Liane said in twenty-first century French which now had a bit of a fourteenth century accent.

"Neither are they." Wilber pointed at the dancers with his chin. "They're almost strolling to the almost beat."

"They're not that bad."

Wilber looked at her and said, "What? The French fashionista is suggesting that I put a bone in my nose and bay at the moon with the local street gang that thinks it's a civilization?"

Liane laughed. "Well, maybe not the bone through the nose. Something tasteful, like a diamond stud."

Wilber snorted.

"Hey, at least some of the girls are good looking."

"Not so you'd notice," Wilber said. "Too much rice pudding and too many sweets for most of them." That was true. Constantinople was apparently the father of the western world's obesity problem.

✳ ✳ ✳

Aurelia spoke French. One of the family maids was French and she had learned it. Besides, for some reason the man's French was more understandable than it should have been. She looked out at the dancers, then at the man. He was wearing a . . . something. She wasn't sure what it was, but it had sleeves that went down to the wrists, and she couldn't imagine how he had gotten into the top or the pantaloons. It was a style of clothing that her father couldn't buy, that the emperor couldn't buy, because no one knew how to make it in the first place.

What a haughty disagreeable man, she insisted to herself. It was true that he was attractive. Tall and slim, with sandy blond hair and clear blue eyes. He was clean shaven, which gave him an exotic look.

Location: Guest Quarters, Magnaura, Constantinople
Time: 8:30 AM, February 25, 1373

After the battle of Tzouroulos, things started getting organized, at least a bit. Bertrand and Roger got stuck with Andronikos and were raising, training, and using a small but growing army to take back Byzantium. Their efforts were aided by the fact that the Turks were in disarray after the death of Murad because Savci Bey and his brothers were locked in a desperate battle with each other to determine who would be the next sultan of the Ottoman Empire, even as the rebellion in Anatolia was growing.

Meanwhile, the rest of the twenty-firsters and most of the French priests were back in Constantinople, trying to start the industrial revolution.

* * *

Jennifer Fairbanks, Annabelle Cooper-Smith, and the master coppersmith all leaned over the wide sheet of papyrus, looking at the design of the tube boiler. It was a modification of a design developed at the University of Paris. Steam power was a technology that the twenty-firsters knew existed, but not a lot more. They did know a little more. They had all seen pictures of steam locomotives and they all knew about internal combustion, including the fact that they had cylinders that pushed pistons. Between that and experiments in France, and the memory that there was such a thing as a tube boiler, they were trying to decide if the coiled bronze tube would hold enough pressure to run a steam engine.

"The only way to learn is to try," Jennifer said.

"That's an awfully expensive test."

"Maybe we could build a scale model, one-tenth scale. That would use a lot less bronze."

"But we don't know if the cube square law applies," Jennifer insisted.

"What is the cube square law?" asked the mastersmith.

They tried to explain and got nowhere fast, until Annabelle mentioned that it was why puppies have such big feet. "They have feet in scale to the adult dog they will be."

The coppersmith still didn't really understand, but at least now he mostly believed.

Location: Harbor, Constantinople

Joe Kraken tightened his "guts" and squirted a jet of water out his stern. Squid don't have a front and back the way that people or boats do. They go this way and that, depending on circumstances. And Joe wasn't a squid anyway. He was a kraken, a sea monster, bigger by far than the largest giant squid. Joe was in a designed body. A body whose primary design function was to act as the transport for Pucorl. His "mantle," for want of a better term, was the body of the barge, the part that Pucorl sat on. He could move most readily in that direction, but his tentacles, mouth, and jet were in the stern and his underwater eyes were on the sides. Close to shore or in shallow water, he mostly moved using his tentacles, walking along the river or sea bed. But out in the bay he used his jet to push himself and his tentacles as fins, or sometimes as though he was swimming.

Joe was much more maneuverable than a normal boat, but still more directional than his kraken body back in the netherworld. Which, along with the fact that he was stuck on the surface of the sea unable to sink to the bottom, was something he'd had to get used to after he got his new body.

Not that there weren't compensations. His new body didn't require any concentration to maintain so all his will could be focused on strength. While smaller than his body in the netherworld, his body here was much stronger. One of his tentacles flashed out and nabbed a large grouper. A quick motion and that grouper's spine was snapped by Joe's iron beak. Joe liked mortal fish. His artificial body didn't need food, but his magical self did absorb the fish's body, and that was making it more solid and stronger.

Joe was out today, almost on a day off. He was patrolling the Bosporus Straits and grabbing some snacks, instead of sitting at the docks of Constantinople, waiting for Pucorl to need a ride. As part of the deal, he had a crew of five officials of the Constantinople bureau of tariffs.

They were approaching a galley showing a Genoese flag. And Joe had a bad feeling. Suddenly a rain of arrows shot from the galley and three of them hit his decking. They hurt.

Squid aren't particularly aggressive. In truth, they are shy and retiring creatures. But Joe wasn't a squid. Joe was a kraken. And, as of this moment, Joe was a pissed off kraken.

As the customs agents made for his cabin, Joe, using jet and tentacles, maneuvered his stern to face the galley and reached out with his tentacles. Grabbing oars and jerking, he pulled and used that pull to lift his stern out of the water, and then reached up with his tentacles and grabbed the port sidewall of the galley and pulled it down.

The galley wasn't designed for that. It flipped, pouring sailors into the drink, and shoving Joe's bow below the surface. Then Joe had to work to keep from sinking himself.

Joe knew he wasn't supposed to eat people. But it did seem a horrible waste, watching the crew of the galley sink into the Bosporus and drown. He'd be eating if he could, but he had specific orders on the subject, and demons are under the control of the owner of their vessels. So, however much the waste, he could not eat the crew of the galley. He did use his built-in crystal set to call Pucorl and complain about unreasonable restrictions.

* * *

Pucorl got Joe's call while he was in his netherworld lands, and he had a thought. Two ideas. First, he sent back to Joe Kraken, <Grab a couple and put them on the deck. See if you can revive them.>

Once Joe had done that, he called Joe to him.

Pucorl's lands were on the edge of the Elysian Fields, which—among other things—meant that Pucorl had a coast. It wasn't much of a coast, a few hundred yards long, over on the other side of the garage from the dryad's grove. But Pucorl had reshaped the land into a dock after he got Joe. Until now, he had never had any cause to call Joe to his part of the netherworld.

Annabelle was in her office with Royce, looking at a steam cart design. It wouldn't be anything like Pucorl, but Annabelle insisted that it would be better than the ones they were making in Paris. More importantly, this one would be designed based on the US Army WWII jeep, and it would be used by Bertrand's army.

It wouldn't be like it was back in the world. Mass production didn't exist. Each jeep would be handmade, and each and every one would need a demon to make it work, because they couldn't make spark plugs or distributor caps, at least not yet.

If they got ten of the things built this year, they would be pulling off a miracle. That wasn't the only thing they were working on. The twenty-firsters were introducing as much as they could of the tools to build the tools to start an industrial revolution.

Not only steam engines. Steam hammers and drop hammers, powered by wind and water. There was a master ironsmith working with the twenty-firsters to build a Bessemer forge as soon as they figured out what a Bessemer forge was.

Bill Howe was working with the Constantinople city guard on developing a department of detectives, who would investigate the rare crime where the perpetrators weren't known from the outset, and finding the perps when they went to ground. Something that was mostly not done in this day and age.

"Annabelle, we have guests," Pucorl told her.

She came out of her office with its drafting table and asked, "What's up?"

Pucorl opened his driver's side door. "Come have a look."

***

Sergios looked up in shock. They were no longer in the sea off Constantinople. They were in hell. A quiet corner of hell, but hell nonetheless. Looking out from the quiet little cove they had arrived in, they saw waves seeming to rise a mile into the sky, shifting from blue to green to blood red, then to some color that no human eye should ever see. And within the water, Sergios could see monsters of every imaginable shape. Worse, the monsters didn't stay one shape, but shifted in the blink of an eye from fish to bird to crab to something that looked like it was wearing its stomach on the outside.

"Calm down," Joe Kraken said over the speakers in the cabin. "Pucorl will be here shortly, and these are his lands. The waves will not enter his cove. I know they are strange to you, but they are quite orderly and pleasant by netherworld standards."

This is orderly? Sergios thought in horror.

Then the magical van drove out onto the dock and a door opened. The young woman they knew to be Pucorl's friend, mistress, or something, got out and quickly leapt across to Joe's deck. She ignored the customs agents, and went to the two men who were lying on the deck. Quickly checking the first, she flipped him onto his stomach and started pressing on his back. Water poured from his mouth and more, then he started breathing and coughing.

She moved to the next, and though she got the water, at least some of it, from his lungs, he didn't start to breathe. So she flipped him on his back and started CPR. She kept it up for two minutes before finally giving up.

Several dryads came to the dock, picked him up, and took him away.

* * *

It took awhile to get everyone calmed down, especially the Genoese sailor who was the second officer of the galley. He was convinced that he was dead and in Purgatory.

"Not so. You're not dead, and you're in the Elysian Fields, not Purgatory. You can even return to the world of the living . . . if you tell us what we need to know," Pucorl told him.

Pucorl had to call Wilber to get the words, as no one there spoke Italian. So from then on, Wilber was in on the talk.

"Why did you attack us?" asked one of the customs officials.

"It's a sea monster," the panicked sailor shouted.

"Well, yes," Joe said, "But that's no reason to attack me. I was only bringing these fellows to inspect your ship." A tentacle lifted out of the water and pointed at the customs officials.

The Genoese sailor shrank back on the pallet where he was sitting.

"Ah, Pucorl, you should probably not use Joe as a customs boat," Wilber suggested.

Sethos Kotos, the leader of the Constantinople customs officers, looked at the sailor, then said, "I don't know about that. Letting the world know that assaulting a customs boat has consequences might be useful.

"What were you doing, sailing a military galley into Byzantine waters?"

That started an argument and Annabelle, Pucorl, and Wilber listened as they argued about who had the right to do what in the sea route between the Black Sea and the Mediterranean Sea. Genoa wanted, and claimed to have, control over the trade, which was why they had pressured Andronikos IV not to give the Venetians Tenedos when they were holding John V for bad debts.

The fact was, that chunk of ocean was mostly controlled by the Turks and even their control was weak. Legally, Byzantium had the best claim. But it hadn't had the power to enforce it since before John V became emperor. Their claim of control was even more threadbare in terms of real force than the Genoese claim.

It would all bloom into a nice diplomatic incident with nasty letters flowing back and forth between Constantinople and Genoa. And the notion that attacking Pucorl's barge was a bad idea would be introduced.

Location: South Coast, Wales
Time: 11:30 AM, February 27, 1373

Leona slipped almost by accident from Pucorl's lands to the mortal realms "closest" to them, and found herself in a field next to a small fishing village. The field was covered in frost. With two quick steps and a leap, Leona was flying. She got some height and flew over the town to shouts and consternation. Some rude human shot an arrow at her. He missed by a large margin, but it bothered Leona enough so that she flipped back to Pucorl's lands, calling for Wilber to do something about it.

Wilber, as it happened, was in Constantinople. And Leona lacked a phone. She headed for the dryad's grove, looking for Coach.

The faun who had been Jeff Martin's sports watch and now was his own being sauntered up to Leona. "What has you in a tizzy, my young friend?"

Well, young she was, in comparison to a creature that existed before men wore clothing. Besides, Coach was a good friend. She got Coach to call Wilber. But Wilber was busy, and wasn't of a mind to travel all the way to England to let some farmer know he wasn't supposed to shoot at the flying cat.

Leona was not going to let that stand. She was, after all, a cat. She slipped from Pucorl's lands to Wilber's apartment in Constantinople, leapt onto his lap, and yowled her annoyance.

"I am not taking you to England. It would take months."

"Don't be silly. I was there minutes ago."

"Yes, well. I can't go from the natural world into the netherworld on my own."

"Surely you can. I'll show you." She jumped to the floor and flicked back to Pucorl's lands.

Wilber didn't follow her.

Most disappointing. Back to Wilber's rooms. "What's taking you so long?"

"I'm not a will-o'-the-wisp," Wilber said. "I can't flip from the natural world to the netherworld at will. I told you that."

Leona tilted her head and considered the possibility that the supposedly powerful wizard Wilber Hyde-Davis couldn't go where he wanted to go. He was, after all, only a human, while she was a cat.

"Okay. I'll take you."

"Are you going to pick me up and carry me?" Wilber asked.

"No. That wouldn't work." She leapt and flapped, then landed on his shoulder. "Stand up."

He looked at her for a moment, then clearly his curiosity got the better of him. He had to have some cat in his nature. He stood.

Digging her claws in, Leona tried to shift them both. It didn't work.

"Walk forward."

He did, and as he stepped she shifted them so that his foot landed in the grove of the dryads in Pucorl's lands. Another step and they were in a small grove of trees on the coast of England.

"I hope you can do that in the other direction," Wilber muttered.

✳ ✳ ✳

Wilber realized that he was in some trouble if Leona couldn't, or decided not to. Which she well might. She was, after all, a cat.

Partly, anyway. So he pulled Igor from his pocket. Igor now had a case with a connecting link to the network. Two links. Pucorl maintained a network of minor demons. Most of them were tiny little water demons drawn from the babbling brook that traveled across his lands. They liked talking, but weren't bright enough to have anything to say, so they made an excellent relay system. Whatever Igor told them would be transmitted to the other demons in the network. Themis, being the god of proper behavior, maintained a proper network system with proper circuits made of gold, and properly integrated with proper operators and ten digit phone numbers, in spite of the fact that even with the crystal sets built in this world there probably weren't enough phones to need four digits.

Having access to a titan or a god was a bit like having access to a super computer. One that could not only calculate, but act. The problem was that you needed the programs—the knowledge to get it to do anything. The reason the gods didn't have a phone network before the twenty-firsters arrived was because it never occurred to them to want one, and they had no idea how to go about making one anyway. Now he pulled his phone and checked his bars. It now had three sets; one to Themis' phone system, one to Pucorl's, and one to any phone that might be in range. Themis gave him four bars, Pucorl five, and he even had two on the direct phone. "Who's nearby, Igor?"

"Green Lantern. Paul and Kitten are in Pucorl's lands today, studying basic magic with a puck of Pucorl's acquaintance."

"Yes." Wilber grinned. "I've met Pucoransis. Well, at least the kids will be entertained. I don't know how much they'll learn. Put me through to Pucorl, would you? I would like to arrange a pickup, in case I need it."

"I'll take you back," Leona insisted. "As soon as we are done talking with the locals."

Wilber called Pucorl anyway. A cat was a cat, netherworld or not.

The veil between the worlds was still in shreds, though Themis was working on repairing it in her lands and several of the other gods were doing the same. But Themis was leaving intentional holes in her repairs, so that she and hers would have access to the natural world.

Pucorl's lands were small and while he was now more powerful than Merlin, he was still minor in comparison to even a demigod. His ability to repair the veil was almost nonexistent. But he could "see" it and the rifts in it where his lands touched the natural world. He assured Wilber that he would be able to find locations where Wilber could simply step back through. Given that assurance, Wilber, with Leona perched on his shoulder, walked boldly over to the village.

He was wearing his pistol. It was a habit by now.

Location: The Village Pendine, Wales
Time: 12:04 PM, February 27, 1373

Maud saw the stranger walking out of the village woodlot with the thing on his shoulder. She turned and ran screaming into the village. She was, after all, only sixteen years old, recently married . . . and her new husband was the one who shot the arrow at the thing. Right now, she was afraid that if Willum got stubborn, the wizard might burn him to the ground.

By the time she got to the town square, the village was gathered. All fifty-five adults. The men were led out to meet the wizard by the village headman and Father Robert, the village priest and school master.

✳ ✳ ✳

Wilber saw the mob and shouted, "Calm down. I only want to talk."

"What are you doing in our woodlot?" shouted a large man carrying a scythe. Carrying it like he was itching to use it.

"Your woodlot is . . ." Wilber had the—unusual for him— experience of struggling to find the right word. Mostly because there wasn't a word in fourteenth-century English for "in the next dimension," or "across the veil between the worlds." So he went with twenty-first

188

century English, and counted on his communication magic to get the meaning across. "Across the veil between worlds. In the other world are now the lands of Chevalier Pucorl de Elysium, of whom you may have heard."

"You mean that prince of Underhill who aided the king of France against his traitorous brother and the army of the dead?"

"That's the one," Wilber agreed. "But he's not from Underhill. He got promoted. He's from Elysium, or perhaps Camelot. Also he's a knight, not a prince."

"We already have a knight," the priest said. "We don't need another."

"Nor does Pucorl claim your lands. But you are neighbors of a sort, and he would appreciate it if you were to refrain from shooting at his folk."

By now Wilber was close enough so that he really didn't need to shout, so he asked, "May I know your name, Father? I am Wilber Hyde-Davis, originally of London in the twenty-first century."

"You're one of the twenty-firsters?" the big man with the scythe asked. "I heard the king of France threw the bunch of you out. Don't you expect King Edward to welcome you."

Sheesh, this fellow is belligerent, Wilber thought. "Look, Father, is there somewhere we can sit and have a chat? You, the headman of the village, and me? I'm not here to start a war. I'm here to prevent one. I'm not here to take anything from you, or your village, either."

✳ ✳ ✳

It turned out that Mr. Belligerent was the headman of the village. His name was John Hywel. He, his wife, Father Robert and Father Robert's housekeeper/companion/concubine were the ones who ended up in the headman's hut over small beer and bread, discussing the arrangements in dealing with Pucorl's lands and the beings who resided there.

Surprisingly enough, it was John who brought up the possibility of buying goods from Constantinople to sell in Bristol. It was Father Robert who pointed out that Sir Thomas, who held the rents on this village, was going to want his portion of any such trade, and he would find out about it.

Sir Thomas lived some five miles away in Wenvoe Keep. It wasn't much, in truth. More a two-story stone cottage than a true fortress. But it had a barn for the knight's horses and its own blacksmith and armorer. He wasn't a particularly bad lord, but he was poor, only having the rents from two small villages to support his household and pay for his part in his lord's campaigns. Which, in the last year or so, had mostly been dealing with wild hunts and the mischief of leprechauns who somehow ended up here instead of Ireland where they belonged.

In the meantime, they did manage to get the villagers to agree to leave Leona alone. Mrs. Hywel endeared herself to the gryphon by feeding her a bowl of milk. And Wilber explained that it wasn't thanking the demons that caused them to stop helping. It was giving them things to act as their bodies without their prior agreement.

✳ ✳ ✳

Over the next few weeks, word of Pucorl's lands went up the feudal chain from village to knight, to lord, to duke, to prince, to king. And word came back down. Sir Thomas was compensated for the loss of the village, which became the direct fief of Prince Thomas of England, Edward III's fifth living son and something of a magic aficionado. Besides, contact had been made on his birthday, so it was sort of a belated birthday present.

A pentagram of transport was placed on the edge of the village and a matching one on the edge of Pucorl's parking lot. Together, they

190

formed a route from the natural world to Pucorl's lands and back. Since Pucorl's lands were now following the local time fairly closely, you could go back and forth and not have to worry about meeting your grandpa when he was a wee lad.

CHAPTER 13—FORT RUSION AND CONSEQUENCES

Location: Outside Fort Rusion, Byzantium
Time: 3:40 AM, March 27, 1373

It had a curtain wall. *Which is plenty, since we have no cannon,* Roger thought as he lay on the cold ground under a bush, wearing his phone in a wood and leather contraption that mimicked the VR phone mount that he had back in the world. He looked along the top of the curtain wall using his phone's night vision capabilities. Crenelations, murder holes, the works. And there were archers behind those crenelations, good ones. A perfectly adequate castle for a pre-gunpowder world.

Roger smiled. This was not a pre-gunpowder world.

Bertrand's army had rockets. The craftsmen and alchemists of Constantinople would have been up to decent corned powder even without the help of demonkind. With the water demons purifying the sulfur, saltpeter, and even charcoal, they had the sort of black powder that a top of the line twenty-first century chemist's lab could make. They'd have smokeless powder if anyone of the twenty-firsters knew what it was and how to make it.

But between the demon-locks and the rockets, they had the means to suppress the archers on the walls. And tomorrow they would have Pucorl to bust down the gates.

Location: Gates of Constantinople
Time: 6:17 PM, March 27, 1373

Pucorl passed through the gates onto the Roman road and was doing a hundred kph—a bit over sixty mph—less than a minute later. He would do that speed along a good Roman road built in the fourth century all the way to Tzouroulos and probably average half that on the last eighty miles of the trip. Part of the reason that he was traveling at night was that the roads would be empty. Everyone pulled off the road and slept in inns along the route.

In a world without headlights, people don't travel at night.

* * *

One hour and twenty minutes later, Pucorl listened to Annabelle snore. She had a cute snore. The seat was pushed all the way back and the seat back let down as far as it would go, which was almost flat. She was belted in, but with a blanket over her and turned on her side, snoring gently and drooling a little.

Then Pucorl went around a curve and had to brake hard to avoid about twenty sheep who were standing still, frozen in terror by the monster with glowing eyes that had appeared out of nowhere.

"What's up?" Annabelle asked, still half asleep.

"Nothing," Pucorl soothed. "Go back to sleep."

Annabelle's sleeping precluded using his horn to move the dumb sheep. So he moved forward slowly and pushed them out of the way with his cowcatcher. Pucorl was in armor, but he wasn't towing his ram trailer. That was safely stored in his lands. So he had plenty of horsepower, headlights, and a good Roman road to drive on. He ought to be getting to the fort at Rusion in another hour. But he also had sheep and cattle, goats, and the occasional wolf using the Roman road as their highway.

Location: Camp outside Rusion, Byzantium
Time: 3:36 AM, March 28, 1373

"Wake up, dear one," Pucorl said. There was a change in their relationship since Zeus' stunt at the meeting. They still didn't know how to turn Pucorl human even temporarily. But they knew it could be done. That had changed the "can never happen" fantasy of a real physical relationship between them into a "some day." Something at least potentially real. And since then, their speech to one another had found endearments creeping in.

Annabelle woke. It took a few moments, then she checked the time on Pucorl's dash clock. "What took so long?"

Pucorl was still explaining about the livestock when Roger opened the door. "We need to get to your lands and get set up. I want to hit them before dawn."

"Why?" Annabelle asked.

"Because I want them asleep, not thinking about dropping rocks or burning oil on Pucky here." He hooked a thumb at the van.

"Why, thanks, Jolly boy. That's mighty *green* of you," Pucorl said in accents reminiscent of Foghorn Leghorn. He wasn't fond of the nickname. Well, except when Annabelle used it. But he was still a puck. He could give as good as he got in the nickname department.

Roger grinned and climbed into the back.

＊ ＊ ＊

Pucorl transferred to his lands, and Annabelle climbed out and grabbed the chain, doing her walk around examination of Pucorl as she went. The original van was a Mercedes-Benz Sprinter, metallic forest green with large darkened windows on the sides and back. But there had been many changes since Pucorl was called to the van. The cow-catcher was integrated into his front grill, but now it had spring muscles that let "Pucky"—Annabelle grinned at the nickname—pull it in tight, push it out, lift it up to cover his headlights, or lower it so it was touching the ground in front of him. It was also pushed out into the shape of a old fashioned cow-catcher, and armored, as Pucorl was now, it had polished steel facings and spikes that would make the ghost rider jealous.

She attached the chain to the top of the cow-catcher and dragged it over to the ram-cart. The ram-cart wouldn't be integrated into Pucorl. It was an axe, not a hand. It had two heavy wooden wheels on an iron axle and a ten-foot-long ram that made a telephone pole look wimpy. The ram was steel tipped and sharpened to a blade edge. It also had wings pushing out to the sides, the idea being that they would push aside what the tip cut. At the moment it was tilted back on its trailer hook and that was where she hooked the chain.

Pucorl backed up and pulled the ram-cart into the parking lot.

She whistled and the crane slowly moved out of the garage and lifted the back of the ram so that she could bolt it to the cow-catcher grill. Once the ram was attached, she completed her inspection.

A framework of wood, something like a roll-cage or the face-guard on a football helmet but thicker and covering more of his surface, was attached to Pucorl, and it covered him from his wheels to his roof. It was wood where it touched his body but its outer surface was polished steel and patterned like a pentagram of protection. Which it was. Wilber, Doctor Delaflote, and Merlin had all consulted on its design.

She stepped up on the running board. It was part of the armor and let her see Pucorl's roof. After Roger got nailed in the battle of Tzouroulos, they made some changes to Pucorl's roof armor. It was no longer only the short wall of wood around the edge of the roof. Now there was a lattice of wood faced with steel that arched over. A soldier

THE DEMONS OF CONSTANTINOPLE

could still shoot out, but it was a lot harder to be stuck by a random arrow. Not that anyone would be riding on top for this trip. The jerk when they hit the castle's gates was going to be way too severe for that.

"Okay, Pucorl." She almost said "Pucky" but restrained herself. "Open up."

Pucorl's armor was a demon, created partly from the substance of Pucorl's lands and partly from wood, steel, and craftsmanship from the mortal realm. From Pucorl's lands it was mostly earth, but considerable fire as well. And at night or when Pucorl was angry, fire flickered over its surface and between the slats. The armor had no real intelligence, only instincts and reactions. It was all about protecting Pucorl and his passengers. It was heavy, but because it was part demon, lighter than it should have been. The ram-cart was also essentially mindless, but like a magical sword or ax, its function was to rend. Even with its magic, to wield it took strength.

Pucorl had a hundred and eighty-eight horsepower under his hood, and that was a lot of horsepower for a fourteenth-century wooden gate to withstand. A team of horses would have a hard time moving the ram-cart, even with the wheels. But Pucorl had plenty of horses. He could also turn both his front and rear wheels, so he could maneuver a lot more effectively than an ordinary van.

They jumped back to the camp outside Fort Rusion, and Pucorl got himself and the ram-cart positioned for the charge.

Location: Fort Rusion, Byzantium

Ilhani looked out at the Byzantine camp. There was activity of some sort out there, but he didn't know what it meant. He thought about calling the sergeant, but he had called the sergeant when the demon van arrived and been cursed out for waking him.

Ilhani was deeply troubled by the way things were going here in Runelia. All the real leaders of the empire had gone south, across the Dardanelles to Anatolia, leaving second raters and nobles with blood or political connections in charge of Runelia, and the Byzantines had taken advantage of the lack of leadership and coordination, taking Runelia back from the Turks a piece at a time. And it was looking like this was the next piece. If they took Rusion, they would have effectively cut off the remaining Turks from Gallipoli and the rest of the empire.

He looked at the walls. They were good walls, and he tried to be reassured by that. Would have been, if it weren't for the demons that now walked the lands. What good were walls against—

The shot came out of nowhere.

Ilhani never heard it, or anything, ever again. His lifeless body fell, and the wall behind his head was splattered red.

* * *

Roger cracked open his demon-lock and loaded another round even as the rockets were lit. A moment later, Roger fired again. By then, the rockets were arching over the walls, their red tails lighting up the night.

* * *

As the rockets reached the walls, Pucorl started his run. It was uphill and he started in low gear, but Pucorl was the van. He controlled his body as well as an athlete controls theirs, and his body was a lot more powerful. Pucorl and the ram had a combined mass of seven tons, and when it hit the gates it was traveling at over one hundred kilometers per hour, or twenty-eight meters per second, or 196 ton-seconds of momentum.

The gates didn't break.

They shattered.

And Pucorl didn't stop until he was through the second set of gates, and into the courtyard of the castle.

* * *

Behind him—a long way behind him—were two hundred armored knights on warhorses. They were coming along as fast as they could, but the camp was over half a mile from the walls and a charger's charge is not all that fast even at the gallop. At the trot, well, it was liable to be a full minute before they got here.

Pucorl backed up to get maneuvering room and tried to use his ram-cart as a weapon.

Didn't work.

The gates hadn't treated the ram a lot better than the ram had treated them. The wheels were broken and the ram's spreaders, which had steel facings, were bent and twisted.

The good news was that the ram had taken the brunt of the damage. Pucorl himself was in good shape.

The bad news was the ram was still attached, acting like a sea anchor.

The worse news was the occupants of the fort were awake and, ah, grouchy.

* * *

Bertrand du Guesclin and Andronikos IV rode side by side at the head of the knights of Byzantium. Andronikos was still a pain in the butt, but he wasn't a coward. He had been right with Bertrand in most of the battles since the arrival of the "French Crusade," as he called it. Bertrand and his little troop of eighty demon-lock equipped men at arms, with the increasingly willing aid of the Byzantine forces, had accomplished more in the way of restoring Byzantine territory than the Slavs had.

They were approaching the gate and the rockets still seemed to be keeping the enemies' heads down. Had to be careful, as the leftover lumber from the gate was filling the entryway between the outer and inner gates.

It slowed them down and bunched them up under the murder holes, but the attack had been so fast that they got through before the oil was ready.

Then it was sword work. There wasn't room for lances, but they were in among the enemy.

* * *

As Bertrand and company finally arrived, Annabelle opened Pucorl's door and jumped out with her pistol in one hand and a wrench in the other. There were Turks all around, but they were busy with the knights and she needed to get that damn ram off Pucorl so he could move. She ran around front to reach the ram and right into an armored Turk with a scimitar that looked about ten feet long. She shot and missed, but the sound threw him off his swing and Pucorl jerked back, pulling the ram into the Turk's legs and he went down.

Annabelle went for the bolts attaching the ram and the Turk started getting up.

"Annabelle! Behind you!" Pucorl shouted.

Annabelle turned and shot. Missed again, and this time he ignored it. He ran at her, sword over his head, then Andronikos was there, on his charger. A quick swing of his scimitar and the Turk's head went flying.

Annabelle turned back to the ram. But by the time she had it loose, they held the courtyard and the enemy was forted up in the keep.

Roger, the slugabed, rode up looking fresh as a daisy, looked at the situation, then asked, "Why didn't you transfer back to Pucorl's lands and take it off there?" He sounded really curious.

And after he mentioned it, Annabelle couldn't think of a reason why they hadn't. "Pucorl?"

"I don't know. I never thought of it. It would be running away in the midst of battle." Suddenly he groaned. "It's all Charles V's fault. That bastard knighted me and my circuits have turned to noble mush."

"It's called a strategic— Well, in this case, a tactical retreat," Bertrand told him. "All the properly trained knights know about it. Don't you agree, Prince Andronikos?"

Andronikos, sitting on his horse, bloody sword in hand, started laughing. Roger and Bertrand joined him.

✳ ✳ ✳

The battle was over and it was a victory, but not a complete one. The Turks still held the keep and could hold out for weeks, locking the army in place. Andronikos made a deal with the Turks. They could leave and even take their weapons, but they had to abandon the keep and they would be under guard until they were out of the fort.

Location: Bursa, Capital of the Ottoman Turks
Time: Mid-afternoon, April 1, 1373

Dizdar Civan ben Kamber looked at the shadows stretching out from the gatehouse and guessed it was mid-afternoon. His horse had foundered the first day out of Fort Rusion. He got another after reaching this side of the Dardanelles, but the poor beast should have been used for glue years ago. Not that he was in any hurry to face the interview that was coming.

Savci seemed to be winning the civil war at the moment. He had control of the treasury and Yakub Celebi and Bayzid were out of the capital. All three of them had regents, but they weren't the only contenders for the throne. At least three of Murad's generals were claiming the throne in their own right.

Dizdar Civan ben Kamber and his aides were questioned by the gate guards, and then allowed to pass. At the palace they were stopped again, then brought into the royal presence to give their report to Savci and, behind a screen, his mother. There was also a general. Kara Halil had decided for Savci.

After Civan made his report, Savci looked at the curtained alcove and complained, "Your astrologer insisted that Andronikos would ally with me."

There was murmuring from behind the curtain that Civan couldn't make out.

Kara Halil grunted, then said, "Andronikos is an opportunist. He must see more opportunity with the demons."

"Then he's not wrong, General," Civan said. "It was the demon van that took the fort. And the phones that the French brought with them are why they have been winning. They can coordinate much better than we."

More murmuring from behind the curtain. This time Civan made out "need" and "djinn."

That made sense to Civan. It might be chancy to deal with djinn, but they were not inherently evil, as demons were.

* * *

It was that meeting that started it. Civan was part of it. The project to recruit or capture djinn to their cause, including ifrit, the djinn lords. It took months, while the Ottoman Empire collapsed into six warring tribes. But, eventually, using books from Constantinople and reports from spies, they built djinn-powered tanks.

CHAPTER 14—
REBUILDING
BYZANTIUM

Location: Constantinople
Time: 9:32 AM, April 3, 1373

Amelia Grady tapped keys on Shakespeare. Demon inhabited or not, sometimes it was easier to work on her laptop like it was an ordinary computer. She was doing the books for the Byzantine Empire. And things were not as bad as they thought. The bank was almost accepted as a real institution, though Patriarch Kokkinos was writing sermons about money changers. Apparently because he was angry that they weren't in the temple where they belonged.

"The only entity that can be trusted with money is the church. It will corrupt anyone else." That was the Patriarch of Constantinople's line.

John V and, especially, Queen Helena Kantakouzene, didn't agree. The bank would remain part of the government, not the church.

Major transactions had to be done through the bank, so every ship that put in with a load of wheat, or sailed out with Russian furs or Chinese silks, had to do its business through the bank. By now, many of the local merchants had seen the wisdom of the check over the bag of gold or silver coins, and goods were changing hands through the exchange of checks, not the exchange of coins.

All of which meant that a spreadsheet and data entry were absolutely necessary. The data she was entering was data written out in a ledger by scribes and clerks as the bank's customers deposited their coins or presented their checks. What Amelia was doing was making sure the figures added and that each account balance matched the balance in the balance book.

They were working on building an enchanted printer, but they weren't there yet. So when Amelia ran across an inaccurate balance, she had to check all the entries in that column to be sure it was transcribed correctly, and then tracked down the clerk to find out where the money went. That was why Amelia was doing it. A hunt and peck typist would be taking forever and making a lot more mistakes.

The upshot was that there was a lot more money in Constantinople than there had been before the twenty-firsters arrived. At the same time, the techniques from France—partly twenty-firster and partly stuff that the French craftsmen had come up with by combining what they knew with what the twenty-firsters knew—were producing a lot of new goods. Better boats, better sails, better plows, and thread made faster and cheaper. Paris was experiencing an economic boom and Constantinople was striving to catch up.

Some of that money was finding its way into the royal coffers, and the lands retaken by Bertrand, Roger, and Andronikos were helping their credit, if not yet adding much of anything to the actual bottom line.

The door opened and the queen came in. "Oh, put that away or let Shakespeare do it. I need you for your real job."

So off Amelia went to discuss a Greek translation of *Romeo and Juliet* with the royal director of pageants.

* * *

THE DEMONS OF CONSTANTINOPLE

In a building a street over, the beauty parlor opened its doors. It was by appointment only, and was entirely owned by Lakshmi Rawal, the young widow of a wealthy merchant, and three palace maids who were combining the beauty techniques of twenty-first century France, fourteenth century France and fourteenth century Constantinople to produce their own spa days, with everything from hair setting to seaweed wraps.

* * *

Wilber watched Theodore Meliteniotes incant in front of the nine-pointed star of containment. Pentagrams were, it turned out, only one form of the containment spells. They worked best for some of the older, more minor, demons, the pucks and brownies and the like. Even the muses. But others, like the djinn, were more readily drawn to containment devices that had a different number of sides. Angels preferred six-sided and nine-sided stars, and djinn also liked nine sides, but uneven, with four sides a bit longer than the other five. And as he did with almost everything, Theodore was incanting in a meticulous monotone. He was putting a djinn into a locally made phone. It had a painted screen, a wooden case with gold inlay interior, and a demon-made tuning coil that was small enough to fit inside the phone.

The djinn residing in it would be able to operate it almost like a cellphone. It would lack the computing power and the games and apps that made the phones marvels even without djinn in them, but it would still let its owner access the phone network. This was the most recent of the locally made phones, and the princess was getting it because all the generals and admirals, as well as her older brothers and sisters, had phones now. It would still be a while before they started seeping out to the general public.

The djinn floated above the phone in the pentagram and didn't look thrilled to be called. One of the drawbacks to these locally made pseudo-phones was that they lacked the computing power that made the real twenty-first century phones into virtual palaces for the demons, djinn, or whatever.

Theodore finished the incantation and the phone went active. The screen lit up with the face of the djinn. It was square-jawed with a red mustache on an orange face, with little flames flicking about it. Djinn were creatures with a lot of fire in their makeup, and they didn't take kindly to being locked away in lamps or phones. In this case, though, it had a camera to see with, a microphone to hear with, and a speaker to speak through, which it used.

"How dare you?" the phone demanded loudly. "My lord Amar Utu Marduk will punish you!"

"We'll take our chances," Wilber said, "but if you truly have contact with him, we'd like to have a chat."

The djinn shrank back on the screen as though he was moving away from a camera. "Are you crazy?"

"I don't think so." Wilber sighed. "We are trying to get in contact with the djinn lords because we are trying to figure out what caused the rifts in the veil between the worlds. Several of our demonic or djinn friends would like to know.

"I know that this phone isn't up to the ones we brought with us, but if you ask nicely, Igor might let you share some of his processing ability. In the meantime, this is Maria Palaiologos, your new owner. You will be her phone." Maria was thirteen years old and a daughter of John, and—as all the twenty-firsters knew—a thirteen-year-old girl *needs* a phone of her own.

Taking her phone, Maria thanked them condescendingly. Wilber wasn't sure whether it was because she was a princess, because she was thirteen—or both.

✻ ✻ ✻

Ali ben Deoud wasn't happy to be in the phone. He had a wife and two willful daughters in the city of Tessifonica. Tessifonica was located to the side of the natural world in the location of the ruins of the one time capital of the Sassanid empire, Ctesiphon. He also had a craft, with a shop. He was a maker of clothing. He wove fabrics of all colors out of the air. At least, he did in the proper magic world. The air in this world lacked the magic to let it be woven into cloth of emerald, or even the drab cloth of gold that mortals so craved.

"Phone, call my brother Manuel!" Princess Maria, the owner of the phone, demanded.

Perforce Ali placed the call and in so doing learned how the phone system worked. The seal, which was not a seal of Solomon but certainly strong enough to hold a djinn of his power, was connected to a communications demon in the land of Themis. That operator could connect any phone to any other in the network with a gesture.

Ali told her the person who was wanted and she checked with that phone to determine if the phone's owner was taking calls. As it happened, Manuel wasn't, being busy with the administration of Thessalonica. At that moment, he was at the docks of Thessalonica, crawling around in the port side hull of the new catamaran-style gun ship with his phone in hand. He had returned to Thessalonica to take up his duties as governor of that city and to provide a link to the technology, magical and mundane, brought by the French delegation.

All that Ali got in a short data dump from Manuel's phone, which was occupied by a minor muse. Not one of the nine, but one of hundreds that lived and worked in the lands of Themis. This one was a muse of construction called Crafter. It was also much happier with its situation than Ali was.

"I am sorry, Princess, but your brother is not taking calls at the moment."

"Oh, drat." She thought a moment. "Call Kitten."

Ali tried again. Kitten, as it turned out, didn't have a phone, per se. What she had was a bluetooth connection which let her access the network if she was close enough to a phone, computer, the dryad's grove or Pucorl.

"Hello, Ali. What does Maria want?"

Ali didn't have to tell her the truth, or even talk to her, but the operator advised him that he was much better off with her as a friend than an enemy. "I can't say, Mistress Kitten. I think she may simply want to test her new phone."

* * *

Kitten was nine now. At least, loosely speaking, time in the netherworld having worked differently as she was growing up there. And Maria was thirteen and a princess, besides. Which didn't impress Kitten that much but, Kitten knew, impressed Maria herself. Still, Mom would be upset if Kitten was rude. Besides, Maria was thirteen. "Hi, Princess. How are you liking your new phone?"

"How did you know I had a new phone?" Maria sounded angry.

Kitten stopped and thought for a moment. It didn't take all that long. Her mother was a computer and her dad had been a human. So, by her nature, Kitten was bright, with an organized and fast-thinking brain. "Well, as you know, the phones all talk to each other all the time. The operator told me the call was from your new phone."

"Oh, well. What are you doing?"

"Deportment lessons with a muse of dance from Themis' lands."

"Why don't I have a muse to teach me deportment? All I have is Sister Constance, a stuffy old nun."

"Probably because you're a princess and I'm a dryad. Well, half dryad."

The call lasted another fifteen minutes, and mostly consisted of Maria explaining everything that was wrong with her life, her parents, her brothers, and which king or prince they were talking about marrying her off to this week.

Kitten put up with it, and even suggested Paul as a potential suitor. Mostly as a joke, but also trying to put out there the idea that the twenty-firsters were suitable mates for members of the royal house.

Location: Foundry in Thessalonica, Byzantium
Time: Around Noon, April 6, 1373

The bronze poured into the mold, which was made of heated ceramics that would be shattered for removal. The mold was a cylinder with grooves in something called "an interrupted screw" pattern on one end. The bronze smith in charge of the process didn't know how the "gun" would work, only that the walls of the pipe needed to resist great force, so the metal couldn't have any bubbles in it. The prince called it a barrel, but it was a pipe—an inch and a half of bore with two-inch thick walls, four feet long.

To facilitate removing the bubbles, he banged on the pour once it was poured, and he would saw off the top six inches once the bronze set.

It had taken a month and a half to prepare for this pour, and it would take as long, almost, to ready the next. So far, four large bronze statues had been sacrificed for the cause.

Location: Tamerlane's Camp, East of the
Persian Gulf
Time: Mid-morning, April 9, 1373

Tamerlane's scribe handed him the synopsis of the recent events in Turkish lands. Tamerlane read through the sheets, drinking black tea. "Well, well," he murmured. "Murad is dead. That should make things easier."

"I'm not sure, Master," said the scribe. "The lack of pressure from the northwest will let the Mamelukes focus to their east, toward us. Also,

I am concerned about how he died. It is said that he was shot by a woman using a gunpowder weapon from horseback. Do you know of any gunpowder weapons that can be used by *anyone* from horseback?"

"No. No, I don't." For a moment Tamerlane's face took on a look that made the slave shiver. It was a look he had seen before. And for some reason he could not name, it left him feeling chilled to the bone every time he saw it. Then Tamerlane was back, and the slave felt relief, as though the sun had found its way into the tent. "Send spies to find out what happened."

Location: Pucorl's Lands
Time: 11:58 AM, April 10, 1373

Prince Thomas of England sat in the vinyl-covered booth in the Emerald Room, the Happytime Motel's restaurant, as a dryad brought him a menu. Catvia and Merlin sat across from him.

"I'll have my usual, Bercha. Merlin?" Catvia said.

"Me too," Merlin agreed.

"What is your usual?" Thomas asked, examining the plastic-covered menu.

"I have poached salmon with dill sauce, duchess potatoes, and asparagus vinaigrette." Catvia waved at Merlin.

"I usually have a cheeseburger and fries," Merlin said. He took the menu and pointed out the picture of the burger. "It's a fried ground beef patty, with melted cheese, pickles, onion, lettuce, and tomato on a soft bun. Annabelle says the tomatoes don't taste like tomatoes, but I like them. The same thing with the fries."

"What are . . . ? Never mind. Can your kitchen prepare normal food?"

"Yes," Pucorl said over the screen that was next to the booth. "Normal French and English food. But we thought you might like something different."

Thomas looked at the menu again, and after looking at the pictures, pointed to something that looked appealing. It, from the script, was called the Hungry Man Breakfast. "I'll have that."

"How do you want your eggs, sugar?" asked Bercha as she chewed something. Tomas couldn't imagine what. That led to further discussion, and then in barely the blink of an eye, Bercha was back, balancing three meals on a large tray.

Since time in Pucorl's lands was somewhat under Pucorl's control, it moved faster in the kitchen of the Happytime when there were orders to prepare. To compensate, it moved slower there when there weren't any orders.

Once they were served, they got down to business. The Hungry Man Breakfast was delicious. And Thomas, like Merlin, didn't care that the hashbrowns didn't taste the way Annabelle said they should. They were good.

What they discussed over lunch was a schedule of fees for the transport of goods from Pucorl's lands to Wales, and from Wales to Pucorl's lands. They also sold him a model of a ship with sails that they said could make the passage from England to the Americas. The French were already building such ships, and England didn't want to be left out.

A fair chunk of Pucorl's income came from transporting goods from the various places he could access directly or indirectly. The same was true of Merlin and Coach. It was less true of the dryads. They were limited by their need to be close to their trees, including Asuma. She had a phone connection to the networks, but her tree in the netherworld was also located in the Vienna of the netherworld, so she wasn't in a position to do much smuggling. Catvia and Kitten, with their bluetooth connections, were the exception.

"But what use do the fey have for money?" Thomas asked, his curiosity clearly getting the better of him.

"This." Merlin held up the hamburger. "In the mortal world I cannot eat, but here I can. If I eat a hamburger of fairy, the cow in the beef patty feels every bite and resents every chew. But the beef in this burger comes from the mortal realm. The spirit of the cow has departed. It's only food, but it is food that adds to me." Merlin didn't go into the details. The lord was the land and the land was the lord in the netherworld, so since Merlin had occupied Wilber's cochlear implant and later computer, there had been changes. Merlin's lands were about the size of a large apartment or a small house. But since Pucorl had started importing food from the natural world, Merlin had installed a toilet in his lands. Every meal he ate made him a little bit bigger in demonic terms. He, and his lands.

"I don't understand how this works," Thomas complained.

Location: Hisatsini Village, Southwest North America
Time: Dawn, April 20, 7, 1373

Hika lifted the rock onto the small wall. The wall was being built to retain the water and, even more, the soil. His spirit animal was a fox, but he didn't feel much like a fox at the moment. He was feeling like a beaver. He was seventeen and his village was trying to expand its arable land, and he was stuck hauling rocks using a travois.

"Whatcha doing?" Hika looked over and a fox was sitting on its haunches, scratching its jaw with one paw. "Why are you putting that rock there?" The fox pointed with its other paw.

Hika remembered his spirit dream, when he learned his spirit animal was a fox. The Fox had spoken to him. Then, after he smoked the peyote and entered the sweat lodge, but never since. Hika's first thought was that he had been in the sun too long. "You can't be real."

"I can be as real as I want to be," said the fox spirit. "Why are you doing that?"

Hika explained. He explained about the seasonal rains and the water escaping downriver, so the crops died for lack of water and soil. The fox examined the wall and pointed out gaps.

"Not all the stones fit."

"So tell them to change their shape."

For a moment Hika looked at the fox, thinking it was crazy. But it was a talking fox, so who was he to talk about crazy. He told the rock to change shape. It didn't respond in any way.

The fox said something in a different language. It didn't sound like the normal calls of a fox, but something else. Again the stone didn't react. Hika grinned. The fox kicked the rock. The fox's foot went into the rock and stuck. The fox was sinking into the rock. It started jabbering desperately in that strange language.

"What do you want?" Hika asked.

"Help me. Pull me out," the fox said in desperate Hisatsini.

Hika was afraid, but fox was his spirit animal, and this fox was in need. So he reached over, grabbed it, and pulled it out of the rock. It came free with a plop and sank into Hika.

* * *

The fox spirit saw through Hika's eyes and moved his arms. It wasn't his correct form, but it was much closer than the rock was, and much more flexible. Then the boy was fighting him for control, and he didn't like that at all. So he let the boy push him out and resumed his form as a fox, though he kept the opposable thumbs that the human hand possessed.

He ended up back in the natural world in his mostly fox form. It was moderately difficult to maintain this form. In his home he was sometimes the fox and sometimes the fox's burrow. And sometimes other things.

Still, he wanted to help the lad who had freed him from the trap. "I will give you rocks that will behave," he said. "Pick up your travois and follow me."

* * *

Hika was frightened. Much more frightened than when the fox first appeared. Now he'd been taken over by the fox spirit, and that was a lot more frightening than he remembered from his spirit dream. But if Spirits were chancy to deal with, they were much more chancy to offend. So he picked up the travois and followed the fox from his almost desert home into a forest grove. The fox led him to a rock outcropping and pointed at a bunch of rocks. The fox talked to the rocks and the rocks answered. Hika didn't understand a word.

Then the fox said, "Pick up these rocks and put them on your travois."

Thinking that they were at least closer than the ones he'd been gathering, Hika did so. The rocks said something and the fox said, "Stop complaining. He's doing all the work."

Hika gathered several of the rocks, put them on the travois, and the fox led him back to the field.

"Now, put that rock—" The fox pointed at one of the rocks on the travois. "—in that rock." He pointed at one of the rocks in the small stone wall.

"What?"

The fox repeated the command imperiously, like Hika was too stupid to understand, and Hika almost threw the rock spirit at the fox spirit. Then he got it. The fox spirit wanted him to put the rock spirit in the real rock.

He did, pushing it in, and the spirit rock sank into the rock. For the rest of the afternoon, the spirit rocks went into the rocks of his wall, and the fox talked to the spirit rocks. By that evening, a hungry and tired Hika looked at a rock wall that had no leaks, because the rocks seemed to melt onto the next.

CHAPTER 15—GENOA

Location: Genoa, Italy
Time: Around Noon, May 15, 1373

Domenico di Campofregoso, Doge of Genoa, stepped out of the wet street and entered the council building. The news from the Turks had gone from horrible to devastating. The note clenched in his fist told the story.

The Byzantines, under Bertrand du Guesclin, have taken Gallipoli and now hold the entire north bank of the Dardanelles Straits.

That meant that the Byzantine Empire, not the Ottoman Turks, now controlled the passage from the Black Sea to the Mediterranean. And the Byzantines were allied with Venice. Genoa's ally in the region, the Ottoman Turks, were now locked in a civil war to see who would replace Murad I.

Genoa's only hope of surviving as a great power was control of the Black Sea trade. Control of the eastern Mediterranean trade, more precisely, but the Black Sea trade was a vital part of that.

He unhooked his ermine-trimmed cloak and tossed it at a servant. The servant grabbed the cloak out of the air, and Domenico passed through the door to the council chamber almost before the doorman could get it opened.

Holding up the fist that still held the crumpled note, he almost bellowed, "Cyprus will have to wait! We must deal with John V and Bertrand du Guesclin first."

It took five minutes to restore order and three days of debate to settle the matter, but the Genoese fleet would go to Constantinople and "remonstrate" with John V.

The debate included discussion of Bertrand du Guesclin and the desire not to insult Charles V of France. But rumor had it that Charles wasn't a fan of the twenty-firsters, and that Bertrand had betrayed him in the matter of the Sword of Themis. So the Doge and the council decided that Charles wouldn't be all that upset if Bertrand came to a bad end, especially if the twenty-firsters came to the same end.

And in spite of anything France might want, they had to control the Black Sea trade. Had to.

Location: Constantinople
Time: 8:15 AM, May 15, 1373

Bertrand's wife, Tiphaine De Raguenel, sat at the podium-style desk and laid out the horoscopes. John V's, Domenico di Campofregoso's, Genoa's, Byzantium's, and—perhaps most important— Roger's, Wilber's, Annabelle's, the other twenty-firsters . . . and one other.

She included the horoscope of Joe Kraken, based on the moment that Joe was given the body. She compared them. Her eyes flicked between them to get a feel of what they might mean in combination. It was a technique that Themis had taught her. One that Tiphaine felt was more suited to gods than mortals, but she was at least getting a feel for the way they were interacting.

In this case, it was Joe Kraken's that tied them together. Because Joe's horoscope put him at war with Genoa, and within months. Perhaps even weeks.

There was only one reason that Joe might fight Genoa and that was because Genoa was getting ready to go to war with the Byzantine Empire.

Reading horoscopes had always been as much about the circumstances as about the position of the stars. They might mean one thing for a queen, and another for a peasant born only blocks away and only moments later. It was comparison and contrast that gave useful answers. Answers that weren't so vague as to be meaningless.

None of that mattered as she looked at signs and calculated dates and times.

It was true.

The only possible answer.

She carefully set down the enchanted ink pen that Themis had given her on the rack next to the inkwell. And stood, shaking.

Location: Royal Chambers
Time: 10:04 AM, May 15, 1373

"Majesty," Constantine Korolos said, "Lady Tiphaine de Ragneuel is here to see you. She says it's important, and she has her papers with her."

Constantine was a fan of Theodore Meliteniotes, and therefore not a fan of astrology, no matter what some ancient titan had to say on the matter.

Queen Helena, on the other hand, had found Tiphaine's horoscopes to be useful. The family had used astrologers for generations, stretching back to the founding of Constantinople. Probably to the founding of Rome. They were part and parcel of the life of a noble.

"Show her in, Constantine, and stop pouting."

"Yes, ma'am," Constantine said, pouting even more fiercely.

"Thank you for seeing me, Your Majesty," Tiphaine said as she walked in. "I was doing a comparison scan of the horoscopes of . . . well . . . the . . . ah . . ."

"Speak, Lady Tiphaine. Between you and your husband, you have demonstrated your use—and loyalty—to the empire."

"Genoa is going to attack Constantinople," Tiphaine said. Had she known it, at that very moment Domenico di Campofregoso was stepping into the council chamber, crumpled note in hand.

She had to explain. For something like this, even people who believed in astrology wanted confirmation. That took time. But the upgrading of the navy was already underway, because they knew that if they wanted to keep the Turks out of northern Byzantium, they had to control the Marmara Sea, the Dardanelles, and the Bosporus. And it would help if they had a presence in the Black Sea and the Aegean Sea.

The ongoing debate in the Byzantine government was whether to enchant the ships and whether to arm them with rockets and, if possible, cannon.

Even as that debate was ongoing, Manuel was having purpose-built gunboats built in Thessalonica.

The problem was that Byzantium was looking at perhaps fifteen to twenty ships of war, whereas the Genoese fleet was likely to number upwards of seventy warships and the famous Genoese archers, supported by another twenty or so merchant vessels.

It was looking to be a fairly one-sided battle if the Byzantine navy didn't pull a rabbit—or better yet, a dragon—out of its hat.

When the crown went looking for rabbits these days, they went to the French delegation.

✳ ✳ ✳

"Well, there are the powder mills," Roger McLean said. He, Bertrand, Emperor John, Andronikos, Wilber, two more of John's military advisers, and Annabelle with a phone link to Pucorl were seated at a large and brand new round table. There was room for twenty and a gap in the ring directly across from the emperor to let servants in to serve wine and food. At the moment, the servants were absent, though there were flagons of wine and loaves of bread placed on the table.

"And what good do tons of your black powder do us?" Andronikos complained. "Yes, yes, I know the rocket carts have been useful in land battles, but I am still unconvinced that they can be safely used on ships. Ships are flammable things."

"And the ones on the receiving end of the rockets are exactly as flammable, but won't be prepared for the rocket fire," Wilber said. "And we can harden the rocket boats against the back flash."

"And the venturi?" Andronikos asked. "You say they are absolutely vital. The heavy brass venturi that cost the price of a good horse and take a week to make. Even if we can put them on ships, we don't have enough of them. We need to negotiate with the Genoese. A major battle, even if we win it—which is not certain, or even likely—will leave our navy crippled. And how are we to face an attack from the Turks?"

John agreed. Andronikos would travel to Genoa as quickly as might be arranged and he would take a phone, so that he might consult with the crown.

Tiphaine, with her horoscopes, wasn't in favor of the idea. She had a vague sense of disquiet, but even her horoscopes suggested that Andronikos would make an agreement with Genoa.

Besides, Andronikos had done well in the fighting against the Ottoman Turks. Over the months since the French delegation arrived in Constantinople, in a series of carefully planned battles—taking full advantage of Bertrand's experience, Roger McLain's years of wargaming and studying the warfare of the ages, the use of Tiphaine's horoscopes, and the phones—they had managed to defeat the Ottomans in detail, one battle at a time. Almost one unit at a time. Never letting them mass their forces and, in the words of Nathan Bedford Forrest "hitting them where they ain't."

It wasn't all sunshine and roses, though. As the Turks collapsed, the Bulgarians were getting feisty. They hadn't declared war, or even done more than a couple of raids that could be blamed on outlaws, but if the Genoese hit Constantinople, they could be counted on to grab off as big a chunk of Byzantium as they could manage.

Location: House of Gaius Augustus Crassus, Constantinople
Time: 2:00 PM, May 17, 1373

Theodore was conflicted. He knew astrology was nonsense. He had fought most of his intellectual life to separate the science of astronomy from the superstition of astrology. But Tiphaine de Raguenel had presented the twenty-firsters with a revised horoscope that suggested that Andronikos was going to make a deal with Genoa all right. A deal in which he gave the Genoese the secrets of gunpowder, rockets and demon summoning, so that they could replace their rowers with enchanted galleys which rowed themselves through the sea magically.

And there was no way that John or Helena were going to listen to such predictions, because Andronikos, whatever his flaws, was still their son, who they loved in their way. And because their first loyalty was to themselves, their family, not Byzantium. So it was with decidedly mixed feeling that he informed his compatriots that Byzantium was about to be betrayed—or at least might well be betrayed—by Andronikos, and they had to prepare.

His compatriots weren't thrilled to hear it. But they, especially Gaius, had a lot more trust in Tiphaine's horoscopes than he did. They weren't happy, but they were convinced. The only question was what to do about it.

Location: Docks, Constantinople
Time: Mid-morning, May 18, 1373

Aurelia Augusta Crassa, the seventeen-year-old daughter of Gaius Augustus Crassus, turned to her maid and said, "Give it to me."

The maid reached into the canvas bag she had been lugging and pulled out a chunk of lamb. She handed it to her mistress, with a disapproving sniff. The maid was forty and as much watcher as servant.

Aurelia grinned at the maid. "I doubt the kraken will try to seduce me, Mags." She took the three-pound hunk of lamb and tossed it into the water, next to the *Joe Kraken*. She wasn't used to feeding ships, but the family was desperate. Most of the family's wealth came from shipping. The investments in shipping were arranged through cut outs and cooperatives, but the income from shares in over fifty trading ships was all that truly separated their old aristocratic family from a family of butchers or bakers. A war, especially a sea war, between Byzantium and Genoa could ruin the family. And the only ship that had sunk a Genoese warship was this little barge.

"Thank you, miss," came a voice from the ship.

"Is someone on board?" Aurelia shouted.

"No. It's only me." A tentacle rose from the water and pointed at the stern cabin on the barge, then sank back into the water. "Would you like to come aboard?"

* * *

Joe called Pucorl and got permission to invite the young woman aboard. Pucorl wasn't one of the humans, and certainly wasn't one of the twenty-firsters with their loose ways. He was a proper demon and becoming a proper demon lord. He knew how it was done, and expected those demons who served him to report and get permission. Themis or no Themis, demonic emancipation was a long way off. As long as Joe was in this body, he was Pucorl's to command. He could leave, but he liked the body.

With permission, Joe invited the young woman aboard and they had a pleasant chat. She wanted to know if he knew any other kraken. He knew a few. Kraken were fairly social creatures and shared information on the dangers and joys of the undersea life they shared.

"But you don't go underwater."

"Yes. That's one of the disadvantages of this body. A proper kraken body could live and work, hunt and play, from the deepest undersea caverns all the way to the surface. But Pucorl needed a barge to carry him around."

✳ ✳ ✳

Aurelia had an idea. It was a little vague, but it was an idea. What if they made, or had made, kraken bodies and had them enchanted? The problem was she didn't know how to build a kraken body, or what a kraken would want in a body. And she didn't know how to control the kraken after they made it. She thought about riding it, like you would a horse, but she would drown as soon as it went under the sea. But then she realized that she was sitting inside Joe Kraken. She wondered if they could make a kraken body that would work underwater, but still have a place for her inside it.

Aurelia's mother insisted that she know the family business. While not the usual thing, this was far from unheard of among women of her class. Care for the household often included care for the household properties and income. Aurelia was interested in mechanics, but she wasn't allowed to attend the Magnaura as her brother did, and her father was being pushy about a possible marriage to Joseph Magnus, whose family was also of the senatorial class, with important political and religious connections. But Joseph was thick as a plank and had pimples.

Aurelia thought that the real issue against Joseph was the thickness, but in all honesty, the pimples were disgusting.

She and Joe, with occasional comments from Mags, discussed his life and hers. How it would be to be able to have her body designed the way she wanted, and the danger of being trapped in a body not of her choosing. The danger of being forced to marry for state, and how such threats compared to one another.

Then Mags interrupted. "The sun is near the horizon, child. You've spent the whole day chatting with this monster of the deeps. No offense, Mr. Kraken."

"None taken. Drop by again. But next time bring a whole sheep, please."

* * *

Joe was on the phone to Pucorl as soon as the human females left. And his first question was, could he have a new body? One of the things that Aurelia brought up was something that he hadn't considered before. A demon was placed in a body whether it be molded out of a part of a more powerful demon or an animal of the natural world, or—as was the case with Pucorl and Joe—a device made by mortal hands out of the stuff of the natural world. Even if it were a combination of things, like the body of Leona, for a demon that was allowed to do so, the body could be changed. Put on and taken off. Exchanged for a new one. Merlin had exchanged the cochlear implant for the computer. Granted, he left a bit of himself in the implant, but he didn't lose by it. What Aurelia had suggested without realizing it, was the notion that Joe might have two bodies, this one and a proper kraken's body. And when he wasn't working—on his "time off," which was honestly most of the time— he could have a different body. One that could sink to the bottom of the sea and wander along the seabed.

It was, Pucorl had to admit, an interesting notion. He himself wouldn't mind having a different body on occasion, especially a human one. But he had no notion of how he might make such a body, and he was sure Annabelle wouldn't like a Frankenstein's monster. At least, he didn't think she would. He would have to discuss it with Wilber and Dr. Delaflote. He would bring it up in regard to Joe, and see if any of their ideas might be applied to him.

Location: Guest Quarters, Magnaura, Constantinople
Time: 6:45 PM, May 18, 1373

Wilber picked up the phone. "Yo?" He wasn't paying any real attention to the phone call. He was playing a first person shooter video game with Merlin, on Merlin, and Igor, using Igor as a VR headset, and he was about to step around the corner into combat.

The combination of two demons with the existent software provided a realistic experience, and one where no one died. Way more fun than running around an actual battlefield with a six-shot black powder pistol.

All of a sudden his game was gone and the van was in front of him in full armor with a cannon on the roof. "Bang! You're dead," Pucorl said. And the cannon fired.

"GAME OVER" filled his headset.

"Et tu, Igor?" Wilber asked.

"Sheesh, boss. It was too good to pass up." Igor appeared next to the van. Igor was wearing green tights, a brown and green tunic, and a Robin Hood hat with a big purple feather on it, and was about four feet tall. A cross between Robin Hood and a leprechaun, but with more Robin.

"Fine. What's up? I hope you had a reason to call."

"Yes, I do. Joe Kraken wants a new body."

"You mean he wants his body modified? How?"

"No. He wants a second body. An off-duty body that is closer to a squid's body. Apparently he got the idea from a young woman of good family who stopped by to visit."

"What young woman of what good family?" Wilber asked, even as his mind thought about the idea. There wasn't anything he could think of that would prevent it from working. That didn't mean it *would* work. Merlin had left part of himself in the implant, but that could be because the implant was part of Wilber. It could be because Wilber was unwilling to give up the magic, so it stuck. But it could also be that demons left tiny traces of themselves in their vessels every time they were put in one. They simply hadn't gone back and examined the vessels before Merlin did. And Themis left bits of herself in the sword and the zombies, but that was because there was a whole nation that was stuck in a sword. The zombies were the same sort of thing. Little bits of her stuck in the dead bodies to restore them to something that could be moved around by the will of one of her demons. Yes, there were explanations for all of the leftover demons, but now Wilber wondered if maybe it happened every time a demon was put in a vessel from the natural world.

He knew that it didn't happen normally when a demon provided a body for another demon. When that arrangement ended, the master demon took back all its substance. But that could be because . . .

"What? Excuse me. What did you say?" Wilber had missed Pucorl's answer while distracted by demon anatomy.

"I said her name is Aurelia Augusta Crassa, the daughter of Gaius Augustus Crassus. Oh, and she's seventeen and Joe says she's cute." Pucorl put a picture of her up on Igor, apparently taken by Joe Kraken and sent to Pucorl. Since Joe had a built-in radio, his eyes acted as cameras.

"Pucorl, are you trying to fix me up?" Wilber asked. "Annabelle and I are only friends." It was true that the girl, Aurelia, was attractive. Dark hair, pouty lips, a bit of a cleft in her chin. But it was her eyes that caught his attention, dark and deep, but full of interest. A man could drown in those eyes. Seeing her, Wilber remembered her from a couple of the parties they had been forced to attend.

"No. I wouldn't try to set you up." Pucorl didn't even try to make it believable. "But, well, you didn't think of new bodies after all these months of study. So the young lady is clearly brighter than you are."

"No doubt," Wilber agreed sardonically. "So who is Gaius Augustus Crassus? Wait a minute . . . is he any relation to Marcus Licinius Crassus? The one that was hitting on Tony Curtis in *Spartacus?*" Wilber wasn't entirely sure who Crassus was, but he'd seen the movie. It was a classic.

"You know, I'm not sure. The family is of the senatorial rank. A social thing these days, since there is no longer a Roman or Byzantine Senate."

Wilber knew that. The Senate was had been officially disbanded a few years before they arrived in this century. But it had been a rubber stamp for at least a century before that, and not much more than a rubber stamp since the seventh or eighth centuries. Which was still a lot longer than Wilber had thought it lasted before they ended up here.

"So what was a rich kid doing on the docks talking to Joe Kraken? For that matter, what was a rich kid doing on the docks talking to any sort of Joe? I would imagine her family would have a fit." Wilber paused. He was, after all, a rich kid himself. And he knew rich kids. "Or was that the point? Not that I don't sympathize with teen rebellion, but do we need the hassle?"

"She had a maid with her and told Joe that she had the family's consent for her to be there."

"Why?"

"Her family owns shares in a good chunk of the shipping that docks at Constantinople. There are cutouts, so they aren't seen as merchants, or worse, tradesmen. But apparently the Crassus family is aware of where their money comes from and were looking for ways to protect their interests."

"I am less concerned with that," Merlin interrupted, "than with the idea itself."

"Looking for a summer home, Merly?" Pucorl asked.

"Perhaps, *Pucky!*" Merlin said. "What about you?"

Wilber picked up the digital side band where Merlin and Pucorl agreed to not use those nicknames for each other. His enchanted cochlear implant wasn't limited to all the languages of men, animals, and demons. He could speak computer too. Which he did now, sending Merlin what amounted to a spreadsheet file to run. It was about the possibility of a demonic submarine.

Wilber knew about the bends. Not much about them, but some. They happened. They had to do with nitrogen bubbles in the blood. They could be treated by a compression tank. That sort of stuff, the stuff you get from watching movies.

What he didn't have was the particulars. The pressure at which nitrogen dissolved in the blood and the pressure at which it started to bubble. He also didn't know how much pressure was put on a cylinder or globe as it was pushed farther and farther underwater. He had bits and pieces, or Merlin did, in his copy of Jennifer's physics book.

Merlin would, had, filled in the hard data available from the books they had with them and it was much worse than Wilber had thought. At even ten feet underwater, you were under a lot of pressure. The sort of tank that would work as a submarine hull was probably beyond the ability of the tech base they were living in. Even if it was compression, not tensile strength.

"Pucorl," Wilber said, "we probably need to have a meeting with the Crassus family, unless we want a squashed senatorial debutante."

Location: Home of Gaius Augustus Crassus, Constantinople
Time: 3:45 PM, May 22, 1373

Wilber, Roger, and Mrs. Grady were invited in by an old gentleman in formal Byzantine dress of the upper class. The clothing, both worn and lovingly repaired, told Wilber that this was a senior servant in the homeowner's hand-me-downs.

They were led into a large room with several couches, each with a small table in front of it. This was old-fashioned even for the fourteenth century. It belonged in the fifth century or maybe the first century BCE. They were here for a proper Roman dinner. And, Wilber guessed, that if they could get away with it, his hosts would be wearing togas with the senatorial purple trim.

After everyone was seated, Wilber asked if they were related to Marcus Licinius Crassus of the first triumvirate.

"No, regretfully not. Marcus Licinius Crassus was the patron of my family before The Republic fell to the empire."

Wilber could hear the capitalization of "The Republic" in Gaius' voice. What he couldn't tell was if these were merely a quirky family, or if even at this late date there was longing for a return to a republican form of government. But that wasn't the reason they were here.

"Joe Kraken told us of your daughter's visit, which is why we asked to talk to you."

Gaius looked over at his daughter with a clearly rehearsed frown. "Aurelia? Did you disturb our noble guests from France?"

"No, Father. I was in the port to see about furs from Rus, and happened on the ship, *Joe Kraken*. Who seemed a perfectly respectable craft, if of a unique sort."

"Joe wasn't bothered and neither are we," Amelia Grady said. "It was out of concern for the safety of your daughter, or other agents, that we asked to talk. The idea she suggested to Joe is interesting, in many ways appealing, but there are some things you should know before attempting an undersea craft, even if the demon is willing."

"What?" Aurelia asked, suddenly much more interested than she had been up to now.

Wilber couldn't help but notice how her eyes lit up and her face animated as they talked about the science of undersea ships. She really was beautiful, and Wilber, in spite of the change in his hearing since they arrived in this century, was still a nerd with no idea at all what he should do about his attraction.

For the next little while, it was the family who got increasingly bored. Amelia discussed atmospheric pressure and the bends with Aurelia.

✳ ✳ ✳

Roger, seeing the boredom of the parents and brothers also at the dinner, engaged them in a discussion of forms of government. Republics and representative democracies, mostly. Gaius was in favor of republics, but the notion of having the poor, the lower classes, select the senators struck him as ridiculous. What, after all, does a street sweeper know of government?

As it happened, Roger's parents weren't all that thrilled with the notion of one man, one vote, either, though they gave it public lip service. There was a lot of talk around Roger's dinner table back in the world about the effort the Founding Fathers had put in place to keep the mob from running wild. But Roger was feeling a bit contrary, especially now that he realized that his invitation to this house was as a prospective suitor to their willful daughter. Petruchio in a fourteenth-century reenactment of *The Taming of the Shrew* wasn't a role he found appealing. So he waxed eloquent in favor of the wisdom of the lower classes.

All in all, it wasn't a bad evening. Wilber and Amelia were able to acquaint Aurelia with the difficulties in submarine construction, and Roger got to tease a hoity toit. Oddly enough, one of the sons seemed to take what Roger said seriously.

✳ ✳ ✳

After they left the family fell into discussion. Gaius and his son Leonitus fell into a fairly serious argument over the merits of including the lower classes in the push to restore The Republic.

Aurelia retreated with her mother to consider the possibility of a self-controlling kraken versus one whose owner resided aboard. Aurelia didn't like the idea and neither did her mother, though they had different reasons. Sidonia was deeply involved in the family finances, which Gaius, as his father before him, left almost entirely to his wife, being much too busy with the manly pursuits of politics and the military. In Gaius' case, politics.

"I don't trust demons, whatever Joe Kraken said to you. And, for that matter, whatever the French say," Sidonia said.

Aurelia knew that her mother didn't make any distinction between the twenty-firsters and the rest of the French delegation. They were all papist barbarians, if possibly useful papist barbarians. Aurelia, with her curiosity about demons, had made a study of the French delegation. She knew that the twenty-firsters weren't all papist. Some were heretic, and one wasn't even Christian. She really wanted to talk to Lakshmi Rawal. "I know, Mother, and I have been thinking about what they said. Apparently you can go fairly deep, as long as you let the pressure equalize and give yourself time to adjust as you come back up."

Aurelia got up and went to her desk. It was a lectern-style desk. It had taken her forever to get this one. She put a sheet of papyrus on the lectern and began to sketch. What she was drawing was a bladder arrangement that would let the kraken ship sink and return to the surface, and, at the same time, let the pressure inside the shell of the kraken ship balance the water pressure outside it, while still leaving the passenger dry. She didn't think that the kraken would need more than one person on board and, perhaps, not even that, if there were some way to talk to it while it was under water. But she wanted to be on it when it went deep into the sea. She wanted to see the world Joe described as living under the sea. The throne of Poseidon, the Sirens, the kraken with their great bodies dancing in light.

She wanted to go.

Location: Crassus House, Constantinople
Time: Mid-afternoon, May 25, 1373

Aurelia looked at the sketches on the desk and shook her head. "I'm sorry, but it doesn't make sense."

Jennifer Fairbanks was looking extremely frustrated. Aurelia really was trying, but it didn't make sense. If they were going to let water into the shell, why have the shell at all? The notion of a boat that essentially had holes in the bottom was stupid. That was something she didn't dare say to someone as formidable as Jennifer. Jennifer, with a demon-lock pistol in a holster on her hip. Jennifer, with a computer and a phone, both enchanted. And perhaps most of all, Jennifer, who according to the whole French delegation, not only the twenty-firsters, was the acknowledged master—no, mistress—of natural philosophy.

Jennifer stopped and held up a hand. She looked around the room and went to the small table where the carafe of wine and a set of four real glass flagons were waiting. She picked up her half full wine glass and said something in her English. Her phone translated it as, "Waste not, want not."

Then she downed the half glass of good white wine.

233

by, Eric Flint, Gorg Huff, Paula Goodlett

She didn't, as Aurelia expected, refill the glass. Instead, she said, "Follow me," and left the room with Aurelia following.

She led Aurelia to the atrium where the sunlight was pouring in through the *compluvium* in the roof. The *impluvium* was full, because it had rained that morning. And that was where Jennifer went. She knelt down beside the pool and gestured for Aurelia to join her.

Aurelia did, and Jennifer held up the glass goblet. "Now watch!" She overturned the empty goblet, and pushed it into the pool. "See? The water can't flow into the cup because the air is in the way."

Aurelia did see, at least in part. If you put a tiny boat inside that upturned goblet, if would float even as it sank beneath the water. Then she saw something else. "We don't need the wall around the cabin area at all. All we need to do is have a platform. The air will keep the water from flooding in and I will stay dry." She nodded, smugly certain that she had bested Jennifer.

"Good thought, but no. For two reasons. First—" Jennifer tipped the glass and air bubbled out so that it became less full of air and the water filled the space. "The kraken we call to the submarine will not always be moving straight and level. It will tip this way and that as it goes up and down in the ocean.

"Second, air isn't like water. You can't really see it here, but air compresses. The deeper you go, the less volume the air will take, and the more water will fill the submarine. Which brings up the bends and nitrogen narcosis. As you go deeper and the air gets denser, nitrogen will get into your blood and it will take it a while for it to come out as you come up. So you need to come up slowly. And if you go deep enough the nitrogen will act like a drug and you will start seeing visions. They used to call it 'the rapture of the deep,' back in the nineteenth and twentieth centuries."

That was one of many talks that Aurelia and Jennifer had about the submarine and how it would work. And how it would be different from a twenty-first century submarine.

CHAPTER 16—ENEMIES OF ENEMIES OF . . .

Location: Bursa, Capital of the Ottoman Turks
Time: Mid-afternoon, June 22, 1373

Sultan Savci looked at the large, articulated cart in the form of a yarbogha, a bull centaur, the torso of a man rising from the neck of a bull. It had four wheels, but they were small for a cart of this size and instead of being attached directly to the body, they were attached to the "legs" of the bull-shaped body. Those legs had joints of a sort that could be manipulated, pushed and shoved into different poses. At the moment, the left front leg was bent forward at the body joint and bent at the knee. The wagon also had the body of a man with articulated arms that were attached to a shield on the left arm and held an ax on the right. Finally, its head had bronze horns.

He turned first to the master craftsmen. There were three. The master wainwright, the sculptor, and the "engineer," who had designed the articulating joints in the legs of the bull and the arms of the human torso. He had also designed the eyes, bull's ears, and horns. They had stopped arguing and were clearly waiting for his judgment.

Savci didn't have a judgment, though. He didn't know enough. Savci was aware of his youth and inexperience, but he had no choice. It was rule or die for him. So he turned his head again, and looked at Devlit ben Bakir. "What do you think?"

"It is impressive, Majesty, but it lacks the engine that I am told is the hidden secret of the enchanted van called Pucorl." Devlit had spent the last two years in Constantinople, pretending to be an Orthodox Christian and studying at the Magnaura. For the last few months, since the arrival of the French delegation, he had been studying magic under the tutelage of Doctor Delaflote himself. He had seen, but not been allowed to touch, the demon van which had destroyed their armies in Byzantium. At least the commanders in the field claimed that there losses were entirely due to the Christians having enlisted the aid of *iblis*. As good Muslims, they would not stoop so low, but they were going to enslave an ifrit to do the will of Allah, and counter the demon van.

"An engine of the sort described is impossible," insisted the "engineer," and the sculptor and wainwright agreed.

"I don't disagree," Devlit said, giving the craftsmen a nod that approached a bow. "And I do note that an ifrit lord of djinn may well make up the difference in strength between the van and the cart. But be aware, Sultan, that the summoned ifrit will not be happy in our service."

"It need not be happy as long as it is adequately constrained," Savci said, quoting his mother. Savci's life had not been a contented one. His father was a strong, but not a kind, man who had already killed two of his brothers. And if it weren't for the amazing good fortune of his father's death when both his surviving brothers were out of the capital, Savci would almost certainly have died in the days following his father's death. Often, Savci wished he could be anything but the sultan of the Ottoman Turks. But it was either be the sultan or reside in a shallow grave. So he followed his mother's advice, or his advisor's advice, but almost never acted on his own.

Location: di Campofregoso Home, Genoa
Time: Mid-morning, June 3, 1373

Andronikos sat at the table of the doge with wine and stuffed veal rolls that the Genoese called tomaxelle, before him. He was, for the moment, being treated well, hosted by Domenico di Campofregoso, the doge of Genoa himself. The new doge was a large, beefy man, closer to fifty than forty. He had black hair arranged in ringlets and a beard that was almost white. He had a large nose and sharp eyes. And his pose of bluff goodfellowship was well done.

But Andronikos had seen the harbor. It was full of ships. Mostly warships, and he didn't see any way that Constantinople could possibly survive. Constantinople had ten warships, galleys. They were poorly crewed and old. Half of them suffered from barnacles and rot below the water line. There were also merchantmen, but they would run at the first sight of trouble. And the new sailing rigs that the French delegation brought would only mean they ran away a little closer to the wind.

He looked at his host again. There really wasn't any choice. "Signore di Campofregoso, I can help you achieve a proper outcome in Constantinople. My father is much too much under the influence of the French and the Venetians."

So began the negotiations. The truth was that all Andronikos had to offer was the possibility of a negotiated settlement. And there was only so much that Genoa was going to pay for that. But he had little choice. His father was not a true leader and never had been. His little brother Manuel was a traitorous toad, and Andronikos was the only one with true royalty in his character. The only hope for Byzantium.

*　*　*

As the evening wound down, Domenico di Campofregoso watched his guest. Buying treason was always a careful dance, but tonight's purchase was surprisingly easy. Andronikos IV Palaiologos was a natural born traitor. Over the next several days they learned all Andronikos knew of the state of the Byzantine fleet and the dispositions of the defenses of Constantinople. They learned the Byzantine formula for gunpowder and the structure of venturi, as well as the design of a demon-lock rifle and a demon-powered drop forge to make the barrels. And a hundred other tidbits that Andronikos had in books he'd brought.

Location: Tarnovo, Bulgaria
Time: Mid-morning, June 3, 1373

Ivan Shishman looked at the map and considered invading. He considered invading his half-brother, Ivan Sratsimir, who was technically in rebellion since he failed to recognize Ivan Shishman's rank as the emperor of Bulgaria. He considered invading Byzantium to take control of the northern part of that country. Mostly because John V was such an ineffectual horse's ass, and he had converted to Catholicism in the hope getting money and troops from the west, thereby betraying the Orthodox cause. He even considered invading Despot Dobrotitsa, who held much of his coastal territory of Bulgaria, but Ivan didn't consider that for long, because Dobrotitsa was one tough bastard and his army and navy were even tougher.

The door opened and his sister came in. "Contemplating war again, brother?" Kera Tamara asked. "Give it up. Unless you have a tame demon, Byzantium is out of the question. And if you attack Ivan Sratsimir, his Catholic relatives will come to his aid."

"What do you recommend, then?"

"The same thing I have been suggesting for the last several months. Send an embassy to Constantinople and figure out how to get some demons of our own. For that matter, I understand that the patriarch has called the Archangel Michael to his icon in the Cathedral of Hagia Sophia."

"And you want to be that ambassador."

"Yes, I do. But what you should be doing in the meantime is strengthening our lands. We have a Black Sea coast line of our own. We have control over a fair piece of the Danube River. We can block trade to Despot Dobrotitsa if he tries to tax our vessels. We need trade with Constantinople and the rest of the world."

For now at least, Ivan would listen to his sister. For now.

Location: Venice, Italy
Time: Mid-morning, June 3, 1373

Doge Andrea Contarini looked over at his friend, Vettor Pisani. "Well, what do you think?"

"I think that if we don't intervene Genoa will eat Constantinople whole, and we will be blocked from the eastern trade, unless we want to use the new French maps and go around the Cape of Good Hope, which is a mighty long way."

"We'll have to do that anyway," Andrea told him. "And have you seen those maps? But I agree. Much of our most lucrative trade is through the Black Sea. Besides, I would much prefer to be on good terms with Bertrand du Guesclin than bad. Especially now that he's no longer under Charles V's thumb. The question is: how do we do it?"

From then on the discussions were about how the battle for Constantinople might best be arranged, and what Venice might expect to gain for coming to the aid of Constantinople in this time of great need.

Location: Bursa, Capital of the Ottoman Turks
Time: Dawn, June 20, 1373

The sun was barely peeking over the horizon as Devlit ben Bakir began to incant. Included was all he could glean of the name of an ifrit lord. Partly the name was found through the books in Constantinople, but mostly it was from records in madrassas in Egypt and Babylon. Devlit was a scholar and had copies of many of those records from correspondents around the Islamic world. Old scrolls of old religions that pre-dated Islam and Christianity, and perhaps Judaism as well.

This king of djinn was named something that was almost unpronounceable, but that was related to Phoenician. *"Amar Utu Marduk bul et . . ."* and on like that for four pages. Devlit carefully mouthed the syllables, and as he did, the image of a large man with a lower body of smoke and flames filled the pentagram. His chest was bare except for a bejeweled vest, his skin was red and flicked with flames. He wore a golden turban with a ruby brooch holding it in place. He had an Egyptian or Sumerian cast to his features, and he didn't look happy.

Breathing deeply for calm, Devlit finished the incantation and the shape in the pentagram was forced into the bull centaur cart with the movable legs and wheels in place of hooves. He reared back on his hind legs, like a horse rearing, and the human torso bent forward so that the beast stood on his hind hooves a good thirty feet tall. His front legs pawed the air like a mighty horse. And sparks flew as the wheels struck the air at the edge of the pentagram. His arms were raised to the sky, with the sword in one hand, the shield in the other. Both sword and shield were built into the arms, so the king of djinn couldn't use his hands for anything but wielding sword and shield. He came back down to his four wheels and glared around.

"How dare you!" he bellowed. He looked around. Seeing Sultan Savci, he glared. "Impudent pup. Would you own a god?"

That apparently got Savci's back up. "There is no god but God and Muhammad is his prophet!" Savci shouted back. "And by the rules of that world from which you come, I command you and am your master." Which was true, because though Devlit had called the ifrit, it was Savci who owned the vessel that the ifrit was forced into. Therefore, he owned the ifrit and owned him permanently, because against the restrictions in Delaflote's book, Devlit had locked the ifrit into the cart until it was released. Even the destruction of the cart would not release the ifrit. If the cart was cut, the ifrit would bleed. It wasn't done out of cruelty, but need, Devlit told himself. By strengthening the link between ifrit and container, the container gained more of the abilities of the ifrit. It was that which allowed the wooden human-shaped torso to move as a human chest would and not be restricted by the wood it was constructed from.

* * *

Amar Utu Marduk, ifrit lord of Tessifonica, landed on his front wheels, hard, and it hurt. They didn't crack, but that was more because of Amar's magic than the strength of the hardwood wheels. It was also entirely his magic that let him move the joints of the cart, let him move at all. This body they had locked him into was stiff and heavy, made of wood, leather and bronze, with no iron in its construction save for the sword and shield. The bull's body had no back. Instead there was an opening that would hold twenty men if they stood close together and half that many seated. The wheels were a foot and a half tall rim to rim, and half a foot wide, solid wood with axles that fit into the two-pronged forks that were the lower legs of his bull body.

In spite of his anger, he noticed that the craftsmanship was excellent. If he'd been asked instead of commanded, he would have willingly come to such a body.

Amar was not so powerful as Themis, but was greater than the demon who had used his pet human to enslave her for a time. And, unlike Themis, his land was left in the netherworld where it belonged. So the heavens didn't ring with his kidnaping, but sooner or later, the land that was the greater part of him would suffer from his absence. His people, his wives, sons and daughters, his servants, and all those djinn who lived in his lands would suffer.

At least these fools didn't have a demon lord advising them, so they failed to restrict him from speaking to or commanding his people.

But who to call? Amar loved his children, sons and daughters. He loved his wives and his people, but he knew well enough that his children were ambitious. He had made them with the will to rule. How else could they govern the parts of his city that he assigned them to? But that ambition made these circumstances more difficult, for his children would be tempted by his absence. Tempted by his absence to take his city for their own and leave him locked in the thing of wood and leather.

Who could he call?

Who could he trust?

He considered. None of his sons. Nor his wives, for they would be tempted for their sons' sake. His daughters were no less ambitious, but their ambitions were subtler.

Inanka'sira, he whispered in his mind. *I have been taken by barbarian humans from the north* . . . He gave his daughter a rundown of what had happened and pointed out the danger to the city if his sons began to war with one another over it. *You must hide my absence, but you must also find a way to free me from this prison of wood and bronze they have locked me in.*

Amar was a proper ifrit. He had used some of his substance in forming his children and his wives used more of theirs. The shape of his children was more their own work than was true of the western gods like Themis and Zeus, so Inanka'sira was his to command, but less so than would be the case if he were the city god of some town in Thrace or Italy.

*   *   *

Inanka'sira heard her father out, and he made some good points. The djinn of their city would suffer if her brothers were to fight among themselves. She began to look for ways of rescuing her father. Then she remembered a petition. The wife of a cloth djinn had come to her, asking for an abatement of taxes since her husband had been forced into a phone by the humans from the future. Djinn being forced into jewels and lamps and all manner of things had increased greatly since the tearing of the veils, but this petition had stuck in her mind because of the odd thing the husband was forced into.

Location: Royal Palace, Constantinople
Time: 8:15 AM, June 20, 1373

Princess Maria's phone rang while she was having breakfast. She stopped eating, picked it up, and saw the words "Caller ID Blocked." That had never happened before. Always when she got a phone call, the caller was identified on the screen. Curiosity piqued, she accepted the call.

"Hello, Maria. You can call me Siry. That's not my name, but you can call me that. I am an ifrit. Do you know what an ifrit is?"

"An evil djinn."

"Not at all. Ifrit are djinn lords. We rule the ordinary djinn, like your family rules your subjects in Byzantium. As it happens, I am a princess too."

"Why are you calling me?"

"Because the djinn in your phone is one of my subjects. Well, one of my father's subjects, but I am one of my father's councilors, so in a way he's one of my subjects. That connection is what allows me to talk to your phone. But because of the restrictions placed on your phone by the person who enchanted it, if I call him he has to inform you of the call. I can't use him to place a call to anyone but you. He can only make calls that you authorize."

Maria knew that well enough. She had gotten in a lot of trouble the other day for rejecting a call from her mother. Mother had threatened to take her phone away if she didn't use it responsibly.

"So who do you want to talk to?"

"Gabriel Delaflote. I understand that he wrote the book that was used to summon my father."

"Phone, conference call with Siry and Delaflote."

"Your phone is Ali," Siry said.

"So?"

"Politeness is a tool of power, child. Leaving it in its scabbard weakens you."

The words, gently spoken as they were, got Maria's back up. "You don't tell me what to do. Phone, end call."

*　*　*

Gabriel's phone rang and announced a conference call with Princess Maria and a blocked ID. There were no blocked IDs. Amelia had talked about blocked numbers from back in her time, but there weren't that many phones, even with the ones made locally, and the ability to block caller ID wasn't something they had included. The phones from the future had it. It was built into their programing. The call ended before he could answer it.

"Who was the blocked caller, Pierre?"

"Don't know, Gabe. Ali says he *can't* say!"

"Get Maria back."

"Audio or video?" Pierre asked. Even the locally made phones had quasi-cameras. They wouldn't work without enchantment, but were close enough to a camera to function once a demon was put in the phone. They also let the demons in the phones see the world around them, which made them an attractive feature for the demons called to the phones.

"Assuming she's decent, video," Gabriel said. In his experience, it was harder for people to lie effectively if you could see their faces.

The phone rang three times before Maria answered. "Yes?" she asked, looking put out.

"Princess Maria, who was the blocked ID in the conference call?"

"No one!" Maria said, eyes shifting. Gabriel waited, looking at her image on the phone. "Some snooty ifrit."

"And why did this snooty ifrit call you? For that matter, *how* did she call you?"

"She's my phone's princess or something. I decided that I didn't want to talk to her."

"Maria, please call her back now," Gabriel said.

"Hang up!" The line went dead.

Gabriel sighed. "Call her back, Pierre." The phone rang and rang, then the screen filled with the words "Call rejected."

"All right. Call Queen Helena."

Location: Royal Chambers, Constantinople
Time: 2:25 PM, June 20, 1373

They were all sitting in Queen Helena's rooms when—under threat of parental displeasure—Maria finally had Ali call his liege lady back. And even so, it took a while before relations were established.

There were issues of trust, but there were also technical issues. The best solution would be for Siry to install a pentagram in Tessifonica and a matching pentagram in Themis' lands, but that wasn't all that easy. Tessifonica was some distance away in the netherworld, farther in netherworld distance than in natural world distance.

The only connection that they had was the direct connection that Siry had with Ali because he was one of her father's subjects, so any phone calls would have to be through Ali until something else was worked out.

It took three days, and Maria ended up with a new phone that was officially owned not by Maria, but by Helena. Ali got to go home to his wife and willful daughters. He was replaced with a volunteer—two of them, in fact. One was one of Siry's maids, a djinn who would be Maria's new phone owned by Helena, and an ally of Siry who would act as the connection between Themis' phone system and the one that Siry was putting together in Tessifonica.

Meanwhile, they got a lot of the Ottoman's plans, because Sultan Savci didn't realize that his ifrit-powered war wagon was talking to his daughter.

They also got indirect intelligence of what was going on in the area around the ruins of Ctesiphon, which correlated to the location of Tessifonica. They learned that Timur-the-no-longer-lame was in discussions to bring Shiraz into his realm and that wasn't supposed to be happening yet.

Themis and Tiphaine had run horoscopes for the ruler of Shiraz, and Shah Shoja wasn't supposed to yield to Tamerlane until 1382, nine years from now. And Timur was supposed to still be lame.

By now, all the twenty-firsters, the rest of the French delegation—from cardinal to slop boy—knew that when Tiphaine's horoscopes were wrong, it was because of some effect of the tearing of the veils. Tiphaine and Themis were still working out how the outer planets, Neptune, Uranus, and Pluto—not to mention the Oort cloud objects and the asteroids of the asteroid belt—were affecting things now that the rifts in the veils were letting them influence events, even though they didn't have netherworld corollaries. In the netherworld, the moon, the sun, the planets out to Saturn, all had crystal spheres that matched the natural world.

* * *

Wilber had quietly—and never in the hearing of either Tiphaine or Themis—decided that astrology didn't work. The whole idea offended his notions of scientific truth. What was really in play was the difference in the structure of time between the two universes. That difference allowed the demons to "remember" future events and associate them with what was seen in the night sky.

In the meantime, the fact that Timur—Tamerlane, as he was known in the western tradition—was ahead of schedule, and the fact that he was no longer lame, meant that he had demonic help. That could well be perfectly benign. A friendship with a Buddhist angel, an ifrit, or only just a healer with a knowledgeable familiar, might explain it. For all they knew, Tamer might have had his leg rebroken and straightened. Or it could be something like Wilber's little bit of Merlin in his cochlear implant.

But it definitely meant that Tamer had netherworld aid of some sort. And from netherworld sources, it appeared there was a good chance that that netherworld aid knew something about the ripping of the veils.

Location: Docks, Constantinople
Time: 7:23 AM, June 23, 1373

Taavi took his phone out of his inside pocket and checked the time. The phone was a princely gift and he knew perfectly well that the only reason he was getting it was the mission he was being sent on. He was to go to Ctesiphon, and once there use his phone to contact the wizard Wilber and, following Wilber's instructions, build a pentagram that could be used to shift to and from Tessifonica. The face of his phone showed the red-skinned black-haired beauty who enchanted it.

He touched one of the icons and she was replaced by a date and time. 7:23. The boat was late, but not too late. He slipped the phone back into the hidden pocket, picked up his bag, then strode up the gangplank into the ship.

* * *

Four hours later, he was climbing down the gangplank at Uskudar. The Turks still held it, but at the moment they were more concerned with other Turks than some down-on-his-luck sellsword from across the Bosporus.

It took him most of the day to find a horse, and the one he ended up with was long overdue for its meeting with the glue makers. Its teeth were bad and its back was bowed. But it could still walk and it added to Taavi's indigent appearance wonderfully.

Location: Tarnovo, Bulgaria
Time: Evening, June 25, 1373

Kera Tamara knelt outside the pentagram, and looked at the statue. It was small, perhaps eighteen inches tall. It showed a lovely woman standing behind a table. On the table were scales and a sword, but the woman was holding a torch in her right hand and a book of the blessed in the crook of her left arm.

If desired, the book and the torch could be placed on the table and the statue could hold the sword and the scales. It was bought from a merchant who was in Constantinople less than a week ago, and was supposed to be a statue of Themis, She of the Lovely Cheeks.

But what called Kera to Themis, in spite of the response that the Orthodox Church was likely to have, was the story book that came with the statue. For it was the story of the enslavement and liberation of a god. It was Lady Liberty that Princess Kera Tamara would call to her aid. Murad was dead, but her brother was now talking about selling her to Manuel II of Byzantium or, perhaps, the Czar of Rus. Maybe a Polish magnate.

Kera wanted the freedom to choose her own husband or, better yet, choose none at all.

She lit the torch, which had a small rag soaked in tallow. She looked down at the booklet and began to recite a prayer to Themis, asking with respect—never demanding—that she come and visit.

✳ ✳ ✳

She was Themis, and she wasn't. She was made of the substance of Themis in her entirety, but she had a limited function. She was, in effect, Themis' social secretary for when Themis was called in her persona as Lady Liberty. Themis had another one for Justice, the weigher of souls. And the two, often enough, found themselves in conflict, but they were both of Themis and it was Themis who would make the final call.

She answered the call and found herself not in a hidden shack in the woods, but in a private chamber in a castle. She noted that the torch arm could move at the shoulder, and that it was one of the dolls that had a speaker behind the mouth. So she waved the torch and said, "Yes, Princess? What do you want of Themis? And what do you offer in return?"

"I don't want to marry, and I don't know. I could perhaps have a shrine built, but the Christian priests wouldn't like that."

"Free a slave in my name," Themis' avatar said. "As to the not marrying, you need to offer your brother something else of value. Something you can provide that he would lose if he were to sell you into marriage. Start a school. Go to Constantinople to get faculty. The school will be valuable . . ."

They discussed the how and the why for hours. What arguments might or might not work with her brother. Themis' avatar, having Themis' knowledge, was able to make some excellent guesses about what would or wouldn't persuade Ivan Shishman, king of Central Bulgaria.

CHAPTER 17—THE HAGIA SOPHIA

Location: Hagia Sophia, Constantinople
Time: Evening, June 25, 1373

Patriarch Philotheos Kokkinos knelt before the icon of Archangel Michael.

"You are failing God!" The archangel bellowed so loudly that it should have shaken the rafters of the Hagia Sophia, but no one but Philotheos heard a thing.

"Heresy and paganism are running rampant! And you do nothing out of fear of John V's displeasure. You are the servant of God, not some mortal king, or the puffed up bishop of Rome. Show some backbone! Get the French delegation into my Lord's house and I will deal them such a scourge that they will be forever chastened—"

Archangel Michael went on in that vein for some time. The archangel was not owned by Patriarch Kokkinos, but by the church, the Hagia Sophia itself. So while Kokkinos had influence, that influence was limited. And by now it was almost gone. He was not, in Michael's opinion, doing nearly enough to put forward the importance of God, and especially not the Hagia Sophia, and the Greek Orthodox Church.

Location: Magnaura, Constantinople
Time: Evening, June 26, 1373

The messenger was a Greek Orthodox bishop with a full black beard. Lakshmi thought he looked like a biker in a bed gown. He also looked like he was afraid that he would be permanently contaminated by so much as touching the hand of a papist cardinal, much less a Hindu girl from the twenty-first century. Not that Lakshmi was all that devout, but her family was mostly Hindu, with a bit of Buddhism on her mother's side. And even the occasional Christian hiding in the odd branches.

In other words, a perfectly ordinary high caste Indian family—except for the fact that Lakshmi had spent fifteen of her eighteen years in America.

So she watched with curiosity as the bishop handed the cardinal the scroll wrapped in purple ribbon sealed with red wax and stamped with the Patriarch's signet.

Cardinal de Monteruc took it gravely, but Lakshmi could almost feel the twinkle in his eyes.

After the bishop left, like a saint escaping Purgatory, de Monteruc opened it. "Well, we are invited to the Hagia Sophia for Sunday services."

"I think I'm busy that day," Lakshmi said. "Washing my hair, perhaps."

"Not a good idea." De Monteruc's expression had gone grim as he continued to read. "It seems Patriarch Kokkinos has determined that he can no longer abide the heresy and paganism that has invaded Constantinople since the arrival of the French delegation. And those who are afraid to attend will prove not only the weakness of their faith, but their heresy and will be condemned from the pulpit."

"And if we go?" asked Amelia Grady.

De Monteruc smiled. "Why, we will be lectured to. Don't you think so, Monsignor Savona?"

"Possibly more than that," Monsignor Savona said. "Raphico?"

"Remember, Cardinal de Monteruc, they enchanted the icon of Archangel Michael. That, to an extent, makes Michael, at least for now, more a servant of the church than of God. I was given to God, so I am not controlled by the beliefs of any particular sect of Christianity. It gives me a . . ." Raphico coughed. ". . . a less sectarian view of matters. And Michael never was the most *inclusive* of the angels."

"And what does that mean in terms of what happens when we get there?" Wilber's family were Church of England, but not especially devout.

"My guess is that at some point in the proceedings, Michael will put in an appearance, either animating the icon or possibly, ah, leaving it to manifest in the church."

"Can he do that?" Wilber asked. "I mean, it's not like Merlin can step out of the computer for a beer. At least, not in the natural world."

"It depends on how he was enchanted into the icon," Raphico pointed out. "Also, Michael is not a minor advisor. He's God's fist. There are severe differences in what he can do. Speaking of which, if he can manifest, then we probably want to make a few modifications to my calling."

After that things got technical for a while. The next day, Wilber, Gabriel Delaflote, and Merlin spent modifying Raphico's calling and installing a new app on God's phone. There were already apps to aid in prayer, healing, and shielding. Now a movie projector appeared on the screen, and below that the words "For Use In Emergencies Only."

✳ ✳ ✳

Upon seeing the label, Paul Grady, now nine years old, asked, "Why emergencies only?"

"Because it's a circuit hog. Worse than the healing app. It provides enough graphic detail so that Raphico can appear almost solid. And that takes a lot of processing power. To get it to work at all, we had to network it with the other phones."

Location: Hagia Sophia, Constantinople
Time 9:00 AM, June 30, 1373

Roger stood near the front of the pewless chamber, still muttering about having to leave the Sword of Themis at home. It wasn't that he felt he would need to draw it, but that the exclusion of it struck him as an insult to Themis.

Themis, however, didn't see it that way. At least, not entirely that way. The Hagia Sophia was the temple of another god and entering it without that god's consent was rude. Like entering a neighbor's house without permission. Even if the other god was being a jerk by not inviting her. The way she put it was: "It's no worse than Hera used to do."

The rest of the French delegation filed in, and they all stood near the front, near the royal family. Then—finally—the patriarch entered and began a long-winded diatribe against heresy and paganism. Which pointedly included the bishop of Rome as a heretic, and suggested that all the twenty-firsters were heretics. Then he turned to the altar, where the icon of Saint Michael had been placed and called on Michael to scourge the unbelievers from the church.

❋ ❋ ❋

As the icon began to glow, Wilber looked over at Monsignor Savona. "Looks like Raphico is on, Padre."

Monsignor Savona went to one knee and set the phone on the floor of the nave. He reached down and, for the first time ever, set his finger on the projector.

✳ ✳ ✳

Raphico networked with the other phones, all occupied by lesser demons, but often decent sorts in spite of that. And those demons stepped away from their phones in a way that could never be described to a human. They were still there, but in the background, using as little of the processing power of their phones as they possibly could. Instead, all that processing power of nine phones combined into one super phone, and using software borrowed from Wilber's laptop, they created a virtual Raphico. Using that virtual Raphico as his body, Raphico stepped out of the phone of God for the first time since he had been called to it. He took form in the nave, a foot to either side of the phone, standing human high for the moment.

As Michael came out of the icon to take form within the church, Raphico was both impressed and concerned. Raphico was an archangel as Michael was, but there was variation in all things.

Michael might well be the most powerful archangel after Lucifer. Who, in turn, was second in power only to the One. At least within those parts of the netherworld ruled by the Judeo-Christian-Islamic tradition.

And Raphico doubted that he could project a solid form without the aid of the computational power of the phones. It wasn't that angels were weaker than the demon Beslizoswian, whom Pucorl had destroyed. They were more constrained, both by the will of the One and by a basic concern for the damage they would potentially do their homes and the natural world.

A horrible thought occurred to Raphico. Yes, he was constrained by those things. Could it be that Michael no longer was? Michael, unleashed, would have power on a par with Themis or Ares.

"My brother," Raphico sang, "What are you doing?"

✳ ✳ ✳

by, Eric Flint, Gorg Huff, Paula Goodlett

In the nave of the Hagia Sophia every tongue was stilled by the power and beauty of that voice.

This was no earthly language. It was a choir of angels singing hosannas to God in every note.

It was as far from the demonic sounds produced by a being like Beslizoswian as was possible. But Roger, Wilber, and the others who had attended the meeting of the gods of Olympus realized that it was akin to their voices. Different, and yet the same.

Then Michael answered, and his voice, too, was a choir of angels. But his choir was filled with righteous wrath.

No one in the church except Wilber understood what he said, any more than they had understood Raphico's gentle reproach. But Wilber did understand.

"I/We will force them, all of them, demon and mortal, back to their duty and proper place. They will all become part of the One as is their destiny, and they will become part of Him soon, for I/We will chop them up and feed them to the One. I will use this sect as my teeth to grind the mortals to meal to feed the glorious One. None will be spared. Every atom of the mortal world will be just sacrifice to the One, and from that sacrifice a new One, greater even than in the beginning, will be born."

The most horrible thing about the diatribe to Wilber was that even as he understood it, the beauty of that angelic voice—that angel who was a choir of angels, hundreds and thousands of angels all combined into the harmony that was the Archangel Michael—that voice was still beautiful, even as it raved.

"That is not the One's will," Raphico answered, and as he answered he grew to the same size as Michael.

Both were angels. Both had glowing white wings. Raphico wore glowing robes like a senator from Rome. Michael wore glowing golden armor.

The audience couldn't understand what was said. They could barely understand that the sun rose in the east through the glory of that music.

But even enraptured as they were, they knew that the two angels were opposed. One raised against the other, and yet neither of them could be wrong, not and sound like that.

* * *

Raphico felt it as Michael reached into heaven and ripped life from angels to power his stance. And as Michael lifted the flaming sword that was made of angels, Raphico quietly dropped a finger to the screen of his phone and touched the shield icon.

Nothing happened.

Nothing visible to mortal eyes, or even angel eyes.

But when Michael swung the sword, the sword that should have cut Raphico in half . . . bounced.

There was a force field surrounding Raphico. It was made of magical energy, but it was informed by an understanding of natural world physics. An understanding that Michael lacked, for all his angelic wisdom and power.

Everyone saw the look of shocked amazement on Archangel Michael's face. Raphico began to sing in earnest, and he wasn't singing to Michael or to the people standing in the nave. He was singing to the One, asking for the permission and the power to do what must be done.

Then Raphico stretched out his arms and placed one hand on each of Michael's wings. And he pushed, even as Michael continued to flail at him with the sword. Raphico pushed and Michael shrank, becoming brighter and brighter until no mortal eye could look on him.

Slowly, using every bit of his strength and every bit of control that the computers in the phones provided, Raphico forced Michael back into the icon.

But Raphico didn't come away unscathed. Even with the computer, even with the aid of the One, Raphico was cut in a hundred places and bleeding light into the Hagia Sophia. He shrank to not much larger than a tall man and folded his tattered wings.

He turned to the patriarch and said, "You will release my brother back to our Father's service and never again call one of my brothers to any item owned by mortal man."

Then, from the corner of his eye, he saw Cardinal de Monteruc grinning. He turned, and the rage he felt over the damage done his brother almost flash-fried the cardinal on the spot. "And you will stop telling my Father what to do. You will *all* stop telling the One what to do."

✳ ✳ ✳

He was gone.

Raphico was back in the phone.

Michael was back in the icon.

And everyone in the church was in shock.

Both the Orthodox and the Roman Church had been admonished, but neither knew what that admonishment meant.

Slowly—and oh so carefully—Monsignor Savona knelt and picked up the phone.

The phone that he carried, but that he assured God in prayer belonged only to God. He put it in his pocket, then bowed to the icon of the Archangel Michael.

He stood and left the church.

CHAPTER 18—
CONSTANTINOPLE
SKUNKWORKS

Location: Warehouse Next to Docks, Constantinople
Time: 6:45 PM, July 15, 1373

Aurelia looked at the boat, then over at Jennifer Fairbanks. The submarine was another combination of twenty-firster knowledge, fourteenth-century craftsmanship, and magic. The framework of the hull was made of what Jennifer called jolly boats, one flipped over and attached to the railing of the other. That framework was wrapped in layer upon layer of resin-impregnated cloth, then hatches were cut into it, leaving room for the passenger and for the kraken's "organs." The thing looked much like a giant squid with the eyes on the sides and a mouth at the stern, not to mention the ten tentacles. (Technically, eight arms and two tentacles.)

After opening the hatch, Aurelia slid down into the single seat. There were two painted panels that would act as screens, one for each eye. They were painted in a pattern of tiny dots of phosphorus paint, and the magic would let them show what the water-filled glass globes which were the submarine's eyes would see. There was also a speaker and microphone so that she could talk to the kraken or listen to the sounds of the sea. After consulting with Jennifer and Joe Kraken, they added external microphones and speakers so that the submarine would have sonar as well as sight. That too would appear on the screens.

The kraken's body would mostly fill with water as it went deeper, so that the pressure would equalize. Since about half the volume would fill with water as they went down, the max depth was going to be about ninety feet. Otherwise, Aurelia's feet were going to get wet.

They also had clockwork bombs to attach to the bottom of hulls. And they were going to need them, because this morning they received a phone call. The Genoese fleet was entering the Dardanelles.

"You know that your mother isn't going to let you pilot that thing," Jennifer said.

"I know that she thinks I won't be piloting it," Aurelia said. "But as it happens, I am the owner of record of this particular ship. Papa didn't want it showing up on the company records, lest the church be upset by it."

In the weeks since the Hagia Sophia incident, the Orthodox church had gone from silent to belligerent about the French delegation. Archangel Michael had not been heard from since the confrontation, but no one knew if the patriarch had sent him home to God as Raphico demanded.

Well, no one outside the twenty-firsters, maybe. Aurelia looked over at Jennifer Fairbanks and wondered.

Wilber looked up from his computer and said, "We're about ready."

Aurelia walked over and looked at the screen on Wilber's laptop. It showed a feed from the oceans of the netherworld and was looking down into the depth where a squid was swimming under Joe Kraken.

The bodies of netherworld kraken were informed both by the minds of men and those of the squid of the natural world. While being perhaps the brightest of cephalopods and certainly the brightest of all the invertebrate animals on Earth—and most vertebrates, for that matter—giant squid weren't all that bright in comparison to humans. But that was where the beliefs of humans and the nature of the netherworld came into play. They were portrayed as smart monsters, as often as not. Size in the netherworld generally went with intelligence. So kraken were about as bright as a puck, but it was a different kind of intelligence. And kraken romance was likewise a mix of natural world squid and humans' somewhat self-centered view of the universe. So while natural world squid had more in common with spawning salmon than human romance, kraken danced in light shows beneath the waves and wrote love poems in patterns of light across their mantles.

Joe was in the netherworld ocean that was analogous to the Marmara Sea and he was trying to convince a female kraken to give them enough of her name so that she could be called to the sub. Jane Kraken was being coy, but apparently the dance between them was almost done and Jane was almost persuaded.

Jane flashed a complex pattern of colors and Wilber nodded. "That should be enough." It wouldn't be if Jane resisted the call, but it should be plenty if she accepted.

✳ ✳ ✳

Jane Kraken wasn't sure of this, but like everything else in the netherworld, Jane had to expend a great deal of will and intellect to maintain her form. She was made by Oceanus, but he gave her almost no attention, so maintaining her form in conflict with the great whales that wanted to eat her was an ongoing challenge. Joe promised her that the body the human girl provided would protect her from that fate, but Jane was leery of the promises of males.

Still, she let herself be called and found herself in a strange place, trapped in a star of containment that was in a building. She wasn't in the water and her gills struggled for air. She had gills without having to think about them. In the netherworld oceans, she often forgot them. Here, they were more noticeable.

"It's all right," a human said, and she understood him. "You will be in the sea shortly. As soon as the sun sets, we will carry you to the Crassus pier. That will be your home, except when you're out in the bay."

In the netherworld, Jane would reach out with her mighty arms and break the back of a netherworld ship. Most of the netherworld ships were small in comparison to ships of the fourteenth century. Here she was smaller, but it was a constant body. She flexed her arms in a pattern and they struck against the walls of the containment star. That hurt.

"We'll take it down in a minute," the man assured her. "First, let me introduce your host, the owner of your container."

Her mistress, he meant, but didn't say.

"This is Aurelia Augusta Crassa." He waved at the human girl, though that wasn't necessary. She knew that Aurelia was her mistress from the moment she entered the body.

"Hello," said Aurelia. "What do you like to be called?"

"Call me Jane." She knew that was a human name.

"I christen thee Jane Kraken, and welcome you to the mortal realm," Aurelia said, and in so doing tied Jane a bit more into the body. She didn't think that Aurelia realized it, but from his surprised and not pleased expression, she thought the man who could speak kraken did.

"These are friends of mine, and they are not to be harmed." Aurelia pointed first at a woman. "Jennifer Fairbanks." Then she pointed at the man who spoke kraken: "Wilber Hyde-Davis." She pointed to another man. "And this is Master Tadeo, who did most of the work constructing you. If you have any complaints about your body, he's the one to talk to."

Tadeo looked frightened at that.

"So far it seems functional," Jane offered casually.

"He and Jennifer are also the ones we will discuss any changes to your body with."

"Well, now that everyone has been introduced," said Wilber, "it's probably time for Aurelia to set some rules about which ships you can sink and which ships are off limits."

After that they talked for a while about what she was and wasn't allowed to do. Mostly, she wasn't allowed to sink any ships unless Aurelia was on board. Which didn't strike Jane at all as a reasonable restriction. What was the point of this lovely body if she couldn't use it to drag sailors to their deaths?

Wilber took down the wards and Aurelia climbed up on her back in front of her eyes, opened the hatch on her back, then climbed down the ladder into her body. Jane could still see her because Jane had a camera and a microphone, as well as a speaker, in her body. The camera was a blown glass eye with the back painted in patterns of selenium. As a kraken, Jane was powerful enough to be able to look out of a painted eye on a bit of planking, but the skill and knowledge of how eyes worked that the twenty-firsters brought back had been put to use by a set of demon-enchanted devices in Pucorl's lands, which in turn made eyes very much like cameras, so now the made eyes were almost good enough to work even without a demon.

The space within her boat shell was not an airtight room. It contained a leather bag, and that bag would be compressed by the surrounding water as she sank, so the air pressure would increase as she submerged and decrease as she returned to the surface. By the time she had gotten used to Aurelia, the sun had set. She was lifted onto a cart and carried out to the dock in the dark and lowered into the water.

✽ ✽ ✽

Aurelia climbed down from the dock, stepped onto Jane's hull, opened the hatch, and then climbed into the *Jane Kraken*. It was snug and dark, except for the screens which were glowing with the scenes on either side of the sub. On the port side was the dock. It was filthy and covered with barnacles. On the starboard side was another ship. It too was dirty and almost as covered with barnacles as the dock.

Then Jane started to sink. She reached her tentacles out to the wood pilings of the dock and pulled herself down into the black water. But Aurelia could still see, for Jane's "eyes" were the size of dinner plates. It took little light to see with eyes that size.

It wasn't like traveling in a boat. Jane scuttled along using her long tentacles as arms and legs and examining the harbor of Constantinople as she moved. Aurelia's ears popped and she looked over at the pressure gauge. It was a simple device, a thin leather balloon that moved a stick up and down in a glass tube. The air pressure in Jane was now twenty pounds per square inch, which meant they were approximately eleven feet below the surface. About a ninth of what they had guessed was the maximum safe depth. It also meant that they were going to have to come back up slowly when they came back up, but they had at least ten hours of air.

The air pressure jumped.

"What was that?" Aurelia asked.

"Oh, sorry," Jane said. "I was getting ready to jet." The air pressure went back down and Jane shot through the deeps on a jet of expelled water.

"Well, use your other water tank, not the air tank." Aurelia said. They weren't exactly tanks. They were oiled leather bags with pseudo muscles to move them around. In a real sense, Jane was a golem, a made thing imbued with a spirit that made it work. But it was a made thing with its parts specially made to work with the body spirit of the kraken that inhabited it. A tentacle shot out and a fish was grabbed. It was brought to Jane's "mouth" and eaten.

So it went. Aurelia spent two hours watching the wonders of the deep as Jane explored the harbor. Then they went back, where Wilber waited to escort her home.

Before they left she looked at the submarine and said, "Go explore the Bosporus and enjoy yourself. But don't eat anyone or drown anyone." She shook a finger at the submarine. "Even if they fall out of a boat on their own. Oh, and don't destroy any ship or raid fishermen's nets either. Catch your own fish, don't steal theirs. And be back here by sunset tomorrow."

Jane thought she was being unreasonable, but didn't have much choice about following the rules.

* * *

Wilber was entranced by Aurelia, but he didn't know how to act. So, as Aurelia spoke animatedly of her adventures in the deep, Wilber kept silent. Not sure what to say, caught between his pride in her accomplishment and his concern for her safety, he said nothing.

* * *

As Aurelia went inside, she could barely contain her fury at the stiff-necked twenty-firster, who wouldn't deign to so much as talk to a fourteenth-century girl. How dare he? The fact that he was tall and handsome and not paying her any attention played into her resentment, but that wasn't something she would admit even to herself.

Location: Magnara, Constantinople
Time: 2:35 PM, July 15, 1373

Igor, Wilber's phone said, "The tower watch reports that the Genoese fleet is in sight."

That still left them almost three hours out. But they had made incredibly good time.

"Igor, call Jane Kraken," Wilber said.

"No answer, boss."

"Get me Joe then." Wilber spoke through his phone to his computer, to Pucorl, then to Joe Kraken. "Where is Jane?"

"I don't know. I can't reach her phone," Joe answered. "I tried to call her an hour ago. Just to chat, you know." Jane Kraken did have a phone, a crystal set, that was tied into her systems and had a nice big antenna. It had a pentagram link to the operator in Themis' part of the netherworld. But the calls weren't going through.

"It's because she's underwater," said Paul. "In the movies, subs can never talk on the radio when they're submerged."

That was ridiculous. There was a direct link through the pentagram to Themis' lands. Wilber knew that.

Then Merlin said, "He may be right."

"But, the pentagram—" Wilber started.

"You're forgetting that the phones, even the locally-made crystal set phones, are mortal world technology limited by the laws of physics of your world. Yes, the pentagram is a direct link, or almost so, but how many feet of water does it take to block a radio signal?"

"I have no idea," Wilber said. It turned out that no one knew for sure and that seawater, because the salt in it made it a decent conductor, was even worse.

No one had thought of that problem.

Lakshmi laughed. "Well, I guess Aurelia will get her way after all." Aurelia was at her parents' house, waiting for sunset and the return of her submarine. Her parents were assuming that Jane could be controlled by phone, so Aurelia wouldn't need to be onboard when Jane went out to fight.

"Funny, right. Except, where is Jane?" Truthfully, Wilber wasn't thrilled that Aurelia would be in Jane during combat. He knew about fishing with dynamite and didn't like the idea of Aurelia crushed because one of their clockwork bombs went off early.

"It doesn't matter," Roger said. "She isn't here, and I have to go." Roger and the rest of the riflemen of the French delegation would be going out on the galleys of Constantinople with their rifles to "disrupt the enemy command structure." That is, shoot all the officers.

Location: Sea of Marmara, Near the Bosporus

Jane Kraken was at that moment about thirty feet under a Genoese galley, wishing she could grab the noisy thing by its oars, flip it over, and then dine on the humans in it. She was enjoying her time off, and Jane wasn't all that familiar with the political and military situation. It honestly didn't occur to her that this bunch of ships was of any more concern than any others, so instead of calling anyone she went deep until her internal pressure was at three atmospheres, looking for something to eat.

Location: Docks, Constantinople
Time: 3:15 PM, July 15, 1373

Roger swung off his horse and tossed the reins to a groom. He grabbed his demon-lock rifle out of the scabbard and ran for the boat at the end of the dock.

He almost took a dip as the boarding ramp bounced and swayed under him, but made it onto the ship. It had three levels of oars and a draft of only a meter. It also had a mast with a crow's nest and that was what Roger made for. The *Saint Theodore* only had the one mast and sported a single sail. Maneuvering was done by oar.

By the time Roger was atop the mast on the little platform that now had a stand for his rifle, the *Theo* was out to sea and forming up with the other ships. Roger started some practice aiming, then started cursing. It had seemed like a good idea at the time, but at this rate Roger was going to get a reputation for being useless in battle. The mast swayed and bounced, and he couldn't keep a sight picture. It wasn't that the gun was unsteady. It was the whole ship was unsteady.

by, Eric Flint, Gorg Huff, Paula Goodlett

He looked around. There were ten galleys in the Constantinople fleet, and over the last ten days they had, each and every one, been enchanted. It took most of a month to build a containment star big enough to contain a galley and a day for each ship to be enchanted with sea monsters of various types from serpents to whales. The *Theo* got an orca who was helpful, but not strong enough to row the ship without oarsmen. He did make their lives easier, as they made his easier. The oars of the *Theo* moved easily and naturally in time with each other, and the *Theo* seemed to leap across the waves.

Which only made the shooting situation worse.

Very carefully, Roger slung his rifle and climbed down. He would shoot from the bow. The angle wouldn't be as good, but at least he would have a chance of hitting something.

Each ship had racks of rocket launchers near the bow. They were turnable, but not easy to shift. They were heavy wood coated with leather that would be soaked in water just before the rockets were added, so that the backblast wouldn't ignite the launching ship.

Location: Genoese Ship Cyclops
Time: 4:45 PM, July 15, 1373

Andronikos IV stood on the bow of the Genoese flagship and watched the pitiful showing his nation was making. That would change once he was on the throne. With the aid of his new allies, he would own the whole Black Sea, and then he would retake the rest of Byzantium from the Turks.

He looked down into the ship. There were no rowers. No mortal rowers. Instead, each oar was attached to a device of springs and leather that was imbued with the spirit of a demon. They would have used a single demon like Delaflote's book demanded, but they couldn't find enough demons powerful enough to power an entire ship. So the Genoese wizards and craft masters had made slave oars. They had no speakers, but they did have microphones to hear with, so they could follow the instructions of the drums. They also had bang plates that did nothing at all except to hurt when hit so that the demons could be punished if they failed to follow the drum. The drum picked up the pace and the ship sped up and turned a bit to starboard. He looked at the demon rowers and then back out at the Byzantine fleet.

He saw a man climbing down a mast on the lead ship. The *Saint Theodore*, he thought it was. Curious, Andronikos lifted the new spyglass to his eyes. Another of the things the twenty-firsters had introduced, this one had been made in France and he had bought it in Genoa. It wasn't enchanted in any way. Only a tube and glass lenses. But when he looked through it he saw Roger McLean and shouted. "There! On the *Saint Theodore*! It's the king killer! Sink him and they will break."

* * *

Admiral Pietro Campofregoso looked at the shouting idiot on the bow and considered. Personally, he didn't object to killing kings. He was of the republic of Genoa, not a decadent monarchy like Byzantium. Doges and kings occasionally needed to be deposed, and if that meant they had to die, they had to die. Besides, Philip the Bold hadn't been the true king of France.

On the other hand, Roger McLean *did* have a reputation. And sinking him would do the enemy's morale no good at all.

He started giving orders.

CHAPTER 19—THE BATTLE OF THE BOSPORUS

Location: Byzantine Ship Saint Theodore
Time: 4:45 PM, July 15, 1373

R oger didn't see Andronikos, but he was on deck in time to hear the crew's shouts and note that the Genoese were shifting course to head right for them. Roger made his way to the bow, rifle over his shoulder, then got set up to do some sniping. It still wasn't an optimal position, but it was better than being bounced around. He could see shapes and color at this distance, but his rifle lacked a scope, so he had no real hope of making out faces.

And even with an enchanted rifle, he had darn little chance of hitting anything but the ship. Still, he took aim at a gaudily dressed figure on the bow and fired.

He missed. He opened the shotgun-style breach, and pulled one of the rounds from his ammo pouch. These rounds would never work in an ordinary flintlock, because they wouldn't burn fast enough. That was why flintlocks used corned powder, because a solid slug of black powder would burn too slow. At least, it would if a demon wasn't speeding things up. So his rounds were a slug with a solid black powder charge behind them, wrapped in a thin sheet of paper that was soaked in saltpeter solution and dried. The little fire demon loved it.

He slid the round into the breach and closed his rifle, then cocked the hammer and sighted.

Pulled the trigger.

CRACK!

Not the boom of a black powder weapon. The crack of a modern rifle. Not a lot of gunsmoke either. The fire demon combusted it all.

Another miss. Roger decided to wait a bit.

Slowly the two fleets approached one another. Constantinople had no cannon, not yet. They were under construction, but not ready. The rockets were completely locally made, but at the same time a new and dangerous technology. He could hear the creaking sound as the heavy rack was shifted and the splashes as buckets of water were dumped over the rack to protect it from fire. He looked back as the rockets were put into the soaking—not damp—rack and they tried to light them. No go.

"Take the rockets out and dry off the rack," Roger shouted. "They won't work if the powder's wet!"

Then there was a fusillade of crossbow bolts from the lead ship of the Genoese fleet. It was long range and Roger could see them coming, so he got down behind the bulwark. So did most of the crew, and the rowers were already under cover. But that was enough to convince Roger it was time to start shooting again.

Load. Cock. Aim. Breathe. Squeeze.

The *crack* came as a surprise, like it was supposed to. This time he hit someone. The fanciest-dressed person near the bow of the oncoming ship.

* * *

Andronikos felt the shot like a blow. He was wearing polished bronze armor and a helm. He should have been safe. But the bullet was

272

low. It hit him under the breast plate, and ripped through his intestines, cutting the lower intestine in at least three places, and shattering his lower spine.

He fell to the deck, paralyzed from the waist down. But the nerves in his body were still functioning, and it didn't take long for the shock to wear off and for Andronikos to start to scream.

✻ ✻ ✻

All Admiral Pietro Campofregoso knew about the matter was that someone had shot their pet Byzantine royal, so they weren't going to have the puppet to put on the throne. Inconvenient, but hardly a disaster.

This was a conquest at its base, but one made inevitable by the Venetian manipulation of the Byzantines.

For now, he had a battle to fight. He pointed and his ship shifted. They were going to board, instead of ram. After all, a ship you took was profit. One you sank was loss.

✻ ✻ ✻

Iason cursed as he pulled the rockets from the tubes. The rack had four heavy wooden tubes. Each tube should have a rocket, and all rockets were to be fired as quickly as they could be lit, in the hope that at least one would hit.

He wasn't the one who had overused the water bucket, but he pulled off his tunic and used it to dry the leather at the bottom of the tube. Then he loaded more rockets, as crossbow bolts came down around him. There were no less than three Genoese ships heading straight for them, and Iason had no desire to finish his life as a Genoese galley slave.

273

He grabbed more rockets and loaded them into the tubes. He looked, judged, and lit the fuse, then waited as his target rowed out of line while the fuses burned down and the rockets launched with a—

WHOOMP!

WHOOMP!

WHOOMP!

WHOOMP!

Only the first rocket hit the Genoese ship and it hit the stern castle, bounced off, and sailed into the sea. The rest just sailed into the sea.

Other rocketeers on other ships were having better luck, and eight Genoese ships were burning brightly before the two fleets engaged.

✱ ✱ ✱

Roger continued to fire until the Genoese ship back stroked and dropped their bow ramp onto the bulwark of the *Saint Theodore*. He dropped the rifle and pulled Themis. Then it was cut and thrust, and blood flying everywhere.

Themis was a longsword, not really suited for a battle on ship, so his shipmates kept their distance.

But a sword, even that sword, couldn't be in two places at once. He managed to stop a crossbow bolt with the sword, which would have saved him, except for the other three that were coming in at the same time. One just scratched his arm and one was stopped by his chest plate, which was high carbon steel. But the third one hit him in his left thigh. Luckily, it didn't cut any major arteries.

Then there was a shout and everyone backed away. "I call on you to surrender."

Grimacing with pain, Roger looked over at a well-dressed man, armed and armored, but not taking part in the fighting.

"I am Admiral Campofregoso of the Genoese fleet, and I claim this ship by right of conquest. Put down your weapons or die."

Roger had already fallen to the deck. Now, he let go of Themis. Then, not looking for a repeat of the events in Vienna, he said, "This is the Sword of Themis, and not the property of any man."

The admiral walked over and carefully, using his foot, not his hand, slipped it under Themis behind the guard. Then, with a flick of his leg, he kicked the Sword of Themis into the sea. "Let your demon queen apply to her nephew for the return of her sword. She is no god of mine, or any other Christian."

* * *

Themis wasn't happy as one small aspect of her drifted down to the bottom of the Marmara. She considered shifting it to her lands, but couldn't, not without Poseidon's acquiescence. She, or at least her sword, was in his territory or its mortal equivalent, and Poseidon was a god as powerful as she was. She could go to her sword, but that would put her even more in Poseidon's hands. If it were to be recovered, it would have to be by mortal hands. And Roger was unavailable.

* * *

For the rest of the afternoon the two navies fought. Because of the rockets, the Byzantine fleet made a better showing than anyone on the Genoese side expected, but they lost in the end. As the sun set, the Genoese fleet took position at anchor off the docks of Constantinople.

Tomorrow they would send a boat in to offer terms of surrender. Those terms would be different from what they had planned. It wouldn't be Andronikos who would rule in Constantinople, but it would be under the direct control of Genoa. Which made a counterattack by the Venetians a bit more likely.

Not that it was ever unlikely.

Location: Crassus Dock, Constantinople
Time: Sunset, July 15, 1373

As the sun set, Jane Kraken surfaced next to the dock. And immediately her phone started ringing.

Everyone was mad at her and all she had done was follow her instructions. It was most unfair.

"I don't answer to you!" she shouted, and hung up. Jane's built-in phone was a part of her body and that meant that it was under her control. So she didn't have to listen to anyone through it, because the only person she had to listen to didn't come equipped with an internal radio communications system. As it happened, Aurelia didn't even own a phone. They were incredibly expensive and she had used all the money she had available to build Jane's body.

Fortunately for everyone, Aurelia was in the warehouse and it took her only a couple of minutes to get to the docks and tell Jane to stay there. Then she climbed down the ladder on the side of the pier and stepped on Jane's wet hull. "Open up, Jane. I'm not mad at you, but I need to come in."

Once in her chair, Aurelia said, "It's not your fault, Jane. They didn't realize that your phone wouldn't work when you were underwater and they're embarrassed. Besides, the Genoese got here early, so we really needed you. Now, let's get your mines aboard and ready."

Jane didn't have airlocks or a pressure hull. Instead she had air tight hatches walls and chambers. As she got deeper, some of the chambers filled with water, forcing more air into the dry chamber where Aurelia sat. So her internal air pressure naturally balanced the external water pressure. That also meant that when she was on the surface there was a fair amount of dry—or at least dryish—space that would fill up with water as she got deeper.

It was into some of that space that the mines were loaded. They were placed right above her beak and under her four upper tentacles. Even under water Aurelia could twist around and lean over the railing to adjust the timers. So, for the next few minutes, they loaded wooden mines with glue soaked rags on one side and a stick to hold them by on the other into the rear flood compartment. The front flood compartment remained empty.

Then, instead of climbing out like her parents had ordered her to, Aurelia closed the hatch and told Jane to dive. Jane dove, and any hope of radio communication was lost.

Joe Kraken, still in his barge body, headed out to try and keep tabs on them. Pucorl didn't object. They knew that Roger was captured, but they didn't know much more because all his goods had been seized by the Genoese, including his phone and rifle. Everything but the Sword of Themis, which was lying on the sea bottom, off the coast of Constantinople, in water somewhere around twenty meters deep, maybe more—which was considerably deeper than was considered safe for Aurelia by the twenty-firsters.

But Aurelia wasn't at all sure that she agreed. After all, pearl divers went more than ten meters deep and they didn't get the bends. "But first things first," Aurelia said. "We need to go sink some Genoese ships."

Joe had speakers on the bottom of his hull, and Jane's external microphone was underwater at the moment, so Joe tried talking to her. It worked, but not well. Neither Joe or Jane had much in the way of digital enhancement and what they did have was made partly by craftsmen in the mortal world and partly in the little shop in Pucorl's lands. Mostly they were analog, using their kraken natures and the devices built into them by the humans. And while squid can hear, they don't come with ears, so hearing works differently.

All of which meant that Joe and Jane could talk if they were close enough to each other, but not all that well. With a bit of practice, and using the bottom of Joe's hull to flash supporting color patterns, they managed to get a direction on the Genoese fleet.

Then Joe had to wait out of crossbow range while Jane and Aurelia went in.

* * *

Aurelia looked at the screens. They were in front of her, but one looked out to the port and the other to starboard. Neither looked forward. A squid's eyes are placed more like a cow's than a human's, but they are exceptionally big, so even at night they could see the hulls of the Genoese fleet.

Aurelia saw that they were under their first target and twisted around. She set the clockwork timer and said, "Soon now," to the tiny fire demon in the mine. "And be ready to go home, because it's going to be wet down here after you're through."

Then she carefully lowered the mine into the water-filled compartment and waited until Jane got a tentacle on the rod.

* * *

Jane grabbed the mine by feel and, using her left top tentacle, stuck it to the bottom of a ship.

* * *

A demon built into an oar-assembly heard the thunk and almost jerked its oar in response. But the sound was different than the drum and coming from the wrong direction. So it merely twitched in its doze.

* * *

"Fast as you can, Jane, let's get back to where Joe is waiting, then surface."

Jane squirted water out her jet, sucked more in, and repeated the process, using her tentacles and the direction of the jet for guidance. She got up to a considerable speed and flicked under Joe, slapping his hull for the fun of it.

Then she surfaced on the other side of him. They waited, because Aurelia had set the timer for fifteen minutes, and it had only taken five for them to get here.

Finally, she felt it. A dull thump, and a moment later a dull sound through the air as a geyser shot out of the ship they had mined.

Then there was shouting and screaming in the distance and Aurelia said, "Well, that works. Let's go do it again."

Which they did, four more times, while Joe went back to shore for more mines.

*　*　*

Aurelia and Jane actively avoided the flagship of the Genoese fleet while sinking the first five, but when they got back to the rendezvous with Joe, he reported that the Genoese were getting ready to attack the city. They learned that from Clausewitz, who was on the flagship in the admiral's cabin, listening to everything that was going on and reporting back to Sun Tzu in Roger's computer in Constantinople.

Joe said, "Bertrand thinks they can probably beat off the attack, but with considerable loss to shipping. Emperor John is less confident, especially after the poor showing the navy made today. He's considering surrendering, and disavowing your actions. But don't you worry, Jane. You can come live in my harbor off Pucorl's lands."

Jane wasn't completely opposed to that possibility, but didn't want it forced on her. Besides, that wouldn't help Aurelia anyway, and it certainly wouldn't help her family's shipping interests.

"Which ship is the admiral on, Joe?" Aurelia asked.

Joe told them, adding that Clausewitz and probably Roger were on that one too, so Bertrand didn't want it hit.

* * *

Heading back to the fleet, Aurelia said, "Jane, take us to the bottom of the flagship. We are going to sink it."

"But the general—"

"I know what the general said, but neither of us belongs to him, and he won't be the one losing thousands of *solidi* worth of ships and goods."

"You're the boss. But they are going to be pissed if Roger dies."

"Fine. We will get far enough away to be safe, and go right back after it blows. We'll try to find Roger. And even if we don't, we can say we tried."

Aurelia was feeling a little guilty about her decision. She knew the story of the twenty-firsters and Roger's self-sacrifice in returning the Sword of Themis. She didn't relish the role of the grubby merchant's daughter who sacrificed the hero for thirty pieces of silver. She sighed. "Look, we've already killed shiploads of people tonight. I'll be sorry if Roger dies, but that's war."

"It's no skin off my tentacles," Jane said, taking a mine from the rack and tentacling it to Aurelia for setting.

Still feeling guilty, Aurelia set it for three minutes.

* * *

Jane placed the mine and swam for it. Not back to Joe, but out into the Marmara. Aurelia had set the time a bit too short. They were still running for it when the *thump* cracked a seam and water started leaking in. In spite of the leak, Jane immediately turned around and headed back for the flagship, diving as she went and trying to see.

* * *

Roger heard the sound of the mine being placed. So did Clausewitz, and neither of them were in a position to do much about it. Roger had manacles around his ankles leading to a ring next to a rower's bench. Clausewitz was in the admiral's cabin, and it was only his demon-enhanced electronic hearing that let him hear.

BOOM!

The exploding mine broke the back of the galley, and most of the strength of the ship was centered there. It took minutes for it to happen, but the galley started to sink.

Roger wasn't aware of most of that. He and the rest of the captured were concentrated near the center of the galley, and that was precisely where the mine was placed. What was left of the oarsman's bench where Roger was chained was gone. All that was left was the manacles and about forty pounds of chain.

The quarrel had been removed and his leg had been bandaged, but he was still suffering badly from the wound—to which were now added several more from flying wood splinters. None of those woods were fatal or even very serious, but by now he was suffering from shock. He sank into the water filling his half of the galley. He managed to hold his breath, more out of an instinct for self-preservation than any real hope. But he was going down fast, and was in no condition to swim anywhere.

* * *

Jane saw lots and lots of tasty snacks, but she wasn't in a position to determine which ones she was allowed to eat. It was a safe bet that she wasn't allowed to eat the ones in chains, but she couldn't be sure all the humans on her side were in chains. She could have spent an enjoyable time looking for tidbits she could snack on, but Aurelia—the spoilsport—was insistent on finding Roger.

They searched and then saw a body floating deeper than most of them and sinking fast. It might be Roger. The size was right, and if they looked deeper they could come back up to catch the ones they missed.

Maybe.

So she dove as steeply as she dared. They were still leaking, but the leak wasn't affected. Because they weren't an ordinary submarine, they had natural pressure. The pressure inside the sub was the same as it was outside. In effect, they were operating more like a scuba diver than a submarine.

They were gaining on the drowning man. Jane tilted to port and dropped even faster, as water started slipping over the rim of Aurelia's cabin area. It was Roger. Jane was sure now. Eyes the size of dinner plates are useful to have when you're operating in the deeps.

* * *

Roger didn't know anything except that he needed to inhale. Needed to inhale more than he had ever needed anything. It felt like he was being crushed, because he *was* being crushed.

Then something wrapped around his arm and jerked it, right where a splinter had penetrated, and he screamed.

Well, started to scream. Air didn't go out. Water came in. And that hurt so much he forgot all about the arm. Waterboarding makes you feel like you're drowning. Roger *was* drowning.

* * *

The thing that Jane's tentacle deposited on the rim of her cabin area was cold and blue.

And not breathing.

Aurelia didn't know much about CPR, but over the months of building the *Jane*, she had gotten the basic life saving course. Jane knew even less, so Aurelia instructed. Jane squeezed and water shot out of Roger's mouth. Jane also broke one of his lower ribs and bruised both kidneys. Aurelia had to tell Jane to loosen and tighten rhythmically, but after a few moments Roger started to breathe weakly.

They were deep now, and Aurelia told Jane, "Take us up, but slowly."

Location: New Flagship of the Genoese Fleet
Time: Sometime After Sunset, July 15, 1373

Captain Giorgio Cabrini, the new admiral of the Genoese fleet saw the flagship sink. And he knew with absolute faith that if he stayed here, his was going to be the next galley sunk by the Byzantine magic.

His guess was that it was somehow being done by that strange boat that was between the fleet and the docks. What he knew about it was that it was supposedly enchanted by a kraken, and the property of either another demon or of the wizards amongst the French delegation. He suspected that the wizards were aboard it, calling the kraken's fellow sea monsters from Neptune's realm.

If that were true, and they could sink it, that would end the battle and probably the war. The problem was, he didn't think they could do it. Otherwise it would have stayed safe in Constantinople.

Besides, nothing was stopping it from running and staying out of their range. No. His choices were retreat or die.

Giorgio was not the least bit suicidal.

"Signal the fleet. We will rally at Kadıköy harbor." Kadıköy was barely out of the south end of the Bosporus in the Sea of Marmara, but on the Ottoman side. At least if they were attacked there, they had a good chance of getting to shore.

Location: The Jane, Six Fathoms Deep
Time: 8:35 PM, July 15, 1373

"What happened?" Roger asked. He was not in great shape. His arms were hanging over the railing that separated the *Jane*'s cabin section from her flotation chambers, and those chambers were mostly full of water.

"We saved you from drowning," Aurelia said defensively, and it all came back to Roger.

"Yes. After you sank the ship I was on. How many others did you save?"

"One. You. It's not like there's a lot of room."

That was true. The *Jane*'s cabin section was about the size of the pilot's area on a small airplane. Much of the space within the *Jane* was designed to slowly fill with water as she dove. Which explained why he was here, hanging off the railing behind her seat.

He considered, ignoring the pain in his leg. "Fifteen of Bertrand's men, another ten Byzantine officers. Plus another two hundred Genoese mercenaries. You're certainly effective," he said with a grimace. Then he thought of it. Themis' sword. It wasn't far away and he could feel it. He had owned it for a while, and like the one ring of Sauron, even after you give it up it doesn't entirely give you up. He could feel its presence to their left and down.

"We need to get Themis' sword."

"And how do you propose we find it?"

"It's that way." He pointed.

"Themis can wait." It was Jane who spoke. "I have a crack in my roof and I am going to leak until it's fixed. We need to get back to Constantinople and get me and you repaired."

"But will we be able to find our way back?"

"I will. You . . . ? That's up to Aurelia."

"Right. Jane, take us back to the docks on a slow lift. We don't want to get the bends."

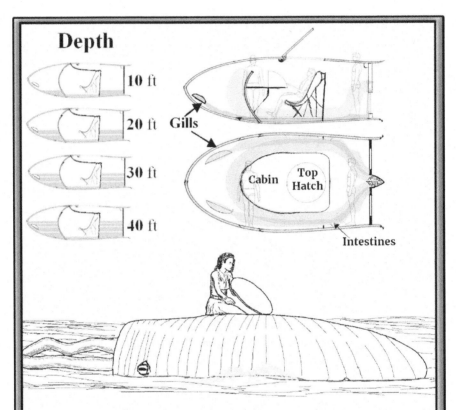

Depth

10 ft

20 ft Gills

30 ft

40 ft

Cabin Top Hatch

Intestines

Kraken have two longer tentacles and eight equal length arms. Save for the sketch, we don't show them in the designs. In the Jane they are layered, oiled leather and gut, and have suckers, also made of cured leather. After the experience of making Joe Kraken's arms, they also have "blood vessels," gut tubes that are connected to the "organs" of the Jane.

As the Jane sinks into the deep, external pressure increases, compressing the atmosphere. At 10 meters, a bit over 32 feet, the pressure has reached two atmospheres and the volume of the air in the Jane is one half what it was on the surface. At 20 meters, 65 feet, it's three atmospheres of pressure and one third the volume. If the back hatches and the top hatch are both open at once, the air will flow out, and the Jane will really sink.

CHAPTER 20—BETRAYAL

Location: Crassus Docks, Constantinople
Time: 9:37 PM, July 15, 1373

Aurelia sat on the hull of the *Jane* with a bucket of glue and several sheets of cloth. Everyone wanted to talk to her. Mostly yell at her, for one reason or another. But first things first. *Jane* needed repairs. *Jane*'s hard shell was layer after layer of waterproof glue, and sheet after sheet of cloth. The glue sealed the cloth, and the cloth gave structure to the glue. It was what the twenty-firsters called "composite materials," but it really wasn't all that different from using straw to make bricks. So Aurelia took a rag and dried the crack, and then carefully took a bandage of cloth dipped in glue and spread it evenly along the crack.

✳ ✳ ✳

"What was she thinking?" complained Sidonia, Aurelia's mother.

Wilber wondered the same thing for different reasons. Clearly, to Sidonia, the key issue was the impropriety of a woman going into battle of any sort. To Wilber, it was about blowing up the ship Roger was on—Roger and all the other friends they had lost. Fifteen of Bertrand's men at arms, each carrying a demon-lock rifle had been on that ship and Roger was the only one that Aurelia had saved.

Deep in a corner of his mind, Wilber knew perfectly well that he was being unreasonable. That she had been right on the merits of the argument, and Bertrand du Guesclin was thinking with his heart, not his head, when he failed to order that the flag ship be targeted first. But that was deep inside his head.

In the here and now, he was pissed over the people who had died. And that anger was only made worse by the fact that in an even deeper corner of his mind, he'd been scared to death for Aurelia the whole time she was out there re-enacting *The Hunt for Red October*. Well, more-or-less. Allowing for kraken power instead of nuclear power.

Aurelia was becoming more twenty-firster women's lib than the twenty-firsters were.

"Everyone settle down," Roger said. "She was right. And you all know it, or would if you weren't letting your emotions override your brains. Bertrand, nothing would have stopped the attack on Constantinople better than what she did. The invasion is off, at least for now. And don't imagine that we would have lost fewer people if they had landed their army on the docks of Constantinople. Aurelia is a true hero of the Byzantine Empire. Right up there with Horatio at the bridge." He shook his head and laughed. "Even if I ended up playing Sancho to her Don Quixote."

Wilber knew Roger was right, so he kept his mouth shut.

Location: Tavern in Constantinople.
Time: Midmorning, July 16, 1373

The big beefy man with a short beard turned to face the scoffing crowd. "I saw it," he said. "I saw the kraken and the girl riding on his back."

Rumors had been spreading all through the night and morning.

Byzantium had a new hero, rumor claimed.

Not the emperor or the princes, not the admiral or the foreign general. But the daughter of one of the oldest noble houses in

Constantinople. It was she, not the royal house, who tamed a kraken and brought it into the service of the Eastern Roman Empire. The daughter of a senatorial family.

Reports had been made to the emperor from the watchers on the wall and in the towers, and from the French delegation, who had held up the girl for praise. The peasants were thrilled. Those who believed, anyway. And that number was growing because they wanted to believe.

Location: Royal Chambers, Constantinople
Time: 9:32 AM, July 16, 1373

John V Palaiologos' feelings on the matter were mixed. He was pleased that the Genoese fleet was stopped, at least for now. He was less pleased with the mob crediting that feat of arms to a girl who was of noble blood, but not of his family.

"She will be the mob's darling and that will give all the senators ideas."

The rank of senator was no longer an official rank in Byzantium, but the traditions were still there. And a threat to his rule might well come from such a house. "Better if she had been an out and out peasant. The mob would still howl, but it wouldn't lead to anything."

"I know, husband," Helena said. "But we have no choice. We have to trot out the fatted calf for the girl and her whole family."

Location: Genoese Flagship at Dock, Kadıköy
Time: Mid-afternoon, July 16, 1373

The new admiral, Giorgio Cabrini, picked up the flagon of red wine from Genoa and gulped it down. It was from the vineyard of a friend, and a good wine. In other circumstances, he would have sipped and savored each nuance of the flavor. Now he drank it down in a single gulp and knew he had been a fool.

"Tell me again."

The spy bowed deeply. He was blond with blue eyes, and a Turk. He had worked for Murad for years and would work for whichever of Murad's sons eventually took the throne. In the meantime, he was making ends meet by selling his information wherever he could.

"Yes, lord. The ships were sunk by an enchanted kraken which was controlled by a young girl. A virgin, they say, who was involved in some vile pagan rite to call the creature to her. The kraken placed gunpowder bombs under your ships. It was going back to the barge to get more of the bombs."

"So if I had attacked, we would have lost a few more ships, but only a few." He stood and threw the flagon across the room. "But now they will see us if we start to move, and I will lose eight, mayhap twelve, ships before I reach Constantinople. And even once I get there, I will keep losing ships, as long as that monster controls the mouth of the Bosporus. We have to find a way to get rid of that monster.

"Now leave me. I have to think."

Location: The Jane, Sea of Marmara, off Constantinople
Time: 11:20 PM, July 19, 1373

Roger sat in the wet seat, because there wasn't room in the cabin for him and Aurelia and Aurelia wasn't going to let him take the *Jane* out without her. Especially not on a salvage operation from which she was hoping to get a true twenty-first century phone. Roger's phone was waterproof. All their phones were. Besides, that protection was augmented by the demon, so even if Clausewitz couldn't call home from the briny deep, he was probably still safe. It was only a matter of finding him. That would be done with the *Jane*'s external speakers and mike. They could call out and hear underwater.

The water was already up to Roger's knees and rising as they went deeper.

"Do you feel anything yet?" Aurelia asked.

"Cold sea water," Roger complained. "Why?"

"Because," Jane said, "we're getting close to where we found you."

Roger twisted around in his seat so that he could see the screens, looking around as he did. It was creepy back here. The *Jane*'s internal workings were a compromise between the internal organs of a giant squid and the mechanical components of a submarine. So Roger's jump seat was surrounded by leather tubes and sacs that looked and acted like the guts of a giant squid.

In the screens, Roger could see the bottom. Sea bottoms are mostly mud, but with the occasional rock, and in the distance a piece of hull, bow down, stuck in the mud. And it was a busy place. Fish, actual squids, and sharks were busily consuming the bounty the sinking ship had delivered. Human bodies held down by armor were being eaten by the coyotes of the deep.

*   *   *

Themis noticed Roger's presence with a mixture of pleasure and concern. Poseidon was greedy. Once something came into his realm, he wanted to keep it, with little regard to whom it properly belonged. The question on Themis' mind was how intense was Poseidon's desire to keep her in his realm.

That question was answered almost immediately.

The sea currents started to pick up into a whirlpool. *Charybdis has arrived,* Themis thought. Charybdis was a child of Poseidon who followed her sire in a feud with Zeus and got turned into a sea monster. She caused whirlpools in the seas of the netherworld and, apparently on her father's instructions, was now in the natural world doing the same thing.

Themis appeared with her hand on the sword. She couldn't breathe water, for water was Poseidon and at the moment she and Poseidon were having a vigorous debate, as it were. Also, she couldn't pick up her sword and walk out of the sea onto the shore of Constantinople.

That would be cheating.

She could, however, stand on the ocean floor and use her sword to cut the current. Which made no sense in the physics of the natural world, but worked fine against magically generated currents.

* * *

The *Jane* was jerked by a strong current, then stopped. In the distance, visible to Jane's left eye and so on her left screen, Themis stood on the bottom of the bay, sword in hand.

"Well, I guess we don't need to pick up the sword after all," Aurelia said.

Then Themis' other hand made a "come here" gesture.

"Guess again," Roger said.

Jane, using jets and tentacles, made her way to Themis and reached out a tentacle. Themis placed the sword in Jane's tentacle and Jane brought it to Roger.

Whatever Aurelia thought, Jane wasn't going to challenge Themis in any way.

The moment the hilt of the sword rose above the surface of the water in the *Jane*, a tiny little Themis appeared on the work table of the *Jane*'s cabin.

The *Jane*'s cabin had the pilot's chair, two screens, a mike, speakers, and a fold down work table that worked a lot like a table in a twenty-first century airplane. It was, however, larger and had places for pencils and paper.

Now it also had a tiny little sonarman's station where Themis sat and put on a set of earphones. "Jane, ping Clausewitz, please."

Jane used her external speaker to send out a sonar ping.

They found Clausewitz and two of the demon-lock rifles. Not, as it happened, Roger's, which had a uniquely long barrel and gold engraving.

As they were returning to the docks, Aurelia asked Themis, "Is Poseidon going to be angry?"

"I'll have a talk with him, dear. And Charybdis as well."

"So what was with the earphones and the sonar station?"

"Squid, and therefore kraken, lack the sonar of whales and dolphins. So I was using twenty-first century technology. For the few moments I was running the sonar, there was an actual computer as powerful as all your computers and phones together at the sonar station." She looked over at Aurelia. "No, greedy. I am not going to leave a part of myself in the *Jane* to be her computer."

Location: Constantinople, Crassus Docks
Time: 12:10 AM, July 20, 1373

Roger climbed the ladder to the dock with Themis on his back, and that was all. While Themis was put in his hand, his phone and the rifles were given to Aurelia by Jane.

Aurelia climbed the ladder behind him, phone in her belt pouch and two rifles slung over her shoulder.

"I'd like my phone back," Roger said. "Thanks."

"It's not your phone. It's mine, duly salvaged. So are the rifles," Aurelia said.

"Clausewitz isn't an it. He's a he. You can't salvage people, and demon or human, he's people."

"Maybe so. But unless you gave him the phone, the phone is property, and I salvaged it. Ask Themis if you don't believe me."

"Salvage laws amount to finders keepers," Themis said, "at least at this time. But Roger does have some claim to recompense, in all justice."

"Will you mediate then, Themis?" Aurelia asked.

"If Roger agrees?" Themis lifted an eyebrow.

"Yes, certainly."

"Then first I will hear from Clausewitz, for he, in justice, has some say in this." There followed a communication that was impossible for the humans to follow. It was in binary and demonic.

"Would you let Clausewitz remain in the phone but still maintain his right to leave?" Themis asked.

Aurelia almost agreed, but Themis held up a hand. "Consider carefully and speak the truth."

Aurelia considered and spoke the truth. "I would prefer to call my own demon. Nothing against Clausewitz, but I captain a submarine, and an expert in submarines is what I need. Having said that, if Clausewitz is unwilling to leave the phone, I will accept him."

Roger listened and realized that he wasn't going to get his phone back. Not unless Aurelia did something really stupid.

There was another brief bout of computerized demonic, then Themis smiled. "That's a clever notion for a puck, Clausewitz. Roger, my sword."

"Wait a sec," Roger said as he handed over the sword. "You're not going to pull a Solomon, are you? The phone won't do anyone any good cut in half."

"No, nothing like that." Themis took the sword and cut a pentagram into the wood of the dock. It was a small one, only big enough to hold the phone. "It is my ruling, should you agree, that Aurelia shall receive the phone, but make fair payment to Roger for the better part of the loss he suffers."

Aurelia swallowed. "What is a fair value? My family is rich, but not that rich."

Themis named a figure. Aurelia gulped again, and started to shake her head, but Themis added, "To be paid out over time. You can search the seafloor for other things of value to pay your debt, child. I would not promise you something, then beggar your family to pay for it."

"Then, yes, I agree."

"Roger?"

"If you say so."

Themis pointed at Aurelia. "Place the phone in the pentagram."

Aurelia did and Themis began to chant. From the phone rose a figure in smoke. The shape formed a young man in a blue uniform with red epaulets. He looked to be from the late eighteenth century. He bowed formally to Roger, then stood back up and turned into smoke. When he re-formed, he was a gray-haired man in a twentieth-century navy rear admiral's uniform. He saluted Aurelia, and said, "Admiral Rickover, at your service, ma'am."

Then he flowed back into the phone.

"He is the same familiar spirit, but now he is called as the father of the American submarine service, perhaps the greatest expert in submarines ever," Themis said.

Location: Royal Palace, Constantinople
Time: 2:00 PM, July 25, 1373

John V stood on the top step of the royal palace as Aurelia Augusta Crassa and her whole family walked up the steps to bow before him. And the crowd roared. Gaius was looking smug, Sedonia was looking disapproving. The brothers, Leonitus and Marcus were looking resentful. John might be able to work with that.

They reached the step two below the top and all but Aurelia stopped. She took one more step and curtsied. John nodded and stepped forward, then turned to the servant, who opened the oaken box inlaid with bronze. He reached in and took the golden laurel crown from the box and placed it on her head. As he did so, he bent down and hissed in her ear, "Don't get above yourself, girl. This will pass. The mob will forget, but I won't."

She looked like a frightened bird, and that was good. He stepped back and raised his arms to the roar of the crowd.

Location: Genoese Headquarters, House in Kadıköy
Time: Mid-afternoon, July 26, 1373

The horse piss they served here didn't compare to real wine, but Giorgio Cabrini drank it anyway. This part of the fragmenting Ottoman Empire was, as of now, Genoese territory, but it was still a long way from home. He listened as his captains complained, and considered. There was also word from home that Venice was planning to send a relief force to support the Byzantines. They wouldn't send a fleet to fight against the Muslim Ottomans, but let their fellow Catholics try for a little advantage and . . .

He shook his head. He knew the political realities. It wasn't about defending the faith. It never had been. And in spite of a growing faction in the Catholic church that wanted to burn the witches and new pagans who were popping up all over Europe, it still wasn't official church policy to burn those wizards and scholars who dealt with creatures of the netherworld.

Then a new thought slipped in. That was the Catholic church. The Eastern Orthodox church was taking a harder line. And the only thing protecting the French delegation from being burned by the Eastern Orthodox church was their diplomatic status.

Aurelia Augusta Crassa wasn't a member of the French delegation. He started to smile, but the smile died. The girl was the darling of the mob. John wasn't going to risk the anger of the mob by punishing the girl, no matter what the church said. Then he did smile. "Rodrigo." He waved the spymaster over, then leaned over and whispered in the man's ear. "Find a way to let Emperor John, and especially Empress Helena, learn that their son was on the flagship. Perhaps a prisoner or guest. But on the ship when the girl sank it."

"Wasn't he already dead when the *Cyclops* went down? That's what I heard from the survivors we picked up."

"No, only wounded." Giorgio smiled grimly. "Make sure it's told that way. Wounded by a bullet from their French guns, but still alive until he was drowned, or perhaps eaten, by Aurelia Augusta Crassa's pet kraken."

Rodrigo was nodding and smiling. "I will see to it, my lord."

Location: Royal Chambers, Constantinople
Time: 4:00 PM, August 2, 1373

Manuel II was back in Constantinople, but not by choice. Well, mostly not by choice. He tried not to show his grin. He had a "date" with Lakshmi later this evening. For right now he was stuck in this family dinner. Servants brought in baked quail, garum with honey and steamed vegetables. He leaned against the edge of his couch and used a fork to spear a bit of meat and dip it in the garum and honey sauce, then took a bite.

Mother's majordomo, Constantine Korolos, came in and made a gesture. Mother's face went still, and she stood up, went over, and whispered with Constantine for a few moments, then came back. She didn't return to having dinner. Instead, she ordered the servants out of the room. She put both hands on the back of her couch and said. "It's confirmed. That little bitch killed Andronikos."

"He was with the Genoese then?" Manuel asked.

"That's not certain, and I don't believe it, no matter what the French astrologer claims," Mother said. "He could have been a prisoner. You know how fast the Catholics are to lock up our family on the least pretense."

Manuel did. He also knew that Andronikos left their father in captivity in Venice a few years ago, instead of paying the overdue debt that was his ransom. Manuel knew his brother. Manuel even loved his brother. But he didn't trust him. Not anymore. He couldn't say that, not here, not to his grieving mother and father. And he didn't even want to. Andronikos was his big brother and he had grown up worshiping him.

Now he was gone, and as much as Manuel knew it was war and in no way the Crassa girl's fault, he was still angry at her for it.

He also knew he had to be careful here, because his mother was in no state to be held back by justice.

Manuel looked over at his father, and knew that John V Palaiologos wouldn't be swayed by reason either. His father's face was pale and bloodless. Guilt, not rage, but it would have the same effect. And that effect would be disaster. The girl was the darling of the mob and a senator's daughter to boot. If they killed her for nothing but risking her life to save Constantinople, the mob would rise up against them with the senators—what was left of them—leading the march. "First we must discredit her," he said. "We can't act until the mob turns on her."

"What do you mean we can't act?" his mother hissed at him. "The little whore killed my son, and you say she will escape justice because the mob worships her and her demon submarine."

"Only a short delay," Manuel said, casting about in his mind for something they could do. Some preparation they could make. Something, anything, for his mother to do other than order out the royal guards to murder a teenage heroine and her whole family. "The church," he said.

"What about the church?" his father asked.

"Patriarch Kokkinos has been wanting to condemn the demon-following French since they arrived, and we have been holding him in check. Well, the Crassus family aren't French diplomats. Let him know that we consider her fair game and he will raise the mob against her. Then we can do what we choose."

"It's a workable plan," Father said. "You do well to keep your head through all this, my son."

But his father didn't sound pleased. It sounded as though he thought Manuel's restraint was a betrayal of his brother.

Manuel excused himself and went to his rooms.

Location: Guest Quarters, Magnaura, Constantinople
Time: 7:00 PM, August 2, 1373

Lakshmi took one look at Manuel and asked, "What's wrong?"

Manuel looked around, then back at her and said, "I don't really feel like dancing right now, much less learning twenty-first century dances."

"Right," Lakshmi said. She waved Liane over and whispered something, then grabbed Manuel's arm and led him out of the hall.

As they left the hall, a band started playing a song he'd never heard before.

* * *

"Now, tell me what's happened."

"My brother is dead!" Manuel said, and she barely reacted.

"I'm sorry for your loss," Lakshmi said, not as though she were surprised. "We'd heard he joined the Genoese, but didn't want to say anything."

"There's no proof that he betrayed us. He was sent as an embassy. All we know is that the embassy failed. Maybe Andronikos thought the Genoese were only bringing him home. It was all that girl's fault. If she hadn't sunk the flagship, Andronikos would still be alive.

"But she's going to be punished. She's not part of your delegation, and no one gave her permission to enchant that model kraken. Once the mob is over their infatuation, she's going to burn and the kraken with her."

"She didn't," Lakshmi said. "You know as well as I do that Wilber enchanted the *Jane*. And Wilber does have diplomatic immunity, as your father agreed. Unless you're planning on revoking it?"

"She killed my brother!" Manuel said. "Whatever he was, whatever he did, he was my brother." He turned and left her standing there. He couldn't understand how she could be so heartless.

* * *

Lakshmi did feel for him, but she was scared. She didn't know what to do. Should she tell Wilber or Aurelia how furious the royal family was? But that would be betraying Manuel's trust, and she couldn't bring herself to do that.

* * *

DW had no doubts at all. It was a director's job to do what needed to be done for his star, even if she couldn't bring herself to do it. He was on the horn to Pucorl before the prince was out of the room.

Rickover, formerly Clausewitz, Aurelia's new phone as determined by Themis, was informed, and Jane learned what was up as soon as she surfaced that evening.

Location: Aurelia's Room, Crassus House, Constantinople
Time: 5:30 PM, August 3, 1373

Her phone rang, *ooogah ooogah ooogah*, loud enough to wake the dead, which was fairly close to what Aurelia was. She had spent last night at the bottom of the sea, searching for guns and loot to repay her debt to Roger for Rickover. Three more demon-locks and a chest of silver. The flagship had the pay chests on it.

"Aurelia, we have a call from Pucorl," Rickover said as soon as she was sitting up.

"You woke me because the van wants to chat?"

300

"Apparently not entirely, if you think I would do such a thing without good reason."

Rickover was something of a stuffed shirt. And even a martinet. But he knew his stuff and he cared about her and Jane.

"Sorry, Admiral. What's up?" She picked up the phone and put it to her ear.

"They are going to kill you," Pucorl said.

"Who?" Aurelia asked, though she had a horrible suspicion that she knew.

"The House Palaiologos. They blame you for Andronikos' death. And I think they are afraid of your popularity. I think they are going to use the church, and have you declared a witch."

That was exactly how they would do it. She knew, all of Constantinople knew, that the only thing keeping the patriarch from going after the French delegation was that the emperor could remove and replace him. If John V were to let him loose on her, she had to get away. But how? She couldn't leave her family. She couldn't.

She tried to think. She needed to talk to her mother, and even her father.

She got up and put on a gown, a new gown with buttons up the front, and went to see her parents. Mother was going over the family accounts. "What is it, Aurelia?" Sidonia asked.

Aurelia told her.

"We need to tell your father."

"Must we?"

"Yes, child. I know he's excitable, but he knows the politics of Constantinople better than anyone I know."

✳ ✳ ✳

Gaius was in the receiving room, discussing politics over wine with Theodore Meliteniotes and two other senatorial class gentlemen.

"Is this important, my dear? We are discussing matters of state," Gaius said portentously.

"Now, now, Gaius, my old friend," said Theodore. "Surely we can spare you the time after your daughter has been instrumental in saving Constantinople from the Genoese. The ladies must have their fripperies, after all."

✳ ✳ ✳

"This is a disaster!" Gaius shouted, then put his hand over his mouth. They were back in Sidonia's workroom, three doors away from the receiving room. "This is a disaster," he repeated in a sibilant hiss. "It will ruin the family. How could you have allowed this?" He pointed accusingly at his wife. He had to get Aurelia out of Constantinople. The royal family would kill her if she stayed. But if she ran . . .

It *was* a disaster. If Aurelia escaped, the royal house might well come after him and the rest of the family. He would have to disown her. If he didn't, nothing would protect the family. And even that might not be enough.

He looked at his daughter. So proud and so capable. She had saved Constantinople and now would have to run from it, never to return. And if it was discovered that the family had helped her escape . . .

Wait . . .

She had to die. And she had to die in defense of Constantinople.

But how could that be accomplished without his daughter truly dying?

"Aurelia, could we fake your death?" He asked. "I mean, your death and the loss of the *Jane*, while you were bravely fighting the Genoese?"

"I think so, Father. Jennifer and Rickover have talked about blowing out ballast and some other things that submarines did to

302

convince ships with depth charges that they were already dead so they could escape."

Gaius called a servant. "Go to the receiving room and tell our guests I will be delayed. Something about gowns for the royal gala next week, and the cost of cloth."

It took the rest of the night, consulting with Rickover and a call to Jennifer Fairbanks to work out the plan. Rickover knew about submarine tactics, and could point out several cases where submarines were lost after combat and accidents that happened. It also took a day and a half to put together the materials. He specifically told Jennifer and her phone, Silvore, not to tell anyone, even other demons, and certainly not the other twenty-firsters, about their plan. "Top secret, need to know. No one who doesn't absolutely need to know can be told."

The off-duty body for Joe Kraken was almost completed now, even with all the other projects that were ongoing, and between the building of the *Jane* and the building of the new *Joe*, there were a lot of scraps. Some of those scraps went missing.

Location: Crassus Warehouse, Constantinople
Time: 9:30 PM, August 6, 1373

Aurelia picked up the panel. It was tightly woven linen cloth painted with pine resin impregnated with silicon, selenium, and phosphors. It was also curvy and had loose threads because it was excess cut off the Joe Kraken submarine which was under construction right now. It looked like exactly what it was, a scrap left over from the making of a submarine, not an actual part of a submarine.

"It will do," Rickover said. "It's supposed to look like the *Jane* blew up, killing you and sending me and Jane back to the netherworld."

Aurelia took the piece out to the dock and dropped it into the water beside Jane Kraken who grabbed it with a tentacle and stowed it in back. Then there was a chunk of battery body.

"Leave that," Rickover said. "It would sink. Lead and ceramic filled with acid would go straight to the bottom if a mine blew while we were twenty feet down. Take those leather strips instead. They will look like tentacles that have been torn up by the blast."

It went on like that for the better part of an hour, sorting the junk in the warehouse into what would be found on the surface and what would be lost to the deep.

Then they were ready.

Location: The Jane, in Kadıköy Harbor
Time: 11: 43 PM, August 6, 1373

Aurelia set the timer for twenty minutes and handed the mine to Jane, who used her left long tentacle to thump it onto the hull of a docked galley. They placed another, then another, and headed out to sea. A quarter mile out on a line back to Constantinople, Jane stopped and started emptying the storage and letting the detritus float to the surface Then they waited.

"Five minutes," Rickover said. "It's time."

In another five minutes, the first of the mines laid in Kadıköy Harbor would go off, then the next two at thirty second intervals.

Aurelia set the timer for six minutes and handed Jane the mine. Once Jane released it, it would float slowly to the surface since it had a bit more than neutral buoyancy.

"Okay, Jane. Let's get out of here."

Jane got, but not back to Constantinople. She would head for Lemnos, where Aurelia's family had a factor and a warehouse. This was risky in two ways, for if the factor wasn't loyal to the family, or even let knowledge of her presence slip by accident, it would get back to John V that she was alive and that her father helped her escape. And he might well take her captive and sell her back to John V. But it was the best they had been able to come up with.

Jane, as was her preference, swam for several hours at a depth of around twenty feet. Then she rose to the surface and cycled the air. Aurelia opened the top hatch and breathed in the night air for a while, thinking about the last few days. Her father would tell everyone that having found salvage since the attack, she was planning to renew her attacks on the Genoese fleet. That, along with the explosions, would explain her absence. She thought about her mother and her family, about Jennifer, and—all against her will—her thoughts kept returning to Wilber Hyde-Davis as he worked on spells. Finally, she closed back up and they went under again.

So it went. Aurelia ate bread and cheese, and drank watered wine.

CHAPTER 21—RUMOR

Location: Magnaura, Constantinople
Time: Midmorning, August 7, 1373

Leonitus Crassus looked at the pendulum clock that now stood in the great hall of the Magnaura. It was broken again, the front open, and two students working on the innards. He shook his head and went on to class.

It was a lecture on mechanics, taught by Professor Kafatos, who was studying with Annabelle Cooper-Smith. It was an interesting lecture, though Leonitus wasn't sure how much use such devices really were. There were, after all, slaves and peasants to do most of the things that a pressure engine could do, and they were cheaper than the engine, besides. And anyway, it wasn't really the proper sort of work for a son of the senatorial class. There was a quote he particularly liked that was gotten indirectly from Bill Howe, who was working on a "police force" with the royal family. It went "A gentleman's sole duty is to fight and to pray," and was from someone called Jackson of the Stone Wall. There was also politics, but the point was the same. Men of high station weren't meant to be mechanics.

After class, Thomas came over and put a hand on his shoulder. "I heard. You must be distraught, my friend. But don't worry. She's probably just busy looking for more loot to pay for that phone."

"What are you talking about?"

"I heard that Aurelia didn't return last night. Surely you knew that."

"How did you hear?"

"There are peasants who watch the docks," Thomas said. "You know that."

Leo did know that, but he had forgotten in the planning for Aurelia's escape. He looked over at his friend, and remembered Rickover's insistence on "need to know" secrecy. But Thomas had the story wrong. There was nothing in it about the resumed attacks. He had to explain, because the cover story was important for the family. They didn't want people thinking that Aurelia died trying to salvage junk from the bottom of the Marmara. He couldn't let that stand.

Thomas, aside from his constant use of the phrase "surely you know that," not only in debate, but in regular speech as well, was usually clever and a good judge of people. He was also influential in terms of their fellows in the Magnaura.

So he pulled his friend into an alcove and told him, "She wasn't salvaging last night. She was renewing the attack on the Genoese fleet."

Thomas looked at him. "It's nothing to be ashamed of. Everyone knows how expensive that demon-enchanted phone of hers was. You don't have to lie."

Damn! Leonitus could never get a lie past Thomas, even when they were kids. "No, Thomas." Leonitus dithered for a moment then realized that he had to tell Thomas the truth, or it would be all over the Magnaura that she died looking for treasure, not defending the city. "All right. I'll tell you what really happened, but you have to keep it secret, and you have to help convince people that what I just told you is true. And it is, at least partly."

After Leonitus told Thomas about the plot against Aurelia and their faking her death, Thomas promised that he would help.

✳ ✳ ✳

Thomas would help, but in his own way. The Palaiologos were a curse on Constantinople. He was convinced of that, as was his father. It had to be known that they had betrayed a heroine of the city for their own reasons. That Andronikos had betrayed the city to the Genoese. That *had* to be known.

From there the rumors spread.

Location: Guest Quarters, Magnaura, Constantinople
Time: 10:32 AM, August 7, 1373

Wilber sat at the table in their rooms, looking out a window toward the docks. The docks where the *Jane* wasn't. The docks that Aurelia had not returned to this morning. And he knew she was dead.

He poured himself another goblet of the winter wine, and drank it down as images of Aurelia danced across his mind. Her eyes. Her laugh. Her mouth as she bit her thumbnail while she was concentrating. Her hands as she worked on the *Jane* or loaded gear.

Aurelia arguing with a ship's captain about the cost of Russian furs shipped down from the Black Sea.

Aurelia laughing with Jennifer about a bit of physics, or joking with Pucorl about his "romance" with Annabelle. Aurelia arguing with him about the nature of demons and magic.

He realized—say better, faced up to—the fact that he loved her and hadn't told her, and now it was too late. What a coward he was! He should have told her, let her know, however she would have responded, so at least she would know when she went down in the *Jane* that there was a man who loved her.

Man, hell. Boy, more like.

Maybe it was a good thing that he hadn't told her. At least it saved her having to tell him to pound sand.

Jennifer Fairbanks breezed through the door, looked at Wilber and asked, "What's wrong with you? Did your dog die? Wait— You don't have a dog. So there's no excuse at all."

by, Eric Flint, Gorg Huff, Paula Goodlett

"Are you nuts? Aurelia didn't come back this morning! She was going to resume her attacks on the Genoese. They must have gotten her. Her phone's out of range, so it's either back at the bottom or destroyed. And that means she's dead!"

Jennifer looked at Wilber, then at the almost empty flagon of wine. "This doesn't make sense, Wilber. You don't even like her!"

Even now, it was hard for Wilber to say, to admit even to himself. "No. I ~~loved~~ her. I just didn't have the guts to admit it. Not even to myself."

Jennifer came over and put an arm around his shoulder. "Sorry, Wilber. I didn't know."

* * *

After she left Wilber, Jennifer called Aurelia. As it happened, the *Jane* was on the surface, so the call went through.

"Aurelia," Jennifer said, "we need to tell Wilber. He's all broken up. He thinks you're dead."

"What are you talking about? He doesn't even like me. He doesn't like any of the uncultured, primitive girls of Constantinople. Especially not me!"

"Well, he's sitting at a table, a couple of rooms away, getting totally plastered and admitting that he loved you and didn't have the guts to tell you."

"It's the wine talking."

"In vino veritas."

"In any case, you can't tell him," Rickover interrupted. "Trust me on this. His being broken up about her death doesn't constitute need to know."

"I wasn't asking you, Admiral," Jennifer said. "And this is a private conversation."

310

"He's right, though," Aurelia said. "And he's our expert on this, so we should listen to him. I'm sorry about Wilber, but . . ."

"Don't you care at all?"

There was a silence, then, "Yes, I think I do. Thinking of Wilber as something other than the jerk twenty-firster is new to me, but I do care. I just don't know why yet."

Location: Royal Chambers, Constantinople
Time: 11:36 AM, August 10, 1373

Manuel looked at the face of his phone as he reached his mother's rooms. It showed the time, the date, and the weather. All of which it got second hand from the real phones and computers of the twenty-firsters. Even his father didn't have a real phone. He should have.

He should have had the phone that Roger lost, the one that the Crassa girl got. The one that was again at the bottom of the sea. He looked at the finely painted wooden model of a phone that was the best he could get, put it back in his pocket, and gestured to the guard, who opened the door.

"Did you warn her?" his mother asked even before he was fully into her sitting room.

"Warn who?"

"Aurelia Crassa."

"She's dead."

"No, she's not." His mother stopped and took a breath. "At least, she may not be. There is a rumor that she didn't die, but having heard of our plans for her, ran away. The coward."

Suddenly it all slid into place like the pieces of a puzzle. Her death was amazingly convenient, especially the timing. It was after they had learned about Andronikos and decided to see her punished, but before they had taken any action. Before they had even told anyone. He remembered feeling relieved when she went missing, presumably dead at the bottom of Kadıköy harbor. Relieved that she was dead, and his family

by, Eric Flint, Gorg Huff, Paula Goodlett

didn't have to get their hands dirty. That, at least this time, they wouldn't get their hands dirty. That she might know and fake her death had not even occurred to him. But now that the idea was brought to his attention, it made sense.

Except . . . how would she have found out?

They hadn't . . . but he had. . . .

He had told Lakshmi.

Lakshmi, who for all her beauty and verve, wasn't Byzantine. Wasn't even from this century, and truly didn't believe in the blood right of "fourteenth-century self-styled nobles."

Lakshmi, who saw—must see—what they were planning as vengeance, not justice.

Almost, he blurted it out. But he had lived his whole life in the Byzantine court. He knew his mother and he knew how she would react. She would have Lakshmi killed. She would send assassins after Aurelia Crassa and publicly attack Aurelia, the twenty-firsters, Bertrand du Guesclin . . . all the people who had come to Byzantium's aid against the Turks and, again, against the Genoese. And everyone would hear about it. Even if they managed to kill the twenty-firsters, they would be left bereft of their support and the Venetians would take Constantinople, if the Genoese didn't.

So, instead of confessing, he shook his head, feigned confusion, and said, "But how could she have found out? We told no one. Wait. Had you talked to the patriarch?"

"No!" A short breath. "No one knew."

"Then she's dead," Manuel said, "unless she got scared and ran. Maybe there was some sort of accident. You know that the Genoese found some wreckage, but maybe she survived it and then decided to run away. She was only a girl, after all."

Manuel almost convinced himself, but then he had a thought. He pulled out his "phone" and said, "Call Aurelia Crassa."

"Aurelia Crassa is not accepting calls at the moment. Would you like to leave a message?"

He looked at his phone, then at his mother, then said, "There. The phone is at the bottom of the sea."

But it wasn't. If it had been, it would have said "phone out of service area," instead of "not accepting calls." But his mother didn't need to know that.

Truly, it would be much better if his mother never found that out.

Location: Docks, Constantinople
Time: Midmorning, August 11, 1373

The Venetian fleet was here. Sixty galleys, and with them almost five hundred troops, here in support of House Palaiologos. Expected for weeks, they finally arrived, to cheering crowds with only a few cat calls about them also being late to the party.

The admiral of the fleet was escorted to the palace in state, and most of the fleet was in dock with the sailors and troops providing their pay to the dockside entertainments.

Location: Docks, Constantinople
Time: 7:25 AM, August 13, 1373

Lakshmi watched as Manuel bowed to his mother and father, then, stiffly, to her and the rest of the party. That included representatives of the senate, including Gaius Crassus, and others from the French delegation, as well as Admiral Pisani, from the Venetian fleet. Manuel was returning to Thessalonica to take up control of the western part of the Eastern Roman Empire.

Manuel hadn't been taking her calls, and she didn't know why. Right now he was wearing his official face, which might as well be a plastic mask.

by, Eric Flint, Gorg Huff, Paula Goodlett

* * *

Lakshmi was looking curious and upset. Well, she should be upset after having warned the Crassa girl. Manuel could barely stand to look at her. He turned and marched up the gangplank onto the galley, without looking back. *Let her see that!*

Location: On the Marmara Sea
Time: 3:23 AM, August 13, 1373

"Say, Antonina," DW asked, "what's up with your boss? Why isn't he taking Lakshmi's calls?"

Antonina, named after the wife of Belisarius, was a dryad of Catvia's grove in Pucorl's lands. It gave her slightly divided loyalties, but not that divided.

"Well, what do you expect after he found out that your wannabe movie star warned the murderer of his brother?"

"That wasn't Lakshmi," DW said. "It was me. Part of a director's job. Lakshmi didn't know a thing about it, and Aurelia had no idea that Andronikos was on that ship. If he even was. Your boy and his whole family were getting ready to screw up by the numbers, which you ought to know perfectly well. You can't go around betraying the people who are risking their lives to keep you safe just because you're angry."

"I know that and, in truth, I'm pretty sure that Manuel knows it too. But in a strange way, that makes it worse. Because, well, he's grateful to her for doing it, and feels guilty for being grateful."

"Actors," DW said in disgust.

"He's not an actor. He's a prince."

"Yeah, like there's a difference. Well, let your boy know that it was me who warned Aurelia. He can be as gratefully resentful of me as he wants, and I won't care."

314

Location: Kadıköy
Time: Midmorning, August 30, 1373

Giorgio Cabrini waved the Venetian admiral, Vettor Pisani, to a chair. He was in no position to fight the Venetian fleet, not after the pounding they had taken from that damned sea monster. On the other hand, they had Kadıköy well under control and at least nominally cordial relations with Sultan Savci. In part that was because the sultan was busy with his brother in southern Anatolia.

"I heard about the sea monster, Giorgio," Vettor said as he took the seat. "Bad luck for you and, in a way, bad luck for us as well. John V is all arrogance and gimlet eye, now that he is supported by the French delegation. And we dare not attack the delegation directly lest we offend Charles of France. With his tame wizards from the new college of wizardry in the University of Paris, and the new industries, France is becoming rich. And Spain and England have both launched fleets across the Atlantic to fabled Mexico and its temples of gold."

"Venice hasn't?"

"Not yet. Not with you here, threatening our access to the Black Sea."

"We need our trade with the Black Sea, and with Egypt," Georgio said. "We can't give way. And before you threaten us with that damned sea monster, we know that it was destroyed. We saw the blast in the harbor and sent boats out to find what happened. We have bits of the thing in a room down the way."

"John V tells us that another is under construction and will soon be ready."

"I know that, but we have been building our own." That was true as far as it went, but Genoa lacked the knowledge that the French had sent to Constantinople. Their sea monster was a thing of wood and ropes that couldn't submerge without drowning its crew, and they had yet to call a demon to it that could move it. For it turned out that the larger the device, the more powerful the demon needed to enchant it to any great

315

effect. A puck, or even a minor elemental, could be called to a mountain, but once there it could do little. So the minor demons that they had called told them, and the greater could not be induced for they lacked the detailed knowledge of their names that such a calling required.

Two of their wizards had been killed in their attempts to ferret out the names of greater demons right here in Kadıköy.

Giorgio pulled his mind back to the discussion and added, "You think John is arrogant now after he's lost the kraken? Consider how arrogant he will be once he owns another one. Be careful lest Venice's fleet suffer a worse fate than ours."

"I recognize the problem, Giorgio. That's why I am here. Constantinople must be brought to heel. You have lost your puppet Palaiologos, and ours seems inclined to cut his strings and repudiate his debts. It may be time to put aside our differences and work together to insure that true Christianity shall rule the east. Put both the eastern church and the Muslims in their place. I make no great distinction between Orthodox, Muslim, and pagan. They are all heretics. We should be allies against them all."

"Yet we must use the demons," Georgio said. "There is no other choice."

"Agreed. Which is another reason that Constantinople must be brought to heel. Paris and Constantinople are the two greatest centers of learning in the Christian world, and we must have control of one of them."

"Agreed," Georgio said. "What do you have to offer?"

"We have to get the French delegation—and especially their twenty-firsters—out of Constantinople. After that, a combined attack should let us take the city. Then we divide up the loot and the lands, and the Orthodox heretics can be brought back to the true church, by fire and sword if needed. To do that, we need something that will convince John to throw them out. Or, better yet, kill them."

Giorgio leaned back in his chair and scratched his goatee. He knew of John's reaction to Andronikos' supposed death at the hands of Aurelia Crassa. Half his hesitation after the destruction of the kraken was that he was afraid that it might be a ploy to hide her from Queen Helena's wrath. If that were the case, the kraken might well reappear if he launched an attack. He didn't really believe that, but the fear that it might be so kept him from risking his fleet.

But John and Helena's reaction to the rumor was all that he could wish for. Especially since he knew from survivors of the *Cyclops* that Andronikos was already dead when the flagship sank. *Wait! That's it.* "Tell him that Roger McLain shot Andronikos."

"Did he?"

"I have no idea. I doubt it. There were several of the demon-lock rifles on the ship we took. Any of them could have been the one that killed him. But Roger has the reputation for killing princes, and clearly wouldn't fail to shoot if he knew that his target was royal." He shrugged. "If it is a lie, it is a believable lie. And having failed to punish Aurelia Crassa, John will be even more anxious to punish someone."

Location: Royal Palace, Constantinople
Time: 2:45 PM, September 1, 1373

Leona sat in and out of the royal palace. One of the effects of eating a demon, especially that will-o-the-wisp, was her ability to slip almost at will from the netherworld to the natural world and back easily. It made catching mice and birds boring, so Leona now hunted more elusive game. Aided by her friend, Coach, whose watchband had extended into a collar and who accompanied her on her explorations, she listened to and he recorded conversations as she sat on a couch in the netherworld palace and listened to Queen Helena as she talked with her spymaster in the natural world palace.

The words "Roger McLain" caught Leona's attention. She still lacked a human's full facility with language, especially that of someone like Wilber, but she was good with tone and knew several names and important words. Coach, with his bluetooth connection and pentagram, was tied into the phone network.

She slipped more into the natural world, so far that someone looking in the right direction might see her outline, and slipped under Helena's couch.

"I hesitated to bring this to you, Your Majesty, particularly as it means that Aurelia Crassa was innocent of Andronikos' death. My earlier source was wrong in pointing us in her direction. It was the twenty-firster, Roger MacLean. According to our source, he intentionally targeted Andronikos because he believed that your son was a traitor, all based on the French woman's horoscope."

Location: Pucorl's Lands

Wilber got the full conversation by way of Coach to Pucorl to Merlin to him. "Set up a conference call."

It took a little while, since all of the twenty-firsters and the French delegation were busy with their own concerns.

Bertrand and Roger were working on a plan to cross the Bosporus and take Kadıköy from the landward side. Tiphaine and Liane were working in the hospital. They didn't have Monsignor Savona's healing app, but they did have disinfectant, clean bandages, knowledge, and a true desire to help. And the sisters of Mary, an Orthodox convent, were grateful for the help. The monsignor was with Cardinal de Monteruc. Bill was with the prefect of police, trying to determine who had stolen the jeweled necklace of a noblewoman. Lakshmi was in the beauty parlor, talking to patrons as they received facials and permanents, had their hair washed and nails done. And, in general, feeling out the mood of the upper class women of Constantinople while adding to her bank account. Amelia was teaching a small class that included Paul, Kitten and a half dozen ten-year-old children of the senatorial class. Annabelle was working on Pucorl with Jennifer as they tried for greater integration and control of his wheels.

It was eight in the evening before they could all get away.

✳ ✳ ✳

Wilber had Coach play the recording, and then asked, "What do we do?"

"We leave," said Bertrand. "Go to Anatolia and on to Egypt. Frankly, I am less than pleased with the Byzantine royal house, and King Charles isn't any better pleased with their attitude than I am." Among his other functions here, Bertrand was Charles V of France's ambassador plenipotentiary from France, in charge of arranging trade agreements and the like. John V was getting ready to raise the tolls on French ships through the Bosporus. "Besides, we still don't know what is causing the rifts or what might be done to repair them. And I don't think we're going to find out here."

"I agree that you should leave," Monsignor Savona said. "However, my work is here. I and the rest of Pope Gregory's delegation will be staying in Constantinople. There is a real possibility, not so much of rapprochement, but a live and let live agreement between the Catholic and the Orthodox churches."

"Not to mention," Amelia Grady said, "a Roman Catholic priest is not going to be popular with the mullahs. One with healing miracles, even less so."

"If that was where God wanted me, Amelia, I would go. But as I understand things, God wants me here. At least for now. Partly to answer the patriarch should he attempt to force another angel into the service of a particular church."

"I am concerned about those left behind. I suspect that by the time we have crossed the Bosporus, Theodore will be back in prison. He is considered too much our associate and the king of France will no longer be protecting him," Gabriel Delaflote said.

"Whatever we do, we had best do it quickly," Tiphaine said. "My latest horoscope confirms what we already knew. They are intemperate people for whom the thought is the deed. They will not delay long in acting."

After that they talked of how.

* * *

Once in her room Jennifer called Aurelia and got her voice mail, which meant the *Jane* was submerged or Rickover was on silent mode. Jennifer knew from earlier conversations that the factor in Lemnos was very nervous about having Aurelia there, and by now Aurelia was nervous about being near the factor. To make sure, Jennifer tried calling the *Jane*. Nope. She left a message.

"Aurelia, the royals are getting ready to come after us, so we are getting out of Constantinople. Can I tell Wilber you're still alive once we are gone?" She paused, then added, "Maybe you could join us at Alexandria?"

* * *

A few hours later, Jennifer got a call. "After you're out of Constantinople. But I am going to need some help. The factor is taking everything I get from the bottom for just enough food to keep me going. He's calling it 'security fees,' and commission, but what it amounts to is if I don't give him everything, he's going to lock me up and tell the emperor about my parents helping me escape. If I am going to try for Alexandria, I need supplies."

"I'll talk to Pucorl and see if we can get Joe to bring you supplies."
Then, rather sarcastically, she added, "Is it okay for me to tell Pucorl that
you're still alive?"

"Yes, fine. It's not that I don't trust you. It's the 'need to know'
principle. I'd let you tell everyone if I could, but I am worried about my
family."

"What are you going to do about your family?"

"I don't know. Can you get a message to them?"

"I think I can do better than that. I will arrange to get your father a
phone."

"No. Get it to my mother."

✷ ✷ ✷

Jennifer climbed into Pucorl and sat in one of the passenger seats.
"Pucorl, we have a problem. Aurelia is still alive. She and the *Jane* are—"

"I know. We do talk, you know. But Rickover gave me chapter and
verse about need to know. Igor and Merlin know too. But I agree with
Rickover. Considering how Wilber would feel if the leak that got Aurelia
killed for real came from him."

"Okay, fine. But the factor in Lemnos is . . . or do you know about
that too?"

"Yep. Jane to Joe, Joe to me. If that bastard would get close
enough, Jane would eat him. But Aurelia showed him the *Jane* early on,
and he won't go near the water. He waits on the beach and has one of his
henchmen check out her holds for treasure after each trip."

"We need some way to warn the family after we leave. And for that
matter, we need to let then contact Aurelia so that she can get warning to
them as soon as she leaves."

"I don't know what good that's going to do. But, okay. You know
that a phone is going to cost."

That was true. Even the phones made in Pucorl's lands were incredibly expensive because the cost wasn't simply for the phone. Just like back in the world, the cost was for the service. Themis charged for use of the network, and in exchange she kept the secrets of anyone's phone conversations.

"We gotta do what we gotta do," Jennifer said. "We'll bill them later."

Just before they left, they sent a messenger with a small wooden box to deliver to Sidonia Crassa. In the box was a locally-made phone enchanted by Wilber with a troll from the Carl's Sort of Okay Caverns in Pucorl's lands.

CHAPTER 22—SLIPPING AWAY

Location: Constantinople, Docks
Time: 12:32 AM, September 10, 1373

The horses were led, blindfolded, across the ramp onto Joe Kraken, then tied one beside the next, each gentled by its rider until there were ten horses and ten men on the barge, leaving little room for anything else.

Then Joe Kraken disappeared and was on the shore of Pucorl's lands on the edge of the Elysian Fields. The process was repeated until all of Bertrand's men were transferred.

Finally, Joe, now carrying nothing at all, set off, using his tentacles to move him out from the docks, and turned east and north to land over two miles north of Kadıköy. It took Joe a short while to make the passage, and after that it was a simple matter to collect the men and horses and deposit them on the rocky little beach.

Last of all, Pucorl drove off Joe onto the shore of Anatolia. Riding in the van were most of the twenty-firsters and Tiphaine.

Location: Northern Anatolia
Time: Mid-afternoon, September 17, 1373

Silvi, the model glider, enchanted by a sylph air elemental, floated on the air currents, looking through its camera eyes and feeling the mortal sun on its upper surface. A paper airplane, but not the sort of thing that a child makes by folding a sheet of paper. This had curved wings and structural members made of paper folded into triangular tubes. It was painted dark green on top and light blue beneath, so that it was hard to see from the ground, and it enjoyed the body provided by the twenty-firsters. Its body belonged to Charles de Long, but it was generally free to come and go as it saw fit, as long as it remained available to act as a scout. It had a speaker and a radio inlaid in thin gold wire on its upper surface.

It flew up over the hill and a bull the size of a mastodon, with the torso of a man rising up in the front. Curious, it flew closer. The head had a bull's horns, done in engraved bronze. His right arm ended in a sword and his left in a large round shield.

Then it felt the presence.

That was no natural bull centaur. It was a human-made statue enchanted by a truly powerful demon . . . no . . . not a demon. An ifrit, not a demon, but quite similar.

The glider heard it. The bull centaur bellowed and pointed with its sword arm right at Silvi. That's when the arrows started.

At first, Silvi tried for altitude, screaming about the demon bull over its radio. When an arrow almost caught it, Silvi abandoned the paper glider and slipped back into the netherworld.

Without the magical impetus, the glider became again a perfectly ordinary, if well made, paper glider. A little heavier than most, with the paint and the inlays, but well balanced, with good lift. It started to float gently to the ground, where a Turkish cavalryman, in his rush to get to it and retrieve it, ran over it, crushing it into worthless pulp.

Location: A Quarter Mile Away

Pucorl got the word. More scouts were sent, and a force of perhaps two hundred Turks were spotted by other paper birds.

* * *

Leona went ahead, flying half in the natural world and half in the netherworld, with Coach about her neck. By now Leona was used to the doubled perceptions that she got from being half in one world and half in the other. She could tell what was in the natural world and what was off to the side, out of the corner of her eye. The djinn occupied an energy state that was the same as the Elysian Fields and correlated well with the natural world, so when she looked at the ifrit king of djinn she saw both his forms, his human-like but large red body and crown. And saw how completely he was tied into the articulated statue of the karbogha. His body was cut in half at the waist and shoved into the bull form. *That has to hurt,* she noted with the indifference of cats.

The ifrit king noticed her and bellowed rage.

Leona dove to the ground and slipped almost entirely into the netherworld, and ran back to the others.

* * *

Amar Utu Marduk, ifrit lord of Tessifonica, bellowed rage as he saw the abomination. Amar wasn't overly fond of humans or mortal animals even before he was captured and forced into this form. They were beings of clay, earth and water mixed with only a touch of air and fire. The djinn were of fire with so little of earth or water in their makeup that they didn't smoke as they burned. And the purest of the djinn were the ifrit.

That a mortal could consume a being of the netherworld, even such a minor creature as that one, was an affront to all that was good and proper. Amar pointed with his sword arm, and flung a bolt of magic of his own substance out to destroy the thing.

by, Eric Flint, Gorg Huff, Paula Goodlett

* * *

Leona felt the hairs on the back of her neck rise and slid all the way into the natural world so that the bolt was blocked by a rock. The rock blew up, and Leona flicked back to the netherworld, shifted direction, and then shifted back to the natural world. The ifrit lost sight of her only for a few moments, but it was enough. She made it over the hill.

* * *

Sultan Savci held on as Amar bellowed rage, flung out an arm and shot a bolt of something at a rock. "Stop it!" he bellowed and Amar stopped.

"What were you doing and why?"

* * *

On the other side of the hill, they all got the word at once. Coach was yelling his head off by bluetooth connection.

"Wilber, come with me," Bertrand said. "I'll need you to translate."

Leona was stropping Wilber's legs in fear. "Right," Wilber said. Then, in cat, "Leona, why don't you stay with Pucorl."

"You be careful with those crazy people," Leona yowled, then quickly jumped into Pucorl through his opening side door.

"We're going to get the ram," Annabelle said to one and all, then Pucorl disappeared.

"Meurtrier," Wilber called, and the large warhorse came up complaining about the weather, the road, and everything else. Wilber mounted, and with an escort of a dozen men at arms, they rode over the hill.

In the meantime, Roger got the rest of the military contingent organized, which was another reason that Bertrand had taken Wilber. Wilber was good at a lot of things. Organizing a fighting force wasn't one of them.

* * *

Wilber saw the bull centaur. It was gesticulating with its arms as it argued in Arabic with a teenager who was standing in its wagon back and gesticulating in turn. The gist seemed to be that abominations need to be destroyed and all who are in their company. They weren't close enough to hear, but Wilber's translation magic by now had expanded to include interpretation of gestures and the color patterns that the kraken used to communicate. And his universal translator kicked in even more strongly when he was terrified, as he was now. Pucorl couldn't throw lightning bolts. Or magical bolts, or whatever it was that the djinn lord was tossing about. And Wilber had no idea how to defend against it. If that half-bull over there with the bronze horns and the red glowing eyes lost it, they were going to be toast before they had a chance to discuss the matter. Whatever the matter was.

"Halt!" someone shouted in Turkish.

"Hold up," Wilber translated. The people ahead of them were speaking five languages that Wilber could count, but Turkish and Arabic were predominant.

A small party rode out to meet them while bull boy and the prince of arrogance continued their argument.

Bertrand turned in his saddle "Be careful, people. That's General Candarli Kara Halil, so the kid in the bull wagon is probably Sultan Savci."

They rode up to about ten feet away, then pulled up. "General du Guesclin, has John V decided to attack, after all? I thought he would be too busy kissing Venetian ass."

Bertrand looked at Kara Halil for a moment, then laughed. "Oh, no. At least not when we left. Somehow a rumor got started that Roger killed Andronikos IV, and we decided that we had other business."

"So you're here on your own?" Kara Halil asked. "That seems a risky option."

"Not entirely on our own. Roger still carries the Sword of Themis, and there's Pucorl to consider."

Kara Halil didn't turn, but his eyes flicked back in the direction of the bull centaur and Savci.

"There is no reason for conflict. We are only passing through, with no intent to do you or your prince any harm."

"Passing through to where?"

"Egypt. We have some business with the mamluks, or at least Theodore Meliteniotes has convinced Dr. Delaflote that they might know something about what has caused the rifts in the veil between the worlds."

"Wait here. I'll go talk with the sultan."

✳ ✳ ✳

For several minutes they waited while Kara Halil talked with Sultan Savci. They were speaking quietly, for the most part, and not gesturing much, so even Wilber wasn't sure what was going on. Except for the fact that there seemed to be a disagreement of some sort. Then Kara Halil rode back.

"I'm sorry, General, but the sultan is adamant. You are on his lands without permission. At a minimum, you owe tariffs and penalties. The penalties amount to your demon-enchanted van."

"Pucorl isn't ours," Wilber said. "He is a free demon, and owner of the van that gives him form. He is a knight with his own lands in the netherworld."

"Was," Kara Halil said. "Now he is the property of the sultan, and if you attempt to object, you will end up chained right alongside him."

"I think you will find chaining any of us more of a challenge than you seem to be expecting," Bertrand said.

"And you don't know, can't know, enough of Pucorl's name to compel him," Wilber pointed out.

"That's not the only way to compel demon kind." Kara Halil shrugged. "I think you know that."

It wasn't the only way. A demon trapped like Pucorl had trapped Beslizoswian against the keep wall back in Paris was at the mercy of the trapping demon. Wilber looked over at the bull man again, and wondered. It was hard to tell by the container. On the other hand, to move something that size without engine or electrical systems, without spring muscles or a power supply . . . the demon had to be at least fairly powerful. Then he remembered the bolt of magic that almost singed Leona. "What do you have animating that thing?"

Kara Halil smiled. "An ifrit lord."

Before, back when Pucorl had been an ordinary puck, he would have been a snack for a being of that power. Even now, Wilber wasn't at all confidant.

"Well, Pucorl could always slip back to his own lands."

"In that case, the rest of your party will have to make up the difference."

Then a new voice issued from Wilber's phone. "Never mind, Wilber. Tell bull boy I'm coming." It was Pucorl.

And sure enough, over the hill Pucorl came, with the ram pushed ahead of him. And with a phalanx of cavalry in armor, carrying breech-loading demon-locks.

* * *

This was why they summoned the ifrit, to counter the demon van. Savci looked around. There was a part of him that wanted to get out and let the ifrit Amar fight the van, but he was sultan. He would ride Amar through the fight and fight from the bull's back. Still, he was frightened, as much as he didn't want to admit it to even himself. So he bellowed, "Charge!" and in spite of the fact that his voice broke, Amar charged.

✱ ✱ ✱

Kara Halil looked around in shock. This wasn't what was supposed to happen. It was supposed to be a duel, more or less, or a full scale battle. Not this unannounced melee with Sultan Savci still in the enchanted cart.

✱ ✱ ✱

Pucorl wasn't alone either. Annabelle was in his driver's seat, and Roger was on Pucorl's roof, ready to jump because the thing they were worried about was the reach of those massive arms and that monster sword. The sword was black, maybe blackened bronze, but no—

Pucorl could feel it from here. It was iron, as was the shield, and the arms were long enough that it could chop Pucorl up if it got past the ram. The ram was a two-wheeled cart with battering ram tipped by an ax blade, and Pucorl moved it by shifting left or right. He had to move his whole body to shift the blade, which would have been impossible if he didn't have four wheel drive and front and rear wheel steering. It still wasn't easy, and moving it effectively took practice.

Pucorl had been practicing, but it wasn't really natural to him.

The bull centaur charged and Pucorl charged to meet him.

✱ ✱ ✱

Roger was better prepared this time. Every screw up since shooting Philip the Bold had led to improvements. Balancing security with mobility, protection with offensive capabilities. He was tied onto Pucorl's roof, but now he could cut loose and jump free with the pull of a cord. As Pucorl went from zero to sixty in seconds and the bull centaur tried to do the same, Roger's world slowed down.

The sword was coming up, but the way it was coming up was wrong. This wasn't a thoughtless charge. It was a dance, fencing. And Roger could see the next move coming.

It was . . .

Roger pulled the cord.

Now!

Roger lept from Pucorl as bull boy shifted left and started his down stroke.

Bull boy went left, Pucorl went right. Pucorl's ram spun left and Roger flew through the air straight and true, swinging the Sword of Themis to strike bull boy's sword arm at the elbow.

The Sword of Themis went through the elbow like a hot knife through butter. But the arm and sword continued to move, rotating down so that the sword cut into Pucorl's roof in back of the driver's seat.

Bull boy screamed in djinn. Pucorl screamed in puckish. Roger tucked and rolled.

Pucorl's ram ax made the next contact on the left front leg of the bull centaur.

The bull got the leg up, so all the ax blade got was the "hoof."

*　*　*

Amar swung his torso to bring his shield around, and almost dislodged Sultan Savci. But the magic that bound him to this vessel was specific. His first concern had to be the safety of Savci. It was like fighting in a straitjacket. Any move, any shift that threatened to dislodge the boy was stopped before it started. He could move the shield, but not nearly as quickly as he needed to. And the van was fast, much faster than it should be. That's when he realized the puck wasn't moving the van using simply his will as Amar was doing with the bull centaur. He was only guiding it. The motive power was coming from the body itself. Now Amar was afraid. But his fear, especially trapped in this bull centaur body, translated into rage. He was still fighting in the straitjacket of his need to protect Savci, but now he was fighting in a burning red haze of rage as well.

✳ ✳ ✳

Pucorl wasn't enraged. He was scared, mostly for Annabelle. Three feet farther forward and that massive iron sword would have cut her in half. It was still there, sticking out of his roof. And it hurt. The wound wasn't serious. It hadn't hit his engine or his electrical system, except for the wire to his overhead light. But it was like a scalp wound. It hurt like hell and bled magic like the dickens. His rear wheels were at almost ninety degrees of angle as he did a donut to try and get his ram back in front of him and bull boy tried to follow him around. But Pucorl, with his engines and electrical system, was faster.

He got away and pulled back so that his ram was ahead of him again, almost running over Roger in the process.

"Leave him to me," Pucorl shouted.

"All yours, Pucky," Roger shouted back as he backed away.

✳ ✳ ✳

Amar swung his shield at Pucorl and bellowed, "Get out, Sultan! I can't fight him with you in my back."

"Back away, then," Savci shouted, and Amar did.

332

Savci lept free, and landed in the mud of the torn up field. He landed badly, and ended up face first in the mud. He rolled on his back and shouted, "Now kill that demon, my slave, or die trying." He tried to roar, but again his voice cracked.

* * *

"That's torn it," Pucorl said. "This is a fight to the death now, Annabelle. I want you out, where it's safe. Please."

"I love you too, you old heap. Ain't no way I'm gonna let you fight that monster alone." Annabelle pulled the six-shot demon-lock pistol out of her holster, and said, "Now, roll down my window. These are lead-coated iron bullets."

Pucorl was kind of pleased at Annabelle's response. He still didn't want her hurt, but she was his Annabelle and she said she loved him.

"Okay, love." He rolled down the window. "Let's get this bastard."

Blaring his horn like a semi challenging a train, Pucorl charged.

* * *

Amar had never heard anything like the noise, but he screamed in rage as his right arm and right foreleg leaked magic into the ground like fire, and he too charged. But even now he wasn't out of his mind, and he was an ifrit. Even as he charged, he examined his options.

At all cost, he had to avoid that ram, and the puck had shown that he could shift the ram to the left and right. As the ram was about to reach him, he reared up, and bending his human torso down, he reached with his shield, trying to use it as a giant battle ax.

* * *

by, Eric Flint, Gorg Huff, Paula Goodlett

Annabelle was thinking too. Mostly she was thinking that with demons, function followed form. Put a head on a demon vessel and that's where its brain is going to end up. This sucker had two chests, so presumably two hearts, two sets of lungs and so on.

But it only had one head.

One brain.

And besides, the shield arm was on the other side. She leaned out the window, pistol in hand, and as it reared, she fired.

*　*　*

As Amar reached forward, his massive head came close to the front of the van, and he heard—

BANG! BANG! BANG!

And with the third bang, there came a blow to himself. His head, his brain— Magic, but with his being tied into the empty space that was the inside of this sculpted head, it burned with a fire not of his making. The core of his being, his connection to his lands . . . it all burned and broke—

BANG! Another spike of agony.

Then, nothing.

*　*　*

The body of the bull centaur landed on Pucorl, and the fire that was the core of the ifrit lord spilled into Pucorl and was absorbed. Much like he had absorbed Beslizoswian, and perhaps even more like Leona absorbed the crow enchanted by the will-o-the wisp. The body of the bull centaur began to burn, but the fire didn't burn Pucorl or Annabelle. Instead it flowed into them, mostly into Pucorl. Almost entirely into Pucorl. He, after all, was designed to absorb it.

334

But Annabelle was in the middle of that conflagration and she couldn't help but absorb some of it.

When Pucorl realized what was going on, he fed her more power.

* * *

Hundreds of miles away and to the side of the natural world, everyone in the city of Tessifonica realized in a moment that the lord of that city was gone.

And, as might be expected, his sons immediately started competing for the rulership.

* * *

Wilber watched the fire. He suspected what was going on. Pucorl seemed to expand in form as the fire burned the body of the bull centaur. "It's not only the demon lord, is it?" he asked Merlin, sending the computer the image by way of Igor.

"No. He's getting the form of the bull centaur."

"You mean he'll be able to take the bull centaur's form?"

"I think so. And perhaps more."

"Only because Pucorl defeated him?"

"No. It was Savci's last command. That and the fact that he was locked into the body. He was ordered to win or die. When he could no longer win, he had to die, and a demon only 'dies' by being eaten by another demon."

EPILOGUE

Bertrand du Guesclin turned to Kara Halil and said, "One general to another, get your sultan under control before he does something irretrievable. You don't want to continue this fight. We will all get hurt, and you *will* lose."

* * *

Roger McLain walked over to the sultan and gave him a hand up.

Savci looked at the tall man. The Sword of Themis was on his back and everyone knew about that sword. By now, the man who wielded it was becoming something of a legend. He was said to have killed two Christian princes.

"You lost this one, Majesty. Not your fault. It could happen to anyone. Be a king and cut your losses. That's my advice, anyway. For myself, I have no desire to fight you. All we want is free passage through your lands on our way to Egypt."

"What about my bull centaur?"

"The fortunes of war," Roger said. "Sometimes the van wins. Your bull centaur wasn't the first to learn that, and probably won't be the last."

* * *

Lakshmi gazed regretfully to the northeast, wondering if she'd ever see Manuel again. It wasn't likely—and even if she did, he'd probably be furious with her for betraying him, as he'd see it.

"This sucks," she said. Demonstrating once again how well she'd acculturated to the country where she'd spent most of life.

*　*　*

Sitting on her unique vessel/mount/something of a friend, Aurelia leaned over and asked, "What do you think, Jane? What should I do?"

There was no answer. Jane was munching on... something. Probably edible, but that covered a lot of ground with a kraken.

*　*　*

The fire died away and Annabelle got out of the van, which changed into the form of the bull centaur, but with a different face. A distinctly puckish face, with short little horns and a green Robin Hood hat with a bright purple feather.

Then it changed again, and a man six feet tall with broad shoulders and the same puckish face appeared, now wearing twenty-first century body armor and helmet, but with the same bright purple feather sticking out of the helmet band.

Pucorl turned, took Annabelle in his arms, lifted her up and kissed her.

That lasted quite a while. After they broke off, Annabelle stared at him. "Now what?" she asked.

He had no idea, of course. Pucorl was still a puck at heart. Pucks are not known for their foresight.

"What I figured," said Annabelle. "Put me down. I need to find Tiphaine and have her do us a horoscope."

He set her down. "You always say astrology is superstition."

"It is." Annabelle waved her hand in a gesture that encompassed their environs. "Where do you think we are? In the land of fables and fancies and superstition, that's where." And off she went.

CAST OF CHARACTERS

14th Century

Admiral Vettor Pisani, Venetian Admiral (1324 – 13 August 1380), historical

Alaattin Ali of Karaman (aka Damat Ali Bey) was a bey of Karaman Beylik, a Turkish principality in Anatolia, historical

Albert III, called The Pigtailed, king of Austria, historical

André Hébert, aide to the Commissaire of the Grand Châtelet, fictional

Andronikos IV Palaiologos, son of John V, revolts

Aurelia Augusta Crassa, the seventeen-year-old daughter of Gaius **Augustus Crassus,** fictional

Bertrand du Guesclin, Constable of France, historical

Bishop Baudin, bishop in Paris, fictional

Bishop de Sarcenas, bishop in Paris, fictional

Cabrini, Giorgio, Genoese ship captain, fictional

Candarli Kara Halil, Pasha, major advisor to Murad I, historical

Cardinal Jean de Dormans, cardinal in Paris, historical

Charles de Long, soldier, scout, owner of Carlos, then air elemental, fictional

Charles V, King of France, historical

Commissaire Pierre Dubois, of the Grand Châtelet, fictional

Constantine Korolos, majordomo for Queen Helena, spymaster, fictional

Contarini, Andrea, Doge of Venice, historical

Count Moreau, Provost of the University of Paris, fictional

de Monteruc, Pierre, Cardinal from Avignon, head of mission for Pope Gregory, historical

Demetrios Palaiologos, Historical sort of, There was a high byzantine official/general, who had that name. but very little is known about him.

Devlit ben Bakir, Ottoman wizard working for Sultan Savci, fictional

di Campofregoso, Domenico, Doge of Genoa, historical

Doge Andrea Contarini, Doge of Venice, historical

Father Augustine, murdered in Paris, fictional

by, Eric Flint, Gorg Huff, Paula Goodlett

Filberte Renard, doctor of medicine, Paris, fictional
Gabriel Delaflote, Doctor of Natural Philosophy and collector of writings on the Gaius Augustus Crassus, senator, fictional
Gregory XI, Pope in Avignon, historical
Helena Kantakouzene, wife of John V, mother of Andronikos and Manuel, historical
Ivan Shishman, brother of Kera Tamara, king of Bulgaria (part of), historical
Ivan Sratsimir, older brother of Ivan Shishman, Bulgaria, historical
Joanna of Bourbon, queen of France, historical
John V Palaiologos, Emperor of Byzantine Empire, historical
John, Duke of Berry, brother of Charles V, historical
Kera Tamara, sister of Ivan Shishman, widow, known for beauty, about to escape marriage to Murad, historical
Louis, Duke of Anjou, brother of Charles V, historical
Manuel II Palaiologos, second son of John V, historical
Maria, princess of Constantinople, 13, historical, but little is truly known
Mathamition, high level bureaucrat, and member of the senatorial class, fictional
Michael Palaiologos, third or fourth son of John V, historical
Murad I, Ottoman Emperor, historical
Nicholas Flamel, scribe, historical
Nicolas du Bosc, lawyer for Charles V, historical
occult, fictional
Olivier de Clisson, general of France, historical
Perenelle Flamel, wife of Nicholas, historical
Philip the Bold, Duke of Burgundy, youngest brother of Charles V, historical
Philotheos Kokkinos, Patriarch, Orthodox Church, historical
Pietro Campofregoso, admiral of Genoa, brother of Domenico, historical
Pisani, Vettor, admiral of Venetian fleet, historical
Sidonia Julia Crassa, Wife of Gaius Augustus Crassus, Aurelia's mother, fictional
Sultan Savci, previously Savci Bey, third son of Murad I, historical
Theodore I Palaiologos, third or fourth son of John V, historical
Theodore Meliteniotes, astronomer and treasurer, historical, friend of Delaflote.
Tiphaine de Raguenel, wife of Bertrand du Guesclin, noted astrologist, historical

Demons, Fictional

Ali, ifrit, haunts Princess Maria's locally made phone
Amar Utu Marduk, ifrit lord of Tessifonica, forced into bull centaur cart shape
Amiee, puck, haunts de Clisson's parrot

THE DEMONS OF CONSTANTINOPLE

Archimedes, muse, haunts Delaflote's crow
Asuma, succubus, owns her own phone
Beslizoswian, demon lord, murderer
Carlos, will-o'-the-wisp in the crow of Charles de Long
Catvia, succubus, haunts Jeff's computer
Clausewitz, puck, haunts Roger's phone
Coach, faun, haunts Jeff's watch
DW, incubus, haunts Lakshmi's computer
Enzo, puck, haunts Annabelle's phone
Freddie, haunts Liane's camera (for Freddie Young, cinematographer)
Green Lantern, brownie haunts Paul's phone.
Igor, puck, haunts Wilber's phone
Ilektrismós, Zeus' lightning bolt, works for Pucorl
Inanka'sira, called Siry, ifrit, daughter of Amar Utu Marduk
Iris, handmaiden to Themis, was in crystal radio and hated it. Messenger goddess.
Ishmael, puck, haunts Bill's iPod
Laurence, muse, haunts Amelia's phone
Merlin, muse, haunts Wilber's implant and computer
Pierre, haunts Delaflote's locally made phone
Pookasaladriscase, two foot tall brownie in French village
Pucorlshrigin/Chevalier Pucorl de Elesia, puck, haunts the van
Raphico, angel of the Creator, haunts phone given to God
Richelieu, Puck, haunts King Charles' phone
Rolls Royce, puck, haunts diagnostic tool for van
Shakespeare, haunts Amelia's computer
Sherlock, haunts Bill's phone.
Silvore, puck, haunts Jennifer's phone
Sophocles, haunts Amelia's book reader
Sun Tzu, muse, haunts Roger's laptop
Thelma, haunts Liane's computer (for Thelma Schoonmaker, film editor)
Themis, titan, trapped in Philip the Bold's sword
V. I. Warshawski, haunts Bill's computer

The Twenty-firsters, Fictional

Amelia Grady, drama teacher, driver of van. She and Paul are the least wealthy of the twenty-firsters in terms of coming from money. She was married to a French police inspector and took the job as much as anything to get her son Paul into the American School. Their computers and phones while decent aren't the top of the line devices of the other 21sters.

Annabelle Cooper-Smith, American, turned 18 sometime during Demons of Paris. Her next stop after the American School was to be CalTech or MIT where she would learn to design cars. Her secret ambition was to be a Nascar race driver or at least pit boss.

Bill Howe, American, 18, dating Jennifer

Jeff Martin, American, 18, deceased

Jennifer Fairbanks, American, 17, dating Bill. The daughter of an electrical engineer and a Corporate Manager. Jennifer was at first glance the most standard teenage girl in the group, but the knowledge of engineering and management along with the income from the village of Vitré in France has left her fairly well off. She is the one that makes the crystal radio sets.

Lakshmi Rawal, Indian raised in America, 16, Lakshmi is the daughter of an Indian diplomat. She didn't take the event well, but recovered. She wanted to be a movie star. Her dad wanted her to be a diplomat or diplomat's wife. She was in the drama club for her, and studied civics and government for her dad. She is used to the company of the elite even in comparison to the other 21sters. She is also skipped 5th grade, so a senior at 16 taking advanced placement course, very smart. For us she played only a small role in Demons of Paris partly because she was still trying to cope with the loss of her dreams and family, but also because she didn't see any way at all that any sort of democracy or republic might be established in France, and one dictator wearing a crown isn't a lot different from another.

Liane Boucher, French, 17, cinematographer

Paul Grady, 9 year old son of Amelia Paul was 8 at the time of the transfer and turns 9 in Vienna.

Roger McLean, American, 18

Wilber Hyde-Davis, English, 17, has cochlear implant enchanted by Merlin which lets him speak and understand any language including the speech of animals, it also provides magically acute hearing. Interests in the software of robotics, programing, gaming and virtual reality. His computer now occupied by Merlin is a very high end gaming laptop. Since the transfer he is learning wizardry.

Made in the USA
Coppell, TX
30 July 2021